'A stunning exploration of love in all its highs and lows, its complications and vulnerability. Gloriously written and one to savour ... I loved it!' Louise Fein

'Delicate, yet compelling, this unusual love story is a little gem' Rachel Hore

'Poignant and unforgettable – Arenz understands the human heart like few others' Louisa Treger

'Ewald Arenz understands the human heart in all its nuances and vagaries ... a masterclass in honest, insightful writing. I seldom cry over books, but this one got me' Gill Paul

'A spellbinding novel about all the colours of love ... told with extraordinary sensitivity as well as breathtaking understanding. A love story for our times, full of wisdom and joy. Surely set to become a modern classic' Maggie Brookes

'Warms even the hearts of cynics' *Der Spiegel*

WHAT READERS ARE SAYING...

★★★★★

'Moving and so profound'

'Reminds me of Anne Tyler ... or Elizabeth Strout. Simple lives so carefully, beautifully examined'

'I hoped I knew where this book was going ... I cried...'

'Vivid, believable and heart-wrenching'

'Ewald Arenz's books always make me look at my own life in a different way'

'So exquisite, so full of hope'

PRAISE FOR EWALD ARENZ

WINNER of the German Independent Booksellers' Award – Book of the Year

***Tasting Sunlight* was a BBC World Service World Book Club Pick**

'Ewald Arenz writes with gentle joy' Iona Gray

'A tender and profound coming-of-age story that's also a gripping page-turner. Gorgeously written … an absolute tour de force' Louisa Treger

'Funny, touching, troubling' *Saga magazine*

'Profound in its simplicity … a remarkable, exquisitely written debut' *Irish Times*

'Hopeful and poignant and lyrically told. A truly compassionate and heartening book' *Culturefly*

'This reminded me of reading Sally Rooney's *Normal People*. It takes a writer of immeasurable talent to make you feel that intensely' Elizabeth Haynes

'Powerful, original and engaging' Susie Boyt

'Written with beautiful simplicity' Doug Johnstone

'Powerful, lyrical and profoundly affecting' Miranda Dickinson

'An exquisitely written, heart-warming story' Gill Paul

'Moving and heart-wrenching, but ultimately uplifting' Carol Lovekin

'Told with honesty and a clear-sighted understanding of human nature … I loved it' Michael J. Malone

'Breathtakingly beautiful' Louise Beech

ABOUT THE AUTHOR

Ewald Arenz was born in Nuremberg in 1965, studied English and American literature and history, and now works as a teacher at a grammar school. His novels and plays have received numerous awards. *Tasting Sunlight* was shortlisted for the German Independent Booksellers' Favourite Novel of 2019, and was on the *Spiegel* bestseller list for more than three years, becoming a word-of-mouth sensation. *Tasting Sunlight* was published in English by Orenda Books and was selected for the BBC World Service World Book Club. *One Grand Summer,* also published by Orenda Books in English, won the German Independent Booksellers' Prize 2021 and was also a number one bestseller in Germany, sitting on the *Spiegel* bestseller list for over two years. Over 1.4 million copies of Ewald's books have been sold in German alone. He lives with his family near Fürth. Follow Ewald on X @EwaldArenz, on Instagram @Ewald_Arenz, on facebook.com /EwaldArenz and his website: ewald-arenz.de.

ABOUT THE TRANSLATOR

Rachel Ward is a Fellow of the Institute of Translation and Interpreting and a freelance literary and creative translator from German and French to English, specialising in crime fiction and books for children and young adults. Having studied modern languages at the University of East Anglia, she went on to complete UEA's MA in Literary Translation. She has previously translated Ewald Arenz's *Tasting Sunlight* and Simone Buchholz's Chastity Riley series for Orenda Books. Her translation of *Hotel Cartagena* won the 2022 CWA Crime Fiction in Translation Dagger award, and she was shortlisted for the Schlegel-Tieck Prize in 2023 for *Tasting Sunlight* and again in 2025 for *One Grand Summer*. Her non-fiction interests include history, politics, art and travel. Follow Rachel on Bluesky as @racheltranslates.bsky.social and Instagram as @racheltranslates.

Also by Ewald Arenz and available from Orenda Books:

Tasting Sunlight

One Grand Summer

Love, After All

EWALD ARENZ

Translated by Rachel Ward

ORENDA
BOOKS

Orenda Books
16 Carson Road
West Dulwich
London SE21 8HU
www.orendabooks.co.uk

First published in German as *Die Liebe an miesen Tagen* by Dumont, 2023
First published in English by Orenda Books, 2026

A catalogue record for this book is available from the British Library.

ISBN 978-1-917764-30-8
eISBN 978-1-917764-31-5

Typeset in Garamond by typesetter.org.uk

Printed and bound by Clays Ltd, Elcograf S.p.A

MIX
Paper | Supporting responsible forestry
FSC® C018072

For sales and distribution, please contact info@orendabooks or visit www.orendabooks.co.uk.

Love, After All

1

How quickly the garden had run wild! In the first few years, she'd kept driving out here, to the cottage. Pruned the apple trees in late winter. Planted things out in the cold frame in March. Picked the blackcurrants in June ... all things she'd never done before. All things that Paul had shown her. Wasn't it supposed to be women who loved gardening? It had never meant much to her, but she'd always liked watching Paul at work. Because, whatever he was doing at any given moment, he was totally absorbed in it.

Clara climbed out of the car. The door slammed more violently than she'd intended. It was unusually windy. Fickle and cool – that was how these early-April days had been so far. Like her. Changeable and chilly. And something had changed, something had been set in motion. That was why she hadn't been here for so long, and that was why she had now spontaneously driven up here.

The cottage looked the same as it had always done when they arrived. The blue-painted shutters closed. Perhaps the roof was a little lower than before. The old grapevine, its trunk leaning wearily against the façade, was yet to bud. The grapes were always late. But the dog rose by the fence, with its tendrils that had gone unpruned for years, looked as though it had cast out fishing lines towards the house. The red of last year's hips was a glowing enticement against the wild, cloud-scudded sky of this windswept, blue spring day. If she photographed the cottage like this, it would surely not be so difficult to find a buyer. She picked up the camera and attempted a few pictures. She could capture a little of the mood. The mood of the house. Not the one inside her; she didn't want to touch that for fear of breaking it. She opened the letter box. The key was still inside it, buried beneath ancient flyers. And then, as if carried in on a fierce gust of wind, it all came flying back just the same. The memories of the many times they'd come, to renovate, to paint, to bring up old furniture that they'd bought at flea markets, and finally, just to spend a weekend here. Those small, almost forgotten satisfactions that only turned into happiness in retrospect. Not having enjoyed the moment enough ... some little thing never quite fitting ... When Clara thought back, she found it hard to believe that, back then, she hadn't sucked it all in, lapped it all up until she was sated with that happiness, full – so full that she'd grown tired and her eyelids had gently drooped with that happiness. She straightened up and lifted the camera again. That wouldn't happen again. Never again.

Later, she sat on the veranda that they'd built together. She'd taken one of the chairs from the woodshed and leant back in it, tipping it against the wall. She loved sitting like that. Always had, ever since her schooldays. In limbo, always around that balancing point that you could only hold for a few moments without leaning against something or falling forwards again. Sometimes the sun shone red in her closed eyes and she felt a fleeting warmth on her face and then, in quick succession, a cloud would pass over and the temperature would drop equally rapidly. She had never sat so alone and so quiet here before. The silence allowed the old pictures to rise up. Let the memories come; they no longer floored her. A gust swept around the corner of the house, hitting Clara, and she instinctively jerked her feet up to avoid tipping over; the chair landed hard on its legs, making her laugh. The memories might not floor her, but the wind could. Reality. The here and now. The mere fact of having survived yesterday was no guarantee that things would work out again today.

She looked through the photos. She still needed to take a few snaps of the interior. The sky was pretty clear just then, so the light inside ought to be nicer.

She walked back into the house. It was like stepping into a

church in winter. The house hadn't been heated for ages and the cold took her breath away. Yet the sun shone through the windows, drawing everything in soft, friendly lines. The pale-brown wood of the low table. The faded cushions on the old 1950s armchair. Even the blurred, off-white tiles in the little kitchen. Everything looked as warm as honey; it photographed beautifully despite the icy cold. She exhaled as she stepped back out through the front door into the open air. The wind suddenly seemed friendly and mild.

The museum of my love, thought Clara. For sale.

2

Elias freewheeled down the narrow alleyway between the cemetery and the oldest houses to the top of the steps that led down to the lower part of town, then dismounted and shouldered his bike. He could have taken the longer way around the cemetery, as he usually did, but this path was nicer. These April days, before the spring came in with a vengeance, were the best. When it was still cool and windy, like today, but the sun was already shining through the racing clouds, lighting up the world, sketching fleeting promises on the walls and the asphalt and the passing trams. Promises of something that he couldn't even truly name. Sometimes that tormented him. Like lost notes from a wonderful song that drifted into your ears, making you desperate to hear it in full. But you couldn't tell where those notes were coming from, and the moment you started in their rough direction your steps made too much noise and you could no longer hear them. At such moments, any small daily satisfactions felt empty. As if there had to be far more.

It was still early and he had plenty of time. He hadn't needed to leave Vera so soon, but sometimes he just couldn't stand being with her any longer. At such moments, when he lay awake beside her, listening to her peaceful breathing, the thoughts streamed through his head – none of which he followed up, of course. It was like watching himself thinking. Those morning moments were when he was most honest with himself. And that was the reason he could no longer bear to lie there – because he had the sense that he was in the wrong place. Standing here in the cool of the morning, at the foot of the steps in town felt right. He mounted and cycled sedately down the road to the town wall. There was a front garden there that delighted him every spring. It belonged to one of the few 1870s villas still standing in the suburbs. There was an ancient magnolia in the garden, its branches reaching higher than the second floor. Every year since the first time he'd been here, he'd looked forward to it flowering. There was something soothing and familiar in the buds opening every year. Sometimes, in winter, when he passed the fence overhung by the magnolia branches, he stopped to study the first hints of the buds. They always returned. The time would come when he would no longer pass by.

He thought briefly of Vera. Don't, he told himself. Why did relationships always have to be difficult? Why couldn't she just let him be the way he was?

He'd reached the garden, and stopped, holding on to the iron railing, his foot braced against the sandstone base. The blossoms had not yet opened. They probably needed another few days. That was how it was meant to be. Nobody tugged at the magnolia buds to make them open. They either flowered, or they didn't. Yes, thought Elias, as he pushed off and pedalled away, people weren't plants and relationships weren't magnolias. But the image was fitting all the same.

Although he was unusually early, Mareike was already on stage, pushing the rubber trees to and fro in their tubs. Elias sat down in the small auditorium and watched in amusement. He couldn't have done anything else. Mareike had amazing ideas, but couldn't always express them in the way you'd expect a director to do. He liked the atmosphere of a theatre in the morning. It had been similar almost everywhere he'd worked. The quiet before the technicians, or the other actors arrived. There was a very faint, dry smell of make-up and the unmistakable odour of burnt dust on the spotlights. Eventually, they'd get LED spots here too, and that would disappear. Would he notice? After all, it often took him ages to notice that something was missing. Like old people, whose hearing grew worse and worse until the birds seemed to be singing soundlessly in the trees above them, and they realised that it had been a long time since they had been able to hear them.

'Does that look better?' Mareike asked breathlessly, once she'd dragged all the tubs into a row at the front edge of the stage.

Elias raised both hands, feigning innocence. 'Depends what you want,' he said. 'If you're trying to tell us that we're not good enough ... that the audience would be better off unable to see us act at all, then you've succeeded.'

'You don't have to see the whole stage!' said Mareike, completely caught up in her idea. 'You guys then clear them away, little by little. Over the course of the play. The same way the truth comes to light, little by little.'

It wasn't such a bad idea.

'So houseplants and rubber trees are our grand delusions. Hm,' Elias said, 'I've always thought as much.'

He'd been joking, but this kind of moment was amazing. As an actor, he loved the applause. Standing at the edge of the stage after an intense performance, gradually slipping back from the role into real life and becoming aware of the audience again and realising that the applause was for you. Yes, that too. But the deepest moments, the most amazing, were generally times like this. Quiet moments when a phrase suddenly echoed inside him as it would in a cathedral. Grand delusions.

'Hey,' he said to Mareike, climbing up from the auditorium to join her on the stage, 'I guess you can't truly live if you're in the wrong life.'

'Good line,' said Mareike thoughtfully. 'Really good. We could use it for the programme.'

'I know.'

For a second, he was tempted not to say anything more.

'It's not mine. It could've been, though,' he added hastily, with a smile.

Mareike grinned indulgently. 'The rehearsal doesn't start for another half hour. You don't have to be in character yet.'

She knew him pretty well, he thought, as he crossed the little stage to the dressing room that almost directly adjoined it. The theatre wasn't large. Hanging on the stairway walls were the posters from last year's productions. A few for young people. A mini opera. A play by Sarah Kane ... they hadn't quite nailed that one. It wasn't bad here, but, all the same, he sometimes missed the bigger stages. The whole apparatus. Always giving you the feeling that everything there revolved around you, even if you weren't playing a leading role. Here, they even had to do their own make-up. But, on the other hand, he got to see Jule more often.

He walked to the window and looked down into the backyard. Around it on three sides were red, windowless façades. It would've looked even more confined if it weren't for the large linden tree in the middle, spanning the few tables.

Back then, everything had felt right. Mona and he having just left stage school. The theatre – a whole new world, and the two of them freshly landed on its coast, full of the desire to explore, to roam, to discover. Everything it held. Everything you wanted to be. But above all, battling and loving.

Stage fights. That's how they'd met. The fencing teacher had been a genuine fencer, and now and then she'd shown them the proper blows, lunges, parries. Mona, who could be so gentle, would go wild. If you came out of a lesson without bruises, it hadn't been the real thing, she'd once laughed. And the two of them always together. Stick fighting. Sword fighting. Stage punch-ups. Those were the best. Once, they'd enacted a fight in the middle of the street. People had come running, called the police, and then, mid- brawl, they'd kissed and run away, hand in hand.

Their first sex had been like that too. Like stage fencing. They'd probably each felt like they were only acting a part, that it was all just a play, could never be serious. And it was amazing. And then when Mona had got pregnant ... they could never have named Jule anything but Julia, Juliet. What else could the daughter of two stage-struck twenty-one-year-olds have been called? And in the same way that they were in love with each other, they were in love with Jule. Until eventually the stage fights turned into real fights. Over the way that life should be, away from the stage.

We can't just act out living together, Mona had screamed. We have to really do it.

But everything is just an act, he'd screamed back, and had meant it. How else could you live your life?

They'd split the same way they'd found each other, but it had been an unequal struggle. How could you parry a real foil with a stage dagger? It breaks, and the foil hits you, and runs you through, and suddenly you can't breathe for the pain because your love has been blown apart, as if by an explosion. Love alone wasn't enough. Love was like a soft metal. It had to be honed in everyday life until it was both supple and firm. Like a fencing foil. Mona had understood that. He'd been content with the emotion, and everyday life hadn't interested him.

He pushed open the window and breathed in the cool spring air, his eyes fixed thoughtfully on the still-sparse linden. Then...

All the same: what a joy Mona had been. For him. For Jule. Because, despite everything, they'd never forgotten how and why they'd first fallen in love. At least that had held true between them over the last fifteen years.

And Mona had been right: you couldn't playact life. That was probably why he'd been early for the rehearsal. Because he was, once again, playing at a difficult relationship.

'But this time...' he confided in an undertone to the tree, 'but this time there's no child.'

3

Clara leant back, put the letter down on the table beside her teacup and looked out of the window at the cloud-tattered April sky.

Bastards!

A letter. They didn't even have the guts to call her into the office for a meeting and say: Sorry, Clara, you know things are hard. Every newspaper has to cut costs. You were only part time anyway. Just look for something else.

No. A letter.

...we regret to have to inform you that due to unavoidable cost-cutting measures ... continued employment would therefore only be possible on alternative terms ... be grateful if you would inform us of your decision within fourteen days...

She knew all that – what newspaper still needed photographers? A phone camera could meet a newspaper's photography needs ten times over these days. You didn't need to employ a trained photographer.

Shit! She'd always assumed that, if the worst came to the worst, the exact opposite would be true. That she'd get to keep her job because she wasn't even full time, so she cost less. But apparently, it was more viable for them to keep Stefan. Besides, he had kids. She got that. Social conscience. Family-friendly employer. Which didn't apply to her.

Clara looked out of the window again. Yesterday, spring had been in the air. Today, fine drizzle was drifting through the grey. Sometimes, the rain billowed in swathes. She liked that generally, but right now, it was making her shiver.

She picked up the letter again. On a zero-hours basis. She might as well be delivering pizza.

She stood up – because she had to do something. Because she

couldn't stay sitting there when the ground had just been whipped from under her feet. She walked through the kitchen to her study and stepped out onto the little balcony. Nice. Now she'd have to work out if she'd even still be able to afford this view over the courtyard. She liked this flat. It had taken almost six months before she'd been able to move out of their old place, which had been way too big for her, and find this one. The two chestnut trees in the backyard. A balcony that let her look out over the rooftops to the broad, friendly-looking copper roof of the school, and its imposing belltower. From here, in the summer, you could see the pair of falcons nesting there, plus, in the evening, the carefree, swooping swallows. And it was a lively area. She liked living in town. She liked living here, in the town, she corrected herself.

A brief moment of panic, then she took a deep breath – there were plenty worse things than this, she reminded herself. This was nothing. She wasn't going hungry. She didn't have to move out on the spot. Her flat was still her flat, and at least the fridge had been stocked up yesterday evening. Besides, there was the cottage. Why did she get like this? Why did she allow herself this entirely groundless fear? Was that how life was, once you weren't young anymore? Yes. She'd been fired. But that was all. She needed to find a new job. And so did thousands of other people.

In reality, it wasn't bad news. When Paul had come home that time, she'd been feeling annoyed that, yet again, he hadn't bought yoghurt. Normally, she was the first up, but that Friday, he'd had to leave so early. The empty yoghurt jar had been left on the breakfast table. One of those little things. Ridiculous, looking back on it today. But perhaps that was how you acted when you didn't know what really mattered in life. You tried to change the other person so that you wouldn't have to become easier-going yourself. You tugged on the other person, without noticing that in doing so, you were demanding that they moved you onwards too. Because when you do a thing like that, you're standing still.

The empty yoghurt jar had mattered more than the real question when Paul had come home from the doctor's. Maybe that was also because you never expect these things to happen to you. You're never part of the statistics you read.

Did you buy yoghurt on your way home? We've run out again. Why...?

He'd been different when he'd unlocked the door. Not pale, like they always said in books. Just different.

No, he'd said quietly. Forgot. I ... the doctor said I should go to the hospital.

What?

Right away. I should go to the hospital right away.

She hadn't understood at first. That's how it goes sometimes. Hearing a thing and understanding it are not the same.

Why?

Paul had sat down at the table and stared forlornly at the breakfast that was still sitting there so cheerfully. The slices of toast on side plates. The boiled eggs, wrapped up in the red pot-holder, the same as ever. The quince marmalade, glowing orange in the morning sun. And, of course, the empty yoghurt jar.

It started bleeding right away, the doctor said. He didn't even get as far as my stomach. There's a growth at the stomach entrance, and it bled right away. You probably have cancer, he said.

Back then, ridiculously, her first emotion had been outrage. How could the doctor just say a thing like that? How could he be so unfeeling, so unbelievably heartless, so cruel?

Today she thought, looking at the letter laying her off, today I'd want people to tell me things straight out.

What an arsehole!

Paul had only shrugged, and suddenly she'd felt terrible. Because of the yoghurt. Because suddenly, everything she'd previously said and done seemed unfeeling. Breakfast. Her minor irritation that had, with all the things left unsaid between them over the years, grown into an undeclared anger at him. An anger that, in that moment, she could only direct towards the doctor because Paul was sitting helplessly at the table.

That arsehole. That can't be right. How the hell does he know that if he couldn't even check your stomach? It could be all kinds of things!

And it had been. All kinds of things. Including stomach cancer. Even in someone in his mid-thirties.

Being laid off was nothing.

She walked back into the room and over to the shelves with the old albums. They all had writing on the spines. The paper had long yellowed, but the dates, in ink, were still clear. She liked the feeling of the heavy slipcase, which had once been black but had now faded to dark grey. She'd always liked it. Rough. A little dusty. She sat down on the wooden floor and opened the book at random, somewhere in the middle. A print showing just four or five empty cups. The magic lay in their precise Art Deco lines: slender, triangular handles on thin, almost translucent porcelain cups, in a whimsical repetition of their triangular pattern. Meanwhile, the light played around the sharp contours of the rims, a fine, barely perceptible haze making them appear soft and turning their shadows into dark pools above which the cups were floating. No monochrome filter on Instagram or TikTok effect could do that. Images like this had made her want to be a photographer. Even as a child, when the albums had still stood in Aunt Elly's studio, these pictures had been windows to look through curiously, into other houses, cities, countries. Other worlds, even. There was something deeply comforting about them, a kind of promise that your own life wasn't all there was.

Probably, that was why there'd come a time when she'd stopped taking photos of Paul. Because the promise had been broken.

She looked at the photo again. How could people a hundred and fifty years ago have thought photography meant the end of art? It just told stories in a different way. The way she wanted to tell stories … which in the last few years, she'd stopped doing.

She clapped the album shut, put it back and stood up. Tell stories.

She couldn't help smiling. She'd never wanted to do newspaper work forever anyway.

4

It was too chilly to sit outside. The morning's blue had long since vanished and the sky was uniformly grey. Elias could see Vera through the large window of the café on Lutherplatz, sitting at the small table that was her favourite. She was reading and looked both engrossed and very beautiful. Her hair tied back in a ponytail, her profile showing a cheeky nose that was maybe a trifle too snub, her book in hand. As if posing for a photo.

I love the image, he thought, as he locked the bike to a lamppost. The images, not her. But that had been the deal. Don't fall in love with me, she'd laughed at the start, on their first few days away together, lying in an overly soft B&B double bed in the early morning.

I won't, he'd replied with a similar smile, suppressing the little feeling of arrogance that meant: I won't, but you will.

She looked up as he walked in and laid the book on the table.

'Long rehearsal? Was Mareike happy?'

They kissed briefly. He sat beside her on the bench. Vera liked it when they sat side by side, when their legs touched, when he put his hand on her back. At first, he'd always sat opposite her because he preferred being face to face when speaking to someone. But perhaps she was right: You like having a table between us, don't you? Always at a little distance.

Since then, he'd sat beside her. But he only did so for her sake. Because she liked it better that way.

'Nah,' he said lightly, 'Mareike's never satisfied. But that's a good thing. I prefer that to directors who never give you a proper lead. Who never tell you what they've actually got in mind. And then you try something and they...'

'...say "no showboating".' Vera completed his sentence. In the same tone.

Why didn't he like that? That had been exactly the way he told it. But it was as though she were laying claim to something that didn't belong to her. This theatre jargon, these old in-jokes that you and your colleagues kept repeating, the whole ... It was simply as though it wasn't her place to speak in that tone. But – whatever. There was always something that bothered you about someone else. Like the way she hated him sitting opposite her. He guessed he'd just have to accept it. Perfection didn't exist.

'Yes, something like that,' he said. 'But I think it could turn out pretty well. You'll see.'

Vera was pleased.

'Did you get me a ticket?'

'Yes. No problem – I'm the leading man.'

She laughed. 'It's a two-person play...'

'Exactly,' said Elias smugly. 'You see?'

She pulled her phone from her bag. 'Will you come with me to look at a house? We could make a day of it. There's a lake nearby. Fancy it?'

There were a few photos; even on the small screen, they looked very pretty. He liked old houses. The pictures reminded him of the large rooms of his childhood, the hallway with the Solnhofen stone tiles that were so wonderfully cool under your bare feet in summer, the heavy oak front door.

'What for? I can't afford to buy a house.'

Why was he so brusque? He'd love a day out. It was ... maybe it was just the way she'd asked him. He pulled himself together.

'Why are you looking at houses? You like your flat, don't you? It's perfect. Especially the bedroom.'

He smiled. Leant over and kissed her. Sometimes that overcame him – a warm feeling for her rising up inside him. Those were lovely moments.

'Oh yes, the bedroom.' She leant her slim leg against his. 'Why were you up so early this morning?'

'I had to help Mareike with the staging.'

It was both true and untrue. He took the thing that had happened later, by chance, as his reason because he couldn't get his head around the reality.

The waiter came over and he ordered. The café was only half full. The music was quiet and unobtrusive. The hiss of the coffee machine, the muffled clatter of cutlery, the diaphanous weave of conversations where you couldn't make out the words and could only sense the mood – he loved all of that.

'So, will you come?'

He nodded. 'Sure. And if there's a lake, we can swim.'

He said it perfectly seriously.

'It's April!' Vera exclaimed before realising that he was just pulling her leg. Her expression brightened. 'Great. I'm looking forward to it. I really am.'

She drained her cappuccino excitedly. He found that so sweet in her. You could see everything about her, every emotion. Her face was an open book.

'Fancy another?' He pointed to her empty cup. 'Mine probably won't arrive till after we've left. Looks like you got priority service.'

'Because I'm prettier,' she said.

He leant back. 'Most waiters judge more by a customer's wallet than their appearance. I've got money on me. You probably haven't. But they don't know that and they think you're loaded.'

'Because I'm prettier,' Vera repeated.

Elias gave an exaggerated sigh. 'If you repeat it often enough it might eventually get through to me. Exploit it then, and get the waiter's attention. I really would like my coffee.'

She waved, and the waiter paid her as little attention as he'd paid Elias. They both had to laugh. At moments like these, when you just stayed on the surface, things felt good and not fake.

5

'Annemarie has gone again. I need to have a lie-down for a while.'

Her father's voice sounded quavery and old. For a moment, as she automatically checked the time on the display, Clara wondered when that had started. Papa had never been the sporty type. Always a thinker. Deliberate. No, she thought, her lips twisting mockingly at the memory, not deliberate. Lost and incredibly slow in all everyday matters. Except in speech. In that, he'd always been forceful, almost fiery. It had probably been the thing that prompted her mother to marry him. Despite being his exact opposite in so many ways. He could speak. He could think. But when it came to practical things, he'd been as lost as she'd been adept.

'Do you know where she's gone?'

'What?'

'Papa!' Clara rolled her eyes. Fortunately, he couldn't see that over the phone. 'Can you please use your hearing aid when you call me?'

'The batteries are dead. You could bring me some. They're those tiny little—'

'Papa, please!' Clara interrupted him. 'Do you know which way she headed?'

'No. I need to go and lie down. My blood sugar's low and now ... can you come? Or are you at the newspaper?'

Now he asks me, she thought. After we've been on the phone for three minutes already.

'No, I'm not at the newspaper. They laid me off. What about Jan? Can't he drive?'

But her father's interest was piqued now, and off he went on a tangent.

'Why did they lay you off? What happened? Are they allowed to just do that?'

Clara smiled, against her will. Why was her father like this? Forgot everything else the moment a subject that interested him came along. She could probably now spend the next half hour listening while he lectured her on what was legal and what wasn't, why the global economy – whatever that might be – was to blame for her being laid off and so on, without any need to say a word. Or, more precisely, without the chance to say a word. That was probably also why, if he had already called Jan, Jan hadn't answered him.

She cut the conversation off brusquely. 'Papa, I'm leaving now. See you soon.'

'That's fine,' he replied, and hung up. No goodbye. Presumably mulling over all the legal implications that his daughter's redundancy might have for world peace.

When she left the house, she felt the fine drizzle on her face. Rain didn't much bother her mother. Better rain than snow. In winter it was always much worse. The days were short and cold and dangerous. Now, in spring, not so much could happen. Unless of course she didn't find her.

It took her over half an hour to get to the western edge of town. Despite everything, she liked these sudden escapes from the everyday. Like a flood, or heavy snowfall on a winter night bringing all traffic to a standstill. An emergency, where other rules applied. Not going to work, breaking off anything else you might be doing, just having a single, clear goal – getting on top of the situation. She was pretty good at that. She had more difficulty with getting back to everyday life.

Her parents' flat was in a rather ugly building in a rather pretty area. You could still make out the village it had once been, even if the 1980s newbuilds had encircled and almost overgrown it, and some of the old farmyards had turned into car parks and supermarkets. Luckily, she'd long left home when her parents had bought the flat.

Where was Mama? She drove slowly down the residential streets, slowly enough that she could glance into the front gardens and driveways too. Someone kept honking behind her; she indicated and made an impatient hand gesture out of the window, telling the other driver to go past. The car revved up and roared by, making it clear that she'd been too slow. She knew that. But she could hardly mount a light-up sign on the roof: *Looking for my mother – she has dementia.*

Her mother generally wandered towards the town centre. But not always. It was equally possible that something had distracted her and she'd walked into the nearest house that had its door open.

Systematically, she drove down street after street, and every time she turned a corner, she had the feeling that her mother would instantly turn up in the road behind her. But not looking wasn't an option either. She crawled past an older man who was walking his dog in the rain. He looked over and gestured to her to stop. Clara braked and rolled down the window.

'Are you looking for someone?' The man pointed back behind himself. 'I just saw an old lady with a cat on her shoulder ... She was somewhat disorientated ... but she wouldn't let me help.'

Clara smiled. 'Thank you. Yes. That's my mother. This way?'

The man nodded and pointed to one of the side streets. A cul-de-sac. That was why she hadn't been down it. Clara turned. In the narrow street, she recognised her mother right away by her determined gait. It was a bitter twist of fate. Her mother had always been afraid of growing frail. And she hadn't. Even now, in her mid-seventies, she didn't look the least like an old woman. From a distance, you could have taken her for fifty. She stopped beside her, looked up at her through the window and felt relief.

'Hello, Mama.'

'Toni!' said her mother. 'There you are at last.'

Impatient, but pleased, as if they'd been supposed to meet up hours ago. Her hair had frizzed slightly with the damp. Her cheeks were red from walking. She had a firm grasp on the cat on her shoulder. She immediately walked around the car to climb in.

'I'm Clara, Mama.' What was in a name? Perhaps a daughter was just a daughter. Whichever one it was. At least she still recognised that they belonged together.

'So, where were you going?'

Her mother pointed to the cat.

'The...' The word failed her. 'The ... flyers. The cat ran away and the flyers were trying to fill her.'

Clara translated in her head. Birds. Kill.

'Mama,' she said soothingly, 'buzzards don't take cats.'

'Yes, yes,' said her mother. Just like she used to do when she wasn't in the mood for a discussion because she completely disagreed and there would be no changing her mind. The fear that buzzards would take the cat dated from before her illness and was at least three feline generations old. Although ... nobody knew when these things started. Maybe that had been a first sign, and none of them had noticed it.

Mama had pulled the belt around her and was now trying to slot the end of it into the air vent. Clara helped her.

'Shall we go for a coffee?'

That almost always worked. Mama had always loved going to cafés. I guess we all inherited that, thought Clara, or else we were conditioned into it from an early age. Suddenly, she remembered a winter morning – it must have been a Saturday. Mama had taken all three of them to a *Konditorei*, where she'd met a friend. But the children only had two cups of cocoa, which they'd had to share. Papa had only just set up his legal practice and Mama had never had enough money. Funny childhood. But nice.

'I'd love to!'

How easy it was to please her. As Clara reversed in the cul-de-sac, she felt a twinge of conscience. Maybe she just didn't spend enough time with her parents.

'You know what, Mama?' she said, on the spur of the moment. 'Forget the coffee. We'll go for a glass of bubbly. You, me and the cat.'

Mama's laugh was like the old days.

6

They went in her car. Elias's car needed work again. As they headed away from the town centre, he looked out of the window in silence, watching as the gardens grew larger, the buildings thinned out and the countryside expanded. He liked this sudden transition into open space. The sky was light grey and there was a pale-green shimmer in the crowns of the chestnut trees that lined the country road. Some of the fields had already been sown while others were still fallow. The juxtaposition of already and not yet was a strange reflection of his inner self. This feeling, which was strongest in the spring, that everything was yet to come. That he was waiting for something. That *this* year, it would come true, fulfil what life was really all about.

'What are you thinking?'

Vera was a good driver. Now and then she glanced at her phone, even though they just had to follow the road all the way.

'About there being emotions that you only feel in spring.'

Vera looked at him briefly. 'Being in love?' she asked.

Her smile opened a door that he didn't want to step through. Why did she keep doing that? Demanding devotion, a confession. Obviously, you couldn't be ... well ... together for eighteen months without having feelings for each other. But he didn't want to be asked about those feelings. Because, at moments like these, he had to admit that he didn't have the feelings for Vera that he should. That he took more than he gave.

'I'm opposed to love,' he answered lightly. 'Love just messes everything up and is responsible for every major war in world history.'

'What rubbish. You just don't want to admit it because you'd be making yourself vulnerable. Because love makes us weaker.'

The landscape was now one of gently rolling hills, and he

thought he should keep this place in mind for a bike ride. He disliked the way the conversation was going, and so he returned to her first question.

'In early spring, everything's open. There's a sense that anything could happen, however huge. There's a kind of ... not exactly a yearning. It's hard to put into words. It's like ... as if it were tugging at you, gently, but you can always feel it. In the distance, and up above, and for a moment you mustn't even breathe because, just for these few moments, you think that there really is some great happiness out there somewhere, glinting brightly in the distance for a second, if you're just still enough. And then you'd know which way you had to go. To find happiness.'

Vera paused for a brief moment, didn't look at him as she said: 'When you talk like that ... I know what I like about you. How can you be that sensitive one moment when you're so often indifferent to everything?'

Elias laughed and put his hand on her thigh. 'I'm an actor. Sensitivity is just playing a part.'

'Idiot,' she said, half joking, half serious, but she left his hand where it was.

They couldn't have been driving for longer than twenty minutes, but they missed the almost-invisible turning twice. The map on Vera's phone wasn't detailed enough, and Elias had insisted that it wasn't a road, just some farm track that would lead them at best to a gingerbread house. They went round in a big loop before ending up back on the narrow street that led into the tiny village. There was a large inn, there was a chapel, and there was a bakery.

'Shall I go in and enquire about gingerbread?'

Elias laughed. 'Yes, I admit it, you were right. It was the right road. But that doesn't mean there aren't witches here. You haven't seen the owner yet, have you? Where's the house?'

They got out. Vera checked the address again.

'Holzgasse 18. It must be back there.'

They walked past the church, across the little village square marked out mainly by the linden tree in the centre of it, and then down Holzgasse. Elias liked the village. Not at all chic. The plaster on the low wall around the church and its little graveyard was swollen in places, and some of it had even fallen away. As he passed, Elias tapped his ankle against one of the blisters. It sounded hollow and he resisted the urge to press on it and crumble the plaster. He'd liked doing that as a child.

The houses down this lane were simple too, and there were even a couple of working farms.

'Look.' He pointed to a stone plaque beneath the gable of a two-storey house. The foundation walls were unplastered, in heavy limestone. Blocks that had been broken, not cut.

Vera looked up and read aloud: 'Rottner. 1896. You like that, don't you?'

Elias raised his hands in capitulation. 'Of course I like it. This is like coming home. I grew up in a village like this. But believe me – it's deceptive.' He was declaiming as if on stage. 'Behind all these pretty walls, it's cramped. Cramped hearts. Cramped emotions.'

Vera laughed. 'Well, now you live in town.'

'No,' he said, in a conversational tone again, 'of course it's beautiful. I often miss this. A garden. Being able to light a fire. To stroll on the terrace naked, if I feel like it. And I know what you like. But you can't afford a house, and I can't afford a house.'

'It's as if we're going round a museum,' Vera said lightly. 'I like it. You see how people live. Their houses tell stories. Just like you do, hm?'

She was right. He did like it. Really. But as so often happened, he now felt obliged to like it. He knew it was childish, an act of defiance, and he couldn't even say what sparked it, but the moment she'd said that aloud, he no longer wanted to go along with it.

They walked in silence for a few metres. Elias counted the house numbers. The lane curved to the left and there was a long piece of ground, a meadow really, with a tumbledown barn on it. It was carpeted in transparent green, no longer the brown of winter. There was a song thrush sitting on the roof, and its lonely song, that inviting, yearning whistle with the jolly twittering in between, reminded him of the way spring had felt to him as a child. He stopped and looked up at the barn ridge. The twin wheel tracks leading inside it, through the rotten doors, had been cobbled with rough stones, grass growing between them. A pretty picture.

'Come on,' Vera said, 'the woman must be waiting.'

'Yes,' said Elias. 'Let's not keep the woman waiting.'

Then came the house. It was small. And decidedly pretty. It must have been repainted a few years ago, but the paint had now gently faded. A dog rose was running wild over the fence, its tendrils reaching up over the small wooden gate. You really could imagine, thought Elias, that if a briar spent a hundred years running rampant like that, you actually would need a sword to cut your way through to the castle. Not that this was a castle. It was little more than a cottage, one and a half storeys high.

'There's a car there.' Vera pointed to the vehicle parked by the fence. 'Maybe she's inside, or in the garden.'

They looked for a bell. There wasn't one. Vera pushed the little garden gate open and they walked up to the front door. It was locked and there was no doorbell here either.

'I'll go round the back,' said Elias.

'I'll wait here,' said Vera, trying to see in through one of the windows.

The garden was large. To left and right, a narrow brick path led around the house. It too looked as though it had gone long unused; green shoots were sprouting amid the brickwork. He ducked under the branches of an elder tree and stumbled, as he came around the corner, slap into the wooden veranda, which was a good twenty centimetres higher than the path.

Clara had heard the voices outside the house with half an ear, but hadn't been expecting them to be the prospective buyers already. It couldn't be as late as all that; she'd left her phone in the car and paid no attention to the clock chimes. She'd walked through the house one last time – she didn't want anything personal on display beyond the furniture. Mind you, everything was personal. The paint on the walls, the tiles, the stripped and oiled doorframes ... all the things you do when you buy a ruin, she thought with a tiny smile. When you have no idea how much work that will really be. Once upon a time, she'd been mad about large manor houses ... Just as well she'd never come into the unfortunate situation of having to throw money down the drain. Even this little cottage had been a money pit – the kind where you didn't even hear an echo from the bottom.

It was icy in the house. She ought to let a little warm air in. She opened the patio doors and saw a man stumble onto the veranda, fall to his knees and immediately get up again.

'It's a long time since I had that happen,' said Clara.

Elias rubbed his knee for a moment, but he hadn't fallen hard. The woman was leaning on the doorframe. She was wearing a skirt suit; it looked unexpectedly fashionable and didn't fit with this little house in the least. Could she be the estate agent? Vera hadn't mentioned one.

'Sorry?' he asked.

Clara glanced at him. It was hard to say whether he was in his mid-thirties or over forty. Younger than her, anyway. There was something boyish about him, but there were a few fine lines around his mouth, which ... well, who knew.

'A man falling to his knees in front of me before introducing himself,' said Clara drily. 'It's a long time since I had that happen.'

'I think it's more fitting this way around. Besides, then I don't have to apologise for just walking into your garden. Should I introduce myself now, or was that sweeping bow enough to go on with?'

Elias had liked her response, and it prompted his cheek. There were some people – very few – who didn't react the way most did. People who didn't act shocked and then ask the blatantly obvious 'are you hurt?', just because it was the thing to do.

'I was expecting a woman,' Clara said now. 'Are you with her, or did you fall over on my veranda by chance?'

'The lady is round the front, waiting for you. I'm just the entertainment. Is this really your veranda or are you the estate agent?'

Clara had to laugh. 'The estate agent? Me? Do I look like I am?'

Elias glanced around the garden. Old fruit trees, and a few younger ones between them. A wonky, ancient shed. A cold frame that had run so wild that you could only just make out its concrete edging. One of the panels in the wooden cover had broken. Then he looked back at Clara.

'In comparison to the garden, certainly.'

She liked the fact that she didn't know right away when he was being serious and when he wasn't. She looked down at herself. How long had it been since she'd had a conversation like this? So light. There was nothing to it but the pleasure of knocking skilful balls at each other.

'I had the choice,' she said, 'between a gardener and a dressmaker.'

Elias smiled. 'If you can afford a dressmaker, why are you selling the house?'

His ball had skimmed the net.

'Think about it,' she answered mockingly, 'or look at my clothes.' He had to laugh. Phew, she thought. She hadn't intended to give a serious answer.

'Come on, we'll open the door for your wife.'

She pushed the veranda door right open. Elias stepped into the house. It was very cold.

'We're not married.'

'Is that a good thing or a bad thing?' asked Clara, already shaking her head with reluctance before she'd finished the question. It was none of her business. It was just revenge for the one about why she was selling the house, and he couldn't help that. He'd asked it as part of their little game, not to hurt her.

'Such a pretty house. I like it when a place isn't renovated to death. When you don't drive the ancestors out of the walls.'

He actually says ancestors, thought Clara. She couldn't help remarking: 'And you don't like answering silly questions.'

They'd reached the front door.

'Nor do you,' replied Elias promptly. 'Nor do you.'

Clara opened the door.

'Hello,' she said, stretching out her hand, 'Clara Wagenbach.'

'Vera Steiner,' said Vera, light-hearted and fresh; and looking at Elias. 'Have you two already met?'

Photogenic, thought Clara, very pretty, and was instantly irritated with herself. Why had that been her first thought? She was neither twenty nor thirty anymore, and, anyway, she'd always hated that kind of self-comparison. All the same. Sometimes, other women were like a mirror to her, reflecting an image that wasn't the way she saw herself.

Elias wasn't quick enough. Clara said, easily, 'Your husband fell on his knees before me. I'm afraid that doesn't mean I can reduce the price though. Come in.'

Vera looked questioningly at Elias.

'I stumbled on the veranda and fell at her feet. Not very elegant.'

Vera laughed. 'Typical. So impatient.'

It wasn't true, he thought; he wasn't that impatient. Sure, he sometimes stumbled, or even went flying, but that was because he didn't like walking slowly. He always ran. Not from impatience but because he liked to. For the first time, he realised that Vera never moved fast. He'd never even seen her walk quickly. Whereas he ... he could never take the stairs slowly. Like his mother. She still ran too.

Clara walked ahead of them into the small living room. The air from outside had finally made it a little warmer and friendlier. Perhaps that was why it felt funny to lead this couple in. Because it was more reminiscent of the place they'd had back then. Cold would have been simpler and more distant. She turned around. The woman had stopped.

'This is lovely,' she said. 'Great taste. Did you do this all yourself?'

Clara nodded. 'It took a few years.'

It had taken ages, and sometimes she'd had the feeling that the shared work was the only thing holding them together. But then events had turned out very differently.

Elias watched Vera as she knelt down by the stove and opened the flap. A draught gusted into the room, bringing the cold smell of extinguished woodfire with it.

'Are you selling the house furnished?' asked Elias. Suddenly he was genuinely interested.

'That depends,' said Clara. 'At any rate, I can't take it with me. My flat is too ... it's already furnished. Of course, I can clear the house if you want it empty.'

'I like some of the things a lot,' Vera said quickly. 'We can discuss all of that later, of course, if we decide to buy it.'

If we decide to buy it! Why had she said that? Was she playing at love, betrothal and marriage?

'Neither of us can afford this house,' he said curtly.

That was unexpected. Clara saw Vera Steiner's impatient, annoyed head movement. And then the return of her winning smile.

'We still have to ponder the finances.'

Elias was on the point of saying that he certainly had no intention of buying a house with Vera, but Clara just replied: 'If there's no disagreement on big decisions, you're not a real couple. Harmony generally means indifference.'

Elias had to laugh. And there it was again, that surprising ease.

Peculiar woman. Vera smiled. Clara went ahead of them into the little kitchen. The Solnhofen tiles were still there on the floor. Elias studied the slight dips worn into the tiles by a hundred years of taking the same path. The wall tiles were in strong colours; they glowed like a present-day accent in this old house. It looked fresh, he thought.

Vera studied the wood-burning cooking stove. 'Is this the only stove? You cook on woodfire?'

'That heats the whole cottage, and the water too. It's kind of the central heating. This place wasn't made to be lived in forever.'

No, indeed it wasn't, she thought, but back then they hadn't known that.

'Nifty,' said Elias. 'And the wood's in the garden? How romantic.'

'When you have to light the fire at six on a winter's morning for there to be hot water, you won't find it so nifty,' retorted Clara drily.

'Ah, there we are,' Elias replied. 'Now I know why you want to sell the house. You're no early riser.'

He'd picked the ball up again. Second set. Whether or not the two of them wanted to buy the house – the man was witty.

'I don't want to sell the house at all,' Clara said, in faux seriousness. This rapid back-and-forth felt surprisingly light and pleasant. 'I'm a social psychologist and I've spent years studying decision-making within couple relationships. The house belongs to the university.'

Vera looked at a loss, glancing from Clara to Elias and back again, not catching on right away.

'Don't worry,' Clara explained cheerily, 'it's not true. I'm a photographer. But your husband seems to like playing games. Would you like to see the upstairs?'

Vera nodded. 'He's an actor. That accounts for it. Yes, I'd love to. If it's as pretty upstairs as it is down here, then we could just stay right away.'

Elias followed Clara and Vera up the steep and very narrow

staircase. Why did she have to say that he was an actor? It was just a job, but she always said it a bit as though she were adorning herself with him. He was being unfair to her. She just liked it when he was on stage. And it was OK to be proud of each other, right? At any rate, in a normal relationship … Pah. He just didn't know what there was between them anymore.

The first floor was little more than an attic with two large rooms. But the generous dormers let in the light and the colour of the April sky, and made everything bright. Both rooms were bedrooms. Simply furnished. A rug. A bed. A clothes trunk in the left-hand room, and a small, rustic-style wardrobe on the right; it hadn't been restored and its doors sagged on the hinges. The pitch of the roof lent a certain air of quiet to both rooms.

Two bedrooms, he thought. Two single beds. The psychology of partnerships … The notion made him smile.

Clara opened the window over the garden. 'You can see the whole plot from here.'

Extensive, thought Elias. But not too open. The wooden fence must be very old. Behind the still-bare fruit trees, you could make out the little church tower. A cottage garden. You could still see the old beds, although they hadn't been planted for years by the look of things, and the paths between them.

Clara and Vera were on their way back downstairs, but he stood at the window for a while. It was lovely here. Truly lovely. So, why was she really selling the house? For a moment he imagined that other life. A place like this. Quiet. Nature. But at the same time, he knew how much he loved being on stage, the buzz of first nights, his life in town. You probably always stood in that tension between two lives.

What was he still doing up there? Clara was making conversation with Vera Steiner. Or, rather, Vera was talking and Clara was being amused. The younger woman was easy to listen to. The conversation bubbled without much contribution from Clara. A little naïve in her views, perhaps, but smart. There was no contradiction in that, and it added to her charm. Clara could understand what he saw in her, and suddenly felt lumbering. You could only be that carefree when life had yet to truly leave its mark on you. Or maybe she'd never had that kind of lightness in the first place.

Elias came down. Clara noticed the way Vera's eyes followed him. As if she hadn't been certain that he'd reappear. Strange.

'Do you like it?'

Clara wanted to go back outside. She wanted to leave the house behind. But you needed a notary for those things. She wished you could just draw up a contract there and then, take the money and be done with it. But things didn't work like that.

'I love it,' said Vera Steiner cheerily. 'Our taste is very similar. It really is gorgeous. But, of course, we have to talk it over a little.'

Elias was now standing beside her. The act was annoying him. It wasn't right to give the woman hope that they'd buy the house. It was downright unfair, but at the same time he didn't want to show Vera up. After all, he'd come along and taken part. And that in itself was typical of him – seeing the right thing, but not doing it. He was furious with himself.

'We have to go. I've got a rehearsal.'

Vera looked at him in surprise. He'd almost snapped.

What's up with him? Clara thought. It would be fascinating to photograph the two of them. They weren't a harmonious couple. And there would be a genuine buzz there – something like an electric forcefield spanned between them the whole time. She suppressed a smile – he was crackling with energy. Vera must get a shock every time they touched ... What *was* up with the two of them?

'I ... Didn't we want to go to the lake?' Vera asked in surprise. Her laughter had vanished.

'We won't have time now.'

Vera said nothing else, but Clara could see that she was unhappy about it. She seemed to pull herself together, turned back to her and beamed, as best she could.

'I'll give you a call. Thank you. It's a very beautiful house, really.'

Clara nodded. Then she glanced at him. As he noticed, he relaxed for a moment.

'Yes,' he agreed, but thoughtfully, 'it is a beautiful house. Thanks for showing us around.'

He stretched out his hand. She took it. No electric shock, but ... good. It felt good and warm.

'Not getting down on your knees in farewell?' she asked maliciously.

Elias immediately released her hand, swept an imaginary tricorne from his head and dropped elegantly to one knee. Then, without a word, he was back on his feet and out of the door ahead of Vera and Clara.

Clara laughed in surprise. 'That's a fascinating man you've got there.'

'Yes,' Vera answered. 'Which isn't always easy.'

Clara was still standing by the fence as they drove away. He didn't look over to her as the car passed the garden. All the same, she was unusually cheerful as she went back to the house.

7

They drove back in silence. Not a real silence but one that sounded, from the outside, like speech. It was just the important things that weren't being said: look, the leaves are coming on the poplars; and: what are you rehearsing this afternoon? and: there's the turning. Sentences that sounded muffled because there was a soft wall of frothed-up expectations between them. Expectant foam, thought Elias, amused by the idea, but if he'd laughed just then, that would have sounded stifled too. Soundproof room.

'We would have had time for the lake.'

Elias shrugged. How could he tell her that it hadn't been about the lake, but about the fact that she ... that he ... Even in his head, all the things he wanted to explain sounded wrong and open to misinterpretation. So he just asked the first question that came to mind.

'Why didn't you tell her? She called me your husband two or three times. Why didn't you correct her?'

It wasn't the real point, but it came a bit closer to it.

Vera kept driving, outwardly calm, but he could see that she was gripping the steering wheel more tightly now.

'Does it matter what some stranger thinks? Does it matter if she thinks we're married?'

Suddenly what was now bubbling up inside Elias was rage. He didn't exactly know why.

'Yes,' he said, his voice hard, 'it does. We're not married. We...' He faltered, didn't say that they weren't even in love. It sounded too harsh. Worse still, he thought, it sounded too sad.

'Yes?' Vera snapped. 'What are we then?'

He looked out of the window. Said nothing. They'd turned onto the brief stretch of motorway, were driving past the business parks. There was no greenery they could have discussed. Yes. What are we?

'You don't want her to think we're married because you always keep all your options open.'

It took him a minute to grasp what she meant.

'You mean, I found her attractive? I wanted to bed her?' He chose to express it coarsely.

'Don't know,' Vera replied, and he could hear that she was suddenly close to tears, and he hated himself for still not meeting her halfway, making it easier for her. 'I saw the way you spoke to her. Getting down on bended knee like that at the end ... What *was* that? That's ... You've never flirted like that with me. Never.'

'We started differently,' answered Elias. It was true, and it was untrue at the same time. He hadn't flirted with her because there'd been no need. She'd wanted him more than he'd wanted her. They both knew it. And they never said so.

'She's older than you. And much older than me.'

She said it with such a defiant naïvety that he had to laugh. And after a second, she did too. In that moment, there was no wall of foam between them.

'It's a pretty house,' he said lightly.

'I knew you'd like it,' said Vera. 'Do you have time to come back to mine? We never did go to the lake...'

Elias nodded in silence. Because I can't say either Yes or No, he thought, fully despising himself.

8

'You want to sell the house? Seriously? Because you've lost your job?'

Jan sounded amused. But that wasn't unusual. The two of them had a particular tone of their own, which other people didn't always understand straight away. He might not have seemed all that concerned, but that didn't necessarily mean that he wasn't.

Clara was standing on a ladder, handing books down to him from the top shelf. The windows in their parents' sitting room were open. It was the first thing they each always did on arriving at their parents' house, and sometimes the fact that they beat a path straight to the windows made them laugh.

'Did it use to smell like this,' Clara asked, 'when we were still living at home?'

Jan grinned. 'Not so much once you moved out. Answer the question.'

He tossed the book carelessly into the box, then took it back out and read the title.

'*Transcendental Meditations on Roman Law. The Near-Death Experiences of Ancient Lawyers*. If Papa notices this is missing, we're dead.'

'That's why we're doing this while he's at the doctor's,' said Clara. 'One day, one of these bookcases is going to topple over and crush him. Why can't he just shelve his books vertically?'

'It goes against his religious convictions,' Jan suggested. 'If it's too easy to take a book from the shelf, just like that, he'll only ever take down the right one. Whereas with his system, for every book he wants to find, ten others that might interest him have to pass through his hands. So, why are you selling the house?'

Clara said nothing for a moment. She could hear her mother in the dining room, talking quietly to herself as she pulled open drawers and counted the cutlery. Jan had put music on for her; that often helped. Something from the early seventies. From the open window the morning sun was sketching slanting triangles onto the parquet. It was such a peaceful atmosphere.

Clara pointed to the chaos on the bookshelves. 'Because I don't want to end up like this. With nothing but ballast. With dusty, useless stuff that fell silent years ago. That doesn't actually have anything to say to me any longer. And besides, I'd put it up for sale before I got laid off.'

Jan smiled innocently up at her. 'Instant karma.'

Clara smiled back. 'Fate sees that I want to sell the house and decides I don't need a job anymore? I don't think fate has any idea of the current cost of living.'

Their mother came into the sitting room. She never looked particularly confused when she was at home.

'What shall I do?'

Jan put another box next to his. 'Why don't you pack the books in this box?' he said gently. 'Look, move them from this one into that one.'

She started at once. She packed a vase in too, along with two glasses that had been standing around, and the half-eaten sandwich in her hand. Then she looked up at Clara, suddenly uncertain.

'Am I doing it right-angled, Toni?'

Jan put his arm around her shoulders. 'Perfectly right-angled, Mama. Toni thinks so too, don't you?'

He looked up at her. Grinned again. Clara shook her head slowly. Sometimes, it was just funny.

Their mother stopped packing, stared wide-eyed at them both, then asked hoarsely: 'Who's Toni?'

Jan and Clara burst out laughing together, and after a moment, their mother joined in.

Later, Clara and Jan were sitting on the little terrace above the garden that was running more and more to seed.

'We should do something,' Jan said thoughtfully, looking at the overgrown hedge and last autumn's leaves. 'Papa can't cope anymore.'

'Yes, we should.' Clara looked at her brother and added: 'But it'll never happen, and we both know that, don't we?'

Jan leant over and tried to push her out of her chair. She fought back, laughing.

'At least I said it first!'

There weren't many people she was this familiar with.

'A couple came to see the house. They were ... kind of weird.'

'What do you mean, weird? Did they ask you if your house had a soundproof cellar, or something?'

Clara shut her eyes. In the moments it broke through the clouds, the April sun was strong.

'That wouldn't have been weird. Everyone needs a cellar like that.'

It was part of their game to make each other laugh. Say surprising things. Lots of people didn't understand that they could be brother and sister and friends too. She'd noticed this same quickness of speech, this rapid wit, in the actor. It was only now that she realised that he hadn't told her his name. Although maybe he'd introduced himself in some truer way.

'No, the weird thing was, they seemed really well suited. Outwardly. But ... inwardly, not at all. There was no ... they didn't chime together, I'd say. I liked the man. An actor.'

'Well, how about that. And about time too, sis.'

Jan had turned to her. She opened her eyes a tiny slit and could dimly see that he was smiling.

'Is he good-looking?'

Clara thought about it.

'Hm. Yes, actually. Not in the usual way. He's witty. And I think he's a good bit younger than me. So there's no need to smile – I don't stand a chance.'

'But why not? You still look good.'

It was a throwaway remark, but Clara sat up abruptly.

'Jan! Never, absolutely never, tell a woman she still looks good. That's the worst thing you could say.'

He stared at her in surprise. 'Seriously?'

'Yes,' she said, 'seriously. If I *still* look good, that means I've got no time left. I'm getting old. I'm running out of chances. Before long, I won't be worth anything on the poxy relationship market. So, if you ever meet a woman, never, never, never tell her that she still looks good. Got that?'

Jan grinned. 'You look great, sis. Your only difficulty is that your actor is clearly part of a couple. A couple that wants to buy your house, start a family and live the dream.'

'Quite apart from that,' remarked Clara, shutting her eyes against the sun.

Mama came onto the terrace.

'There you are!' She greeted them as if they'd only just arrived. 'I want to go home now.'

'You are at home, Mama,' Jan said cheerfully.

Their mother looked around and pointed at the back door. 'But they're walking old,' she said.

Clara pulled out a chair for her. They were lucky really. A lot of people with dementia got ever more aggressive. Their mother had been nicer over the last few years.

'Even so, Mama. You live here. Have done for ages.'

'Well,' their mother replied. 'Well...'

Jan picked up the thread again. 'But maybe he likes you too. However old he is.'

He was just being nosy. She knew him.

'Jan! What do you want from me? Are you into older women?' she asked. 'Do you know anyone who's with an older woman? Have you ever been with an older woman? Men look for younger women. Unless they're kinky, and I don't want a relationship with anyone kinky. How could I ever be sure he wouldn't get sick of me after five years and leave me for someone younger after all?'

Mama was listening with interest.

'I lost my virginity to an older woman.' Jan sounded vehemently defensive. 'She was thirty-two and I was eighteen.'

'You always were a late starter,' Clara mocked. 'But yes, I found him attractive. And I don't even know his name. It's not worth thinking about. Anyway, he has a very pretty girlfriend. A bit naïve, but not stupid, and – let me say this one more time – pretty.'

Jan leant back. Like he'd won.

'What?' Clara asked, somewhat uncertainly. '...What?'

'All I can say,' Jan pitched his voice high, imitating their father, 'is that this isn't the end of the matter.'

'Idiot,' said Clara. But, she thought, if I'm really honest with myself, it's kind of sexy. Not the end of the matter ... perhaps ... no. The start of something. It should be like that. A thrill. Something lovely. And right now, I wish I was younger.

'Jan,' she said firmly, as if to assure herself, 'I don't even know his name. There. And now, let's go.'

'Yes!' their mother exclaimed joyfully, standing up. 'At last!'

9

Elias jammed the paper bag from the bakery between his teeth and unlocked his front door as quietly as possible. Jule was bound to be still asleep. She'd come for an unexpected visit this weekend.

'I'd like to see your opening night,' she'd said on the phone. And that she'd skip her classes the following afternoon, so they'd have a bit more time together. He'd been really pleased. Things were much better between the two of them now. When she'd been twelve or thirteen, it had often been difficult. He'd been far too far away, at the Landestheater in Schleswig-Holstein. She'd been in the middle of puberty, and then Mona had started seeing a new man, who'd actually been quite a decent bloke, but God, he'd been uptight. Elias had seen way too little of Jule, and when he had, he'd always felt guilty about it. It was lucky that he'd always got on well with Mona. Looking back on it now, she'd had to field a whole lot of stuff.

He pulled off his shoes and walked into the kitchen to make tea. The flat wasn't huge, but he liked that it was up high enough that you had a great view over the town. Especially on a day like today.

I enjoy making my daughter breakfast. Why does it take so long to figure some stuff out?

He opened both sides of the double window. The air was cool but you could feel that spring really was on its way. The spires of Michelsberg Abbey towered over the rooftops nearby. This view had been the main reason he'd taken this flat. Suddenly, he found himself thinking about Clara Wagenbach. The way she'd stood on her veranda. In that severe and elegant suit. He found himself thinking about her the same way that you suddenly spot a picture on the wall and ask yourself in surprise if it's always been there.

That was how he felt in this moment – like the thought had always been there.

He put the kettle on. Took the plates off the shelf and put the rolls in a basket. It was still so quiet. He loved the soft sounds of getting breakfast. The measured movements. It was like a dance of small things.

Music. Quiet and non-demanding. It intensified the cool hush, made his movements weightless, as if he were underwater. Did she like swimming? He remembered her suit and laughed to himself. She'd wear a one-piece, never a bikini. He'd like to see the way she swam.

He paused, walked quietly across the hall to his study and opened the door a crack, just as quietly. Jule was still asleep. The flat was too small for her to have her own room here. So when she came to stay, she got the study. She looked very like Mona back when they'd first met. Jule was only four years younger than her mother had been then, when he'd fallen in love with her. Twenty-one, both of them. It had all been so absolute in those days. No alternative. Mona, the love of my life, he'd thought. He shut the door again. Well. In some ways, it had been true. Mona was ... he couldn't exactly call her a friend. She was both more and less than that ... Either way, she was one of the few fixed points in his life. Not just because she was Jule's mother. There'd been times when he'd been too broke to pay the maintenance, and she hadn't said a word about it. Because she was one of those very rare people who, even after a relationship ended, never forgot why you'd once been in love.

He poured the tea. Lifted the eggs out of the water. For a moment, things were in equilibrium.

Jule was still looking sleepy over breakfast, and Elias reminded himself that, as a teen, he'd always slept in late too. It was a long time since he'd been able to manage that.

'Vera might come this evening too. Is that all right with you?'

Jule laughed and pulled her knee up onto the chair.

'Papa, you always have some girlfriend coming along. It doesn't bother me. Seriously.'

Even so, he was a bit uncomfortable about it. If Jule was going to be there, he didn't really want Vera to come. He wouldn't go to hers, either. They were two separate worlds and he wanted to keep them apart.

'Is she your actual girlfriend?' Jule cut a roll in half and looked enquiringly around the table. 'Is there any ham?'

Elias stood up, raised his index finger admonishingly and declaimed: 'Listen up, kiddo: I was a vegetarian before the Greens even knew what the word meant. Before you were born. Get thee back to the hell whence you came, Spawn of Satan, and lead me not into temptation!'

Jule laughed. 'So it's in the fridge?'

Elias nodded and put on an offended tone. 'I'm very sorry for having forgotten this once.'

Jule took the ham from the fridge, filled her roll, bit into it and then, with her mouth full, asked: 'So?'

He hesitated, then shook his head. Not to deny Vera, or because he didn't want to tell Jule. But because he wouldn't have wanted his daughter to be in a relationship like this. No commitment. No certainty. No letting the other person into his life. He wanted her to introduce her boyfriend to him. Or girlfriend. Either way. And he wanted her to fall truly in love one day, and to throw herself into a love like that with everything within her, everything she had. Suddenly, the little sense of unevenness inside him seemed huge. You can't truly live if you're in the wrong life ... Great. And constantly repeating this without doing anything about it didn't help either.

'I...' he began, pouring himself another cup of tea. 'I don't think I'm cut out for love. Not anymore, anyway. Things with Vera are more...'

Jule clapped her hands over her ears and sang loudly and tunelessly 'Lalalalalala ... I can't hear you ... I don't want to listen to my father discussing this stuff ... lalalala!'

She got that from him. But it was funny all the same.

He laughed. 'I'm not planning to talk about sex.'

'Lalalalalala!'

'Want another egg?'

Jule nodded, took her fingers out of her ears and shrugged.

'It's always the same with you. Some date comes to the first night. It used to bother me because I ... I always used to think that I didn't want a new mum. That I didn't want anyone to tell me what to do. But it was never like that. So, is she the one?'

'Maybe there's no such thing,' he answered hesitantly. 'Or if there is, it's only on the stage. The one, true, real love of your life. You wish for it, dream about it, but in reality ... maybe you just always have to make compromises.'

Jule hunched her shoulders again and stared hard at him. 'Do you really think that? That there's no such thing as your one true love? I think there is. Maybe you don't find them, that's possible. I don't know. But I do believe that that kind of love exists. So, she's not the one for you.'

It wasn't a question. It was a statement.

Jule's words had a strange effect on him. Her certainty. It was rare for them to have this serious a conversation.

'I'm really not a great role model.'

He'd meant it to sound light, merry, but somehow, it didn't come out like that.

Jule stood up, leant over the table and kissed him on the cheek. 'Papa, you're a great actor. And I've managed to turn you into a good dad. And maybe one day, you will be someone's one true love. So, what more do you want?'

She dropped back into her chair. Glanced down at her phone and took another roll. She was at peace with herself.

He wasn't. And his daughter could see it. He tried to smile all the same. It wasn't enough, he thought soberly. It wasn't enough to be able to play two parts well. Nobody would hire an actor who could only play two roles. I should be good at everything. Or try to be, at least.

'Shall we go out somewhere? I don't have to be at the theatre till six.'

She looked up for a moment. 'Nah, don't worry. I've got a bit of schoolwork to do, OK?'

He nodded. Sometimes it was hard to find the right level of intimacy. What had he been like at seventeen? Definitely not as certain as she was. But also not as ... young. As light-hearted.

'Do you have a boyfriend, kiddo? Or ... a girlfriend?'

It was a spontaneous question. Just because he'd been thinking about his younger self. In those days, pretty much everything had revolved around it. And, to be honest, still did. If there was anything that fundamental in Jule's life, he ought to know about it, right?

'Nosy Papa! Mama keeps asking the same thing. Mind you ... she only ever asks about a boyfriend.'

Jule grinned and tore off a lump of croissant.

'I'll tell you in the fullness of time, old man,' she mumbled through a mouthful, maybe to hide any little awkwardness. 'Not right now.'

A feeling of real warmth flooded through him, lifting him out of his seat. He stood up, came to stand behind his daughter and ran both hands through her hair.

'Ow,' she laughed. 'Is that your clumsy attempt at showing your love for me? By pulling my hair?'

'I ought to take you out of school,' Elias retorted, 'you're already too clever by half.'

He fled before the bread roll could hit him.

10

Teeth clenched, she pulled herself up on the rings. One more. She could do one more. She had to do one more. Eighteen, she repeated soundlessly, eighteen. When she'd started, she couldn't even manage one. She didn't know many women who did pull-ups. Even so, it was a battle she couldn't win. Nobody could win.

'Fuck,' she gasped, hauling her chin level with her hands with the last of her strength, then lowering herself in exhaustion and letting go of the rings. Panting, she walked over to the open kitchen window. The rings hanging from the ceiling in the hall had provoked plenty of comment, mostly along very similar lines – not exactly original. She took a deep breath. The air was cool and good. The morning sky was clear; there might even have been a frost overnight.

Sit-ups now. She went back to the hallway, lay down on the mat and set her feet against the front door, then raised her arms, not linking her hands behind her head. Three, six, nine, twelve, fifteen ... She counted sets of three, trying to come up as high as she could. Sixty-nine, pointless, seventy-two, pointless ... It was like a paradoxical mantra. Doing something in spite of it all. Wasn't all of life like that? Doing things even so? Despite? Regardless. Now, of all times.

She'd always done a bit of running. And cycling. But she'd started exercising properly back then. After Paul.

Paul had sometimes said such wise things. With a smile, but still serious.

There's something inside you that I can't reach.

Then he'd thought about it and corrected himself.

Or that I can't get out. And nor can you. But it's there all the same. Maybe someone else could – another man.

Or nobody could, she'd replied. It was hard to say anything else when you were lying side by side in bed, after sex. Funny. She only remembered those moments of intimacy. She couldn't remember what had gone before them. Showering together? Or had she come home late and cuddled up to him, still chilly from the evening air? She couldn't remember. She'd forgotten the sex too, but not the conversations afterwards.

Something inside her that he couldn't reach. And nor could she.

She found herself thinking about the actor. About his laugh. She'd only heard it once. Not many people laughed that freely, that genuinely.

Eighty-seven, ninety, ninety-three. Don't think. Keep it tight. She'd only turned the exercises into a proper training programme after she'd first noticed signs of dementia in Mama. That it was more than just absentmindedness or quirks intensified by age. Her father still refused to believe it. But it had been a shock to her back then. And to her siblings. Mama. Of all people. Mama, who'd always been so strong. Who'd taken them on holiday alone because Papa never managed to get a locum in time, to cancel his meetings, to arrange his diary. As if the summer, and the holidays, came as a complete surprise to him every single time. Mama, who'd done Papa's accounts, who'd always known which cases were due when, which clients were coming when, which family-court judge would be in charge.

But that was just how it went. Nobody knew that better than she did. Nothing was certain. Nothing was forever. And because of that – or rather in spite of that – she'd started training. Every morning. Almost without fail, the only exception being when she was travelling. And her exercises had increased over time. Push-ups. Pull-ups. Sit-ups. Forearm plank – thirty seconds to start with, then a minute, then a minute twenty ... she was probably unusually fit for an unemployed photographer. Or unusually mad.

A hundred and twenty. Done. She lay there, breathing fast, stretching her arms out sideways, as far as she could. Then she stood up and tidied the mat away. Feeling a strange mix of pride and self-mockery. As if exercise prevented dementia. Or ageing. Or was a guarantee of or against anything. They always won in the end. Death and forgetfulness and illness and ugliness and weakness. It was unavoidable. But for today, she'd held them all at bay. For today, for now, it felt good, this moment of strength. Tomorrow was tomorrow.

At the newsroom, she cleared her desk, which had actually never been hers. It wasn't much. A few folders. Chargers, her spare camera bag. Accumulated junk that suddenly didn't matter a damn. She threw almost all of it away. There wasn't much going on in the large office. She'd been careful to get there as early as she could, so as to dodge the usual conversations. I'm so sorry ... I'd never have thought ... Why, you? You're way better than ... I can't understand it ... We should ... Someday ... If I hear of anything that might suit ... She'd had enough of that already, after Paul. They all meant well, but she could do without it. Clara packed everything in the little wheely suitcase she'd brought with her. She wasn't actually out of a job for another two and a half weeks, but she had leave to use up, and there was no way she'd go in for the three days after that. What could they do – sack her?

On the stairs, she met Richard. Richard was OK.

He gestured towards her suitcase. 'I heard. Want me to shoot someone for you?'

Clara laughed. Richard was undoubtedly the last person who could ever shoot anyone. She liked him. Meanwhile, he was probably in love with her. Or so he always claimed, in a joking tone beneath which lurked a hint of unspoken pain. He was about her age and had somehow become the chief political editor. Nobody had a clue why. He was way too nice. He had none of the supposed attributes of a boss. Elbows. Toughness. And he was a hopeless leader. The rest of the team probably only did what he said because he asked them so nicely.

'I'm glad to see you one last time,' Clara said. It was true. 'Call me once the paper finally goes bust and you need a job.'

'That's my line,' Richard said with a smile. Sometimes he had a real sense of humour. 'I'll miss you, you know.' He hesitated a moment, then said hastily, 'Would you like to come to the theatre with me this evening? The arts section are all busy. I've got two tickets. And then we can go for a drink and I'll convince you that I'm the man for you, OK?'

Clara had to laugh because Richard knew perfectly well that he had absolutely no chance, although maybe he was putting on this awkward charm just to console her. Sometimes, his manner reminded her a little of Paul.

'I don't know. I...'

She didn't actually have plans. Far too many evenings were long and empty. She sometimes left the flat if the weather was nice, but then didn't really know what to do with herself. She wouldn't be in the mood for a pub or the cinema, but sitting around at home felt like throwing away perfectly good food. A waste. She was still good too, wasn't she?

'OK,' she said in the end. It might not be a bad thing. 'Then we can raise a glass to me getting sacked. I can't talk you into a drink right now, can I?'

'Hmm,' Richard mused, 'it's only nine-thirty. The days of the booze-hound journalist are long gone. Or were only ever a cliché.'

'I probably won't go out with you then,' teased Clara, picking up her case.

'I'll pick you up!' he called down the stairs after her.

She felt as though the evenings had suddenly grown lighter. After the gloomy winter, when dark afternoons shaded almost imperceptibly into early night, and after a very cold early spring, which had brought the snow that had been missing all winter, early April abruptly held the promise of summer. She leant on the iron railing around her tiny balcony and tried to taste the clarity of the air, which was yet to contain any of the sweet scents of the coming spring. It tasted more like melting snow than rain, and not yet like the first grass cuttings or linden blossom or evening showers on hot asphalt. This clarity had no flavour, but its beauty and freshness opened up her chest.

The bright evening sky, restless with high, scudding clouds and wild colours above the sharp, almost-black outline of the school roof … she suddenly felt like she'd done at fifteen. Roaming the town at night, always searching for life, which had to be out there somewhere. Alone, but not lonely, with total certainty that everything was yet to come. Everything.

The doorbell rang. Richard was here. She left the balcony door open as she walked back into the flat. She wanted to feel this clear air in every room when she got back later.

11

First night. No matter how big or small the theatre, this feeling – a mix of nervous tension, joyful anticipation, furious rage at the one scene that hadn't been properly finished – this feeling was always the same. Before the party, Elias thought, that was it. The feeling you get before a party. Mareike wasn't even trying to hide her nerves. She was smoking one cigarette after another, and was in a filthy mood. He'd worked with her once before and knew that she'd rather be hiding. She couldn't stand watching the finished play with the first-night audience because, for her, it never was finished. She gave him a quick wave when she saw him, but it confirmed what he already knew – better to leave her in peace.

In peace.

Vera had offered to give him a lift.

Then I can get a drink while you finish getting ready.

I love being in the theatre so early.

I like the vibe.

Me. Me. Me. She didn't notice how often it was all about her, and she'd have denied it vehemently. It didn't fit her self-image. And ... obviously she didn't want to be like that. But she was, again and again. So, he'd declined. Because of all that, and because of Jule. And more gruffly than strictly necessary. Besides, he'd been out all afternoon and been almost running late by the time he got home.

The cottage ... After this morning, he'd been drawn out there again. His car was still at the garage, so he'd got on the train with his bike. He hadn't even originally planned to go out there. He'd liked the area that first visit, and so he'd ridden through the cool, bright afternoon, enjoying the wind on his face, and after a while, had found himself in the village.

The cottage. As he stood outside it, the song popped into his head. Maybe it was the roses in the hedge. Julie London. 'A Cottage for Sale'. Her melancholy, casual, smoky voice. All the yearning, all the pain wrapped up in that effortless sound. He wished he could act like that.

He sang to himself as he leant the bicycle against the fence and walked into the garden. "*Our little dream castle...*" You never heard anyone singing in the street these days. If anyone sang in the street, people would look at them like they'd got a screw loose. Drunken caterwauling maybe. Football fans. But they didn't sing, they yelled their heads off, thinking it was a song. Not even kids. It was a long time since he'd heard anyone in the street just singing for the joy of it.

"*Where you planted roses...*" Hm, well probably nobody had planted the dog roses. They grew by themselves. His sleeve snagged on the tendrils and a thorn stabbed him as he climbed over the fence.

He could hear the humming even before he reached the veranda, where he'd fallen to his knees last time. The buzz filled the garden, and it was as though everything in his belly, in his chest was vibrating with it. It was like the drone of a mighty organ. The plum tree, which had still been bare the week before, had turned into a cloud. A cloud of white, a cloud of blossom in which danced tens of thousands of bees. He stopped. Perfectly still. The buzzing surrounded him, as if he were standing inside an invisible bell that had struck noon, the reverberations of which were setting him vibrating gently too.

Yes. Trees probably sang like that.

A single, thousand-voiced, thousand-winged hum of joy that spring was on its way.

Elias stood there, as if he could fill himself up with the sound of it.

Later, coasting back to the station through the late afternoon, it was still tingling in his fingertips. These spring evenings grew cool very quickly, and he stood up on the pedals to ride himself warm. Spring is coming, he thought. It's really coming now. Sometimes that was all it took. A tree in blossom and a swarm of bees and their shared song.

Elias was made up and in costume, standing by the little attic window above the stage, looking out into the small square outside the theatre as it filled up. Mareike smoked on first nights; he went up to the attic. There was no fly loft here, the theatre was too small.

They were standing down there with bubbly and beer. Indecipherable scraps of conversation rose up. Laughter.

Lots of woolly beanies, sloppy caps, smart hats. Colourful waistcoats. Second-hand coats and so many pairs of black trousers on women and men alike. The very definition of indie theatre, and a handful of more mainstream types too. If you considered yourself an artist, you went to the theatre to feel even more artistic. More artistic even than the actors on stage, who never got anything right, if the interval conversations were anything to go by.

Elias took a deep breath. He wasn't being fair. Maybe he was the one who wasn't where he wanted to be.

He thought about the buzz again. And the song.

Our little dream castle ... with every dream gone...

Then he grinned. No mirror, nothing. Straightened himself up. Now for the opening night.

Showtime!

12

They were late. Apparently, the arts section had only left one ticket at the box office, not two. Richard – far too nice, as ever – had offered to wait down in the bar for the play to be over. He was visibly horribly embarrassed.

'Absolutely no way!'

It was much easier to stand up for other people than for herself. Clara walked up to the box office. Polite, but very firm.

'It's never completely full. Even if it's sold out – there's always someone who doesn't turn up.'

The woman behind the desk was already on the defensive. She didn't know exactly who'd made the mistake – the newspaper or the theatre. She was looking for a way out. That was good. Clara made her tone more conciliatory and offered her one.

'It's ten to eight. You can just let me have one of the tickets that haven't been picked up.'

Tickets generally said 'available for collection until fifteen minutes before the performance begins', but box office staff pretty much always waited until the last bell rang. The cashier hesitated, then took one from the little pile and handed it to Clara. Richard looked at her with an admiring sigh. Now he really does look a tiny bit in love, she thought. He'd divorced years ago. Or rather, his wife had divorced him. And after that, somehow, things had never worked out for him.

'There's no way on God's green earth that I could ever manage that perfect blend of polite determination.'

Clara smiled. Was that a pretty compliment?

'You don't have to. Just find the right woman to do it.'

He smiled. It was only then that she realised that was open to misinterpretation. But what was said was said.

The ticket situation meant they weren't sitting together. She wasn't upset. Maybe she shouldn't have come at all. She didn't want to get his hopes up. She wanted a relaxed evening. But maybe he did too. Just a nice evening, nothing more. To feel not *wanted*, but at least not *un*wanted for a few hours. And not to feel alone. She turned to give Richard a quick smile. Of course, he'd let her take the seat nearer the stage, but it wasn't a big theatre. The auditorium was more like a cinema, with folding seats. Her knees were almost bashing the seat in front, but on the other hand, the atmosphere was friendly.

There was no curtain. On the still-dark stage stood large pot plants – African hemp, rubber trees and miniature lemon trees – like a hedge. Clara picked up the programme. She'd always liked *Death of a Salesman*. About a life – a successful life in actual fact – that unravels because people always prefer to live a different one. The wrong life. Then she realised that there were only two names. *Death of a Salesman* as a two-person play? How could that work? Her expectation of a relaxed evening was dimming along with the lights. She really wasn't in the mood for experimental theatre.

She glanced over her shoulder at Richard. He was holding the programme right up to his face and didn't notice her. He looked kind of lost ... It was just as well they weren't sitting next to each other.

Suddenly, there was a commotion in the back rows. At first, she thought someone had come in late. The man pushing his way between the seats, mumbling constant polite apologies, seemed as helpless as Richard had earlier. But he was getting ever louder as he forced his way through to the stage, clapping one person on the shoulder, shaking hands with another, and then finally squeezed between the pot plants and onto the stage.

No way! she thought in surprise, and with a touch of amusement. What are the chances? It was the actor. The one whose name she still didn't know, even though he'd got down on bended knee to her. It couldn't actually be that much of a coincidence; after all, he had to be working in some theatre. But for her to turn up to see him perform ... She glanced back at the programme, looking for his name. Elias Kornfeld. A strange feeling flooded through her. Had he recognised her on his way through the audience?

He was telling stories. You didn't know who he was speaking to. The plants and artful lighting meant that you could only make out vague silhouettes, so she couldn't even see if he was alone up there. He was speaking about a car crash that he'd just been in. Because of the low sun. And because he'd been so lost in thought. The way he talked, he could have told her the same story back in her garden the other day and she'd have believed him. And that was pretty good. He wasn't acting as though he was acting. Then there was movement among the plants. A young woman started pushing them aside, one by one. Elias in the role of Loman ... no, Elias as Loman, was talking and talking. He gave an exaggeratedly hearty laugh as he told his invisible sons about his successes, none of which were real. As he spoke about their amazing careers, which would never happen. He was funny. He was self-deprecating and not at all as tragic as she'd always imagined the travelling salesman. No Heinz Rühmann. No Dustin Hoffman. An entertainer, but one who'd never made it onto the stage.

He moaned that he was always in a race with the junkyard and accused the fridge – actually just a door fastened to the wall – of breaking the minute he'd paid it off. As he spoke, he turned to the audience, saw Clara and winked. Everyone laughed. So did she, without even really knowing why. Even so, she didn't know whether he'd recognised her and that was why he'd winked, or whether that was part of the play and he'd have made eye contact with someone at that point either way.

The interval was already half over before Richard got back with the *sekt*.

'The bar staff seemed a little taken aback that there were people wanting interval drinks. Speed is not one of their best qualities,' he said, handing her a champagne flute. 'To a pleasant evening.'

'Thanks for inviting me,' Clara said, taking a sip. 'It's much better than I expected. The leading man ... he makes it ... I don't know how he does it. The whole time you feel like he...' She paused. Seriously, how did he do it? He simply came close to her. She simply believed him. Even though he was telling tragic stories as if they were jokes. You laughed, but at the same time, you knew that there was more there.

'He's not acting on a head level,' Richard said, offhandedly. 'He's acting on the level of your emotions.'

Clara gave him a quick look of surprise. Sometimes, he got right to the heart of things, without even realising.

'And that's why you like him,' he added, with a slight, rueful smile, then raised his glass a little.

'Oh, how lovely to see you here!'

It was the woman who'd viewed her house. Elias's girlfriend. Clara couldn't immediately remember her name.

'Vera,' the woman said cheerfully. 'Vera Steiner.' She held out her hand to Richard.

'And you are...' She glanced quickly from Clara to Richard and back again. 'You're married?'

'About as much as you are,' Clara said, with a half-smile. 'We're colleagues. Were colleagues,' she corrected herself meticulously. 'We've come to the theatre to celebrate me being sacked. Will you buy my house?'

Why was she doing this? There'd been no need to make the woman feel awkward. Vera Steiner hadn't meant anything by it. It wasn't her fault that Clara had been laid off. But it didn't seem to faze her; either that, or she was politely ignoring the needle. She wasn't smiling anymore, just looking directly at Clara.

'Where did you work, then?' she asked. 'And I ... I owe you an apology. We don't have the money to buy your house at the moment.

It was just so ... the listing online made it look so lovely that I really wanted to see it. But we just can't afford it. Not at the moment, anyway. I'm really sorry to hear you've lost your job. I had no idea.'

Vera was quite upset and, above all, so childishly honest, that although Clara found her irritating, she couldn't be angry. And, after all ... but no, she wouldn't let herself think that. But the thought wouldn't be repressed. It was only in the back of her mind, but it was there. Because 'after all' there was Elias. She would never have met him if this Miss Steiner hadn't wanted to see her house ... Stop. It was just a funny coincidence, meeting at the theatre like this. Still, it was hard not to read things into it.

'What do you think of him?'

Clara hesitated and Richard answered. 'Very good. I think it's ... yes, very good. Very different from the way the play is usually staged. But ... no. Really good.'

But Vera Steiner hadn't asked what he thought of the play. She probably didn't care about that too much. She was interested in what people thought of her boyfriend. And Richard probably thought Clara wasn't enjoying the play, so he'd wanted to jump in for her.

She found herself smiling, so she hastily hid her mouth behind her glass. Her hesitation had had nothing to do with that. It was just that she ... she hadn't wanted to tell Vera Steiner how good her boyf... she hadn't wanted to feed her pride. However much she was trying to hide it, Vera couldn't help displaying this possessive pride. What must it be like when people could read pretty much everything from your face?

Vera turned to her. 'How about you? You're not so keen, are you?'

The bell rang just in time.

'I'll tell you once he's died,' Clara replied, and then couldn't help adding, a touch maliciously, 'if he manages that as well as his dropping to his knees, then I'll like it very well indeed.'

He managed it. Clara didn't know quite how he did it. She could still see the man who'd been there in her garden. But that man was also Willy Loman, teetering as uncertainly on the rim of the planter as on the mountaintop of his lies and delusions. Willy Loman, who no longer understood his sons because constantly comparing them to other boys meant he couldn't see them properly anymore.

Clara was sure now that he'd spotted her. Whenever he spoke to his unseen wife, his unseen boss or his unseen sons, his eyes constantly darted to hers; sometimes they met. Just for one word, perhaps. And then he laughed again and tried, as if it were a game, to drop seeds into the cracks between the boards, so that he'd have something in the ground before it got dark. Clara found herself thinking about Paul. How much he'd enjoyed planting things. And how that still moved her...

Loman grew very quiet at the end. He was almost merry as he sat on the stage between his plant pots, in the evening atmosphere, listening to his sons' grand plans for the next day. Except that nobody was speaking. Whatever they were saying could only be deduced from his half-answers, his nods, his strangely skewed, false pride, which shone around him there, without dimming. They'd probably left long ago. Because they hadn't been able to bear him always looking at the wrong sons. His entire life being an utterly unnecessary lie. Then he stood up with a smile and disappeared behind the wall of weeping figs and rubber trees and African hemp, and you heard a car start up. The young woman came and suddenly the pots were easy to move; they were on wheels, but it was only now you could see that. You heard Loman's car engine in the distance as the actress arranged the plants at the side of a grave that gradually appeared. First as an outline and then clearer and clearer. Then the engine cut out abruptly and it was very quiet. His name glowed faintly on the projected gravestone. The woman stood at Loman's grave for a while. Looked around. Waited. But nobody came. Then she left too.

It took a while for the applause to begin. Elias and the young woman stepped up to the edge of the stage. Held hands. Bowed. The applause didn't stop. Clara was clapping too, but she found it hard. Not because she hadn't liked it. It had been amazing. When had she last been that caught up in anything? What kind of strange emotion was this? His acting had been so incredibly intense ... she remembered what Richard had said. He's acting on the level of your emotions. Clara remembered what she'd said to his girlfriend during the interval and that robbed her of some of her enjoyment. Stupid. Stupid and thoughtless.

Never mind, she thought. This was now. She was clapping properly by this point. Almost defiantly.

13

He took his time over removing his make-up and getting changed. Not to find his way back out of the role. Sometimes colleagues said that stuff. Affectation. If you needed time to find your way back out of the role, you weren't fully in it. It was more to put the second performance off a bit longer. Nobody told the truth on first nights and so, by the end of them, he never knew whether they'd pulled it off. How well they'd pulled it off. And least of all, whether he'd been good enough.

How funny that is, he thought. I know what I'm capable of. I know that I was good. But good enough? I never know that. The distance between good and very good is always decided by others.

Jule knocked on the doorframe. She was out of breath, like she'd been running, and she looked like she was over the moon.

'You were great, Papa. Really great.'

She hugged him.

'Did you think so?'

'Yes,' said Jule. 'And the thing with the plants was a good idea.'

'You think the plants were better than me?' He raised his eyebrows. Followed up with a long, drawn-out 'shit!' But he was still proud to be praised by his seventeen-year-old daughter.

'Are you coming down?'

Her excitement was infectious. But she'd seen him in heaps of plays. She was so used to the theatre that she'd once destroyed a production with a single word: boring!

He grabbed her playfully by the back of the neck and felt a little swelling.

'I'm coming! And what's that there?'

She ducked away, laughing. 'Papa, you're a freak. I'm not having you picking my spots. Get a grip.'

'I can do what I like,' Elias answered majestically, 'I'm a star! And you can't let yourself be seen like that. It's bright red.'

Jule pulled away and backed out of the dressing room.

'Horrible old man! You and Mama – you're obsessed. Nobody else picks their kids' spots.'

He followed her. She hastily changed the subject.

'Which of those two women is Vera then?'

He stopped, not understanding right away. 'Sorry? What do you mean, those two women?'

'There were two women looking at you the whole time. I was watching them.'

He pushed her towards the stairs. 'Ah. Now your enthusiasm starts to make sense. You didn't even see the play. But if it comes to being watched – everyone was looking at me. That's what we call an audience.'

'Not the way those two were. So, which is she?'

Yeah, that's my relationship with Vera, he thought fleetingly. After almost two years, my daughter has to ask me what she looks like.

He raised his arms in a gesture of resignation. 'You'll probably meet her in a minute. Bide your soul in patience.'

Music and laughter and the wild chaos of conversation rose from downstairs. Jule jumped down the steps. Like a child. A warm yearning welled up in him and he thought: this moment. She's so grown up. If I could keep this moment, it would be enough for the whole evening. This light familiarity between him and Jule.

'Come on!' she called impatiently. 'Everyone's waiting for you.'

He took a deep breath.

'I'm coming.'

14

'You were very good, Mr Kornfeld.'

It was loud. At best, what you could hear from the loudspeakers over the bar was scraps of some kind of classic rock. People were talking, laughing, drinking, shouting. The noise ebbed and flowed, sounding a bit like you were by the sea. So, you had the choice of shouting too, or leaning in very close to the other person if you wanted to speak at anything like a normal volume.

Elias nodded seriously and said 'It's all first names and "darling" at a first night. We can drop it again tomorrow if you want to. But for now, I'm Elias.'

'I know,' said Clara. 'I read the programme. I'm Clara.'

She'd wavered when Richard had suggested going for dinner after the play. But she'd known very well that she wanted to stay.

'Did you really think so? Nobody ever tells the truth at an opening-night party.' He smiled and looked down. 'And I wouldn't want to hear it tonight, either. So lie to me.'

'You were terrible. I've never seen such a wooden performance.'

She liked the way his head jerked up, almost in shock.

'Seriously? I was wooden?'

'You wanted to be lied to.'

They both laughed. Clara looked over to the bar, where Vera was standing, chatting to someone.

'What did your girlfriend say? Did she think you were good too?'

Clara had had a glass of wine with Richard, standing at one of the tall, round bar tables, and observing. Had watched as Elias, his co-star and the director had walked into the room. As Vera had hugged him after the three had been applauded ... she'd had the sense not to join him immediately. Had watched after that, as Vera's every movement, her every glance, her every smile had declared Mine. Mine. Mine.

'She doesn't like the play. But she likes me in it.'

Elias didn't know exactly what it was. There was no hint of … competition, jealousy, or anything like that in her question. She'd just asked it. He'd seen her watching him earlier. But it hadn't been like someone staking a claim in some unspoken way. Not like … no, not like a hunter watching their prey. Rather, it was as though her interest lay not in his relationship with Vera but in the way they looked together. No more. No less. The way Mareike had thought about the stage, and about the plants.

'Too dark?'

Elias shrugged. 'I don't know. She doesn't like the way Loman lies right up until the end. She likes honesty. That's one of the…' He couldn't say it was one of the nice things about her. But it was, wasn't it? It was a nice thing. And she generally was honest. More than other people, a lot of the time. But she bore her honesty like a glittering shield that preceded her. So he left the sentence unfinished.

'We all lie to one another. And she isn't always entirely honest, is she? After all, the two of you looked at my house when you don't have the money for it.'

She smiled at him. She didn't mind. People were like that. At least it meant they'd met. She liked him. That much was clear.

'Being honest with oneself is overrated. Why are you talking to me?' Clara pointed mockingly towards the group of young people at a large table right next to the little buffet, which looked pretty bare by this point. A sad remnant of a very organic-looking quinoa salad was all that was left. 'All the little girls who admire you … don't you see the way they look at you? Of course you do … Why aren't you over there?'

Elias looked at her. Her face matches her name, he thought. Clear. Not conventionally beautiful. You could never have called her pretty. A severe beauty, perhaps. There wasn't much softness in those features.

'Well, for one thing, because one of those little girls is my daughter. See, over there.'

There was a little stab in Clara's stomach. Daughter. Now he'd shown her, she could see the resemblance.

'She's not much like Vera.'

Elias had to laugh. 'That's probably because she's not Vera's daughter. I'm one of those stupid artists who had a kid far too young because in their sheer exuberance, they don't think things through.'

Clara looked from Elias to his daughter and back again.

'Has anything changed about that?'

She couldn't quite suppress the smile as she asked that. Elias liked the way it softened her lips.

'Not much,' he said, with a kind of self-deprecating honesty. 'Not very much, I'm afraid.'

There was a little pause between them. The music was turned up a notch. Elias saw Vera glance at him. Smile at him. Kiss her hand to him and blow it through the air. For me, he thought briefly, or for Clara? So she knows what she's up against?

'This time you didn't answer my question.'

Clara had been thinking about their first meeting.

'What?' Elias asked. He didn't catch on right away. 'What do you mean?'

'Why you're speaking to me.'

Elias raised a hand melodramatically to his brow and declaimed: 'Do I have to have a reason for everything I do?'

Clara tilted her head slightly. He was being evasive. Why?

'Not for everything. But your girlfriend is standing over there, kissing her hand to you. I don't want ... I don't want to play this game.'

Elias grew serious. 'Me neither,' he said. And then, without thinking about it: 'I was at your house again this afternoon.'

Now Clara was truly surprised. 'Why?'

Elias shrugged. She found this little, helpless gesture touching.

'I couldn't tell you. I don't know. I liked the garden. Did you know your plum tree is blossoming?'

Suddenly, right out of nowhere, she felt knocked off balance. Until now, everything had been open and right. The play. The evening. The conversation. Pleasant, a little poignant perhaps, because the play had been so intense, while this party was so casual and alive. But whereas so far this evening, she'd been on solid ground, though fleet of foot, yes, almost dancing overland, she was now suddenly standing on the coast of an unknown sea. Turn back, or get into a boat?

'Why?' she asked again. But the question sounded very different from her intended tone, almost a whisper.

Elias sipped his *sekt* as if to liberate the mood again.

'Oh,' he said, as lightly as he could, 'I was merely on a quest for truth.'

Amid all the noise around them, at their table you could suddenly have heard a pin drop.

'Shouldn't I have said—?'

Clara cut him off, pointing to Vera. 'If you're looking for truth, you'd be better looking at your girlfriend's place.'

Elias put his glass on the table. How serious she was now.

'I didn't plan it. I went out on my bike. I often do, before a first night or whatever. And then ... yes, maybe I was just drawn back there,' he ended up helplessly. It didn't sound very like an explanation. Perhaps that was what Clara found so moving.

'Go to your girlfriend. She's been looking over to you this whole time.'

She was smiling as she spoke. Elias felt strangely relieved.

'But you'll stay a while, won't you?'

Clara didn't have to think about it.

'Yes,' she said.

15

Fewer and fewer of the small groups who drifted out to smoke were coming back in. The music had got louder and Richard had left long ago. She'd felt a bit sorry for him. She didn't know whether he'd been expecting more from the evening, although of course, if that had been the case, he'd been far too polite to let it show. A brotherly hug at the end: I'm really tired now.

Maybe he had been. Tired of waiting. Was she?

The space was expanding. This was the moment, the turning point in every party, that determined whether it would fizzle out or pick up steam. Go somewhere or other. Elias looked around for Vera. It was good that Jule had already left, he thought. Somehow, the chance for the two of them to meet had never quite arisen. To his relief.

There were posters all over the walls. Clara was standing, glass in hand, in front of one of them, studying it intently. Elias looked between Vera and Clara. There was something definite about the things Clara did. Great concentration. And she was alone.

'Shall we go?'

Vera had finished her wine and was no longer entirely sober. Elias pointed to Mareike, who was standing a little way down the bar with her boyfriend and the technicians, still on a high from the success of the evening, and still drinking.

'I'll stay a bit longer. But you can go if you want to.'

It sounded more unfriendly than he'd intended.

'Will you come over later?'

She nestled into him. He could feel her warmth, which he liked, actually. Actually. There was always that little word between them. He liked having sex with her, actually. He liked travelling with her, actually. He liked going out with her, actually. But there was always something that made the difference between actually and really. Really liking going out with her. Really wanting to be with her – with no limitations.

Ha. That was probably what people meant by love, he thought.

'Don't know. Don't wait up for me.'

'Why are you being so unkind?'

It was true. He'd sounded harsh. But it was also true that he didn't know. And she'd been drinking, which he always found hard to deal with. Because then ... then she stopped hiding her feelings. The more she pulled on him, the more he pulled away.

Our little arrangement is another of those lies, he thought. You're in love. I'm not. I act like I don't notice your love, and you act like my chilliness is love too, just well hidden.

His voice softened. 'I didn't mean to hurt you.' That was certainly true. 'I truly don't know. I can't leave just yet, anyway.' He pointed again to Mareike and her friends, who'd started to dance. And saw Clara putting down her glass.

'OK,' said Vera. She pulled out her phone and looked at the time. 'You know where the key is. Come later, yeah? Or message me.'

He walked her to the door. Helped her into her coat. He liked to be polite, and she liked that he did that kind of thing for her. Held the door for her. Stood up when she came into the room. Let her walk ahead of him.

'See you later,' she said, and kissed him.

Don't say that, he thought. Why do you do that? See you later means: I'm expecting you.

'Yeah, maybe,' he replied.

'Were you arguing?'

Elias had joined her at the table. With two little bottles of beer.

'No. Yes ... kind of. But not out loud. Sometimes that bores me to tears.'

Clara smiled and raised her beer. 'To you. You were amazing. Really amazing.'

Elias clinked. The bottles met with an honest, robust sound.

'Why can't it be easy?'

Clara laughed. Freely.

'Because it's never easy. Life isn't made that way.'

The music grew louder still. Electronica. Cool. With a compelling, pulling bass and melodies made of whispering voices from the Charleston era. It made you want to move.

'Dance?'

He nodded.

16

It must have been two a.m. by the time they left the theatre bar. Inside, people were still dancing and drinking. It had been a clear day, so the night was chilly. You could see a handful of stars, despite the town lights. Clara breathed out white. The cold was doing her good.

They hadn't spoken much. Danced. Drunk a little more, then danced again. Mareike had been so unbuttoned and so full of happiness that she'd swept the two of them along with her, and everyone else too. In the end, the whole place had been dancing.

'Your director has a good sense of humour.'

Elias nods. 'She needs one. I think working with me is pretty tough sometimes. I can't stand it if the director doesn't know what they actually want to do with the play. I'm a much better actor when I know what's what.'

They both looked up into the sky for a moment. The air was so clear.

'What now?'

Clara didn't want to go home just yet, but the evening really was over.

'Didn't I just tell you that I need clear instructions?' Elias grinned at her. 'What do you think? How are you getting home?'

She shrugged. 'No idea. Richard gave me a lift here. Taxi maybe. How about you?'

He imitated her. Quite well. Raised his shoulders like she'd done. 'No idea! Taxi maybe?'

She had to laugh.

'Wait here a moment,' he said, 'I need to pop back in.'

Clara leant against the brick wall. Once upon a time, she would've had a smoke now, at the end of the evening. But that really was way back when.

Elias reappeared and walked towards the bike racks by the gate. Clara followed him. Elias pulled out the theatre cargo bike. An e-bike with a big crate on the front.

'Taxi!' he said with a laugh. 'Want me to run you home?'

Clara laughed too. What a nice idea.

'Can I do the cycling? I've only ridden an e-bike once.'

Elias slipped readily into the crate. His legs dangled over the edge.

'That was the plan from the start. You do the cycling. I'm just ballast.'

Clara wheeled the bike onto the street, push-started it, then got into the saddle. They swayed a bit and almost toppled over, but then she got into the swing of it and they picked up speed.

The streets were empty. It was so easy to pedal with the assistance of the motor that they were going really fast and Clara was riding herself warm. Through red lights and crossing roads on the diagonal, cutting across all the lanes, further and further east. Cycling through the cold spring night was great.

'Does this thing have a hooter?' she called out as they swerved around a drunk who'd just lurched off the pavement into the road.

Elias shook his head, dug in his pocket and pulled out his keys. Clara saw him hold one up to his lips, the bit upwards. A sharp whistle.

'Will that do? Or I can just shout.'

She laughed. 'A whistle will do. I feel like a train.'

She turned off suddenly, and Elias had to hold on tight as they rattled over the cobblestones, down towards the park.

'Do you live in the park? In a tent or something?'

Clara steered onto one of the smaller paths. Cycling here was against the rules. But tonight, there were no rules.

'I've got a country cottage. When I'm not out there, I just sofa-surf with my friends,' she said, deadpan. 'I don't need a flat.'

'That explains how you can afford such expensive clothes. Do you raid their wardrobes while they're in their kitchens, making you a coffee?'

These games felt so easy. This kind of chatter was like playing it as a child – running for sheer fun, trying to catch one another, nowhere in particular to go. Play for play's sake. Running for running's sake. Nothing more.

'Fancy a little tour of the town?'

Clara was heading back onto the road, towards the posh end.

'Always,' said Elias. He wrapped his coat more closely around him. It was pretty cold if you were sitting still. But there was nowhere he'd rather be than in this bicycle crate.

'I've lived here years though. Show me something new.'

'That was the plan,' said Clara.

They rode through the town's nocturnal hush. It was cold enough to almost smell a little of snow. In April ... A slender moon hung aslant over traffic lights that blinked forlornly to themselves. They were almost out into the suburbs when Clara turned at a petrol station and rode uphill. Elias didn't know this area very well, and he didn't know the little park they were now entering at all.

'This isn't how a tour works,' he called back to Clara. 'You have to explain things. Something like: OK everyone, so here we can see the very spot upon which Erich the Skinny had his fifth wife beheaded, after which, in his disillusionment, he threw himself from the castle battlements.'

Clara was breathing fast. Despite the motor, she was having to work hard here.

'The beheading stuff is a myth. In reality, she pushed him and then faked her own execution with the assistance of a watermelon to which she had glued her own hair. Tour guides always get that wrong. She was actually a nasty con artist. Anyway, we're nearly there.'

They were still heading uphill, up a winding lane, beneath the birch and linden trees and their first, delicate leaves. A squat tower appeared around the last bend; Elias had never seen it before.

'Where are we?' he asked, as Clara stopped. He got out cautiously to avoid tipping the bike.

'The observatory. Have you ever been here?'

He shook his head. She lowered the kick-stand. He handed her the bottle of beer that he'd smuggled out of the theatre.

'Everywhere looks different at night anyway. But no, I've never been here. It looks ... it's very pretty.'

There was a sudden strange shyness between them. Maybe, thought Clara as she took a swig, that's because we're definitely not on anyone's way home anymore. This is like the start of something.

The tower was low but very broad. Glittering very faintly around the generous entrance were plaster flower tendrils. In the dark, you could barely make out the hint of gold. Art Nouveau. The first-floor window was slightly oval. The elegant railings around the roof terrace looked black, but you could tell that they were actually dark green.

'It's probably quite nice in the daytime,' he remarked mischievously as they walked around the tower.

Clara smiled. 'Yeah. But by day, you can't see what I want to show you.'

She'd found the key safe, tucked away behind the small back door, and typed in the pin.

'Oh wow,' said Elias. He liked this. 'You're full of surprises.'

'Nah,' she answered as they headed back to the main entrance. 'This is my only one. But I bet you joined some club or whatever when you were fifteen or sixteen, right?'

'The usual,' he admitted, as he followed her up the stairs. She didn't put the light on. So they wouldn't be dazzled, she said.

Standing on the terrace were six telescopes of varying sizes, on very robust-looking stands. Clara joined Elias at the handrail and they both looked up into the sky.

'Some things never change,' he said quietly. 'There are things that never lose their fascination. Fire. Running water, the sea. The sky on a night like this.'

'Fresh-baked bread,' said Clara. 'Wine. Sex.'

They fell silent. Then she went over to one of the telescopes, removed its case and adjusted the height.

'Look,' she said, pointing to the telescope. 'I bet you've never seen the moon like this before.'

As he gazed through it at the moon, she rested her hand gently on his back. A familiar gesture. But it felt erotic too. Clara was right. He had definitely never seen the moon like this before. It was a tiny crescent in the sky, yet he could see the whole thing through the telescope. Shadowy, but whole.

'Does it zoom in?' he breathed. 'Can I see more of the surface?'

'Come over here.'

Clara uncovered a different one.

'With this, you can even see the man in the moon.'

She adjusted it for him. He laughed softly.

'What?' asked Clara.

'Oh, terrace, starry night, two people looking at the moon. It's like some kind of *Romeo and Juliet* moment.'

'How kitsch,' she said. But despite her ironic tone, she'd been thinking something very similar.

He walked over to the telescope. 'Sometimes, I'm all for kitsch. It often works on even the most educated of audiences. Oh!'

The last part was addressed to the moon. The sharp rims of its craters, the hard interplay of light and shadow, the utterly alien surface structure that no longer looked like the safe, familiar moon he knew – it was strangely fascinating. He took a step back.

'Do you often come here?'

'Haven't done for ages. I used to like astronomy. And photographing the stars. Then, at home, if I couldn't sleep, I'd look at the hundreds of different night skies. Maybe that's why I became a photographer. The unendingness always amazed me. How small you are, and yet you exist.'

There was no breeze up here. It must be getting on for four o'clock. When had she last pulled an all-nighter, Clara wondered.

'Thank you,' Elias said. 'We sometimes forget how big the world is. It's a long time since I looked that far. It helps.'

'Helps what?'

Clara covered the telescopes again. Why did people talk about different stuff at night from in the daytime? It was as though you had a different voice at night. More open. Lighter.

'Think more clearly,' Elias replied. 'Although to avoid that, we could have another drink.'

A strange familiarity. Could you call it that? The atmosphere between them. They were talking like they'd known each other years, yet there was still that prickle of newness.

They were standing side by side at the edge of the terrace, looking into the sky. Clara could feel the warmth from Elias's hand seeping into the railing beside her, they were that close. Not touching. Just the warmth.

'The magic of new beginnings,' Elias said quietly. 'Why can't it last forever? Why can't people always keep that hint of being strangers, so that you never lose the real closeness?'

Clara could see Mars glowing red. When she was younger, fifteen, she'd wished for a great adventure. Like being the first woman on Mars or something. Where had that yearning for adventure gone?

'Because they always want to know everything about each other. Because they think *that* is true love,' she said with slight disdain. 'Because they can't bear secrets.'

Yes, thought Elias. It was a great relief to hear Clara speak out what he'd thought so often.

'Come on,' he said, 'I'm cold. Let's get a drink.'

There were no pubs still open. They went to a petrol station, where a weary attendant sold them two considerably overpriced bottles of bad vodka that they clinked ceremonially together, standing by the bike. A distant church clock was striking five.

'Hardly worth going to bed at this point.'

Elias had one foot resting on the rim of the box. He looked good, Clara thought. She could suddenly feel the years there must be between them only too well.

'At my age, you need your sleep,' she said, keeping it light.

Elias looked at her in surprise. 'I have no idea how old you are. Does it matter?'

'Sometimes.'

Clara looked at him. He looked at her.

'Age always matters,' she said.

'Yes,' he agreed, 'maybe it does. But…' He didn't know how to put it at first.

'Have another swig,' she teased, 'and then you're sure to think of something charming to say.'

He drained the bottle. The bad vodka burned its way down to his belly, and the sensation was the same as back then, aged sixteen, when everything, everything, had felt so incredibly exciting. And for that still to be a thing – for him to feel it … He hurled the empty bottle far away and shouted: 'No calendar gets to tell me how to feel!'

Clara laughed out loud.

'This is me.'

Clara dismounted and Elias climbed out of the crate. He rubbed his hands. He was really cold now. There was a very faint trace of dawn in the east, but it was still too dark to see properly.

'Will you get any sleep?' he asked. 'I don't know whether I'll go to bed now.'

'We'll see,' said Clara.

They didn't know how to say goodbye. And they were standing too close to each other. If she … then he'd turn to face her … she turned to him, and the air between them crackled with electricity that could no longer be discharged with words. There was a tension between their bodies crying out for release.

What must she be feeling? thought Elias, as he said, as lightly as he possibly could: '"O, wilt thou leave me so unsatisfied?"'

He wants me to make the first move, she thought, and turned to unlock the main door, to win herself a little time, before she turned back to him again and answered in a tone that defied categorisation, somewhere between irony and smiling: '"What satisfaction canst thou have tonight?"'

Elias raised a hand as if to wave. 'I'm so glad you know your Shakespeare.'

Clara swept a theatrical bow. 'Many thanks for the taxi service, Romeo. I'll happily travel with you again.'

Elias bowed too. 'Any time, my lady.'

Then she shut the door and Elias got on the bike for the last time that night.

This isn't true, Clara thought, as she climbed the stairs to her flat, this really can't be true. Oh, shit. I've fallen in love.

17

There were so many things that went with losing your job that she'd never thought about before. Or wanted to. She didn't feel unemployed, but she still had to go to the Job Centre if she wanted any money.

'Please take a ticket!' the tired-looking security guard at the entrance had said. Security guards at the entrance. The last time she'd been to the Job Centre had been for careers advice at the age of eighteen, something the school had made them do. There hadn't been security guards on the door then, and there hadn't been ticket machines either.

'I have an appointment,' she'd replied.

He pointed to the long queue at the door and the rows of chairs in the corridors, all fully occupied.

'You still have to take a ticket.'

So she'd taken a ticket. And, almost an hour later, she was sitting in an utterly faceless office, facing a women ten years younger than her. At least.

'*Abitur*. University, dropped out in the eighth semester, switched to the College of Photography in Hamburg...'

As if she didn't know her own qualifications. She was utterly bleary-eyed and a Job Centre appointment was pretty much the last thing she wanted right now.

'Can we skip this part? I'd been considering going freelance anyway.'

The young woman at the desk looked up from Clara's application form for the first time.

'You have to show that you're actively looking for work if you want to claim unemployment allowance. If you then register as self-employed, you are required to inform us.'

Yes, she'd do that. Not a problem.

'Once your application goes through, one of my colleagues will call you and make an appointment for a consultation. You need to put your account details down here. You are initially entitled to a year of unemployment allowance.'

'And how much is that?' asked Clara.

The young woman shrugged her shoulders. 'Of course that depends on your most recent salary, and there are a few other factors that get taken into account. If you like, I can calc—'

Clara's phone buzzed. It shot right through her. Could Elias...? She looked at the display. Unknown number.

'Excuse me,' she said hastily, 'may I take this quickly, please?'

The young woman nodded even as Clara took the call and gave her name.

'I'm calling from the Southern District Police Station,' said a not-unfriendly woman's voice at the other end, 'in relation to your mother...'

Clara wasn't exactly shocked, but she instantly tensed on the inside, as if readying for any attack.

'Yes? Has she run away? Did my father call you?'

Her father did that sometimes if he couldn't get hold of either her or Jan. He had a boundless confidence in the police that his children didn't exactly share.

'No, she's here with us. But you will have to come and pick her up. She shouldn't be driving.'

Apparently, her mother had taken the car again. And of course, Clara was the one left dealing with it.

'I'm on my way. But it will take a while.'

Clara hung up and looked at the adviser. The call hadn't been such a bad thing. The perfect excuse to cut any boring appointment short.

'I have to collect my mother from the police station. She has dementia. Are we done for now?'

The woman was suddenly transformed. Interested. Friendly. Polite.

'I can complete the application on your behalf,' she offered. 'Just sign here. I've got your number, so if I need anything else, I can just call you back.'

People can be like this too, thought Clara as she signed. But why did it always take some little catastrophe or emergency to bring that out?

The woman even walked her to the door of her mini-office.

'Good luck with your mother.'

Luck, thought Clara, walking down the stairs. Luck was no use to them anymore. Dementia was dementia. Five years ago, Mama could've done with luck. Now, it was too late.

'Hello, Clara!'

Mama was terribly worked-up. Her cheeks were a brighter red than ever, and her hair was all over the place. And it seemed like she'd wet herself. There was a large damp patch on her trousers. Great. But on the other hand, she'd got Clara's name right this time. You couldn't have everything, she supposed.

The policewoman was perfectly friendly, but adamant.

'The doctor should have declared your mother unfit to drive long ago. She was going twenty-eight kilometres per hour over the limit in town here. It was lucky we had a speed-monitoring team out. How can you let your mother get behind the wheel in her condition?'

Like she was living at home and her mother's carer.

'Where were you trying to go, Mama?'

'Home!' her mother replied, still agitated, and full of an anger that she couldn't put properly into words. 'These bears, they ... I was stopped myself. I ... They can piss off.'

Sometimes things were clear as day, however.

'Mama,' Clara tried to soothe her, 'they can't help it. The police have to stop you if you go too fast.'

'Fast!' Mama laughed scornfully, and Clara couldn't help laughing with her. Her mother had always driven fast. Probably, she'd just thought she was going at an appropriate speed for the situation.

'We have to inform the licensing department. Your mother must not drive. You can collect the car anytime, but your mother must not be driving.'

Why did she keep repeating that? Mama was totally out of it either way. Although there were some things she still understood.

'How did you even find me? Did my mother tell ... did she give you my name? Or her own?'

Maybe there were still times when she was more lucid than Clara had thought.

'The number plate,' said the policewoman. 'We couldn't get hold of your father, so we called your brother and you.'

Sometimes it was uncanny that the police could just find you, call you anytime. Clara looked at Mama. Those wet trousers must be horribly uncomfortable.

'Is there anywhere ... can I give my mother a shower?'

The policewoman shook her head regretfully. 'The shower is for staff only. I'm afraid that's not possible. I'm afraid it's staff only.' She really did constantly repeat herself.

Her mother had an iron grip on the car key. Where had she even found it? Her father was supposed to keep it locked away. But, yeah ... Papa. He'd probably put it down on the table like he'd always done. And driving was the only thing her mother could still do. She didn't know where she was going, but until now it had gone all right, so long as Papa had been sitting beside her. Clara had had no idea that she sometimes took the car out on her own.

'Come on, Mama, time to go.'

At this moment, she felt terribly sorry for her. And suddenly there was the memory of the time her mother had collected *her* from the police station; the time she'd been caught with the weed.

The way she'd stood up to them. Loud and certain and firm. What do you expect? I'm sure you've never done anything wrong in your lives! I'm sure your children are all perfect, well behaved, never even cross the road against the lights. This is my daughter and I'm taking her home now.

The police hadn't had much to say in return. They'd been pretty surprised that she hadn't been ashamed, or furious with her daughter. Rather, she'd acted as though it was her job to free Clara from their clutches. Her mother had always been so determined when it came to her family. It was so unfair...

It was only later, as she showered Mama and got her dressed again, that she realised how much help she actually needed. Perhaps, as a daughter, you just didn't want to face up to it. Mama was standing there helplessly, her jumper in her hand, not quite sure how to put it on. That shitty phrase about adults becoming children again came to mind as Clara guided her arms down the sleeves. What was that? She certainly had no desire to become a child again when she got old. She didn't want her mother to be a child again either. Even so – there was nothing she could do about it.

'They'll send the medics to check up on her. Or a psychiatrist or something,' said Papa darkly. 'They might try to take our house.'

Clara rolled her eyes. 'Papa! You're a lawyer. You know perfectly well that nobody can take your house from you unless you sell it. And evidently someone has to come. We need care for Mama. Things can't go on like this. I can't go looking for her every second day, or keep collecting her from the police.'

'If they declare her non compos mentis, they'll do the same to me soon.'

Sometimes her father was unbearable.

'Seriously, Papa! Seriously. Even if there is a global conspiracy, why would they be out to get you two, of all people? Why would they want your house? Can you please, please, be logical for once? Think? If Mama isn't going to go into a home, we need round-the-clock care. You can barely look after yourself. Let Jan and me sort it out, OK?'

'You have no idea how many loopholes there are in the law. And I'm more important than you think,' her father mumbled, somewhat mutinously. 'Whether you two believe me or not. This is all part of the big plan.'

A demented mother and a psychotic father – no wonder she'd turned out like she had. At least Papa still had the lucidity to laugh at his own persecution complex from time to time.

'You could go undercover with them,' he said now with a smile, 'then you can get to keep the house. I'm sure a journalist like you can manage that, huh?'

'I'm a photographer, Papa. And out of a job. But I'll gladly give it a go. Will you two be all right now?'

Her father nodded. Maybe it was because it had been a very long – or short – night, but today, she could really see how vulnerable he'd become too.

'Fuck old age,' she swore with quiet bitterness as she walked down the garden to her car. A glance at her phone told her that Elias hadn't texted. Looked like, today at least, part of her problem with ageing was that she was behaving like a fourteen-year-old.

18

There were standing at the station. Jule had still been asleep when Elias got in. Sometimes, watching her sleep, he felt something like a beautiful, painful longing, or almost like a breathless fear that he'd never known before. She wouldn't be a child much longer. Was barely still a child now. Why hadn't he felt that more strongly before and enjoyed the time? It was so amazing to have a daughter like Jule.

'You look pretty knackered,' said Jule. 'When did you get home?'

'And you're pretty cheeky. Half-five, six, or thereabouts. I have absolutely no idea how any of the bakeries around here are still in business, seeing that they don't open till seven.'

They strolled to the platform, where Jule's train was already waiting. He put his hand on the nape of her neck as he'd done when she was little.

'Look after yourself. And Mona. Well ... not that she needs it.'

'Will do.'

Elias had to laugh. 'Don't say "will do" in my tone of voice. Say it like you mean it. Promise! And come again soon. It was really lovely having you here.'

Jule threw her backpack through the door of the train. 'Yeah, I liked it too, Papa. Thanks for the money.'

They hugged, suddenly semi-embarrassed.

'Text me when you get home!' he yelled over the beeping as the doors closed.

Jule gave him a mocking salute. The doors were shut. The train was pulling out.

As Elias watched the train depart, it suddenly became clear to him that he had to break up with Vera today if he wanted to be in any way honest with himself – and with her. OK, so he didn't know what that had been last night, but one thing was certain: there'd never been anything like that with Vera.

Probably because I'd never have wanted anything like that with her either.

That night, he and Clara had been closer than he'd ever been, or wanted to be, to Vera.

All around him, people were pushing their way through the station forecourt. Suitcase wheels clicked over the cracks in the paving stones. Automated announcements about delays and platform changes echoed through the space. Elias stopped, hearing and seeing it all. What had he been expecting? A dramatic soundtrack? All the travellers and every train in slow motion because he suddenly had the feeling he'd come to a terminus? That he couldn't go on with his life like this? He started moving, and all at once, he couldn't help smiling. In actual fact, the station, with its pretzel stands, the smell of thin coffee from the bakery stalls, the florists, the bookshop and the everyday bustle, the thousands of emotions among the passengers – relief, happiness, pain, annoyance, joys both tiny and huge – was a wonderful place to escape a wrong life.

He stood outside her flat and rang the doorbell. Vera should be home by now – Friday was her short day. He knew where she hid the key, but it no longer felt right to use it, as if he could waltz in and out however he liked.

Vera opened the door, looking as friendly and open as ever.

'I was expecting you last night. But now is good too. I've just got in. Would you like a coffee?'

Apparently, whatever his age, he'd never learn how to have this kind of conversation. Suddenly, every familiar thing was uncertain. Was it still OK to let her make him coffee? He nodded.

He followed her into the kitchen, sat in the place he always sat, fiddled with the sugar shaker like he always did. Even so, she could sense his unease.

'Why didn't you come?' she asked, spooning coffee into the little basket and screwing the moka pot together. 'Would you like cream?'

'No, thanks,' he said, shaking his head, his mouth dry. 'Just black, please. I…' He didn't know where to start. He was rubbing nervously at the itchy, slightly swollen spot on his ring finger from the thorn he'd caught it on in Clara's garden. That seemed much longer ago than just yesterday.

'Well?' she asked, sitting opposite him. 'No kiss? What's wrong? Are you pissed off with me for leaving so early?'

'It wasn't that early,' he answered. 'No. I'm not pissed off with anything. I … This isn't working. We can't go on like this.'

Even before the coffee was done! But in conversations like this, there was no diplomacy and no right or appropriate. In conversations like this, you could only ever get everything wrong.

'What do you mean?' asked Vera. 'Are you breaking up with me?' Her voice was still calm, but he could see in her face that she was upset. 'Did you … did something happen last night?'

Yes. Something had happened last night, but he couldn't have said exactly what. He didn't know. He was silent for a moment.

'Did you sleep with that woman from the house? Clara?'

'No,' he said. 'But I was out with her for a bit.'

'She's way older than you!'

She sounded incredulous. Suddenly, he was almost furious that she'd said that. What did her age have to do with anything?

'I don't know. Maybe,' he said. Why was she talking that kind of nonsense? He tried to get his thoughts together.

'Vera, we aren't in love. Or … I don't know if you love me in some way. I … I…' It was so hard to say the right thing. 'I don't love you. We somehow ended up a couple because at first, we both … I don't know. All I know is that one of the first things you told me was that I absolutely should not fall in love with you.'

There were suddenly tears in her eyes. She stood up and took the hissing coffee pot from the hob. Put a cup down for each of them. Poured. The coffee smelled way better than the stuff at the station.

'I've been in love with you for ages,' she said. 'And actually...'

He knew what she wanted to say. Yes, he'd actually known that, and he'd only acted as though he was taking her at her word. But it had been obvious that she was in love. And that he wasn't. It was that simple, and that wrong. She sat back down.

'Is that it?' she asked. 'After last night, you come to me and tell me that you're ending it? What happened in between? What ... have you fallen for her?'

Elias looked outside. It had started to snow. April weather. There'd been a smell of snow last night, but the sky had still been clear. A strange feeling of unreality suddenly seized him.

'I don't think so,' he said, realising at that same moment that he couldn't say that. He just didn't know. But even that was enough. He had no idea how he could explain that to Vera.

He launched into a helpless explanation. 'It's wrong, what we're doing. For both of us. You're kidding yourself that we're a proper couple, and I'm acting like I don't notice.'

Now she was really crying. He couldn't help standing up and taking her in his arms. She let him, and leant her face against his shoulder.

'You just don't get involved!'

She was right. He'd never let himself get involved with her. Right from the start. And she'd encouraged him in that, maybe because she'd known that things would never have gone any further between them if she'd insisted that he did. Back then, almost two years ago.

'Because I ... It doesn't work. I can't. And if I did, it would be fake.'

She jerked her head up. Sudden rage amid the tears. 'That never used to bother you when we slept together. Never.'

Yes. That was true. Of course it was true. A wave of shame welled up in him.

'I know,' he said softly.

She said nothing for quite a while. Her tears gradually stopped, but her face was still resting on his shoulder. It was as though this embrace would never end, as though you could never free yourself from it.

'I'm sorry,' he whispered. 'I should never have let it get this far.'

She misunderstood him and raised her head.

'What did the two of you get up to then?'

'No, that wasn't what I meant,' he answered hastily. 'I meant us.'

'Even so, something is different from yesterday.'

'Maybe,' he began hesitantly, 'maybe there are moments in life when you suddenly know that something has to change. That you yourself can't go on like this. We ... in a way, we always knew there was no future for us, didn't we?'

'Because you didn't want one! What happened last night?'

'It was yesterday evening. Before I even went on stage. I realised that that's me. That I'm Loman. That nothing distinguishes him from me. That I'm leading the wrong life too. Probably that became really clear to me last night. Because I...' He hesitated, but now was the moment for him to be honest. 'Because I preferred being out with Clara to being with you. Even though nothing else happened.'

That wasn't really true. You didn't have to kiss. You didn't have to touch. It all began much further back. Began with avoiding one person's company and seeking out another's.

'You always thought we could still come to something. That I could learn to love you.'

Vera stood up abruptly. 'Didn't work,' she said brusquely, her voice heavy with tears. 'Go. You can go. You don't have to sit here and watch me cry.'

It was so obvious that that was exactly what she didn't want. That she wanted him to be with her. But there was no way out.

'Vera,' he said helplessly. He hadn't wanted to hurt her, but to stay in a bad relationship just because the other person thought it was a good one was as wrong as cheating on the other person. And of course – he'd liked that she loved him more than he did her. That meant you were always the stronger one. It was only at the end that that didn't hold true.

'I'm sorry, Vera,' he said very quietly. 'I shouldn't have let it get this far. I should have ended things much sooner.'

Honest, but stupid.

Vera stared at him in disbelief. 'You mean you've been wanting to break up for ages? Since when? How long have you been lying to me for?' There were red spots on her cheeks.

'I don't mean it like that! I meant that for a long time there's ... that there's an imbalance between us, and I should have said so.'

'You did, all the time. And yet you kept coming back to me. Isn't that love?'

Yes. This wasn't the first time they'd broken up. Sometimes him. Sometimes her. But this time was different.

He said nothing. Not because there was nothing to say. The words and phrases stacked into towers in his mind and he didn't know where to start, to explain the thing that they actually both knew: even though there had been lots of good times, moments of intimacy, glowing with light; carefree days, passionate nights; a train is still heading to the wrong destination if you walk through it, against the direction of travel. Because eventually, you get to the end of the train and realise: I've been lying to myself the whole time. I was just on the wrong train. That was today.

How lovely the snow on the windowsill looked. It only snowed like this in spring. Hard, throwing down huge, heavy flakes, as if the winter was in a hurry to get rid of all the snow that hadn't happened over the real winter months. The sounds of the town couldn't make it up to the window. The silence between them was thickening, and every word, no matter what, was heavier, even before it had been spoken.

'I...' He had to clear his throat. His voice was choked. 'I'll be going now.'

'You'll be back anyway,' she said, in childish defiance. 'That's always the way. Why do you do this? Does it give you a thrill?'

'You know it's not like that,' he said helplessly. 'I'll be going now.'

He stood up. Hesitated another moment, but then walked into the hallway and took his coat. He hadn't even taken his shoes off. On stage, that would have been a sign that he didn't want to stay. He walked back to the kitchen door.

There was no right way to say goodbye. Farewell was far too dramatic, see you inaccurate, bye too flippant. She took the choice from him.

'Have a good life. I don't want to see you anytime soon. Or ever.'

Now, perhaps because the pressure was so immense, he found himself trying not to laugh. Melodrama. As if they were teenagers. That was so very Vera. But then he saw himself in her place, as if in a snapshot. What she was feeling. What else could he have said if he'd loved her?

19

It's been so long, thought Clara. So long that I can't remember what people do when they're in love. Thoughts and emotions are swirling and suddenly everything is music.

There'd been nothing to keep her in the flat when she'd got back from her parents'. It had started to snow on her journey home and the traffic had slowed to a crawl. There hadn't been a single day in the whole dreary winter when it had snowed like today. A bit of powder for a couple of weeks maybe. A few mornings with slushy stuff that soon melted. Mostly it had just been grey. Foggy, never properly cold and never properly sunny. But today it seemed unstoppable. She'd quickly popped upstairs to fetch her gloves and camera and to put on her boots. She'd stopped in the front garden, on the steps down to the street and was looking up into the sky. Or rather towards it, because all she could actually see was the endlessly falling snow. It was as if she could watch as millions of flakes were created out of nothing up there, thirty, forty metres above her head, because that was the limit of her visibility. And it was very quiet. The snow had come so unexpectedly that she couldn't hear any of the usual winter sounds – the scratch of snow shovels on asphalt, the hectic rasp of spinning wheels, the ugly din of snow-blower engines. There was a faint orange light blinking through the snowy air from the ring road, but you couldn't hear the snowploughs either. She walked down the steps and along the street, uphill. It was fantastic. Thin ridges of snow, ten, fifteen centimetres tall, rested on twigs and branches. She took photographs of the way the houses of the Old Town, the crest on the town wall and the onion domes on the towers were softened into silhouettes; the way the snow leached the colour from everything, creating a picture of its own. As paradoxical as it sounded, you needed colour photos here, to do justice to every nuance of the whiteness: the little splashes of red from a parked car that had almost entirely disappeared beneath the snow, the glowing yellow of an outsized anorak almost drowning a little girl as she slithered in delight along the pavement. She had to smile as she lowered the camera. That was exactly it. This feeling of exceptional circumstances. That today, everything was different from normal. And that was exactly it too. Storm outside. Storm inside her. A small, friendly catastrophe. Nobody would be on time for work; the trams weren't running and nor were the buses. And inside her, a whirlwind of feelings that she'd never have believed herself still capable of.

Everywhere, little bunches of children and teenagers were drifting through the snowy town – looked as though the schools had closed early, or never opened at all. Exceptional circumstances. And almost everyone Clara saw seemed in a good mood. Nobody could help it if they were unpunctual today, didn't turn up at work; it was as though, for one day only, all obligations had been revoked. Clara started to photograph the people. The schoolkids having a snowball fight. The old lady in black gloves that were far too big for her, feeling her way uncertainly, step after step, until one of the girls offered her her arm – an old-fashioned gesture. She really was in luck today: it was rare to be able to capture these moments. The scene was almost romantic.

She would have loved to share her joy at such a sudden outbreak of friendliness. With Elias.

She stopped and took out her phone: *Little winter walk after being up all night?*

She hesitated before pressing send: Sorry, Clara, it was really lovely, but you know I have a girlfriend. Sorry, Clara, I can't today. Or tomorrow. Or the day after that, or ever, in fact. Sorry ... no name. Number blocked. Hey, Clara, it was actually quite...

No. No more actually.

She sent the message. If they weren't going to see each other again, she'd cope. Maybe not today, but she'd manage. She had to grin at herself. Who was she kidding? She'd cope, but it would hurt, and of course she was hoping that—

Her phone buzzed.

Yes. Where are you?

Suddenly, there was an excitement deep in her belly. Like a little inner kick. She thought a moment. Then a little smile, just for herself: on a day like today, when everything was different anyway, you could perfectly well play the tourist in your own town.

I'm walking to the Domplatz. I'll wait there. OK?

It took barely a couple of seconds for his reply to come through.

Thirteen minutes. See you soon.

Thirteen minutes! Anyone else would have put either ten minutes or quarter of an hour. Was that pedantry or just precision?

She could have taken the narrow alleyways up to the Cathedral Square, but that would probably have taken longer than thirteen minutes, so she went via the steps. If anyone had come up here ahead of her, the still-falling snow had covered their footprints long ago. Her feet had to seek out the stone; the steps had turned into little rounded hills into which you sank deeply and you might easily slip if you didn't sweep the snow aside a little. She was getting warm and really looking forward to walking through this winter's day in spring. She took the last few steps and came onto the square. A car was rolling almost inaudibly, at a very cautious walking pace, right over the snow-covered cobbles. The whole town was a wintry fairytale in mid-April. Good luck driving down from here, she thought with a touch of schadenfreude. That would not be fun.

Up here, on the large, open square, the flakes were whirling so vigorously that the two cathedral towers were no more than fuzzy lines. Could you capture that? She took the camera in hand again.

'You look like Anna Karenina.'

Elias had seen her on the steps ahead of him a minute earlier and slowed a little to watch her. It was the first time he'd consciously seen her from a distance. She moved in a unique way. Most people didn't know how to walk. The joy of the interplay between muscles in walking, jogging, running, had always been important to him. Because on stage, you could express so much through your body alone – hate and love and despair and courage and satisfaction – without needing to say a word. But in the outside world, you first had to find someone who could walk properly and not just propel themselves forward in some weird way. Someone who could simply, naturally walk without looking wrong. Clara walked like that.

She didn't turn round to him, just kept trying to photograph the towers.

'Anna Karenina didn't have a DSLR camera and she wasn't a photographer either.'

'Oh, shit,' Elias said, 'I'd been hoping that you hadn't read that book, at least. Were you a bookseller in a former life? And you're not afraid of animal-rights activists and their paint bombs?'

'They won't find me today,' she said, unbuttoning the coat. 'Too much snow.'

She opened it as if unfurling her wings, he thought. What an image amid this snowstorm.

'It's my mother's astrakhan. I don't think me not wearing it will bring the sheep back to life. Seeing that I haven't had a chance to wear it all winter, I've got to make the most of this merry spring day.'

She gave a twirl. Elias laughed.

'Kiki the coquettish cocotte,' he declaimed.

'What?' Clara didn't understand. Elias pointed to her lambskin collar.

'Astrakhan comes from a sheep known as the karakul. Doesn't sound as cute as a baby baa-lamb … Anyway, it's a diction exercise for actors. "Kiki the coquettish cocotte craves a cosy khaki coat with a karakul collar. Cold Coco the kid crunches coconut clusters…"'

Clara was laughing now too.

'Shall the three of us, you, me and my karakul collar, take a turn around the rose garden together?' she asked.

It was this winter day in spring. The birdsong was out of kilter with the whirling white. It sounded like a promise made when you were least expecting it. A promise that everything would be different. That things inside him wouldn't have to stay cold.

They strolled through the gates from the Bishop's Palace to the courtyard, and from there to the rose garden. Clara stopped in the entrance archway.

She has an eye for a picture, thought Elias. Or else it was entirely unconscious. If so, it was all the more beautiful.

She looked into the garden and then at him.

'It's a good job there's snow. It's far too early for roses. Just bare branches.'

'Yes,' Elias agreed, 'this is much more romantic.'

They walked between the flower beds to the wall. The snow on the narrow paths was ankle-deep and pristine. There was nobody here but them.

'Does that matter?' Clara asked out of the blue, even before they'd reached the wall with its view of the town.

'Does what matter?'

Elias didn't understand right away what she meant.

Clara spun around as if to encompass everything. This white sky hanging so low over them. The soft white silhouettes of the rose bushes. The extravagant snow cupolas on the wall, beyond which lay the rooftops of the whole town. How often did you see everything like this? Every few years at most.

'That it's romantic. Does that matter?'

Elias followed her movement and thought for a moment. Why was she asking? And did it matter?

'I think it matters that it's beautiful. Yes, actually. It does matter.

You have to take up, take away, take in all this beauty. There isn't that much of it, is there?'

They were standing side by side looking over the town. She picked up the camera. Even if the photo could never be the same as what she was now seeing. No panorama, no wide-angle. She could only ever capture a part of it. The camera never saw the whole, partly because it could never capture emotions.

'I didn't mean it like that,' she said with a smile in her voice. 'I've noticed that you ... that you always crave beauty,' she concluded, deliberately hamming it up.

Elias inclined his head, ever so slightly, and smiled at her. 'I do,' he admitted. 'That's probably why I'm standing here.'

'That's why Vera is your girlfriend?' Clara asked. Instantly, she was annoyed at her question. But you couldn't take it back. And ... well, she wanted to know.

'Was.'

Elias's tone was dry. It felt funny to say that. It was awkward telling Clara. Because then she'd have to think it was all because of her that he'd...

'I had to ... I split up with her. After last night ... and yesterday evening ... I...'

He was stuttering. He couldn't find the words.

Clara was surprised. And strangely touched. Because of me? It was on the tip of her tongue. A tingling yet fearful feeling in her stomach.

'Because of last night?' she asked instead, hesitantly. And then, hastily, to strip the question of its meaning, she added: 'We didn't even have sex.'

He didn't laugh. They both had their hands in the snow on the wall. Side by side. Not touching. Elias watched the snowflakes melt on the backs of them. The snow was cooling the little cut on his finger, which was inflamed. That fitted ... he was inflamed too.

'Not for that reason ... or not only. I ... It's hard to describe. I just couldn't do it anymore.'

She said nothing. The silence was almost perfect. Only the birds were still singing, despite the snow. In the end, Clara took a deep breath and plucked up her courage.

'Elias,' she said firmly, 'I think ... I've fallen for you.'

He waited. Very surprised. Didn't know whether to say anything. She was so clear.

Clara looked at him and, in that moment, she knew that she'd like everything about him. That made it even harder for her.

'I've fallen in love with you. I don't know how you feel.'

He wanted to say something, but she raised a hand as if to tell him to wait a moment.

'So ... if it's...' She exhaled completely, then started again. 'If it's the same for you, then ... I hope you feel the same. But if you do, we can't start like this.'

The snow was gradually easing. She straightened up but left her hand lying next to his. They were gradually melting their way through to the stone. Ice cold. She could hardly feel her fingers.

'But as you said – we didn't even have sex. Would you have preferred ... Should we have started like that?'

Tone light, but he didn't want to rob the conversation of any weight. She didn't answer.

'What do you think?' he asked eventually, into the white silence between them.

Clara looked at their hands, side by side, and smiled.

'That it can't start like this. You can't just stumble out of one relationship into the next. Just saying.'

They took their hands from the wall almost simultaneously. Elias turned to her.

The parallel prints look good, he thought.

'Why not?' he asked. He'd never had to think about it, had always taken things as they came. But right now, it felt as though something inside him was being turned head over heels. It was different from before. Everything was. He observed her, and her face with the slight dry twist to her lips looked clear and open and as wonderfully contradictory as the snow on this spring day. 'What makes the difference? Do you think it would be different if I waited a month, or three, or a year?'

Clara leant forwards, but she didn't kiss him, as he'd expected for a moment she would. She was so close to him that he could take in her lovely scent. It was somewhere between bitter orange and bright, fresh wood. Her lips were so close to his ear that he could feel their warmth.

'I'd be a year older,' she whispered with mocking pleasure. Then she stood up again.

'Me too,' answered Elias. 'But no wiser, and probably not very different either, and I have the feeling that ... no, I *am* standing at a fork in the road. Now. Here. Today.'

Clara looked over the rooftops. It had almost stopped snowing and the sky was starting to clear. Was that true? Now? Here? Today? Her breathing was suddenly trembling, as if she'd run up to the cathedral.

'Is that how it feels to you, then? Do you know which turning you want to take?'

Clara saw the smile waiting in the corners of his mouth. He nodded.

'Yes. I can stop here at the fork if you want. Three months. A year, as far as I'm concerned. But I know that I don't want to take a turning. I want to go the right way.'

He was smiling properly now, and looking down. He's jittery, Clara saw, to her amazement. He's trembling.

'Then the only difference will be that you're a year older,' he added in the same mocking tone as her, 'and do you want ... do we really want us to ... not experience that year?'

He said we, Clara thought.

'In a film, this would be the moment we kiss,' she said, putting her hand back in the impression on the wall. 'It's so annoying that nobody can ever do anything romantic ever again, because you always feel like you're just copying films and photos.'

Elias laughed. 'I'm the actor. That's my line. But do you know what?' He stepped behind her and put his arms around her. 'I don't care. We were here first. And I don't know any film that happens during an April snowstorm.'

She felt his crossed hands over her stomach. Such a lovely gesture. When had she last felt this enfolded? Years ago.

'This is all very pretty,' she said. 'But what about that kiss? If you're so blasé about clichés?'

They were both trembling. He could feel her tension. Because words weren't enough to convey the emotions.

'I'm still standing at the fork in the road,' he reminded her. His voice shimmered. 'The traffic lights seem to have got stuck on amber.'

Clara let go of his hands and turned to face him.

'Green light,' she said, her tone misted, like someone waking from a long sleep. 'On all of my roads.'

20

'That has to be the shortest space of time in which anyone was ever single,' said Jan, his voice deeply serious. 'The man breaks it off with his girlfriend and, ten minutes later, he's fallen into your arms. Should I be worried?'

They were standing on the terrace outside the hospital cafeteria, beneath the incredibly blue, bright April sky, drinking coffee from the inevitable and indestructible ceramic mugs. It wasn't as terrible as she remembered, but you couldn't have called it good either. The snow had almost entirely melted, leaving only little drifts along the sides of the paths, which lay ridiculous and forgotten in the spring sunshine. April. Total transformation from one day to the next. It was still thawing and dripping and drizzling from the rooftops, but the old elms in the hospital grounds were veiled in fresh green. It was the first time since Paul's death that she'd visited Jan at work. Superstitious and silly, when you got down to it, that she'd never been back here. After all, it wasn't the hospital that had killed him. They'd done everything possible to help him here, it just hadn't worked.

'I think you'd need to be worried if he hadn't immediately fallen for my charms. He's ... he's deeply light-hearted and serious all at once. It's a funny thing.'

They were standing shoulder to shoulder.

'Is it wrong, brother-dear? Do you think we should have ... *I* should have waited?'

Jan took a sip and thought it over. She loved that so much about him. He didn't feel the need to speak, just for the sake of words. When he was serious about something, he took his time.

'I don't know him,' he said in the end, 'but isn't that good? That he knows right away that he wants to be with you? After all, there aren't that many guys who'd want that...' he added maliciously.

'Aren't you risking a reprimand, meeting a woman on the terrace when it's not your break?' Clara retorted. 'And if you say we're family, I'll burst into tears and say you grabbed me.'

Jan laughed. 'Maybe Mama's dementia is just because she wants to forget her children,' he mused aloud. 'At any rate, I'd gladly wipe you from my memory.'

'You would not,' she answered wryly. 'You don't have anyone else you can talk about absolutely anything with, like you do me.'

'Nor do you,' Jan replied. 'How's the sex?'

Clara had to laugh. 'How would I know? We only snogged a bit.'

It was true that they could tell each other everything, but even so, she had to rob the kiss that she and Elias had shared of some of its the significance by calling it snogging. As if it hadn't been quite serious. Because she couldn't yet share that special, accentuated feeling. Like the negative of a special picture that you mustn't take from the developer too soon. The photo had been taken in the snow, but its contours were only just starting to form within her. It wasn't quite all there yet.

'His hands feel good.'

Jan threw up his arms. 'Hands! Hands! Hands!' he cried theatrically. 'But you want sex, don't you?'

Clara elbowed him in the side. 'That's the difference between you and me,' she said with a laugh. 'As a woman, I can have as much sex as I like, anytime. No problem. It's harder for you men.'

Jan had shut his eyes and turned his face to the sun. He looks good, she thought, he has a sharp profile. If you didn't know him, you'd never believe how quick he is to laugh. He often seemed way more earnest than he was.

'I know,' he said. 'But I don't even remember the names, if you ever told me.'

'There haven't been that many!'

Strange feeling. Something between quiet pride that she could have a man if she wanted and something like … embarrassment?

Because she always knew from the start if the first few nights would turn into something more? Because she often lost all interest in getting to know the man after the first time? Because sex was so easy and sometimes just sad, but talking was so exhausting?

'Wait,' said Jan, taking a last swig of coffee. 'I'll happily count them up for you.'

He put the empty mug on the ground, took a notebook from the breast pocket of his white coat and started making notes.

'That teacher from Braunschweig. The one you met on Tinder.'

He grinned mischievously. Clara grabbed the pad from his hand and threw it over the balustrade, among the trees.

'Jan!' she threatened, laughing. 'Stop that. Go back in this instant. Your patients will be dying on you.'

'Good job I'm not an emergency surgeon,' Jan said calmly. 'In orthopaedics, our patients generally don't die until years later.'

'I should have learnt a proper profession too. When you're twenty, you always think yourself a genius ... and then you end up an unemployed photographer.'

So much was going on at the moment, that she was finding it hard not just to know that she was out of work, but to believe it. It didn't feel true.

'Do you need money, by the way?'

How lucky she was to have a brother like Jan.

'Not at the moment. I'll let you know if I want to shower my lover with expensive gifts.'

Jan set one foot on the balustrade and studied the trees in the grounds.

'He's not your lover yet,' he teased, 'you have to have had sex for that. What's the problem?'

Yes. What was the problem? Was there one? On one hand, she definitely wanted it. She wanted to know what he felt like. Plus, she'd been missing sex for such a long time. On the other hand ... she didn't want it to ... them to ... shit!

'I guess I don't want ... I just don't want to be disappointed.'

'A frequently expressed wish,' Jan remarked, with feigned restraint. 'I'd happily prescribe you a packet of Satisfactio Forte right now, but it seems like someone's thrown my pad away.'

'I don't think you'll prescribe me anything, because then it would all come out that you're not a proper doctor.'

Jan gave a plausible jump, looked dramatically all around him, then hissed: 'Not so loud!'

He was watching her, as if waiting for applause. Then they both burst out laughing.

The last time she'd been here, almost ten years ago, she'd thought she'd never laugh again.

'When are you seeing each other again? Tonight?'

Clara could hear the birds in the elm trees. There was always a morning in spring when it was like they were suddenly all singing. Even as a child, she'd experienced it. Everything was beginning. From then on, the days were suddenly getting long.

'Probably not. He's on stage every evening, I think. I don't know.'

Jan turned to her and started patting her down. She laughed in surprise, fending him off.

'What are you doing?'

'Aha!' he exclaimed, triumphantly pulling her phone from her inside pocket. 'You *have* got one.'

'What?'

He held the phone out to her. 'I can gladly show you what used to be the hospital's very own telegraph office. It's been the computer room for forty years now. Modern communications and all that. This is a te-le-phone. Nowadays, it's much easier to let people know that you'd like to see them. Text him.'

Clara went to take the phone from him. 'It's his turn to text,' she said.

'*Dear Elias*,' Jan pretended to be typing, '*let's have sex today*.'

'Jan!'

He handed her the phone back with a smile. 'I have to go. Just text him. There's nothing you can do wrong. You don't want to play games, and you don't want anybody who does play games. So, don't. If he's not serious, at least you'll know from the start. Text him. You have to get to know him before you can properly fall in love and potentially end up unable to get out of it. I…' He hesitated a moment, then added quickly: 'I don't want you to be unhappy.'

They had a quick hug. Clara stood in the sun a moment longer. Somehow, it was always easier to give other people advice. Everything always looked much clearer from the outside. She had to smile. Jan was right. She wanted to get to know Elias. From within and without. And from without as soon as possible.

21

He would gladly have texted her, but it wasn't possible just then. His phone had to be switched off in the studio, or you'd hear it ticking on the recording, even if you couldn't hear it at all on the monitor. And this morning, when he'd cycled over to the radio station, he'd considered it too early. He didn't want her to feel pressured. Even so, he'd stopped along the way and started a message. It was still really fresh, but it was going to be a sunny morning. A proper spring day. Yet in his mind's eye, he could see snow and her wearing that funny karakul collar in the rose garden, and her strong hands, which were anything but slender, on the snow-covered wall. He didn't know what it was about her that fascinated him so much. Was she exciting? Interesting? At any rate, she was attractive. In a sharp, closed way. But with those intermittent and always surprising moments of openness. I think I've fallen for you. Nobody else would say that right away. Everyone was always cautious with their feelings.

'Sorry, can we do that again, please? You didn't quite stress that line enough.'

'Oh, sure. Sorry.'

The director was getting on his nerves. But yeah, maybe he wasn't entirely focused. Clara ... What was wrong with him? He didn't usually lose concentration like this. He hadn't been like this since Mona. Everything right now was reminding him of that time. Back then, everything had been interwoven too. Reality. And the play they were in together. Love and the fighting. Everything had always been half acting and half reality, and sometimes they hadn't been able to tell the two apart. Whether the argument they'd had in the play hadn't also been real. Whether the love scene in the play hadn't strengthened, reflected, intensified their nights of love together, resounding between them in a way no one else had even picked up on. The magic of what was so secret and yet so apparent. Except that today, there was no longer any reason to hide his emotions.

'The last paragraph again please. You just … Could you concentrate please?' The director's voice in the monitor sounded amused. 'You just said Clara instead of Aouda.'

A sudden heat surged through him. But there was something like joy there too. An encompassing cheerfulness. Had he really? Clara? Wow, it would be so lovely to be outside now, and to cycle to her. There were no windows in either the studio or the control room. The sun was probably shining endlessly, and he was trapped here for the next three hours, reading the part of Phileas Fogg, who was currently in India, having just rescued Maharani Aouda. And his lines of dialogue with her were sometimes so incredibly silly that he couldn't help asking himself whether Jules Verne had been that daft, or if it was down to the translation, or even the radio dramatisation. Or had Jules Verne just wanted this Phileas Fogg to be too stupid to recognise that he'd long been in love with Aouda?

Aouda. Clara.

Yes. Shit. He was in love too. If only he could text her now. Time suddenly had such a weight to it! Suddenly, three hours was ages again. Like back when he'd been unable to wait for life. When everything had had to be at once, because everything had been so new and so wonderful and so magic. And he'd never have dreamt that life would one day feel like that again.

'Again please.'

He had to smile at himself. Amazing feeling.

'"Aouda, I won't be able to leave you in Bombay. The danger is too great for you…"'

Feeble script. But the emotion in Phileas Fogg that lay beneath that line, that was genuine.

They had the studio until midday, and the two chapters really did take them almost all of that time. He sighed with relief once he could finally step out of the building. It stood in huge grounds, almost a private park. You could see the buildings clustered in clearings among the trees. If it hadn't been for the enormous transmission tower between the TV and radio sections, it could've been an expensive rehab clinic. Elias liked the broadcasting centre. It was so very fifties. The control rooms still had their old tape-splicing equipment. The editing blocks had been so solidly installed back then that it had probably been too much trouble to rip them out again. As a result, the monitors for the digital mixing desks stood on panels on top of the reel-to-reel tape machines that you still needed if you wanted a particular archive recording.

As he walked to his bike, he switched on his phone and message after message popped up. None from Clara. There was one from Vera though, which startled him for a moment. But she'd just sent him a photo of a newspaper review, with no other words. He was curious, but he couldn't read it yet. If it was rubbish, then he was ... He hated that bad reviews still got to him. If anyone claimed to be unbothered by them, he didn't believe them. He could still remember pretty much every hatchet job he'd ever read. And it had always bothered him, always. Even if he considered the criticism to be wrong and unfair, it still got to him.

And then there was a message from Mareike:

The Hamburg Theatre Festival wants our play. Not because of you. Because of the excellent direction. Shall we succumb to cheap fame and commercialism? Also, do you have time for two performances in Tübingen, Sunday/Monday? It would be filling in for a cancellation.

He'd known that Mareike had invited a few artistic directors, but it didn't generally come to anything. Least of all this soon. This was so cool. God, a real success. It had been such a long time. He grinned as he messaged back:

I don't know … I'm really above that kind of thing. Hamburg! Hamburg is cool! And Tübingen could be arranged.

He pictured Mareike; no way would she be sitting quietly at her desk. She was probably dancing around her flat. Hamburg!

And now he knew what he could text Clara about: *Fancy a visit to Swabia? Sunday and Monday?*

22

Clara was looking for a parking space near Elias's flat. Not that easy, in the middle of the Old Town, but she was glad to have an extra five minutes. She was full of the jitters. She must have been eighteen the last time she'd felt this way. At any rate, she couldn't remember being in this sort of mood any time in the last twenty years. An inner adventure.

She was in the middle of manoeuvring into a very narrow gap between two parked cars, when her mobile buzzed. She answered without looking. She was a bit late.

'Elias?'

But then she could hear just from the pause that it wasn't Elias, it was her father.

'Clara?'

'Papa, I really don't have time. I'm just—'

'She's gone again.' His voice creaked. Had it always sounded that elderly? 'I only nodded off for a moment.'

Good God! Why couldn't he ever manage to lock the door when he had a nap?

'Is the car still there? Is she out in the car?'

That wouldn't be good, wouldn't be good at all.

'Wait,' her father said, terribly slowly, 'I'll go and see.'

She heard him shuffle down the hall to the door. Sometimes, she hated his roundaboutness. He'd always been like that. He'd never done anything quickly in his life. Maybe that's what had attracted him about Mama. Nothing had ever been quick enough for her. Clara couldn't help pulling a face. Probably that was why she'd gone again. Because she'd never been able to sit still.

'The car is still there,' her father reported back. 'Can you come?'

She could have screamed with impatience.

'Papa! I ... I'm about to drive to Tübingen. I really can't come now. Couldn't you ... Have you tried calling Jan?'

'No, he'll be at work,' said her father. 'Well then, I'd better call the police.'

Clara rolled her eyes. The police?

'Papa, they won't even start looking for another couple of hours. Hold on, I'll call you back. I have to sort things out.'

She got out and slammed the car door. When had she last gone away? Millions of years ago. And now, of all days, when she...

She was looking for the number. It was on the corner. An older building, like hers. A bit more everyday, perhaps, with the charm of the unrenovated. She found his name by the doorbell. Right at the top. Fourth floor, then. She rang the bell. The door opener buzzed almost at once.

The stairwell smelled of old wood. An enamel sign on the second step of every flight: *Caution! Freshly waxed!* The plaques couldn't have been true for at least forty years. She took the stairs two at a time. Get it over with.

Elias, sorry, I was so looking forward to our date. I wanted to go away with you. But I have to look for my mother. She has dementia. I'll probably get it too one day. But I'd really, really, really have liked to sleep with you first. Looks like it's not meant to be. I'm sorry.

She heard a door open upstairs. Elias's face appeared above her. He was laughing.

'Hey! I was about to come down. How lovely to see you. That you're coming along!'

She was disarmed. Full of rage at herself and Papa and ... no, not at him. She stopped on the half-landing.

'Listen, how much of a hurry are we in? When do we have to be there?'

He didn't know what she meant by that. Was she ... did she want ... He hesitated a moment.

'We're not in a hurry. You're welcome to ... would you like to come in?'

Clara looked up at him. Then the absurdity of it suddenly made her laugh.

'For a coffee? To see your etchings?'

Elias looked at her. How vibrant she was!

Clara plucked up her courage. 'Elias,' she said, still from the half-landing, 'honestly – there's nothing I'd rather do. I'm dying to see your collection of etchings. But unfortunately, I have to go and look for my mother. She's just run away again. And I have no idea how long it'll take.'

'Were you planning to introduce me to her before we drive to Tübingen together? I'm glad you like to do things the old-fashioned way.'

Clara smiled at him. Teasing. 'I do hope that before you go to bed, you still kneel down on the rug and say your prayers. No, my mother has dementia,' she explained.

Elias did some quick sums. Just under three hours' drive. Mareike wanted to sort the lighting and do a run-through at four. They had time.

'I'll come,' he said. 'If it takes too long, you can always drive me to the station.'

He went into the flat, fetched his bag from his room and found himself on the landing, standing in front of Clara. Who abruptly took his face in her beautiful hands and kissed him.

'We can make time for that,' she said.

'I think,' Elias quoted as he put on his baker-boy cap, 'this is the beginning of a beautiful friendship. There. Now, please introduce me to your mother.'

How relaxed the tone was between them. Almost the way it was with Jan. Not like they'd only just met.

'We have to find her first,' she replied. 'Shall I take your bag, or can you manage?' She reached for the handles.

Elias pulled it towards him. 'Don't you dare. I had a very

traditional upbringing. It's enough that you kissed me before I had a chance to take the initiative. You've called my masculinity into question.'

They walked down the stairs.

'That,' said Clara, 'is something I was planning to do later.'

'Where does she normally run to?'

Clara was driving, slowly as ever, through the suburban streets.

'She doesn't run *to* anywhere. She mainly runs away, whenever my father is too preoccupied with his latest reincarnation as a French Revolutionary judge to remember to lock the door.'

'Is your father a judge?'

'Barrister,' said Clara. 'Or was, anyway. He's mainly a ... no idea.' She glanced over to him. 'He's always been odd. He never had a glittering career. Somehow, it was always the crazy cases that interested him. He was some kind of mystic in a robe. What about your parents?'

Elias leant back in his seat.

'I'm glad to get this cleared up right at the start. Mine are odd too. Although they're still working.'

Clara was strangely touched. His parents were a weak point, then. Yes. It was simply a chink in his armour.

'Seriously? Looks like we're from two completely different generations. I'd have thought you were older.'

Elias felt her slight uncertainty, and it surprised him. She normally seemed so self-assured, almost arrogant if you didn't look closely.

'My parents were very young when they had me. Constantly repeating the same mistakes seems to run in the family.'

They were both scanning the pavements.

'You have to look in the gardens too,' said Clara. 'Sometimes, she just walks into people's gardens if there are dogs or cats there. She's always loved animals. She got bitten once, but we only realised a few days later when the wound was so infected that she had to go into hospital. Then my brother spent the nights in her room so she couldn't run away from there as well. She wanted to, you see.'

They drove past a red VW campervan; an old woman was rattling at its doors. It took Elias a moment before the image took on meaning.

'Stop!' he said. 'Is that her? Is that your mother there?' He pointed behind him.

Clara angled the mirror and saw her mother. 'Yes. That's her. She probably thinks it's hers. We used to have one like that.'

She pulled up to the kerb and stopped the engine.

'Come on,' she said, voice full of irony, 'let me introduce you to my mother.'

It was weird, getting to know this side of Clara so quickly. Seeing where she'd grown up. Meeting her father, who wasn't as odd as all that. And to be introduced to her mother, which hadn't been necessary at all, because she'd immediately greeted him with a hug and a friendly smile. Hello, Paul, she'd said. Where's the dog working today?

Normally, you got to know a person divorced from all context. OK, if you met them in the theatre, or through friends maybe, then you might have heard a bit about them from other people. But most of the time, all the rest of it came later. Visiting the parents. Travelling to where you lived as a child.

They were on the motorway. Clara was driving fast, focused. And swearing, very casually, whenever anyone cut her up or some stubborn idiot hogged the middle lane in their SUV, despite everyone on either side going faster than them. It was good to be on the road. It was a bright day, even if the sun hadn't really come out. She listened, he thought, to the right music. But the main thing was that they were on the road together, and, for the first time in ages, it didn't feel like he'd rather be anywhere else.

'Why did your mother call me Paul?' he asked, after a while. 'Is that your brother?'

'Did she?'

Clara glanced at him. She hadn't heard that, she'd been busy lying on her stomach on the street, trying to encourage the scared cat to come out from under a stranger's van. Mama had probably been pleased that the cat was under the car, where it would be safe from the birds of prey she always imagined darkening the skies above their town.

'Paul was my husband,' she said briefly, surprised at herself. If she was in love with this man beside her, then she'd tell him about Paul either way. Perhaps it was just the timing. He'd already learnt as per style sheet so much about her today.

'Have you ever been married?' she asked hastily.

Elias shook his head. 'There's never been anyone before ... almost never. And I've never been the right man for anyone to marry.'

Clara smiled.

'No one is *the* right man or *the* right woman. And "before" – should I take that to mean that that's about to change?'

Elias turned to her. How he liked that little line around her mouth. That little line that spoke of experience.

'Yes. It can mean that, I think. It really could mean that. When did you split up?'

They were at a junction. The slip road was at a standstill, which gave her time to get her thoughts together, before she replied: 'We didn't split up. He died. Widow. Sounds weird, doesn't it?'

Elias listened without saying anything.

'*I* think it sounds weird. The word "widow" always makes me think of old women with black headscarves. I could never imagine it. And you always think it only ever happens to other people. Of course, you know that's not true. But you don't believe it.'

Yes, he did always think that – only to other people. But to yourself, no ... Whenever you thought about it, somehow a magical protective shield appeared around you. Allowing the idea of a genuine misfortune happening to you would punch holes in it.

'What did he die of?'

Clara watched the road.

'Not nice.' She paused. 'There are these films, you know. *Knockin' on Heaven's Door*. *Love Story*. One of them has only three months to live and then, because nothing matters anymore anyway, they have the best time of their lives with drugs and sex and going to the seaside and having a quick baby ... It's all a massive crock of shit.'

Elias would have liked to touch her, but this might not be the right moment. Clara took one hand from the wheel and sought out his. Only to give it a short squeeze. She didn't know if she could tell him everything.

'It's all shit because it's all just shit. They removed his stomach... That's possible, you know. You just have to get used to it. You have to eat very small portions, but you can live that way. But he was always ill. Continually. At first, I thought it was because of that. Because you have to get used to it. And of course, he kept getting thinner. But mainly...'

Fuck. It was so long ago now, but talking about it still made her freeze on the inside.

'Mainly...?' Elias asked softly.

Clara took a deep breath in and out.

'Mainly, nobody told him that he had no chance. They opened him up, saw that the cancer had already spread everywhere, but they still took his stomach out. Because by some miracle, that might still have helped. I don't know why they even did that. Shit story, isn't it? We can talk about something else,' she added hastily.

'No,' Elias said calmly. 'Tell me. I want to know.'

'I'll keep it short. There comes a time, you know, there comes a time when you think: this isn't right. He ought to be getting better. And then you realise that they haven't even sent him for rehab. And then you ask questions.'

Elias tried to imagine what Clara had been like in those days. What it had meant. She suddenly gave him a helpless smile.

'I'm telling you all this and we don't even know each other properly. Don't you find that strange?'

Elias unbuckled his seatbelt so that he could turn his whole body towards her, not just his head.

'That's what getting to know someone means,' he said quietly. 'No. I don't find it strange.'

'We ... I almost left him. You know, we got together quite young. And it was actually over, but we didn't have the courage to see that. Or to split up. And then, along comes cancer and says, no need to worry about that, your boyfriend's going to die anyway.'

They'd passed Heilbronn and there were blue holes forming in the thin blanket of cloud. The tarmac shone grey and smooth. Being on the road together like this was lovely in a very special way. The way travelling with someone can be, thought Clara. When you travel together and chat because there are so many things you want to talk about with the other person. With Paul, she'd run out of topics after a while, and maybe it had been like that for Elias and Vera for ages too.

'Could you talk, you and Vera?'

He already kind of knew this about Clara, and he liked it. The way she could suddenly put a new twist on a conversation.

'That was a pretty screeching conversational U-turn,' he said even so, with mild surprise. 'Yes. We could talk. About art and the theatre and we … yes, we liked visiting castles.' He grinned at Clara. 'Oh yes, and houses too, sometimes. Pretty old cottages in picturesque villages, being sold by beautiful women.'

'Do you think I'm beautiful?'

Clear question. Straight up and no coquetry. Elias studied her. There were more and more stretches of sunshine along the motorway, which was definitely helping.

'Not in the classic sense. Not averagely beautiful. You have … it's a tart beauty. I'm afraid there's nothing sweet about you,' he concluded in a tone of feigned malice.

'If you don't like sweet things, why Vera?'

He was silent a moment. Struck, because she was right. Why Vera? Clara looked at him for a second. She was driving very fast again, through the rolling landscape. Like a painting, he thought. It's such pretty countryside.

'I need to ask right now,' Clara said quietly, 'so that I know why you'd pick someone like me at this point in time. And I need to know that because the two of us are starting something here, and I want it to start out right.'

It's so hard to explain properly, he thought, but she has a point. When, if not now?

'Yes,' he said slowly, 'she's truly pretty. And sex with her was nice. We had good sex. But, well, you don't have to talk to each other, doing that. So from the outside, lots of things fitted. There was a lot that we both liked. But…'

'But?' asked Clara.

'But I didn't love her,' Elias said simply.

They were driving further south-west in silence. The midday sun slanted down on them. If you looked up, you could see the scraps of cloud blow away and dissolve. Elias opened the window a crack. The air streamed in; it was fresh and smelled green.

'Will you tell me the rest of your story later?' he asked. 'We got a bit sidetracked.'

Clara nodded.

'Doesn't matter. You know the most important part. I'm a widow. I'm free.'

She smiled in that special way, between mockery and merry melancholy. A smile that really meant something. A smile that you could fall deeply in love with.

Clara took her right hand from the steering wheel and rested it, open-palmed, on his thigh. Elias took it and held it for the rest of the way.

23

'If we fall in the water, we'll freeze in an instant,' Elias said. 'It's April. Did you ever see *Titanic*? You can survive maybe five minutes at six degrees.'

They were standing on the boat-hire jetty.

'I'm not planning to stand arms outstretched in front of you in the boat,' Clara replied drily. 'And if you don't make any inappropriate movements, we won't capsize.'

The landing stage had become his stage. He was speaking that tiny nuance louder than necessary. For the audience made up of the two boat-hire men and a young family about to take out a pedalo. How different he could be in front of other people. How much pleasure he had in acting a part ... Was it for her benefit? It was nice being out and about with him. He stood out. Like she did sometimes. She enjoyed it when people looked at her because she was well dressed. And the pair of them – she'd noticed that from the glances they got checking in at the little hotel – they really did make a handsome couple.

It had cleared right up. The Old Town lay across the River Neckar. The boat-hire place was under the bridge; it had looked shut, but Clara had insisted on checking. Neither of them had been to Tübingen before.

'I feel like a tourist,' said Elias as they pushed away from the jetty and he began to row.

'We are tourists,' Clara answered. 'Deal with it.'

The sun shone warm but the air rising from the river was very cool. To their right, the colourful fronts of the old houses stood proudly over the embankment wall. Elias steered between the low-hanging branches of a willow and Clara took photos of him. Very romantic, all of it. Him among the branches, in a rowing boat, a casually unbuttoned shirt collar above an unbuttoned waistcoat.

'You know you look good,' she said. 'Most people freeze when you photograph them. You're always posing, even when it doesn't look like you are.'

Elias stopped rowing a moment.

'That's my job. My face, my body – they're the tools of my trade. So they both have to do what I want, or it doesn't work. Incidentally, that's one fear that all actors have, I think. Of some stupid accident happening. Your voice failing. A stroke, aphasia ... whatever. And not just because of the women you'll no longer be able to impress.'

He looked at her with affectionate mockery.

Clara let her hand run through the very cold water. Elias was rowing quickly and strongly. She could see the muscles working on his forearms.

'Everyone has that fear,' she said inattentively.

Elias sat up. She could see that the subject really bothered him.

'Yes, maybe. But in other professions, you can do a lot to compensate, or you can work in a different area. You can sit at a desk with a torn ligament, but you can't get up on stage. If you lose your voice in the office, that's annoying. All I'd be able to do would be to work as a mime. This deep fear of your body – lots of people don't really get it. I need it to live, in just the same way as a medieval peasant. If my body fails, I'm out. That's that. Like a peasant, there's nothing else I can do. Poor. Out of work. My face, my body, they're my entire capital. My tools. My equipment.'

'Speaking of equipment,' she said, 'shall we have sex today?'

Elias looked up. Smiled. Kept rowing.

'Let's definitely have sex today,' he said. 'You might have deployed your senile mother as a way of putting it off a bit longer. But today has to be the day.'

They were passing a small island between the branches of the river. An ancient tree-lined avenue ran parallel to them. Between the massive, crooked trunks, you could see the Old Town rising steeply uphill. The afternoon sun set the windows sparkling and the faded painted façades glowing with colour. Today, I'm a tourist, she thought. A traveller. There's no yesterday and no tomorrow.

'Although, to be honest, I am a little scared.'

She lowered the camera in surprise.

'You're scared of sleeping with me? I ... Yeah. Me too, a bit.'

Of course she was scared. Whatever he said about her tart beauty, her body was not that of a thirty-year-old. Excuse me please, Vera, may I borrow your body? It's just that he's used to it and I don't want to disappoint him ... No, thank you, I'll keep my own face. Tart beauty, he said. Whatever the hell that means.

'Why are you scared?'

It burst almost sulkily from her. Elias lifted the oars from the water. The drips left an attractive trail in the water to either side of the boat. Didn't she get it?

'Of course I'm scared. Like any man. Fear of failure. I'm ... I think I'm anxious, you know. No idea what you think of me, but I ... One-night stands, for example. That was never my style. Doesn't interest me. But even so. The first time ... I'm just anxious.'

He paused a moment. The boat drifted to the side and ran onto the gravel. The two of them pushed it away from the bank. He rowed them back out into the middle and smiled awkwardly.

'But even so, there's just no getting around the fact that we have to have sex today.'

'Finally,' she sighed, only semi-ironically. It was nice that he wasn't quite as sure of things as he seemed.

The elongated island beside them came to an end and the Neckar flowed back together. Suddenly, the river was broad.

'All this talk about sex,' Clara said slowly, 'is making me hot. Row me back.'

Elias rolled his eyes dramatically and dropped the oars in outrage.

'Row! Shag! Act! Anything else?' He screamed his protest over the river.

Clara laughed. And took over the rowing.

The window was half open. The sound of a piano wafted in from across the street. Nothing amazing. Just an etude. But it sounded the way a late afternoon in spring ought to sound. Sleepy and self-contained. Life in equilibrium for a moment.

They were lying side by side. Their naked shoulders and hips were touching. Clara had one leg crooked, her hand resting on his crotch. His hand beside it.

'In a film, this would be the happy ending. The story is done once they go to bed. We ... for us...'

She left the sentence unfinished. Elias lay very still while everything in him tingled and it felt as though he could feel his blood fizzing gently, like freshly poured sparkling mineral water tinkling against the glass when it's very quiet.

'In the light of past events,' Elias said solemnly, 'I think we waited far too long. We should have slept together right away.'

He rolled onto his front and looked at her. Her shoulders were broad and firm.

'Do you swim?' he asked.

She nodded. 'I used to be on a team. But now ... far too rarely. It's good that summer's on its way. And yes. I think we should have had sex right away too. I've had too little in recent years.'

'Is sex important?' asked Elias.

'Yes,' Clara replied at once. 'Sex is very important. I know people always say that women talk about this stuff all the time, but to be honest, I don't have that many female friends. Hardly any, in fact. So I don't know exactly what it's really like for other women. But I think everyone actually wants good sex and that hardly anyone has good sex.'

Elias shrugged. Smiled apologetically. He looked very charming, Clara thought.

'I told you I'd be anxious. Sorry that it didn't quite...'

'You're as shy as a little princess,' said Clara. 'Anyway, it was worth the wait.'

'Oh,' Elias replied hastily, 'it wasn't that great for me. You should have put more effort...'

She was on top of him at once, pressing the pillow into his face.

'Say it was the best sex of your life.'

'It was the best sex of your life,' he parroted obediently, his voice muffled. 'But in general, I'd prefer to be smothered by pillows.'

How easy it could be.

'What's the time?'

Elias startled up. He'd fallen asleep. Clara had been lying next to him, looking at him. He wasn't much taller than her, but what you might call wiry. All his muscles were for use, not show. Good legs, like a dancer. And arms. Did he dance too? He'd mumbled in his sleep but she hadn't caught any words. How peaceful this was. She'd been afraid of the hours after sex. Until today, she'd only ever had one desire afterwards: to leave. Just to get up and go. It was different with him.

'Half past four. You only slept fifteen minutes. Do you have to go?'

He sank back in relief.

'Soon. There's a technical run-through at half-five. And a short rehearsal. Shall we meet in town afterwards?'

'It's kind of good that we first slept together in a hotel, isn't it. It's like neutral ground. Doesn't belong to either of us.'

Elias looked at her. Sitting cross-legged beside him, her back straight, naked. He hadn't been sure if he'd like everything when she was naked. Like he hadn't been sure if ... There was always something that you could dislike about somebody else. Something you had to overlook. But Clara … you could see that she worked out.

'Or belongs to both of us,' he said. 'I hereby declare this hotel room the personal boudoir of Clara and Elias, for their sole use for all time. Amen. Nobody will ever be allowed to shag here again.'

'Nobody but us. Tonight.'

Elias laughed.

'Yes,' he said. 'I see you have a plan.'

24

The stage in the vaults of the Zimmertheater was almost smaller than their own at home. Mareike had already set it up and everything was looking good.

'How's your room?'

Elias smiled. 'Really nice. Really very nice. Shall we start?'

As they went through the scenes and the blocking, Mareike getting him to come down the stone stairs to the stage instead of through the audience, and they practised the costume changes, a great joy spread through him. It was as though he'd lost his way this whole time, only to discover to his complete surprise that he'd arrived in the exact place he'd been wanting to go from the outset.

Happiness. Truly. It was simply just happiness. No rush of pride as on a first night, not the breathless, tearful liberation of Jule's birth, nor the low-level satisfaction of the evening after a good day. But a deep, quiet happiness. Quiet and true and all-pervading. It was a very long time since he'd last felt like this.

The narrow streets of the town were full of life. There were groups of young people everywhere. It was nice to watch them. Clara was sitting at a pavement café at the bottom of the market place. White wine to match the early evening. Her phone buzzed. Jan. The message was brief. A question mark. She couldn't help smiling as she typed an exclamation mark in reply. He texted back almost immediately: *Good girl. I'm proud of you.* She sipped her wine and fiddled with the phone before messaging: *Remis. I'm catching up. Your move, late starter*.

Sex always changed everything. With that teacher ... things had looked good at first. Going for a coffee. Going for dinner. Once they'd even gone to an exhibition she'd suggested. She could overlook it if someone didn't share her and Jan's sense of humour. But if you couldn't even laugh during sex when something went wrong – and it had gone wrong – then what was left? And it had been pretty similar with the others.

The clock on the market place struck seven. It was really bustling now. A mild evening, and full of scents that promised the summer to come. Coffee and the female students' not overly expensive perfume, the wooden shutters that had been soaking up the sunshine until just now, and drifting smoke. She watched the young couples, young men in shorts – which she'd never been able to stand – and young women in short skirts or long, light, wafty dresses. Paul and she had probably looked like that once. Fifteen years ago. I'd like to be able to just let myself fall. Spread out my arms and fall into the other person. No rope. No parachute. No bungee relationship that pulled you back just before you reached your goal, after a flight that was only pretend. Some things were more apt in English than German, she thought. *To fall in love.* That really is what it is. But we just add a prefix: *verlieben.* That fits too though, in my opinion, Clara thought. Falling in love is dangerous, and nothing much good starts with the prefix *ver-*. *Verloren. Vergangen. Verderben.* Lost. Bygone. To go bad. *Verliebt, verloren:* in love, lost.

She drank up her wine. The colourful life all around her. A group of young people were sitting on the fountain steps, drinking, laughing and celebrating youth. The evening sky was changing colour above the Town Hall tower.

This is now, she thought, standing up. Would Elias be as good tonight as the first time she'd seen him act? Could he enchant her again?

Congratulations, Elias, she said to herself in a tone between self-mockery and despair, you won't have it easy with me.

After the performance, they'd let themselves drift through the town; further and further up, via the market place and the Town Hall and down the narrow lanes and up the steps until they'd ended up in a garden behind some tall, wide building. An old school perhaps, or a former monastery – in the dark, it was hard to make out what it was. Lying there like a large, contentedly sleeping animal, thought Elias. It wasn't a large garden. A few trees, the early blossom shimmering faintly in the light of the town beneath them. A cute little wall above the steep slope, on which lay scattered a few little orchards. Four deserted benches, which gave the place a quietly municipal air.

They were standing by the wall, looking down on the town. Although it was pretty late by then, an occasional laugh or shout would ring out and up to them from the still-busy streets. The sky spanned above them, moonless and endless.

'I like being on the road with you,' Elias said quietly.

'It's certainly a very romantic backdrop,' Clara teased. 'And when you're travelling, it's always easy.'

Elias put his arm around her and pulled her to him.

'Every love story needs a backdrop. Every love story needs beautiful images. And music of course. There's nothing wrong with that. Believe you me,' he added in a deep, soft voice, 'believe you me, I speak the truth.'

Clara had to laugh. 'Even so. Love cannot live by beautiful pictures alone.' She pulled away from his arm and made a sweeping gesture that took in the town and the castle above them and the garden they were standing in. 'All this is desperately pretty. But it's only pictures.'

'Says the photographer,' Elias retorted.

They were silent a while. How could she suddenly be so dismissive again? This afternoon, he'd had the feeling that they were breathing in synch. The whole time. As if they'd actually sung together. But now it was as though he wanted to sing and she wouldn't join in. As if she was suddenly, yes, ashamed of their song. He looked over the town. The reflections of the lights in the Neckar, as it flowed so sedately away. The cool night air around them both. The huge, expansive darkness of this new-moon night. He stepped behind her and encircled her. As he'd done in the snowy rose garden. It seemed longer ago than it had actually been.

Clara let him. It felt good and yet, at the same time, it was as though none of this was allowed.

'Look,' said Elias softly, very close to her ear, 'I stopped believing that this kind of thing could happen. That it could feel so true.'

'Do you say that to all the girls?' Clara asked. She'd meant it to sound playfully ironic, but it hadn't.

'I'm saying it to *you*. But for me...' How could he best tell her it?

No, Elias decided. I'll just say it. Leave nothing out and tell no half-tales, or make anything less of it than it was. Not with you.

'When you meet a person,' he began slowly, 'everyone always acts like they've never had a past. Like there's never been anything before you.'

Yes, thought Clara, that was true. The men she'd met had ... they'd always wanted to float in mid-air. With no past. That only ever emerged gradually. And as for her, she was sick of always feeling so heavy with her history.

'But I've been with Vera, as you know. And there have been a couple of other relationships, if I can even call them that.'

'Everyone knows what these actors are like.'

This time it came out right. Light. He was correct. Neither of them had lived in a monastery.

'And for you,' Elias continued, 'for you, it presumably won't have been any different. You're very attractive. Very. It wouldn't surprise me if ... No,' he grinned, 'it would actually disappoint me if there hadn't been anyone.'

'One of them was a teacher from Braunschweig. Will you despise me now?'

Her almost imperceptible resistance to his embrace was

softening. He kept holding her and she enjoyed the feeling of his hands crossed over her belly. It had been the same in the rose garden.

'What are you actually trying to tell me?'

Elias took a deep breath. He sat down on the back of the bench behind them. She sat next to him. They were close to one another. Shoulders, hips, legs. It felt tender.

'I fell so deeply in love with Mona, back then. Jule's mother. That was ... It felt like a great, true love. The way you are when you have no idea. But not yet knowing anything about the world doesn't make the feeling any smaller. We were like Romeo and Juliet. That was how it felt. And you never forget that first love. It stays forever. Was it like that for you too, with Paul?'

Clara's face softened as she thought back to that time. It really was a long time ago. Her. Beate. Jan. And...

'Not Paul,' she said, 'that was later. Johann, his name was. Not that I noticed right away. But it was something similar. Not Romeo and Juliet. We saw ourselves more as Bonnie and Clyde. But it felt just as ... imperative.'

'But not with Paul?'

She could talk to him. He really listened and he asked the right questions. Did he feel the same about her?

'With Paul...' She hesitated. The town had grown quieter. One tower after another struck the quarter-hour. The varying notes sounded in tune.

'It was much more grown-up with Paul. Perhaps you start thinking that way some time. That you have to be more grown-up. That a partnership consists of all kinds of things because it can't just be one big emotion. Of friendship and trust and shared interests and—'

'Ah yes, I know that one,' Elias interjected with a theatrical sigh.

Clara instantly dug her elbow into his ribs, none too gently. 'Listen!'

Elias jumped up, struck a pose in front of her and swept a bow, almost to the ground. 'Certainly, my lady. I do beg your pardon.'

'Are you always acting?' she asked him with a laugh.

'Always,' Elias answered, 'but that doesn't mean it isn't true. Go on.'

This time he sat on the bench at her feet. Leant against her legs. The darkness made it easier for her to talk.

'I think,' she said, 'after a certain point, I simply didn't want to conduct a relationship along those adult lines anymore. With no great emotions; with just this friendly "I love you" that has barely any meaning left. And then one morning, I was standing at the bathroom mirror and I thought: this can't be it. This mustn't be it. But of course, there was also: I know that you get days like this, and you can't just sit down at the breakfast table after all these years and break up.'

Yes, Elias thought, that's how it is. Exactly like that. It was a relief that she'd felt the same way. He wanted to say something, but she laid a hand on his shoulder, as if to mean that he should wait. She was speaking more haltingly now.

'I wanted to give myself a little time. Not just throw in the towel because of one day's emotions. To be fair – not to spring it on him. But life isn't fair. Life is faster than you and it cuts you off. It sends your boyfriend home from the doctor with stomach cancer.'

She took a deep and somewhat trembling breath.

'You know, at the start, everything revolves entirely around treatment and the operation and the hospital – and that's normal. You want to be caring. Everything else takes a back seat. You can't then be selfish enough to say: so, I was actually about to dump you, deal with your cancer alone.'

It was only now, here with Elias on this bench, that she realised that this was the first time she'd told this story like this. That until now, it had gone untold in her head.

'But that's good,' Elias said softly. 'It's good to be like that.'

At that moment, it shot up in Clara, the way a freak wave can sweep you off your feet, and she almost screamed.

'No! It's not good. It's a fucking shitting lie and it makes nothing any better. You know,' she said, breathing hard because it was suddenly as though she couldn't get enough air, 'he then asked me if I'd marry him. Two weeks after he got out of hospital. At that point I didn't know that he ... that he was going to die. He didn't either. For him it was the way things are when you've just got through a serious crisis. That always makes you think that now something has to change.'

Elias could feel her whole body trembling. He laid a hand on her knee.

Clara was still speaking, hectic and fragmentary. How was it possible that all this had caught up with her again?

'I couldn't say yes and I couldn't say no. I said let's wait. But it was important to him. And at the same time, I could see him declining. And that the nausea wasn't easing. Back then, I thought it was due to the chemo. Until one day, when I went to pick him up from an appointment at the clinic, one of the doctors randomly gave me the address of a hospice in Stuttgart. You'd better give them a call, she said, we won't be able to do much more for him soon. She probably thought I was his wife. She shouldn't have said it otherwise, I don't think.'

Elias could feel her agitation, but didn't want to say anything. Imagined what it would have been like for him ... with Jule. Not a good thought. He took a deep breath and sat up straight. Everyone always said that death was everywhere. You just didn't want it to be true. He would have liked to take her in his arms, but felt that it wasn't the right thing to do. She stood up again and walked over to one of the trees. Laid her hand on the trunk. Elias stood beside her and rested his hand next to hers. It was almost like something that belonged only to them. Laying their hands side by side.

'And then you did get married?'

Clara's breathing eased. It was good to be standing. Nothing around her but the night. She would have liked to hug Elias and tell the rest of her story into his shoulder, but the Clara of ten years ago was reaching through time to her and holding her back. You can't split up with yourself. No divorce. Nothing. You just have to keep on living with yourself. When she spoke again, her voice sounded cold, even to herself.

'I then did something very stupid. I told him the truth. I told him that he was going to die. And you know why?'

She's furious, thought Elias. She's really furious. He'd never seen her like this. Her voice rose again now. But it sounded stifled. As if it was costing her a lot of strength not to yell everything out.

'Because I thought I had to be honest. With myself. That you can't be untrue to yourself and all that. That you're too good for a merciful lie. Because it's only for your own benefit. Hey, the other person's dying. You want to be left with the good feeling: look, I told him the truth. I did everything right. I was true to myself. I'd never do it again. Never.'

'Clara,' Elias said gently. 'Clara.'

She paid barely any attention. It was all back. How livid Paul had been, despite being so weak.

'You don't believe in me. That's what he said. You don't have faith in me anymore. Do you want me to die? He was ... it was like until then, he'd thought everything was going to work out. That it would just take a while. Because it only every happens to other people. Never to yourself. Because you can't imagine that. He hated me.'

'But how...?' Elias didn't quite understand. 'But you did then get married, didn't you?'

Clara could picture it. The room in the Town Hall. Her parents. Her mother had still been well then. Jan and the others. Paul's family. Only a very few friends. A circle of friends shrinks rapidly when someone gets cancer. Another of those clichés that turn out to be true. And Paul with a headscarf. Like a pirate. A sick, miserable pirate.

'We didn't speak for a couple of days. And then I couldn't bear it any longer, and I asked him if we wanted to get married.'

'To show him,' Elias said slowly, 'that you *did* believe in him. That he was going to get better.'

Clara nodded, full of disgust with herself. 'The greatest lie.'

Elias took her hands in his. She yielded reluctantly.

'But you did it out of...' Sympathy was perhaps the wrong word, he thought. 'You did it for him. That's a good thing.'

Clara ripped her hands furiously from his. 'Nothing about it is good!' She really was screaming now. 'Nothing! It was wrong and only because I couldn't bear it ... and he died anyway. He was in pain. He had such a miserable death and I hadn't loved him for a long time by then. It was only another ... It was all wrong. In the end, I was only hoping that it would soon be over.'

Elias heard the tears in her voice. She'd gone over to the wall and was looking down, without seeing. Why had she let herself go like this? Why had she said that? She was trying to get the tears under control when Elias joined her and took her in his arms.

'Perhaps it was wrong,' he said after quite a while. 'Perhaps. But this is now. We can get it right, this time.'

She didn't know what she was feeling. It was good to be so close to him. And yet...

'I don't know if I can,' she whispered. 'I don't know if I even can, if I can at all.'

'I think so,' said Elias, kissing her softly. But maybe only to bridge the little uncertainty that her words had provoked in him. I don't know if I can.

'How would you know?' she asked.

'Because you're like that,' Elias said simply. 'Even if it didn't feel that way to you anymore, it was a kind of love that you stayed with him to the end.'

'I shouldn't have married him,' Clara said, composed again.

'Maybe not,' Elias replied. 'But that was what he wanted, wasn't it? In a situation like that you probably can't do anything right. Doing the right thing would presumably mean being able to stop the other person from dying. And that's not possible. Everything feels wrong when someone dies before their time. And you were there for him.'

Clara straightened up and looked at Elias. 'Not inwardly. That was wrong ... You can't take it away or talk me out of it. I know that it was wrong, and you do too. You wouldn't want me to stay with you out of sympathy or a guilty conscience, would you?'

Elias smiled and said something that he hadn't been able to say to anyone for a very long time:

'I would always, whatever happened, want you to stay with me. Can we go and get a drink now?'

Her tension dissolved so suddenly that she had to laugh. He was good at that, this man. She kissed him fleetingly.

'Asking that question at the right moment will definitely increase the probability of me staying.'

25

Church bells all over the place. They'd left the hotel room window wide open overnight. The air was fresh and cool.

'Monday,' said Elias. They were still lying in bed. How intimate it felt. That might also be because he didn't feel like he had to leave. Like he mustn't let them get too close. Soulmates, he thought mockingly, but there was a grain of truth in it, even so. He turned to her. She had her eyes shut and looked, in the morning light, extraordinarily beautiful. Even as an old woman, she'd be beautiful in that sharp, unaccommodating way. A feeling of warmth washed through him.

'Hey, you,' he said tenderly. Nothing more. In that lay everything.

She didn't open her eyes, although she'd heard it. The words sank warm and deep into her. Until she caught hold of them, just before they reached her core. Don't. Don't touch my innermost being. I don't know if I can bear it. If I can be the right person for you.

He was lying close beside her. The morning sky was thinly veiled but the day might well turn out fine.

'When I was little, in the village, we lived next to the church. I never needed a watch. In winter, the evening bell rang at six, and in summer at eight. I like the sound of bells.'

'Me too,' said Clara. 'There's something so peaceful about it. What's that there?'

She took his hand and studied the ring finger, which wasn't looking good.

'A souvenir from your house,' said Elias. He pulled his hand away and eyed the swelling. 'When I climbed over the fence, I got a thorn from your dog rose in it. It's pretty. It reminds me of you.'

'If you need reminding of me when you're lying right next to me, there's something wrong with your memory, my dear. I've got enough dementia in my life already. Shall I lance it? It looks infected.'

Elias sat up.

'I can't imagine anything more romantic. Are you some kind of a freak? Why do you want to cut me? And what with?'

Clara stood up and pulled her wash bag from the bathroom.

'The wise woman makes provision for the future. I generally travel with a scalpel. It's handy to have relatives at the hospital.'

'Other women travel with lipstick or tampons or perfume, or whatever. You have scalpels. Should I be worried?'

'I've got tampons too,' said Clara drily. 'Using the scalpel often results in loads of blood. Wash your hands and then come here. Oh yeah, and there's a body bag in my suitcase. Bring that over too, would you?'

Elias jumped out of bed with a laugh and a devil-may-care salute, then walked into the bathroom. Clara took the scalpel from its sterile packaging.

'OK,' she admitted as he came back, 'maybe I am a bit of a freak. I can't stand the sight of anything like that. Not even spots. I want to perform surgery right away. Put your hand on my knee and hold still.'

'I'm very glad there's a hand on a bare knee,' Elias said. 'Otherwise, this kind of scene would never get shown in a romance. Ow!'

Clara had made a small, rapid cut at the side of the nailbed. Blood and a little pus oozed out. Clara dabbed at the wound and sprayed it with disinfectant.

'I hope I cut deep enough,' she said as she wrapped the scalpel in paper towels and threw it away. 'Keep the wound clean.'

'How can I touch you then?' Elias asked maliciously. He knelt before her. His hand was still on her thigh. Clara pulled him to her.

'Hands are overrated,' she said.

The morning was quiet. There was a fine mist over the river and it was still chilly in the streets. You could hear the birds singing on the other bank. They were leaning against the quay wall, looking silently into the water. It's good to be quiet with him, Clara thought. She turned and looked up. The grand houses on the slope lay in huge grounds, almost like sparse woodland, still bright green. It all looked expensive and very pretty and unattainable, but that didn't matter. It was enough for her. It was as though the town was only there to make this morning more lovely for her. Elias was still looking into the water, but she could hear him reciting quietly, as if to himself, in a tone somewhere between singsong and everyday: '...the red bricks of a wall in the first light of dawn...'

'What's that?' asked Clara. 'It's very beautiful.'

'It's a song.' Elias didn't look up as he started to hum the tune. The waves were playing on the bank and the morning breeze was ruffling the surface. 'My attempt to translate it into German. "Waters of March" it's called.'

It fitted well, even though it was April, and even that was nearly over. She took the lens cap off the camera.

'Stay still a moment.'

Clara was searching for a good angle for the photo. Him, his forearms resting on the wall, his eyes fixed on the water. The gently moving willow twigs above him. The shore with the wealthy gardens behind him.

'May I take a photo of you for a change?' Elias asked, holding out his hand for the camera. Clara shook her head.

'I'm not photogenic. I love the camera, but it doesn't love me. There are no good photos of me.'

'There are in my head,' said Elias. 'But as you so charmingly informed me this morning, my memory is shocking and I would therefore like a few photos.'

'Out of the question,' said Clara. 'Paint yourself some.'

He tried to grab the camera, but she ran off like a shot. And she was fast. He didn't catch up with her until they were on the bridge, kissing breathlessly.

Sunday love, thought Clara, briefly but full of joy.

They'd ended up on the avenue of plane trees.

'You probably miss all kinds of stuff if you don't read the town guide, but I enjoy just drifting around a new city.'

Elias simply nodded because he generally did the same. He liked the way she walked beside him. He'd noticed it before but now that he'd seen her naked, her gait was like confirmation. She found joy in her strength, in her body.

'You have a nice walk,' he said.

'That's not for you to determine,' she said majestically. 'But thank you. I'll add it to the stock of compliments for bad times. Waste not, want not.'

Their conversations were like fencers' training bouts. Playful, but you had to be fully present at all times. Alert. Inventive and skilful. She kept him on his toes, and he hadn't experienced that since Mona.

The sun had never quite come out, but you could tell that it was there, behind a thin blanket of cloud. All the colours were a little muted, none stood out. Between the ancient tree trunks, the shadows lay hazily dark on the brighter green of the fresh grass. The split Neckar flowed past at its leisure, dark silver arms either side of them. Good light for photography.

'Why do we always want to be on an island the moment an island's there?'

'Because it's there,' she answered at once. 'Why don't cats just sleep once they're full and out of danger? If evolution was only about the survival of the species, that would be wise, wouldn't it? But cats are curious. They're one of the few creatures that enjoy finding stuff out. So they think, *Evolution can bite me. I want to know what's going on on that island.* Some people are like that too. You. Me.'

'Are you comparing me to a cat?' Elias was flattered.

Clara looked at him with a grin. 'Cats don't have a taste for sweet things. They just don't. That's why they don't go for chocolate. You do. Stand next to that tree there.'

'When will you let me photograph you?'

'Never,' she answered curtly, dropping to her knees. She really liked how naturally he could take a pose, could understand the kind of image she had in her head. A man who had truly kept his boyish insouciance and didn't only sometimes act that part, to impress others. A true lack of inhibitions that meant he had no fear of looking silly. He didn't stiffen up in the face of the lens as so many people did.

'Unlike me, you're very photogenic.' She tilted her head. 'You look even better in photos than in real life.'

Elias stepped behind one of the large trunks; it had split and was held together by a strong metal band.

'Photograph the tree. You don't get to see my face anymore.'

She lowered the camera and walked around the plane. He was leaning his back casually against the trunk. Suddenly, her chest was seized by a slight breathlessness at the sight of him.

'Spending time with you is so beautiful.'

Yes, he thought, yes, yes, yes.

'Is that a declaration of love?'

She kissed him lightly on the lips.

'Yes,' she said with a smile, 'I think it is.'

26

Toni and Jan were already there when she arrived at her parents' house. Since Toni had moved to Augsburg, the two of them hadn't seen as much of each other. And they'd never been quite as close as her and Jan. Even so, Clara felt their intimacy as they hugged. A sister was a sister.

'Sorry that you had to come in the middle of the week. Long drive, huh?' she said to Toni.

'I needed to pick a few things up anyway. So it actually worked out quite well. When exactly is this guy coming?'

It sounded dismissive and was presumably meant to. This guy ... the way you always fell into a hostile attitude, even before you'd met someone. The man was only doing his job. But you immediately felt as though the family was under threat. When it was only a conversation with their mother. Clara looked at the letter from the district court that had miraculously escaped being lost without trace amid her father's bizarre chaos of flyers, doctors' bills, newspapers, increasing numbers of new folders, and old files.

'His name is Dr Henschel. Expert witness. Ten-thirty. Where is Mama, anyway?'

Toni pointed towards the bathroom. 'Jan's helping her get dressed. What do you think? Is the dementia really that bad?'

Clara shrugged. Toni had been away for over two years and her mother was always on her best form when the family were there; you could sometimes even have a conversation with her then.

'It's not great. But I think it's OK still. Papa can take care of her to some extent.'

'I wouldn't have expected that, actually,' said Toni, walking into the kitchen to make herself a coffee. It looked like the old days, thought Clara. Their house had always been kind of chaotic. Mama had never really liked housework. When Toni had been little and wanted to know where their mother was, she'd never asked 'Where's Mama?' It had always been: 'Where's Mama reading?' It was so unfair that all that was being lost. People always said that keeping your brain active helped. So their mother was probably just a statistical exception. She'd always been different, in lots of ways.

Clara followed Toni into the kitchen. 'Make me one, please?' she asked. 'And what wouldn't you have expected?'

'That Papa would end up taking care of her one day.'

She opened the drawer on the coffee grinder and tipped the powder into the pot. The espresso machine they'd given their parents years ago stood gathering dust in a corner of the worktop. Papa had never been able to get on with it. All at once, there was the overwhelmingly good smell of fresh coffee.

'I mean, once upon a time ... they both lived their own lives. Mama and Papa never even went on holiday together.'

Clara laughed. 'No, because Mama didn't want to wait for Papa to pack. But yes, he's doing ... he's going to a lot of trouble. I wouldn't have expected it either. But he can't cope any longer.'

Toni poured on the boiling water in silence. Clara suddenly found herself wondering what it would be like with Elias. Would she want to care for him when he was old? Would she even ... She'd never been able to imagine being with anyone that long. Was that sort of thing even still possible?

'Voilà,' said Jan cheerfully as he and their mother walked into the kitchen; he took her by the shoulders and twirled her around. He'd put a dress on her, which he must have found in a wardrobe somewhere. Mama had always preferred trousers. And he'd combed her hair. She looked as fresh and contented as if she were perfectly healthy. Almost like the old days. She loved having her children around her. Always had done. Toni hadn't had it easy when she'd wanted to go to university in England.

'You scallywag!' laughed Mama, and Toni and Clara found themselves laughing too. Sometimes it was just funny.

Perhaps it's actually all right. Perhaps she's more stable now. Perhaps ... Clara didn't want to think any further.

'Where's Papa? He's meant to be here for the chat too, isn't he?'

Their father was probably down in the depths of the cellar, looking for some kind of helmet, or some other thing he considered necessary for talking to a psychiatrist. Or maybe he was only taking off the hideous dressing gown he sometimes kept on into the afternoon.

'I'll get him,' said Toni as the doorbell rang.

'I'll come too,' said their mother.

'You'd better stay here with us, Mama,' said Jan. 'There's a man here who's come to speak to you.'

Her brain might not work quite right anymore, but apparently her instincts were still wide awake.

'I don't want visitors! Only children have their plates in my house. Only children!' she repeated insistently, but Jan had already opened the door.

'Do you know what year it is?'

Dr Henschel was very professional and didn't smile. Papa, Toni, Jan and she were sitting at the dining table with their mother, almost like the old days. Clara was writhing on the inside; it was so unpleasant having to watch this. It was even worse than that day at the police station. It was as though their mother had been stripped naked. She could see that Toni and Jan were feeling similar.

Item after item was ticked off on the pile of papers that Dr Henschel had placed on the table in front of him.

'Mrs Wagenbach, what money do we use here in Germany, euros or marks?'

Mama's cheeks were flushing bright red.

'I don't have to ... I can tell you something ... The cat led our water astray. You can't get me under the table here!'

The angrier she got, the less sense she was making.

'Mama,' Toni tried, 'you only need to say what money you use. Euros or marks.'

'It's all my own money!' their mother shouted furiously, jumping to her feet and tipping the chair over.

Jan and Clara had to laugh. The only clear sentence had to do with money. But their laughter was only because everything was so tense.

Another little cross on Dr Henschel's list.

'Do you know what day it is today?'

He was implacable, and the worst of it all was that none of them around the table had wanted to admit how adrift their mother was from the world. She, who'd always been so very strong. Who'd always stood up for her children if anything happened. Clara still remembered the time she'd phoned after Paul had been in a car accident.

Mama, listen, you might get a call from the police in the next few days.

Mama's instant response had been: What shall I say? Not what had she done. Not what had happened. Not if she'd killed anyone. Just: What shall I say?

Suddenly, she had tears in her eyes. Jan was pale and Toni's cheeks were nearly as flushed as her mother's. Only their father seemed the same as ever.

'Four o'clock!' Mama screamed. 'Hush now!'

She ran out of the room and slammed the door.

One last cross. Dr Henschel looked up.

'As you have observed yourselves,' he said soberly, 'your mother has severe dementia.'

He tidied up his papers. With small, precise, almost pedantic movements. He actually has a briefcase, thought Clara, like in a film. Brown. Ugly.

'The district court will appoint a legal guardian for her,' he said as he stood up. 'Of course, the family will be taken into consideration first, if you are happy with that. So, you,' he turned to their father, then nodded towards Jan and Toni, 'and you too, of course, if you are willing. It's not easy,' he added with a sudden and entirely unexpected smile. Maybe he was human after all. How pleased she was to see such a silly little smile. As if that changed anything.

They led him to the door. All of them. As if to make sure he would really leave. Except he couldn't take the dementia with him. That stayed here.

'Where is Mama?' asked Toni.

Jan looked into the kitchen. The back door was open.

'Is the cat there?'

Clara knew that it would be gone too, even before the others had searched every room. It was probably sitting on Mama's shoulders, and Mama had run away again.

27

Everything had changed. Everything felt new. Every song had meaning. He'd finally been able to collect his car from the garage, and they were on their way to visit Jule.

'Don't you think it's a bit soon to introduce me to your daughter?'

Clara had taken off her shoes and jammed her feet up against the dashboard.

'You introduced me to your parents almost before our first date. So if anything, I'm late.'

Thinking of her mother, Clara looked out of the window for a moment. The mountains in the distance.

'I can introduce you to my mother anytime. It's always new for her.' She took refuge in dark humour.

'It won't be like that for long, will it?'

She'd told him how long it had taken them to find her mother the last time. And that it had been hours later that they'd discovered the bite wounds, where she must have stroked some dog she'd thought was theirs. Like a child who couldn't explain where it really hurt, she'd kept saying tummy ache. Clara had seen Toni crying, for the first time in years.

'Probably not. We've got a place in a home for her,' she said. The home was like some kind of life insurance for her mother. Literally. Assuring her life. You took out life insurance as a superstition, so that you'd never die. You arranged a place in a home so that you'd never have to take it up.

She stretched her hand out to Elias, and he took it. His grip always felt good. Never tentative. She could feel that he liked working with his hands.

'I don't want to die, Elias. Not now. Not later. But especially not now.'

He looked at her. Laughing. Fearless.

'Nobody dies. We've only just found each other. It wouldn't be worth the trouble.'

She joined in with his laughter.

'What a compelling argument. Fate will have to bend to your logic; it has no other option.'

Elias bowed slightly and put the music on. Clara shut her eyes.

'I like cafés in the morning. When they've only just opened and it's just you and the waiters. The tiny sounds as they put flowers on the tables or straighten the chairs. And the right music to go with it.'

Clara listened, her eyes still closed. If Elias looked at her, the yearning struck him in the chest.

'I love that ethereal mood,' he continued. 'Being on the cusp, able to tip any which way. When the music is as though certain notes contain a bud of happiness. And it sways in the sound as if in a morning breeze.'

He has a way with words. Tell me more. Drive me through the morning and tell me more about you. The light flickered before Clara's closed eyelids, sometimes bright, sometimes not so bright.

Elias's voice softened a little, became more tender. He could see all that before him.

'And now, one of them...' His pause wasn't to find the right words, it was more as though one was necessary to give the thought enough space. 'Thanks to you, one of those buds has opened and it's starting to unfurl its petals. When I think of you and hear certain music, it's exactly like that. If I could compose, I'd write you a song like that. Just a light, uplifting melody based on the notes of those buds.'

That's the most beautiful thing, Clara wanted to say, but she couldn't because she didn't want Elias to hear the sudden tears in her voice. That's the most beautiful thing, she thought, that anyone's said to me for years. Absolutely the most beautiful. But she couldn't speak so she undid her seatbelt so that she could lean her head against Elias's shoulder.

It was hillier now. Clara had often driven in this direction, but always via the motorways.

'I prefer the country roads if I have time,' said Elias. As if he'd known what she'd been thinking. That kind of coincidence was nice.

'It's beautiful here, isn't it?'

'To the photographer's eye, or does it look that way to you personally?'

She liked the way his mind worked. Not like other people's. As if he had another angle on things and people. From below, or sideways on, or round about.

'I'm a photographer. I don't distinguish between business and pleasure. If a thing is beautiful, it's beautiful. I wouldn't want to think a thing beautiful just because other people see it that way.'

'You can tell that from your house. And especially your garden. Do you want ... we've got time, haven't we?'

'It's your daughter. If you want to leave her in tears at the school gate ... Do you ever miss her living with you, by the way?'

'Yes,' he answered. 'I do. I miss her. More now than I used to. I think I could be a better father to her now. I used ... I was always very focused on myself. I always wanted to be a good dad. But then things just didn't work out that way. We've been on holiday together a lot, and of course she always came to stay. But looking back on it now – it wasn't enough. Not for her, and not for me either.'

They were silent a while. Clara could easily imagine him as a father. Yeah, he'd be a bit different, but she could see what he meant.

'It's this ... you can't call it lust, can you? This greed for sensation. For life. And you always think it ought to be even more intense. More direct and more violent. The way you feel in dreams sometimes. With that incredible ferocity.'

They came to a crossroads and Elias turned off.

Yes, he thought. Yes. She gets it. She knows what it's like.

'I feel that,' he said. 'When we have sex, I can feel that.'

'And because we're like that, we don't always think enough about other people, do we?'

'Probably not,' Elias admitted. 'But it's been different the last few weeks. Since I was in your garden, actually. Yes. That was one of those moments when you think: this can't go on. You can't keep living your life like that.'

'Wasn't intentional,' Clara said lightly.

Elias looked at her. It was a look full of warmth.

'No,' he said, 'I know. But it happened all the same, and that's amazing. We're almost there.'

They were driving up a steep road. Clara read the town sign.

'Gößweinstein? The church?'

'The church is pretty too,' said Elias, 'but we're actually heading up to the Kreuzberg. The view is amazing. And I like it there.'

'Have you brought all your other women here too?'

It was a malicious question, but he had to be able to deal with that.

'I've only ever been up here alone before. But if you like, I'll call them, OK? Maybe they can make it in time,' he said, grinning broadly.

'Give me their numbers,' said Clara, 'and I'll happily do it for you.'

It was good that it didn't feel weird to either of them to leave their pasts in the past.

They were driving through the small town, past the pilgrimage church. Elias turned onto a side street and parked up. There were only a handful of tourists to be seen. A small group with a total age of about six hundred were cycling cheerfully up the steep hillside on e-bikes. Mid-morning on a Wednesday, almost early morning still. The quiet around them like a very lightweight cloth. The church bell. Now and then, a car or a tractor on the road.

'What do you like about it here?'

He didn't answer and they climbed the gently winding road in silence. As if the hush of the place was very slowly rubbing off on them.

There were a few half-timbered houses dotted around the little market place below them, but most of the buildings had simple, painted façades that bore witness to their history as farmhouses. Neither splendid nor as cute as the little doll's-house towns like Dinkelsbühl or Rothenburg ob der Tauber. Clara thought about her own cottage.

They were only a few hundred metres from the top, on a narrow path past the church. There were iron railings on either side.

'It's not that dangerous,' mocked Clara, pointing at the rather gentle slopes beyond the railings. 'All very picturesque and within reasonable bounds. It's not much of a mountain, either.'

'Doesn't need to be,' answered Elias. 'What enemy would bother climbing up here, just to conquer a few fields?'

They'd reached a small, circular look-out point. There was the cross and a bench beneath it, and no room for much else. It was almost like standing on the prow of a ship.

Elias made a sweeping gesture with his arm, to take in the entire landscape beneath them. You could see for miles from up here. Some of the fields gleamed brown, freshly harrowed in the morning sun. Others were already a fresh green. In the forest on the other side of the valley, you could see the crowns of the deciduous trees, not yet in full leaf, like pale, delicate dots amid the dark pines. Behind them, the tall cross was like a mast.

'I like the simple beauty here. And the beautiful simplicity.'

She leant against the iron fence. He stepped behind her and took her in his arms. Did he know how much she already loved that gesture? He'd done it from the start, with the kind of intimacy that you normally only have once you're so certain of the other person that you don't need to keep looking into their face. As if it had always been that way.

They looked out together at the small town beneath them. The wide roof and twin towers of the basilica. The valley. The hills over there. He was right. Nothing special. Just a quiet place on a spring morning. That was all, and it was everything.

'I've never brought anyone else here before,' said Elias. 'I always wanted to have this to myself. You know how it is. Some places belong just to you. Places where you were once happy. It's mostly...' He hesitated a moment because he didn't know if she'd understand. 'The times when you're truly happy ... you're almost always on your own. When the world is in balance for a moment or two and there's no before and no after.'

'And this is that kind of place for you, where you were happy?'

She got what he meant. The moment on a sunny October day when you stood stunned and alone in a golden rain of falling linden leaves. When, at the end of a night that you'd finally slept through, you woke up from a bright dream, got up early and stepped out naked, onto the balcony on a clear January day. Moments of happiness like that.

'This,' Elias said quietly into the nape of her neck, 'is a place like that, where I have been happy and where I am happy now. And that's why I have to share it with you. That makes the difference, doesn't it? That I suddenly want to share something with you, something that used to be locked up inside me like a ... well, like a treasure,' he concluded lightly.

Clara looked into the sky. Not a perfect blue. Thin wisps here and there. As though yesterday, someone had turned a blind eye and not swept the sky clear ready for today. A sky like a friendly, messy flat, where you were welcome to turn up unannounced.

'I've got out of the habit,' she said. 'Of sharing like that. Or maybe I never really learnt how.'

It was only as she said it that she realised. It really had been like that. She had never shared those moments of true happiness.

A light wind gusted up and stirred the branches beside them. The banners of smoke from the chimneys below were suddenly all aslant.

'Here you are,' said Elias with a slight bow, as if he had arranged it.

'Thank you very much,' she said. Added a 'darling' without thinking.

Thank you very much, darling. For this place and for you. But she couldn't yet say that aloud.

'Hell and damnation!' he shouted out of the blue. 'We have to go!'

She couldn't help laughing.

'No need for overblown romantics, young man.'

He kissed her stormily.

'Yes, there is!' he said firmly. 'Come on.'

'I've never been to Bayreuth before,' said Clara as they stood outside the school. 'This looks like something out of an old film.'

The nineteenth-century sandstone façade, the imposing front steps, the entrance composed of three narrow doors with high arches, the broad windows – all of it exhaled a sedately bourgeois, cosy refinement. A beautiful building. She remembered her own school – also a grammar, but hers had been a hideous 70s concrete monstrosity, with brown needlefelt everywhere. It must be very different to learn in attractive, high-ceilinged classrooms, where generations of pupils had sat before you. If you looked out of the windows here, it would be into the tops of the old trees surrounding the school.

'How did your daughter end up here?'

He could hear in her voice that she was nervous. So was he. He wanted Jule to like her. That was it; it did matter. Nobody could live their life in splendid isolation.

'When Mona retired from acting, she happened to be here. And she stayed. She went back to university and retrained as a teacher. Maths. The woman is an enigma.'

He laughed as he saw Clara's expression. It was probably reflecting her surprise that she'd felt a tiny flicker of jealousy. Jealousy that he'd loved Mona. And her surprise that she had that jealousy within her. Because it was saying: you ought to love me like that too.

'No, she isn't really. But acting and maths don't go together that often. How is it with photography?'

Clara reached for the camera.

'Physics. It's only physics we need to be good at. But I liked physics first, actually. And still do. It's hard to remain an atheist if you dig into it.'

Elias thought he needed to correct her mistake.

'You mean it's hard to believe in God if you dig into physics and—'

Clara interrupted him. 'If I meant that, I'd have said it.'

She dug him in the side. He pretended to collapse to the street.

'Was I a ticket inspector in a previous life? Why is God punishing me with scientifically minded women?'

Clara pulled him up. If he was trying to ease her nerves, it was working pretty successfully.

'He isn't punishing you with them. We're a blessing. Did you know that there are such things as entangled photons?'

The late morning, the cool, blue-veiled sky above them, the town-centre trees – it was like being on holiday. They were walking the length of the school building.

Elias took her hand. 'Only for a moment,' he said, 'then you can walk free again. What are entangled photons?'

'They're actually a single entity. But if you split them, even if they fly apart at a speed of over three hundred thousand kilometres a second, they remain tethered to each other in the most wonderful way. If one has vertical polarisation, then the other will immediately be polarised horizontally. They stay entangled forever. Even light years apart. And nobody knows why.'

That was a nice thought. Do you want to tell me what I think it's meant to mean? He squeezed her hand before letting it go.

They heard the school bell. End of lesson. How strange that she immediately remembered the feeling. The sound of thirty chairs being scraped back at once. The laughter and surging conversations. The smell of school bags, the taste of wood and graphite when you chewed a pencil. How closely interlinked exhilaration and despair, sorrow and rage had been in those days, and for what tiny reasons. A bad mark. A meaningless argument because the girl next to you hadn't let you copy her work. Or then again, a look from Kurt – pretty Kurt – that had lingered a second longer than necessary. Happiness for the whole day. Had life been better then? When she'd thought she knew everything, yet had been so innocent?

'Would you like to be back at school?'

The doors flew open. The first groups emerged. Younger kids running, bags flying behind them. Older ones deep in their phones, or with studied nonchalance, unlit cigarettes in the corners of their mouths.

They stood at the foot of the steps and waited.

'I don't think so. It wasn't that great. There were one or two OK years. But things didn't actually get good until later. I don't think I was actually a teenager until my twenties. With all the associated shenanigans. There's Jule.'

He pointed to the entrance, and Clara recognised her at once, even though she looked totally different from at the theatre. A tiny jolt of shock in her belly.

'Job interview,' she said with quiet irony.

'You've got this!' Elias answered brightly, then added in a perfectly ordinary voice: 'Do you think this isn't making me nervous too? I want you two to like each other.'

Jule had seen them, pulled away from the group of schoolfriends and came towards them.

'Hey, Papa!'

It sounded cheerful. She gave him a hug and a kiss on the cheek. Hmm, thought Clara, I've never greeted my father like that. Jule stretched out her hand.

'We met once at the theatre, didn't we? You're Clara.'

Clara nodded. 'Yes. Hello, Jule...' She hesitated a moment, but then she said: 'I'm a bit anxious about meeting you.'

Jule put her bag down, glanced over to Elias, then back to Clara.

'Me too,' she said. 'Papa's never introduced me to one of his...' she corrected herself hastily, 'a woman before. That's something special.'

She's cautious, Clara thought. Holding back. I would be too. But at the same time, she was smiling inwardly. One of his many girlfriends, she'd been about to say. That little, unthinking criticism of her father's life. How old-fashioned people still were, deep down, despite all the openness of youth. All at once, she felt very close to Jule.

'Yes. It must be.'

'Hello?' Elias exclaimed in mock outrage. 'I can hear you, you know that? Would you two stop talking about me?'

Jule took his arm. 'Deal with it, old man,' she said. 'How long do you guys have? Let's get a coffee.'

The sun slanted down on the school. It was a spring day as it should be. A day when you could feel new, even if you'd been around for almost fifty years. A day-trip day.

'It'll probably bore you to tears, kiddo,' he said, 'but Clara has never seen the Hermitage. Fancy a visit?'

Jule picked up her bag. Colourful and knitted, with pompoms on the bottom corners. What goes around comes around, Clara thought with amusement. When she'd been eight, she'd had a bag like that for her flute lessons. She'd hated it. Today, it would probably cost you a fortune on eBay.

'It's like the cathedral to you,' Jule told Elias. 'When did you last go into the cathedral? We went to the Hermitage once in primary school. I'd like to go again. It's just I'm meeting…' She paused, flushing a little. 'I'm meeting at six.'

'Meeting someone,' Elias teased her. 'Why am I sending you to a grammar school if you're not learning any grammar? I'm meeting someone. Meeting needs an object.'

Jule turned to Clara with a grin.

'Does he do that to you too? Correcting you and all that?'

Clara smiled. 'He doesn't dare yet.'

'This is going to be a very sad afternoon,' Elias said glumly. 'The women in league against me. Can we go?'

'I don't remember the park at all,' said Jule as they walked past the geometric topiary hedges and the perfect oval pond in the middle. 'I don't like everything being this straight. This pressed into a mould.'

He felt the same. Elias was walking between Clara and Jule. He looked over to Clara and then back to Jule. They were both a little tense, but it seemed they were going to get on. And it was a nice feeling that his daughter sometimes thought along similar lines to him.

'But you wear a bra,' he remarked mischievously, all the same, 'so you have no right to complain about anything being moulded into shape.'

'Papa!'

Jule's outrage wasn't real. Or not entirely, because she was laughing.

Never, thought Clara. Never would Papa have spoken to me like that. Sometimes, it would have been better. This lightness – I often missed that when I was young.

'Does he always talk to you like that?' she asked Jule.

'He used to embarrass me hideously,' Jule answered. 'Because he's always so loud. These days, I sometimes think he's cool. Sometimes.'

Clara had to smile again.

I feel like I hadn't laughed for years, it occurred to Clara. But that's not true. It's just – I'm noticing how often I smile now. That he can make me laugh. Without meaning to. He makes me smile, just by being there. By being who he is.

Elias pointed to the bare pollard willows.

'You can see we're a good bit higher up here. There aren't many leaves on the trees here. And the oaks are bare.'

Jule shrugged. 'Everything is always four weeks behind here. The trees. Spring. My dad's visits.'

Clara looked hastily from father to daughter.

'You can tell you're father and daughter, just by how you speak to each other. I only have that with Jan. My brother,' she explained to Jule. 'Most people don't take such a direct approach.'

Jule sighed dramatically. At that moment, she really was very like Elias.

'I went to the school of hard knocks.'

Elias dragged her over to the fountain and tried to push her in. Jule fended him off, laughing, then ran away. He chased after her. Clara watched as they vanished behind the tall hedges, then popped out again; like a pair of kids. And although she felt very clearly that she shouldn't be there for these five minutes of play between father and daughter, she sensed their light-heartedness. Because it was a joy to watch them.

Elias was still out of breath when Clara stepped back onto the path about a hundred metres further along.

'A bit out of shape, old man,' Jule teased affectionately.

They were standing by the Temple of the Sun. The trees might only be starting to green here, but the air was warm and the sun was strong. Elias leant against one of the mosaic pillars and watched Clara walk towards him.

'She has a nice walk, doesn't she?'

He looked at Jule.

Jule nodded. 'I think I like her.'

'That's good,' said Elias after a short pause, 'I like her too, you know.'

'For real?'

Jule wasn't looking at him. She was running her fingers over the uneven surface of the colourful mosaic tiles.

'Yes,' said Elias. 'Really for real. Like I like you, I think.'

He saw Clara raise her camera to take a picture of him and Jule. Jule came to stand even closer to him. Laid her head on his shoulder for a second.

'And she likes you?'

Clara was too far away to hear what they were saying, but it looked very intimate. She knelt down to steady her hand. She wanted to capture this moment. The pair of them under the gleaming golden finials to the pillars of the little octagonal palace. The almost impressionistic fuzzy colourfulness of the mosaic façade as she saw it through the long lens. The gentle blue of the pieces of glass. The tiny movements made by Jule and Elias as they talked. Did she look like that too sometimes, with him? Could you tell by looking, how close they were? She had enough pictures. She stood up and joined them as Elias said, 'I hope so.'

'What do you hope?' she asked him. She would have liked to kiss him, but after that moment between father and daughter, that would have looked like jealousy. And it wasn't. She didn't have to show that Elias belonged to her. That was the special thing they had – they didn't belong to each other just because they were in love.

'That we can finally have that coffee,' said Elias lightly. 'The two of us have been standing around here for hours, waiting for you. The kid needs feeding and changing. Where've you been all this time?'

'Did you really change my nappies, Papa?' Jule seemed genuinely surprised.

Elias acted hurt. 'You can't imagine how often. Back then, I still believed fathers ought to do stuff, to strengthen their bond with the child. Doesn't seem to have worked.'

Clara shoved him between the pillars. 'I think you could strengthen the bond between us by getting us something to drink.'

As they stepped into the sun, Clara stopped a moment. The greenish water in the large, round central fountain glittered as a light breeze ruffled the surface. Scattered along the colonnade and around the terrace in front of it were café tables, mostly empty at this time of day. Glowing in the flower beds on the lawn, which sloped slightly downwards to the middle, were heartsease, tulips, daffodils – spring colours. The promise of summer. The wind tugged at the unopened parasols. They looked as though they had long, pale skirts playing around their legs. The clouds seemed sketched on the sky with a casual hand. None of it was anything special. Nothing unusual. But that was the whole point. That with him, a simple spring day, a little trip out could be so perfect that, for a moment, she forgot to breathe.

I love you, she thought. I love you, you loud, silly, tender, amazing man.

Later, the three of them were strolling through the gardens. Elias had persuaded the café staff to sell him three mini bottles of prosecco without charging the bar rate.

After all, we're not making any glasses dirty, he'd said. And we'll clear up after ourselves too. He'd smiled so charmingly that the burly, unfriendly woman had conceded. Perhaps that was why. She probably didn't get that many smiles.

It was properly warm now. Clara took photos of Jule in an airy wooden, green-and-white painted gazebo as she twirled obliviously to a music that only she could hear. Elias couldn't help himself; he stepped behind Clara and kissed the back of her neck.

'Don't,' said Clara, 'I'll blur everything.'

'If you were a real photographer,' Elias declared, 'you could take photos and let someone kiss you at the same time. But you're probably only some delinquent strumpet that I've fallen for like an idiot.'

'What's a strumpet?' asked Jule, coming up breathlessly.

'A lady of easy virtue,' said Clara. 'So, see what your father's let himself in for. Can we drink the fizz now, please?'

They found a bench, not far from the old palace, from which you could see for miles. Somewhere, there was a little gilt wooden roof, glinting between the trees in the slanting sunlight. After a clink of glass on glass, they drank their prosecco straight from the bottles.

'Nice to meet you,' said Jule. 'I was a bit scared of it.'

'It didn't show,' said Clara. 'And I was too.'

'You? Why?'

Clara took a little sip because she didn't immediately know how to explain.

'I've got unused to being introduced to people. It's like an exam that you can't really revise for.'

It really is, she thought, like a first little test of your relationship. I'm showing you to my daughter. Because I'm serious about you. And how serious are you?

'Because it's apparently important to your father that you don't find me utterly impossible.'

'And maybe also because I want you not to find my daughter utterly impossible. I've only got the one. I can't offer you any alternatives.'

Jule looked at Clara. 'I find you possible,' she said. Then she glanced at her phone.

'Do you have to go? Who's your date?'

Elias couldn't help it; he had to ask. Everyone always said so, and it was true. It was a weird feeling the first time your daughter brought someone home. But that's probably how she felt about Clara and me, he thought.

Jule stared past the intricate sandstone figures in the fountain, across the valley.

'It ... I'm meeting a girl. From class twelve,' she said, almost defiant.

'Then I'm afraid I'll have to cast you out,' said Elias casually.

'Papa! That's ... I don't even know...' She turned away.

Elias stood up and rested a hand between her shoulder blades. It was a nice gesture.

'Are you in love?' he asked, his tone serious.

Jule shrugged. She still wouldn't look at him.

'Don't know. I don't even know ... well, what that feels like. But I think she's great.'

Clara was very quiet. This was entirely a matter for the two of them.

'If she's pretty, you're welcome to fall in love,' said Elias. 'But if she makes you unhappy, I'm afraid I'll have to shoot her. I think I'll come along this first time.'

Jule had to laugh.

'You're such an idiot!' she said.

'He is. I can confirm that,' said Clara drily. 'Shall we go?'

'Let's finish our drinks first. I'm not having my daughter standing around nervously, waiting for her first date. We shall be late. Let *her* wait.'

How proud he is of Jule...

Clara wasn't sure how she'd have reacted. If she'd have been able to say the right thing. At that moment, she was glad not to have children, while at the same time, she got an inkling of that huge feeling of being so closely linked to someone, to have known them since birth, to have longed for them to be born.

She must have made a funny face, because Jule asked straight out: 'What?'

'I think that was the briefest coming out I've ever heard of. You're a strange family.'

'I don't really know about that,' Jule answered curtly, '... I don't know yet. I just like her.'

'I didn't mean...' Clara began, but then she saw that Jule was suddenly close to tears.

Without thinking, she reached for her hand.

'It really doesn't matter,' she said quietly. 'Really. If she's the one, nothing else matters at all. Nothing else has anything to do with it. I didn't mean to ... You know what? You're doing this well, Jule. I don't think I could have managed it at your age.'

Jule didn't answer, but Clara got the impression that she was relaxing slightly as they walked back to the car.

Once they'd dropped Jule off and were out of the town, the evening light was almost summery. Elias was humming to himself at the wheel, the images of the day whirling through his head. Clara was sitting beside him very quiet, deep in thought.

'Did you know?' she asked after a long while.

Elias didn't answer at first. He needed to think it over.

'I think I had an idea, but I hadn't really thought about it. So, it *did* come as a surprise just now. But like you said, it's not important. Mona might not like it. She comes from a very small village. You might never really shake that off.'

'Conservative? An actress?'

Elias looked over to her and grinned. 'But now she's a maths teacher. So she's within her rights to be conservative, don't you think? But in the end, she won't kick her out or anything. She loves her.'

Yes, Clara thought, it's not that hard.

The veil of cloud at the horizon had thickened slightly. The sky was starting to burn.

'You're a good father,' Clara said tenderly.

'Too late,' said Elias. 'I should have been that a long time ago. And been able to have all this.' He moved his hand as if to catch the whole day. 'Too late.'

'Late perhaps,' answered Clara, 'but not too late. Like us.'

Elias put music on, took his right hand from the wheel and rested it by hers, so that their little fingers touched. As always.

'If I hadn't already fallen head over heels in love with you,' he said warmly, 'then it would definitely have happened today.'

28

Elias was woken by the lovely sound of her rapid breathing. He drifted up very slowly from sleep to wakefulness; a few scraps of a perfectly peaceful dream were still at hand. He spent a few moments on the edge of daytime consciousness, tracing back the images, then opened his eyes. The breeze coming in from the window was so strong and so cool that he pulled the covers over his shoulders. A storm had come up overnight. The sky was almost entirely blue, but you could hear from outside the singing of the gusts in the TV aerials and the wild roar of the treetops.

'Do you do that every morning?'

He'd sat up and was watching Clara do push-ups.

'Not that it's any of your business,' she answered in curt, breathless gasps between movements, 'but at my age, you have to do something.'

Elias rolled onto his front and watched her over the edge of the bed.

'You look so incredibly sexy. I don't think I could manage that many.'

'Don't distract me,' she panted, couldn't help laughing, and lost all muscle tension. 'Go and make tea.'

'Not for the world would I miss a beautiful, scantily clad woman working out on her mirrorlike parquet floor.'

He propped his chin in his hands. Clara looked up at him, her eyebrows raised derisively.

'Mirrorlike parquet floor ... every morning I'm down here, I see that I ought to hoover again. What about that tea? In return, I'd be willing to senselessly fritter away my dole money and go out for bread rolls.'

Elias stood up. 'Not without me. Shall we go like this, or are you getting dressed?'

He kissed her on each bare shoulder. Then he walked into the bathroom. Clara watched him. How naturally he moved around her flat, even though it was the first time he'd been here. And it was nice to have him here. There'd been a tiny hesitation inside her yesterday, when they'd got back late in the evening. She had let none of the men she'd met since Paul's death into the flat. She'd always gone somewhere else with them. She'd never wanted to open the door to herself to anyone.

She went into the bathroom. Elias was in the shower.

'Come in,' he called. Laughed.

But she only pulled the glass door open a crack, reached for him and gave him a tempestuous kiss on the lips.

As he dried off, he opened the window. The storm burst in, strong and cold. The satellite dishes were swaying on the roofs all around. A young falcon hovered high against the blue above the tower, barely having to move its wings as the wind carried it higher and higher. He felt a wild happiness. It hit him like one of the gusts of wind sweeping in through the window. You couldn't call it anything else. Wild happiness. He wished he could spread out his arms and soar like the falcon. That was how it took him. The image of her, breathless, doing push-ups on the parquet. The kiss in the shower. Her ever-surprising laugh.

Clara, he said to himself quietly. Only to himself, because it sounded so amazing. Clara.

They were walking through the windswept morning. There were branches and twigs all over the roads and pavements.

'I like storms,' said Clara. 'They always seem to finally set everything in motion.'

'"There swirls the storm, a rearranger"', Elias quoted, '"swirls through the woods and throughout time. And everything is as if ageless."'

'I'm not,' put in Clara.

'Shut up,' said Elias, digging her in the ribs, 'I haven't got to the best bit yet. "The landscape, as the Psalmist's image, is depth and weight and all sublime."'

'If you elbow me in the side again, you hopeless romantic, I'll knock you out with one well-aimed blow.'

She'd grabbed him by the lapels and was very close to him. He couldn't see her smile, but he could hear it in her voice. Actually, it's like way back when, he thought. Like being sixteen. You need to keep touching. And if you're not kissing, you're bopping each other, play-fighting, shoving.

'Do you have a show this evening?'

She kicked a branch off the path. She'd have to sweep the street at her parents'. But not yet. She didn't give the thought space.

Elias nodded. 'Yes. I'm glad you didn't ask me how I can remember all the poems. All actors hate that – how do you learn so many lines? And: what do you do all day long? As if that's what makes up our profession.'

Clara unlocked the door to her building, then her letterbox, took out the post and the newspaper.

'That was such a long sentence for you. How did you get it down without mistakes...'

He wanted to nudge her again, but wasn't quick enough. She was already fleeing up the stairs. We're like children today. No school because of the storm. No one checking up on us. Today, we can do what we like.

He came up behind her, noticing as he did so that he really was a bit out of shape.

They'd left the window open. The whole flat was chilly and smelled as fresh as only a stormy day can manage. Clara put the coffee machine on. Elias started boiling water. It was only ever in the morning light that you first saw a flat properly. In the evenings, everything was soft and imprecise. It was only in the morning that you could see how someone really lived. If there were darkened jars for storing the tea, for example, as there were here, or just a pile of boxes in the cupboard that had long ago leached out all the scent. If it was a flat you could only visit in the evenings, or one where you'd want to have breakfast with someone in the clear morning light.

'I like the way you live,' he said. 'I like your house too, but here ... you get a sense of you there too, but here, I can see what you're like.'

It was true. He only became aware of it as he said it. Her clarity was reflected in her flat. There was very little fussiness. The many nudes – large, black-and-white photos on the walls – gave the rooms an air of cool eroticism, but there was something halfway public about them too. As if nothing could hide here. He watched as she laid the table with quick, measured movements. Honey. Butter. No jam. A little cheese. Fruit.

'And,' she asked, 'what am I like?'

We want, no we *have,* to see ourselves through the other person's eyes. We have to know what they think about us. That's something that, ideally, never stops. Because then we keep seeing other people anew and don't stop with an image that eventually goes flat and loses all the colour of love.

She was waiting, leaning against the kitchen counter. The tea was steaming in a jug. In the morning light, her silhouette, her arms propped behind her, her legs long and toned, crossed at the ankles, looked like a hasty yet skilfully dashed-off sketch. He wished he could photograph her like that.

'You're the one,' he answered simply.

She poured the tea into a pot, took hold of it and sat down

opposite him. They'd had breakfast together on several days, but even so, today felt special. She sipped the tea and reached for a roll.

'Mascha Kaléko always ended her letters to her husband with *L.d.m.e?*' she said.

'What does that mean?'

He'd pulled one bare foot up onto the chair. A nice picture, she thought. He feels comfortable in my home.

'*Liebst du mich eigentlich?* "Do you actually love me?" That's what it means. No sign-off, no kisses at the bottom of the letter, just always that one question.'

Clara drizzled a thin line of honey onto one half of her roll.

'I always wonder if that's her seeking confirmation? Is she uncertain of his love? Or is it something else?'

Elias couldn't help himself. He stood up, walked around the table and kissed her.

'You only ask that if you already know the answer. It suggests a very deep trust in the love between the two of them. It's something special if you can write that.'

Through the open window, they could hear the laughter of a green woodpecker through the chirping of the sparrows; to her, that was the sound of spring.

They fell silent. It was a light, listening quiet, full of the soft little sounds of a peaceful morning. Elias had pulled out one of her photo books. Was drinking tea, fully immersed in it. She was opening her letters. There was one from the Job Centre. Not nice – she weighed it in her hand. She didn't want to let it spoil the morning, but then she ripped it open. If he and I ... if we're real, then a morning like this has to be able to deal with these things.

Dear Ms Wagenbach ... within the remit of the Federal Initiative for Labour Mobility ... we are pleased to be able to offer ... unusual opportunity...

She had to read it again before she could take it in. Elias saw her expression change.

'What?' he asked.

'I'm invited to apply for a post as head of department, photo editor, in Hamburg.' She read the letter through a third time. 'Apparently there's a nationwide network of employment agencies.'

She didn't know quite what she was feeling.

'Magazine or online or newspaper?'

'It only gives the publisher here. Bogen and Peters. That's big. Apparently, they want to establish a new magazine, and need someone to head up the photography department.'

Elias put the book aside.

'But that's amazing, Clara. That's a great opportunity!'

He was really thrilled. She had to laugh, despite herself.

'Elias! But you know ... God, how do I put this? If I apply, and they take me, then I'll have to move to Hamburg.'

Elias had stepped behind her chair. Hugged her. Nobody had ever done that for her before. Nobody would ever do it again. This gesture belonged solely to them.

'Hamburg's great. I love Hamburg.'

'Yes,' she said, harshly. She had to be harsh. 'And are you going to move there with me?'

Suddenly, the mood was very different. Elias could feel it, but couldn't have said why.

'I think you should start by applying,' he said. 'I was in a play in Hamburg once. It really is a great city.'

'Yes,' said Clara, and asked again: 'And are you going to move there with me?'

Elias let her go. Walked around the table and sat down. Drank a swig of lukewarm tea.

'I'm still employed here,' he said slowly. 'My contract has another two years to run. And Hamburg is a lot further away from Jule. I'll have to think about it. But...'

He saw her starting to close down, but he couldn't answer her question so quickly. He needed time to consider it.

'Do we have to talk about it now?' he asked, rather helplessly. 'You don't even know ... you don't have the job yet, and you don't know when it would start either, do you? If you get it, that is.'

Clara handed him the letter.

'September. October at the latest,' she snapped. 'And yes, we should talk about it now. You know what,' she said frankly, 'I don't know if I'll ever get another chance like this. This offer is really unusual. If I got the job, it would be like winning the lottery. I mean, I'm out of work. I'm not in a great job, applying for an even better one. I'd have been happy if it had just been another—'

Elias interrupted her. 'Would you move with me if I got a job in Berlin? Or Leipzig?'

She felt stung. 'But that's not the question. The question is—'

Elias interrupted again. Raised his voice, without meaning to: 'Is the question how much we love each other? Or if we love each other? If it is, then for my part, yes. I'm sure of it. Yes. But I can't leave here right now. But that doesn't mean that will still be the case in two years. And it's all ... I mean, all you've got is a piece of paper, that's all. So why do we have to talk about it now?'

Because if we don't, we're only putting it off, she thought. Because it'll be coming between us the whole time. Because I need to know where I stand with you. That's why. But she couldn't say it – as had so often been the case.

'No, we don't have to,' she said. It sounded much sulkier than intended, but then, it wasn't what she wanted to say.

'I really want to be with you,' said Elias. 'But will you please give me a little time so that I can think about it?'

'Do you need time?' she asked crossly.

'Clara!' cried Elias. A cry like an urgent plea. 'Of course I do. We aren't the only two people in the world. There are others apart from us. You have your mother. I have Jule. I...'

He didn't know how he could explain to her that it wasn't about whether he loved her. But about there being other people around you that you loved too, who you couldn't just abandon.

'We can't be like Bonnie and Clyde,' he said, trying for a lighter tone. 'Nobody can.'

'No,' answered Clara after a short silence, 'probably not.'

She didn't want to be distant, and she couldn't say exactly what had hit her so hard. He had the right to think about it. He also had the choice of how much he loved her, if he did at all. Completely or not at all – as if that was really a thing. He was right about all of it. But even so – it was like jumping into water on a sunny day and it suddenly being much colder than expected.

She looked across the table to him. He looked back frankly. Frank and sad.

'Yesterday was such a nice day,' she said spontaneously.

Like an outstretched hand. Elias took it even though he didn't know exactly what it was meant to mean. Yesterday, yes; today, no?

'Yes,' he answered all the same, 'it was. A really nice day.'

29

Can we talk?

He didn't see Vera's message until he walked off stage and into the dressing room at midday. Mareike didn't like it at all if you brought your phone to a rehearsal. And it was bad manners, even if the play they were currently rehearsing wasn't that gripping. Mareike just wasn't as good at comedy as she was at high drama. Or it might be because he wasn't at peace with himself. Everything felt a little unreal at the moment. Like the way you felt after a sleepless night – a little too light. Since that conversation, they hadn't seen each other in five days. It wasn't such a long time and they'd both been busy. Clara with her parents, him learning his part for the new play and performing every evening. If that morning had been different, it wouldn't have meant a thing, except that they'd have been looking forward to seeing each other. But it hadn't been different. And her messages ... if he couldn't hear her voice in what she wrote, it made his own texts sound wooden. It was as though he couldn't reach her with what really mattered. And he missed her. Every day. So he'd felt a start of joy when he saw that he had a message. Only then had he spotted that it was from Vera.

Can we talk?

He would have liked to go down to the courtyard, but Mareike was out there, smoking with Fabian and Johanna. There were five of them in the play this time. He wasn't in the mood for those little chats, halfway between work and personal stuff.

Can we talk?

The message was almost four hours old now. For a moment, he was annoyed. She knew very well that rehearsals always began at ten. But she probably hadn't found it easy to text, and had therefore not been paying attention to the time. But that still created trouble for him because it looked like he was ignoring her message, and he didn't want to give that impression.

But what did they have to talk about? What could she want? Can't we try again? We've broken up so often in the past. Don't you want ... can't you ... don't you think...?

A sudden, deep weariness overcame him. If only he could lie down somewhere for quarter of an hour. He thought of Clara.

Hamburg. Oh, Clara. I can't tell you right away. I'm probably not the kind of person who totally loses himself in love. And you're even less so.

His thoughts were all over the place. He looked back at Vera's message. Despite everything, a conversation was only fair.

They'd agreed to meet in the café on Lutherplatz. Of course, he thought, as he chained his bike to a lamppost, she always did like to create a story for us where there wasn't one. He'd asked her briefly *Where*, and she'd texted *In our café* in reply. It was no such thing. It was just a café where they'd often met. He thought about the park in Tübingen at night. About the hotel room. Was it only him who saw those as shared places? Perhaps things between him and Clara were no different, except that this time, he was on the other end. The one who was loved less. The thought took an icy hold of his insides. That would probably be only fair, he thought bitterly.

She was sitting on the bench in the large window, which today was open wide in the sunshine. And she'd dressed up. As if for a date. He stepped up to the outside of the window.

'You look pretty.'

He said it lightly, to ease the tension. And because he knew that she liked it when he noticed that kind of thing.

'Hello,' she replied without a smile. 'And you look tired.'

He simply climbed through the window to the bench inside.

'I am,' he admitted. 'It's a tiring time.'

'With your new girlfriend or at the theatre?'

It hadn't taken her long to show how hurt she was.

'Can I sit down and order something first?'

He was trying to keep the tone light, not to answer too quickly, even though she'd hit him unexpectedly hard. It was true. Things were difficult between him and Clara at the moment.

Vera waved her hand. He sat down. The tables on the square outside the café were all full. People were sitting in the sun, drinking coffee and Aperol and beer, and chatting. The newly retiled roof on the church glowed deep red. It was a gorgeous day. For everyone else. He wished he could be part of it, but it was as though he could only see the other side through a thick pane of glass.

'Vera,' he began, even before anyone came to take his order, 'I'm sorry. It must have been very sudden for you. That it was over.'

'You'd been funny for a long time before that,' she said. 'This is all nice and easy for you, isn't it? A brief conversation and the thing is over, and you can concentrate on a new woman. Did you ever think about me in the last few weeks – ever at all?'

'Yes,' Elias said shortly. 'A lot, in fact. I was trying to understand where I went wrong. Why we carried on with a relationship that wasn't right.'

'Wasn't it?'

Sharp. Furious. He'd rarely seen her like this. She mostly kept this side hidden. She'd only been this direct on the very rare occasions that she'd had a bit too much to drink.

'For me it was, Elias. For me, it was a relationship that *was* right. Not some non-committal thing. And it would really, really have been ever so nice of you if you'd told me a little sooner that for you it was just about the fucking or whatever.'

She was loud. Elias leant back deliberately. Let people turn their heads.

'Vera,' he answered after a brief pause, 'do you remember? We said at the start that we wouldn't fall in love. That it would be just that – non-committal. And that—'

She interrupted him. 'Yes. But that was at the start. And then ... don't tell me that you weren't in love with me too. You just forgot about it because I started to bore you. Because then, suddenly, an exciting new woman popped up, who you maybe couldn't have so easily. You're always like that. You can't help it. But that's not a real emotion – you know that, don't you?'

'Are we rerunning the conversation from a couple of weeks ago?' Elias retorted heatedly, partly because she had, yet again, hit a secret uncertainty harder than he liked. Were his feelings unreal? He noticed that the waitress wanted to take their order but didn't dare approach the table because she could see that they were arguing. He gave an involuntary laugh and waved to her. Vera misunderstood.

'Is that funny?'

He took a deep breath, ordered and turned back to her. The sun – he couldn't help noticing the detail – was turning the colourful cups and their blue-black shadows into an Impressionist painting.

'No. It's not funny. Vera ... there were a lot of good days. But they never added up to a whole. They were only ever individual beads. Wasn't it like that for you?'

'No,' she said loudly. 'No. I was in a relationship. You apparently weren't. Wasted years...'

She drank hastily. He noticed that he was trembling slightly with the tension. Were they really wasted years?

'What is it you actually want?' he asked. Not reproachfully. He really wanted to know.

It was as though he'd disarmed her. Suddenly, she was having to fight the tears, and he was feeling guilty and, yes, ashamed. She was right. It would have been honest to have ended things a long time ago.

'What should I want?' she asked, her voice choked. 'I don't want it to end. I miss you. I hate myself for it, but I just miss you.'

The way it burst out of her made her words move him all the

more. He'd never wanted to hurt her. It was just that, at some point, all the carefreeness of the beginning had dwindled into superficiality that didn't permit depth. A shiny, pretty superficiality made up of a series of days that he'd been satisfied with because he'd never striven for depth.

'I'm sorry, Vera.'

He meant it.

'I don't want you to be sorry for me. I wanted you, but nobody can have more than half of you.'

Her voice had caught. She blew her nose – images of sorrow are always the same, he thought fleetingly. He could never stop making a note of that kind of thing for the stage. That was a part of him, that constant observation. His phone buzzed. He glanced at the screen – Clara. It would be! He'd so wanted to speak to her, but it wasn't possible right now. It would look like he was deliberately hurting Vera even more. He didn't know if she'd seen it, but she leant in towards him.

'You know it'll be exactly the same with this Clara, don't you? You're incapable of truly loving. You're way too caught up in yourself to ever truly love anyone else.'

She's hitting out, he thought, she's just hitting out because she's so sad. It's not true.

She was much calmer now, and looking straight at him.

'Actually, I'm sorry for you. Because you think you're in love and it's the love of your life, and in three months you'll have the first doubts, and in six you'll start to get bored. And then it won't matter who you're with: suddenly, they won't be the one, yet again.'

A million years of human history, and we're sitting here fighting about mating behaviour. He couldn't help it, the thought was suddenly there, and maybe that was only because she had – yet again – hit a sore point. Yes. It was true. That was pretty much how it had always gone.

'Not this time,' he replied, but wasn't sure of himself. He didn't know if he was just sitting at the top of a rush of emotion that would be over in three months. If he could trust himself.

'If that happens,' Vera said, paying no attention to his reply, 'I'm here. I love you, you know, even though you're like that. I still hate myself for being so weak and because it has to be you, but there it is.'

'That's not weakness,' said Elias, almost automatically. 'But all the same. I ... that won't happen.'

He stood up and gestured to the waitress that he wanted to pay.

'I have to go now, Vera.'

'Yes,' she said with sudden certainty. 'I thought as much. I'll wait. See you, Elias.'

He didn't turn back to her as he walked to his bike. He was shaken up – the conversation had knocked him further off balance than he'd been expecting, and he didn't want her to see that.

See you, Elias.

No. It was Clara. It had to be Clara.

He got onto his bike and cycled back to the theatre. Confused, unhappy and riddled with doubt. Perfect conditions for rehearsing a comedy.

30

We think you'd be a great fit.

After the interview, she'd walked. Along the landing bridges for a way, and then towards the Dammtor. She wanted to stroll through Planten un Blomen and her route to the botanical gardens took her past the elevated railway station towards the Bismarck memorial. She'd come here on a school trip once, with Johann too. Graffiti. Getting stoned. Being in love as if there was no tomorrow. She'd never felt that way since. Until Elias.

Walking was good. It helped get her thoughts in order. Or didn't. At the moment, the memory was only helping to bring her thoughts into disarray. To set everything within her in motion, stir things up, so that she could see what was happening to her. She'd never had a difficulty with precise thinking. Precise feeling was another matter. Perhaps it was good to dig that old love back up again. Just for purposes of comparison.

She stood on the circular base, looking up at Bismarck. They'd renovated him, but he was still leaning on his massive sword. She pulled a face. Back then, they'd sprayed *Happy Happy* on the bottom of the plinth. One each. Because that was how it had felt. And anytime she'd been in Hamburg in the last couple of decades, she'd had to come to see Bismarck. Not so much because of Johann as because of the feeling. She'd listened to 'Mercy' over and over. *You got me on my knees...* The graffiti had remained over all those years, but she'd thought a feeling like that would never come around again. Now the plinth had been cleaned, bright and untouched. Back to the beginning. She thought about Elias. This, yes, was one of the places she'd been happy and that she'd never wanted to share with anyone, not even Paul. She would bring Elias here. Could have brought him here. What tense, what timeframe, was she even in now? Before or with or after Elias?

She sat down on the bench. A breeze blew up from the Elbe and rustled the trees. The flecks of sun on the gravel eddied chaotically.

I'm not doing anything by halves anymore. Never again. If I ever love again, it will be completely and forever. No more compromises. Not with myself and not with the other person. And if that can't be done, then it can't be done.

She looked up at Bismarck, who seemed to be thrusting his sword down into the earth, and thought about herself thirty years ago. But then she erased the mental image of the young Clara and brought her current face to mind. Her face in the mirror this morning.

No, she thought almost furiously, no. Love doesn't only belong to the young. Love doesn't, and nor does unconditionality. Love doesn't and its unconditionality doesn't and nor does full, entire happiness.

She stood up and straightened her spine.

Love like that or no love at all.

We have another two interviews today, but we think you'd be a great fit.

A ship's horn sounded from the nearby port, incredibly deep. You couldn't hear much traffic noise up here. But the quiet wind was rustling the trees and there was the choppy shadow theatre of the leaves on the wooden bench, on the plinth, on the pale chippings covering the square, the flecks of sunlight playing nonchalantly over the steps – it all had such a peaceful beauty that a yearning for Elias welled up in Clara, its sudden impact almost taking her breath away. Shit! Where was he? She wanted him to be here, here beside her. To shout with him in delight at the beauty of the world. Just to shout out and to cheer and to give that delight a voice. That would be possible with him.

She breathed deeply in and out. Then she sat on one of the benches in the sun and looked back up at Bismarck. The statue was so monumental and warlike, and yet, to her, there'd always been something playful about it. Perhaps because back then, she'd told Johann the story of how Bismarck and his mistress, a Russian princess, had almost drowned in the sea and been rescued in the nick of time by a lifeguard. They'd concluded that he'd been given the monument for stupidity. For the stupidity that arises from endless infatuation, and for the things you do when you're in love. She hadn't thought she'd ever feel the same again. *Happy Happy.*

We think you'd be a great fit. We'll let you know tomorrow, or the day after at the latest. Aren't you happy?

She pulled out her phone and called Elias. It only rang twice, then he declined the call. She looked at the time. He couldn't still be in rehearsal. She would have loved to hear his voice.

Come here! she typed on the spur of the moment, but immediately deleted the message. He might take it the wrong way. It could also mean 'come to Hamburg with me'. And it did bloody well mean that. If she got the job, how was she meant to be without him?

She found a café in Planten un Blomen. She had almost an hour and a half before her train. The café was half empty. Too late for the parents meeting up for a morning coffee after kindergarten drop-off, and too early for the old ladies who didn't know what to do with themselves after lunch. A quiet time.

How could you not want to be outside on a day like this? The halyards were beating a bright, even rhythm against the flagpoles. It almost sounded like a sailing yacht. The water in the fountains and ponds was still fresh, not green and viscous and tired, like in late summer. The tall ferns, the exotic trees and of course the tens of thousands of flowers, colourfully arranged in the beds between the paths. Everywhere this cool, sunny midday was bright green. Some things never wore out. Spring days like this. The scent of fresh bread or coffee – always much richer than the actual taste. Drinking cold, clear water. Was there such thing as a love like this? That didn't wear out?

'I have no idea,' she said aloud.

'Sorry?' asked the surprised waiter who'd approached her table from behind. 'Should I come back later?'

Clara had to laugh. 'No, I didn't mean you, I meant my absent boyfriend.'

'Then have a drink while you wait for him. That helps us both out.'

He was very young. A student perhaps, but self-assured and rather cheeky. She liked that.

'In that case, I'd better have a glass of *sekt*.'

The waiter pointed to the fountains you could see from here. They looked as though they sprang from the base of the TV tower.

'That's why we had the lake put in,' he said with a smile. 'Everyone who sits here on the terrace with a view of the fountains orders *sekt*. I'll hurry.'

He really did hurry. His white apron flew out. Elias would have liked that, and would undoubtedly have flirted with him. The way he flirted with everyone he found amusing or interesting, with a little twinkle in his eye. She looked at her phone and pressed Jan's number; she let it ring, was about to hang up when he finally answered.

'It's not a great time,' he gasped. 'We're in the middle of ... Nurse!' she heard him shout. 'Clamp it! The abdominal artery ... shit, can't you see? The blood's on my glasses ... Nurse! We're losing him!'

'Since when have you been allowed your phone in theatre? And why am I surrounded by men who think they can act?'

She could practically hear Jan grinning.

'You have no idea of the hospital daily grind. I had to jump in to replace our star surgeon, who was in an accident. The fatality rate in emergency surgery is climbing at an alarming rate. Seriously though,' he added, 'I've got the day off today. I'm in a café with Mama.' He laughed. 'She's stolen three spoons so far.'

She often did that. Nobody knew why, but since the dementia, their mother stole cutlery from wherever she was. She'd always said that her grandmother's silver dinner service was the only thing they'd been able to save.

'Where are you?'

'Also in a café. In Hamburg. What's the weather like with you? The sun's out here – it's glorious. I just had my interview.'

'Did you have to sleep with them?' Jan asked in amusement. 'Mama says: did you win?'

The young waiter brought her drink with a hint of a bow, and then left without interrupting further.

'They've got a couple more candidates but it looks like I have a good chance.'

She was actually almost certain that she'd get the job. She'd been good. But something in her wouldn't allow her to say such things. It was almost a superstition. Unbidden. Touch wood. Don't tempt fate.

'Of course you have a good chance,' Jan exclaimed. He seemed to be in a really good mood. 'You look stunning, hopefully you wore a short skirt, you're funny and...'

'And I'm a very good photographer, you sexist pig. Don't you have a gender-equality officer at the hospital? I ought to speak to them.'

'Yes,' he retorted, 'that's Mama. Want to put in a complaint to her?'

'Not now,' she replied. 'Jan, if I get the job, should I take it? What do you think?'

'Are you crazy?' he asked in reply. 'Of course you should take it. What else did you go up there for? That's such a good ... You always sold yourself short at the paper. I always thought—'

'But what about Mama?' she cut him off. 'I mean, Hamburg is a really long way, and Toni isn't around either.'

She could hear his voice grow more serious.

'Sis,' he said, 'if you get it, take it. Are you going to wait for Mama to die? Or Papa? We'll just have to find a way.'

Jan could sometimes be incredibly direct, but that was exactly what she loved about him. His deep loyalty and his absolute consistency. That was why they got on so well.

'Yes,' she said. 'But then there's Elias. I don't know if I can. A long-distance relationship like that. Or if I want to.'

'I think the question is more whether you want Elias. If he wants you. Am I right?'

Yes, that possibly was the question. She was silent a moment, listening through the telephone to the sounds of the other café and her mother talking nonsense.

'When's the hearing?' she asked. Not least to change the subject.

'Tomorrow morning. Will you be back by then?'

'I'm coming home today. They weren't in that much of a hurry to keep me here.'

'See you tomorrow then, sis. I'll make sure I get Mama out of the café without us being arrested.'

He hung up. She shut her eyes and lifted her face to the sun for a moment. It was good to have Jan.

31

She'd often been in court, even though photography wasn't permitted during most proceedings, but never before in the family court. Very few divorces, adoptions and guardianships were interesting enough for the newspaper. Strangely, Mama was in an excellent mood as they met at the entrance. Papa and Jan were with her. The security guard at the checkpoint was very nice, patiently explaining to her father exactly what he had to put in the grey box before he could walk through the gate.

'There never used to be all this,' he informed the guard, making a painfully long-winded business of freeing himself from his excessively long belt. 'I often used to come here – barrister, you know.'

Jan and Clara glanced at each other. Jan rolled his eyes. Did your parents never stop embarrassing you? Clara was about to say something when the security man's face changed.

'Oh, it's you, Mr Wagenbach!' he exclaimed cheerfully. 'I didn't recognise you at first.'

It took less than thirty seconds for him and her father to be so deep in conversation that he'd practically forgotten that the rest of them were there. Jan simply shepherded Mama through on his own, and Clara followed.

'We'll go ahead, Papa,' she said to him. He nodded, as distracted as he'd always been on meeting anyone more interesting than his own family, and continued gossiping happily with the guard about judges past and the food in the canteen.

'I'll have coffee with snow,' Mama said. A surprisingly clear sentence, not so hard to translate.

'Whipped cream?' Jan asked.

She nodded. Clara took her hand.

'We'll go to the café later, Mama. When we've finished here. Probably won't take long.'

'Yes, yes,' she answered, but not grumpily. She just liked to be with her children, even if she didn't know which of them it was. Clara's stomach clenched. It was so easy to make her happy. What would happen if she actually moved away?

Their mother pointed to a picture of a Norwegian fjord on the waiting-room wall.

'Four, five big wet,' she said contentedly. 'Look.'

What went on in her brain, Clara wondered. Water was still water; it was just that the word for it had gone. But then the brain picked one from the next drawer along. You understood what she meant. Sometimes, anyway. Did she still realise? At first, four, five years ago, she'd been full of rage at the way she forgot so much. Once, she'd hit her head against the sideboard. Her energy had still been there, but the one, most important part of her body had just left her in the lurch.

Her father eventually stumbled out of the lift. He was having dizzy spells increasingly often, and he steadied himself against the wall. Was that how it was when you were old? She found herself – as always – thinking about Elias. What would he be like, what would she be like in later life? Was a thing like that even possible together? You could only enter into a partnership if you constantly lied to yourself. The wheel of thoughts started spinning in her head.

It won't be that bad. I'm sure I'll age differently. I keep myself fit. I've never seen Papa ride a bike in all my life. I'll simply kill myself before it gets that far.

How could you think, even for a second, that you could demand a thing like that of someone else without pining away for shame and self-loathing? She would never, never, never want Elias to see her the way she was seeing her mother or her father right now.

'Wagenbach family? Please come in.'

The judge was a surprisingly young woman, tall and on the skinny side.

It was all very impersonal and prosaic. It wasn't even a courtroom, just an office, and Jan had to fetch an extra chair from the waiting room so that they could all sit down.

The judge spoke politely to their mother, asked her name and her date of birth, but didn't make a fuss when she answered incorrectly.

'Mrs Wagenbach,' she said then, with calm focus, 'I am appointing your husband and your son Jan to be your guardians. That means that they can, together or individually, decide on where you live, open your letters and do your banking. Do you understand what that means?'

'Yes, yes,' Mama said impatiently. 'Of course. I'm not old.'

Clara looked down because she wanted to laugh. Sometimes Mama was her former self.

The judge handed Jan and Papa each a sheet of paper that looked like the old, green driving licences, only twice the size.

'Your certificates of guardianship,' she explained. 'We will meet again in two years, when we will check whether the guardianship continues to be necessary.'

Because of course Mama will be fully healthy again by then.

The judge got Jan and Papa to sign various other things and explained their duties to them. Clara was no longer listening. She was watching her mother as she arranged the pens on the judge's desk in parallel lines and squared the files off at right angles to the edge. She'd always liked to do that, even when Clara had been little. The cutlery had to be straight on the table. Was that how it started? Or was that just a reflex that persisted?

Oh, Mama, what the hell shall I do?

Her phone buzzed. A message from Elias.

How's it going? Has your mother roughed up the court?

He'd remembered the appointment.

She's peaceful, she texted back. *Quite unusual. See you later?*

Like a schoolgirl, she thought, slightly annoyed at herself. But his answer came only a few seconds after she'd sent it, which reconciled her with herself. Why did she have to keep making sure of him? She wanted to be sure. Perfectly sure. Not to have to ask him or herself questions.

Absolutely love to.

We're going to the café after the court, she typed hastily. *If you want, come and join us.*

Once they were all back out in the fresh air, Mama linked arms with her and Jan.

'Where to?' she asked cheerfully. Clara exchanged hasty glances with Jan. Mama's good mood was wonderful and bitter at the same time, because she no longer understood what had been decided on her behalf.

'Well now, Mama,' Clara said, 'seeing that Jan gets to decide where you live, we'd better go to his choice of café too.'

'Good potato,' said Mama.

They were sitting on the roof terrace of the café by the market, with its view across the town. Rooftops in the morning light. A perfect day, in fact. Blue. Bright blue, far and wide. Swallows in the sky. One by one, the church clocks struck half past ten. If you pulled the chairs into the sun, it was a pleasant place to sit. Clara couldn't remember the last time almost the whole family had been together in the morning. Her mother had always used to love that. For her mother, going into town had always also meant meeting up with one of her children. Clara remembered what Elias had said in the car. About what it was like to sit in a café in the early morning. And that he thought about her as music. The yearning suddenly made her draw a deep breath, as if she was short of air. Like being fifteen.

Jan stood up. 'What do you all want to drink? Maybe the waiters are too scared to come to us. Mama?'

'*Sekt*,' said Mama firmly.

Jan laughed. 'OK, bubbly all round then. And coffee with snow for you too, Mama.'

As Jan walked inside, Clara's father suddenly turned to her. 'So, how are we going to manage the move? Will we need a van? And what about me then? I'll be left on my own.'

He said it with such outrage, as if it had only just occurred to him. Which perhaps it had. Her father's mind worked in different ways to normal people's. And he didn't care that her mother could hear him.

'Papa!' She pointed to her mother, whose ears had pricked up at the word 'move'. 'Can we discuss this later?'

But he paid no attention. 'Everything has to be organised. It's not as easy as all that. What about the furniture? And the house!'

His lack of practicality was legendary. Clara leant forwards.

'Papa, Jan and I will do that. There won't be that much space in the home anyway. We'll take a table and a couple of chairs. And everything else will work out. For as long as you want to stay in the house, you really don't need to worry.'

Pointless; her father always worried. Probably about whether it would be easier for the CIA to find him if his wife went into a home.

Her phone lit up. It wasn't a message from Elias; it was an email. *Dear Ms Wagenbach ... come as no surprise that we ... welcome to the team!*

She scanned the rest of the message, her hands feeling suddenly cold with nerves. She'd got the job.

Jan came back. She passed him her phone. Said, more casually than she felt, 'They want me.'

'Who wants you?' her father asked, as Jan read the mail.

'I applied for a job in Hamburg,' she explained. 'But I'm not sure ... I don't know how it'll be for you all here. I wanted—'

He mother looked past her. 'Paul!' she exclaimed happily.

Clara turned and saw Elias. Her smile was just there. Teasingly, she too exclaimed 'Paul! At last,' and then was shocked by herself. Her mother couldn't help it, but for her, it was … like she'd broken a taboo. Like she'd made an irreparable mistake.

Luckily, there was Jan. He looked from her to Elias and back again, then asked laconically: 'You really can't make up your mind, can you? You told me about Elias, but you never mentioned Paul. Clara,' he added, as dark as the grave, 'Mama's right, you're throwing yourself away.'

Elias clutched his heart. 'I knew it!' he groaned.

But then he laughed, bent down and kissed Clara on the lips. She grabbed hold of his arm as if she'd been about to fall. When he straightened up, he looked around the table. Clara's mother had jumped up and was pulling him by the sleeve, down onto the chair beside her. He nodded to the two men.

'I'm Elias. Nice to meet you.'

Clara's father had stood up, but now sat down again. Jan came to shake Elias by the hand.

'Jan,' he said. 'No need to stand on ceremony, right? Clara has told me a bit about you. But you look much better in real life.'

'Jan!' Clara laughed. She'd got over her shock. 'Let him sit down before you start.'

There was a strange bond between Clara and her family. Elias had never had that. And Clara looked oddly emotional. He put his hand next to hers on the table, so that their little fingers touched.

'Not an easy morning, right?' he asked as quietly as he could.

Clara's father looked over to him. His voice was faltering with age, but still full of life. 'You're an actor? Thank God for that. There's a terrible lack of artistic spirit in this family. Have you ever considered that, in a past life, you—'

'Papa!' Jan broke in on him. 'Here's Clara with a sensible man for the first time in decades, and you're trying to scare him off right away? He hasn't even had a drink yet. At least hold off on your theories of reincarnation until he's so deeply in love that he can't get away.'

He didn't exactly wink as he silently begged Elias's forgiveness for his cheek, but rather pulled a kind of quick face that said: we understand each other, right? I'm on your side. Elias gave him an almost imperceptible nod. He'd liked him right away.

'I'm already lost,' he said. 'But what do you mean, Mr Wagenbach? Your daughter is a great artist!'

Clara intervened, half laughing, half shy. 'Could we maybe not talk about me? You should be bombarding him with questions. That's normally how it goes.'

'We met!' Clara's mother exclaimed triumphantly. 'The other day, in the tent.'

Jan stroked her hand. 'I sometimes think you're just faking it, Mama,' he said with tender mockery, before turning to Elias. 'She might be remembering the time you found her.'

But she was already looking nervous again, searching for something under the table and in her handbag.

'Where's the cat?'

'What do you mean?' Clara's father asked. 'At home, of course.'

Elias got the impression he was genuinely surprised by the question. Like he didn't have the least belief in his wife's dementia.

'None of them think homeopathy works. None of them. Conventional medicine then makes up a condition, and they call it dementia. Schinkel, the architectural genius, when they did a post mortem on him, they found practically no brain left. Imagine that!'

Elias could see Jan roll his eyes for a moment. Beside him, Clara sighed.

'Is that so?' Elias asked politely.

'Don't encourage him,' Clara said. 'Would you like some fizz too? We're celebrating my mother's incapacity.'

Jan shrugged. 'What do you want? She's alive. She's got us. And she's not stuck in bed or whatever. It could all be much worse. We're sitting here with her. We can drink *sekt* with her, and you're not unhappy, are you, Mama?' Again, he reached for her hand. She smiled at him.

How tender he was with his mother. Elias thought about Jule. Would she be like that one day?

Clara leant gently against him. 'I got the job,' she whispered.

'But that's amazing!' he replied. 'That's great.'

She rested her head against his for a moment. The sun gleamed on her hair.

'Shall we talk about it later? Do you have time?'

He nodded and gave her hand a quick squeeze. No, Vera was wrong. It was more than infatuation. He loved Clara. That was all.

32

Doves were cooing from the rooftops. Huge flocks of starlings were wildly swooping up and down between the towers. It was shady in the narrow lanes of the Old Town; there was only the occasional strip of sunshine when you came to a gap between the tightly packed buildings, or at the end of a side street. There was a cool scent in the air, like water.

'A few weeks ago, the snow was still lying knee-high,' remarked Elias. 'Springtime is always like a miracle. Everything happens so fast.'

I shouldn't have drunk that *sekt*, he thought. He had that strange feeling of lightness again. As if he were struggling to grip the ground beneath his feet. He shook his head to dislodge it.

Clara was walking beside him. With that wonderfully firm yet swinging gait that had fascinated him from the first. If small things could destroy a partnership in the long run, then there must presumably also be small things that never stopped reenchanting you.

She was very quiet, looking up. The small section of sky between the roofs was a cool blue. You could never, never, never photograph colours exactly as they really were. Even the most beautiful photo was only a pale reflection of the beauty of reality. And despite that, she took pictures of the sky again and again.

Elias, lost in thought, said, almost incidentally: 'You have a fascinating family.'

They were turning down Concordiagasse. Ancient, crooked houses. Cobbles that had a dark glow in the beam of sunlight. First-floor windows standing open, reflecting the light; you could probably jump up and touch them if you judged it right, the houses here were that low.

Concordia, thought Clara. Two hearts together. The way hers

was currently beating, it couldn't possibly be in time with anyone else's.

'Elias,' she began helplessly, 'I don't know what to do.'

He said nothing. Just looked at her and put his arm around her as they walked.

'This job in Hamburg ... I mean, a chance like that will never come up again. It's the sort of thing you normally dream of and never get.'

They turned again and crossed the river via the Mühlbrücke. They were heading to the little wooded park on the left-hand arm of the river. Elias had only been there a couple of times. Clara knew the town so well. Probably because she'd been all over the place, taking photographs. Whereas, if he had time, he always felt the draw of the countryside.

'We're living in the twenty-first century,' he reminded her with a slight smile. She sounded so grave. 'There are trains. I've got a car. Hamburg isn't outer space.'

'Six hundred kilometres,' Clara replied. 'You don't just drive that on a whim.'

'I do,' said Elias, 'if it's to see you.'

Suddenly, she was almost furious at his naïvety. Was he only pretending, or did he really not get it?

'Elias! Can we please be realistic for once? It's six hundred kilometres. You're an actor, and you have to act at the weekends. I'll probably only be free at the weekends. I'll have to travel a lot. And now and then, you'll want to visit Jule, or she'll come here. How often will we see each other then? Once a month?'

She was walking faster now, because she was so worked up and the energy had to go somewhere. She was right, but still...

'If we wanted to be realistic, we should never have let ourselves fall in love, should we?'

They were passing along the narrow road beside the river now. There were almost no cars here, and fewer and fewer tourists.

'Clara, I know that this is an amazing opportunity for you.

You're going to take the job. Yes, I admit that I didn't think it through at first. But I'm doing that now. What's wrong with offering to come and join you later? We're talking about eighteen months, or two years.'

He suddenly had the feeling that she was slipping further away from him with every word.

'Two years. Eighteen months...' she snarled at him. 'You say it like it doesn't mean a thing. Do you really believe we'll survive that? Or, more to the point, that you will? Do you know any weekend relationships that truly work? I don't. It'll be six weeks here, two months there, in places we can't be together, and anyway, do you seriously think two days a month are enough to create anything deep? Quite apart from all the young women who'd love a word or two with you after every performance. Be honest: will you always say no? Nobody could even blame you,' she concluded bitterly.

Elias had to admit that her words hit him hard. Yes, he'd been like that. Until now. Until her.

'I'm no innocent, naïve fool,' he said, uncharacteristically sharply. 'Everything you say is true.' He increased his pace so that he could stand in front of her, look into her face, as he continued furiously: 'Or it would be true if I didn't love you. Do you really have so little faith?'

She didn't reply. The anger was ebbing away, and he took her arm, so that he could reach her better.

'Clara,' he asked, and it sounded like an entreaty, 'is this really about whether we can be together? Is this deciding for or against us?'

Again, she didn't reply. They continued on, walking side by side now, and, for the first time, there was an oppressive silence between them. As they reached Hain Park, it had solidified to the point that they were afraid that if one of them spoke in this moment, only he or she would be able to hear it.

Flecks of sunlight shone on the gravel path. The lawns, the

hornbeams, the forsythia – still in bright-yellow bloom – and the tall, abundant shrubs, leaning in on either side with their thick, white clustering flower heads ... as if they wanted to scatter mocking petals in their path, he thought.

'Elias,' Clara began, her voice breaking, 'I simply don't know what to do. I don't want to be with you if I can't be *with* you. I couldn't bear it, and I don't want it.'

'Me either!' He was shouting. 'I ... have no idea.' He was hunting for the right words, but right then there were none. 'Clara, how is it possible that suddenly everything is up in the air? You're demanding too much. Seriously. Of yourself and of me.'

There was a gazebo in the middle of the wood. The tall trees above it, the playful dance of light and shade on the lawn, always in motion, the abundant white blossom on the bushes all around – it was a peaceful image, through and through. They were both walking towards the summerhouse without thinking about it.

'Neither of us can walk past it, can we? This is like the islands. You want to go because it's there.'

'Yes,' said Clara.

There was the warm smell of old wood, and a dash of the roof tar in the sun. The coming summer was already in the scent. They stood side by side, leaning their hands on the balustrade. Not close enough. Their hands should be touching, he thought fleetingly.

'Yes. I'm demanding more than we can have right now. I'm just too old to wait for real life, real happiness, real love. What's eighteen months to you? Less than it is for me, at any rate. No, don't interrupt me. We can't talk the age difference away. It's just a fact. And how's it supposed to work? I'm not Jule, for you to visit every couple of weeks. You're father and daughter. That's a very different bond. You can't help loving her.'

'I can't help loving you either.'

How long had it been since she'd heard anything like that?

Decades. But he just didn't see as clearly as she did. I have to brace myself. He's just making everything harder.

She fought the thick sensation in her throat and tried for an even voice.

'I won't get a job like this again. I don't want to keep worrying about whether I can make this month's rent. Running to the Job Centre. How do you think my chances will develop if I stay here? If I don't take the job? A provincial photographer in her late forties? In a few years ... who employs a woman in her mid-fifties if they can have a thirty-year-old? I know it shouldn't be like that, and nobody says it out loud, but that's the way they all think. Even the women. Especially the women.'

'Clara—' he began, but she interrupted him breathlessly.

'No, wait. I almost can't help ... no, I want the job.' She was speaking faster and faster, to get everything said. 'It's a chance in a lifetime. A dream job. I don't know what will happen with us. I don't know if, in two years, you'd prefer a younger woman too. I hope not, and I don't want that and I ... but I don't know. And I don't want to be left standing alone in two or three years, still out of work or in some bloody part-time job, or freelance, just about scraping by. That's it. And it's nothing to do with feminism or anything like that, if that's what you're thinking, but solely to do with my life. Nothing else at all. Only my life.'

She was trembling. She was breathing fast, as if after a race. There was a sudden flush around her cheekbones. Elias had stepped back from the balustrade and longed to take her in his arms, but that suddenly wasn't on.

'I'll come with you to Hamburg. I ... It's not even two whole years now, but that's how long I'll be here. Can't we survive that? Less than two years? I'll come too.'

'And then what?' She was almost screaming with tension, with rage at herself and at him and at everything. 'What will you live on? Where will we live? That's ... We're not sixteen any more. I'm certainly not,' she added with sudden bitterness. 'But the main thing – and I've only just realised this myself – is that I don't want to spend every day that I don't see you living with the fear that I'm getting too old for your love.'

That almost bowled him over. Like she'd slapped him.

For a few moments, he couldn't find the words. There was a cobweb in the semi-shade between one of the wooden struts and the roof. A few last dewdrops hung from it, glittering. The fresh scent of water came up from the river. Why was the world allowed to be so lovely when everything was going to shit?

With an almost physical effort, he took her hand. 'Clara, I've only just found you. It's the first time in a long time that I feel like I've made the right decision. That I'm living the right life. And that's because of you. Can't you just trust in my love?'

Could she? Was that it? Something was raging inside her. She'd almost forgotten how rupturing this fury at the world and herself could be. She took a trembling breath and tried to speak calmly.

'To be honest, I want to. But, to be equally honest, how can I? Or you? You left Vera after one night with me. In a moment. How can you, how can I, be sure that something like that won't just happen again? Neither of us can. And maybe it wouldn't happen if we each had time for the other. But we won't have that. A thing like that can't work over just two weekends a month, and that's being optimistic, isn't it?'

He pulled his hand back. She was right, and she was wrong.

'And you don't even want to try, right?' He could barely control the sudden anger in his voice. 'Yes. I left Vera after a night with you, when we didn't even kiss. Because I knew that you were the one. But you don't want to be, do you? I know that I don't ... Maybe I wouldn't trust me either. Vera said that. That after six months, I'll have fallen out of love. Apparently, it didn't even take you that long.'

'How nice that the two of you are talking about me,' Clara said with forced calm, deeply hurt, but cold and sharp. 'Do you see each other often?'

Oh God! She was taking everything the wrong way!

'She wanted one last conversation. You were in Hamburg at the time—'

She cut him off. 'I remember. I tried to call you but you rejected it. I wanted to tell you how it had gone. You know what, Elias?' She turned away from him and buttoned up her jacket. 'Maybe it's just as well that we cleared this up now. I don't want this kind of thing.'

She walked out of the gazebo. No, she practically ran. He wanted to follow, but stopped in mid-stride. There was no point.

She didn't understand. I have no idea what else I can say.

Everything in his head was chaos. He didn't know what was right anymore, what was wrong. Should he not have met up with Vera? What the fucking hell had he actually done wrong?

'Clara!' he yelled after her. 'Clara, wait!'

But she didn't stop. She didn't even turn around.

He suddenly felt so weak that he had to sit down on the wooden floor. The planks were ice cold.

33

He hadn't been able to get to sleep, and when he woke up the next morning after a hideous night, he felt ill.

No wonder. He hadn't been feeling good even before that, and then he'd gone home freezing. Had been freezing all afternoon, the way it goes when everything looks warmer than it really is. And he shouldn't have had a drink, but after the performance, he hadn't wanted to go home. There was nobody there waiting for him. And he couldn't go to Clara's anymore.

Clara.

Why wouldn't such a simple thing go into his head? She'd split up with him. Split sounded as sharp as a knife. Split up. Such a shit expression. It was as if he'd been split in half down the middle. No blood. No pain. It was simply as if there was a void where the other half should be. For the first time he thought he might understand what it was like to lose a hand. You want to ruffle your hair or shake hands with someone or pick up a cup but there's no longer anything there to do it with. The cup just sits there, untouched. Like he could no longer get to grips with anything. Like he suddenly had no emotions left.

It was hard to get up, but he needed to make some tea. His head was heavy. The kitchen was cold. He'd left the window open overnight. Outside was a non-day. The sky was apathetically grey. Thanks, weather. Perhaps things would have been even worse if today had been lovely. Yesterday had been the perfect spring day. Sun. Wind. Split.

I don't get it, I don't get it, I don't get it. A mantra. Put the kettle on, don't understand. Pour the tea, don't understand. Take the cup back to bed with you, shivering, don't understand. The feeling that he couldn't touch anything was in his head too. He couldn't hold on to any thoughts.

He noticed that he was running a temperature. The cold planks in the gazebo. And Clara, walking away without turning round. He'd fucked everything up. Somehow, he'd fucked everything up and he didn't even know how.

34

Fickle and cool.

It seemed much longer than the six, seven weeks since she'd last been at the cottage. It had been windy then, everything in motion, and she'd had the sense of something beginning. Why did she now have this bitter sense that everything was ending? She was going to Hamburg. Everything was changing. Draw a line under everything. Under Paul and the grief and the house.

Paul. The last time they'd been here together, he'd only been able to walk a couple of steps. From the car to the veranda.

Get a move on, he'd snarled impatiently at her when he'd wanted to sit in the chair and she hadn't had the cushion in hand in time. Already so thin that the seat hurt him. She understood, but it had still annoyed her. Maybe he'd felt it and just not said anything. That she'd stopped loving him. For the first time, it occurred to her that Paul might have seen things very differently. That he might have believed she could no longer love him because he had cancer. But that he'd had no choice but to love her. Because she'd be the last woman in his life and he needed her. She didn't want to be that dependant on another person. She didn't want to make herself that vulnerable.

Is age like cancer? But much slower and crueller? The weather was fickle and cool. And she probably was too. Elias might think so. But she couldn't do anything about that.

She leant against the fence, waiting for the lorry. Her mother was in the garden. One last trip out with her. Not 'one last', she corrected her own thoughts hastily. Just one more time before she moved into the home.

In her head, 'home' sounded more like 'prison'. As if you wouldn't be allowed out anymore. And it might be like that for Mama. Dementia patients were in a secure section. Why do we do that? So that she doesn't get lost, doesn't get lost someday. Because I won't be able to go out looking for her every week. Because Papa can't do it anymore. Because Jan's too busy. Because I'm going to Hamburg. That's why we're locking Mama up.

In her best interests. What a load of shit. It's in our best interests, isn't it. Because we just won't put the effort in. Because we want our lives ... Shit. Shit. I'm thinking about Mama just so that I don't have to think about Elias. Is it the same with him? Because I want to live my life without thinking about him? It's not the same. No. It's not the same. Is it?

Pull yourself together.

It's only been a couple of weeks.

I've been through worse.

'Mama!' she shouted, almost relieved as she looked over the fence and snapped out of her thoughts. She'd given her mother a pair of secateurs for the ivy on the wall, so that she'd have something to do while the people from the house-clearance company cleared the cottage. But her mother had apparently dealt with the ivy as quickly and thoroughly as she always had. And then she'd turned her attention to the blackcurrants. She'd cut every branch off the bushes.

Mama looked helplessly at her. Uncertain. Shocked. Wordless.

Clara came closer. 'Doesn't matter,' she said hastily. She suddenly had a lump in her throat and longed to hug Mama and pull her into her lap like a child, just the way her mother had done for her, long, long ago when she'd cut her knee.

'Doesn't matter, Mama. Keep going,' she said, as tears ran down her cheek. 'It's only the bloody blackcurrants. Cut them down. Cut them all down. They'll grow back.'

But her mother dropped the secateurs and touched her wet cheeks with muddy fingers.

'Raccoon,' she whispered soothingly.

'Yes, Mama,' Clara had to laugh, despite the tears. 'Raccoon.'

It had been much easier than she'd been expecting. The house was empty. Only the range, the kitchen table and the chest in the bedroom were left. Because the table and the chest had been in the house when they'd bought it. Because they pre-dated her and Paul. No significance. She walked through the rooms. She hadn't got much for the rest of the furniture. Nothing at all for the carpets and curtains. But that didn't matter. Memories weren't worth much when you sold them on. What was the asking price for a second-hand life? It actually felt good to have everything finally gone. Now she just had to sell the house itself, but there was time for that.

Exhale. It's over. Everything decided. Exhale. Set yourself free.

But as she stepped through the glass door onto the veranda, the memory ambushed her with full force. It was here that she'd seen Elias for the first time. On his knees. In front of her.

Leave me alone. Leave me alone. Leave me alone.

'Toni?'

Her mother came out of the garden. She'd found a sack that she'd tied around herself like an apron. She spoke very seldom now, and generally only one or two words.

'I'm Clara, Mama,' she said, hating herself for being so close to tears again. She hadn't even properly cried over Paul, and Elias wasn't dead. But she was standing here with her mother, who moved through a grey nothingness from which nobody could pull her back. She was standing here and had a dead husband behind her and an empty house and a lost love, and ahead of her ... no. It was no grey nothingness. She had decided on a life, and Elias had simply acquiesced to it. He hadn't said so, but it was true. So it was simply better to make a clear, sharp cut than to be in a relationship that would lose its way into just that kind of grey nothingness. She didn't want that. She wouldn't go through that again.

'Come on, Mama,' she said. 'You and your jute sack and I are driving home now.'

At once.

When can you start? She'd read the email through again once she'd got home. On the day that Mama had lost her right of decision and she'd broken up with Elias. Full of rage at herself and at him. Trembling to her core. When had she last felt like that? Like suddenly swimming into a river current that you hadn't noticed. That you couldn't see from the bank, where everything around you was the same as ever. The long willow leaves, bright green, stroking the water. The sun glittering on the tiny waves. A dragonfly hovering beautifully above you, and you know that all that will still be there in ten minutes, when you've drowned. And then this feeling, out of nowhere, right out of the blue, of having to swim for your life, because otherwise you'll just go down without a sound.

At once.

She'd typed it with flying fingers. On her phone. Standing by the mirror: this is me. A woman in her late forties. More than halfway through. How much time is left? There was no alternative.

At once.

Now she was sitting in the kitchen, a cup of coffee in front of her, making a list of the things she wanted to take to Hamburg with her. She could stay with Katrin for the first few days. She had a large flat. And then she'd see. She could keep her flat here for a month or two. It couldn't all be done in one go anyway. Next Monday. She twisted her face into a dry smile. She could store her furniture at her parents'. That's how it went. You moved out of home, and then, sooner or later, your furniture found its way back to your parents' house.

When her phone buzzed, it shot through her belly. Still and always. Because, every time, she thought it would be Elias texting. As if. She didn't text either, and then ... what was there for him to say? What was there for her to say? But still, she always reached immediately for her phone. But it was only a message from Jan: *Are you dead?*

She wasn't in the mood to chat, and he'd called twice without her answering. He seemed to have some kind of uncanny sense for when something wasn't right. They could go for three or four days sometimes, but this time, Jan had tried quite often to get hold of her.

No. I've got a lot to do. Packing. I'll call later.

She couldn't find the light tone they normally used with each other. It rang almost at once. Jan.

'What's wrong, sis?'

She hesitated.

'Nothing. I'm just ... I have a lot to do. I don't know what to take—'

Jan interrupted. 'Madam, would you kindly get off the phone and fetch my sister? I'd like to speak to her.'

She laughed against her will.

'Maybe you could just tell me what's wrong? Have you had a fight, you and your new boyfriend, whose pretty name I can never remember?'

She took a deep breath.

'We split up.'

'Ah,' was all Jan said.

Neither of them spoke for a while.

'Over Hamburg?' asked Jan.

'Partly,' she replied.

'Clara!' Jan said loudly, a touch of impatience in his voice. 'Stop that right now. Don't turn this into a case of getting blood out of a stone. Did he dump you? I'll kill him for you. What's wrong?'

'I did. I dumped him.'

'OK,' said Jan after a moment of surprise. She'd disconcerted him. In the end, he asked cautiously, 'Would you like to tell me why? It looked like you were pretty happy. You both looked happy. What happened?'

Clara drank a swig of coffee. It was cold. Then she tried to tell him what had happened. It wasn't so easy to put into words. That she didn't want a relationship that wasn't one. That on top of that, he'd been meeting Vera. That ... she didn't know how to make her feelings clear to Jan, this feeling that she'd rather be alone than ... whatever. She fell silent.

'Clara,' Jan said in the end, 'I have to go back in and we can talk later. But what I don't quite understand is...' He stopped and started again. 'I think there's only one question really, isn't there? Do you love him?'

Him too! It made her livid that he didn't really understand either.

'Of course I love him. Or ... maybe I don't anymore, or I don't want to love him if there's no point. Don't you get that?'

She was shouting, but Jan could deal with that.

'You're not giving him a chance, you know that,' said Jan. 'The way I see it ... Clara! OK, he should have told you about the thing with his ex. But you ... you're just asking too much. I—'

She cut him off. 'No! No, Jan, it's not asking too much. Or if it is, then I don't want less. I want real love, not some fling, and not just shitty "quality time" every four weeks and the occasional holiday together or something. And who are you to give me advice? What's up with you?'

'I have to go,' Jan said shortly. 'We can talk later.' He hesitated a moment. She waited. Then he said hastily, 'That wasn't fair, Clara. It really wasn't. I know I'm no expert on successful relationships. But I haven't given up. You apparently have. Speak later.'

He hung up.

She'd done an excellent job there. Now she'd screwed up with Jan too. She was about to put her phone away when a message came in.

*Sorry, sis. You're a total idiot. But at least *I'll* still always love you.*

What the hell? Why was she fighting tears at the least little thing these days? She really had to get a grip on that by Monday.

35

He didn't have a cough, but his head ached and he had a temperature. Elias felt as though he had flu. It was hard to wake up from these horrible dreams, and when, now and then, he had to go to the bathroom, everything felt unreal. The dreams ... he remembered that from childhood. If he'd had a temperature, he'd always dreamt that he had to count, just count, endlessly. Now it was different. He spent the whole time dreaming about her cottage. The steps were winding and he was constantly late so he had to keep climbing and climbing and running down and along the corridors that were way too long for the small house. He was looking for the room she was in. But he ran and went up stairs and back down more stairs and had to squeeze through tiny doors. Then he had a dry throat from all the running and wanted to turn on the tap, which, strangely, was sticking out of a photograph on the wall, but he couldn't grasp it. His hand always went through it. Again and again.

It was a constant oscillation between wakefulness and fever dreams, and it was such an effort to stay properly awake. He lay in bed and couldn't think clearly. He didn't even know for certain what day of the week it was.

It took a while for him not to be quite so woozy. He normally wanted to be alone when he was ill and couldn't stand having someone constantly with him. But at the moment ... he had absolutely nothing left in the fridge. There wasn't even any tea. He felt far too weak for anything; shopping was out of the question.

He reached for his phone, which was lying on the floor beside the bed. Clara. He couldn't call Clara. How would that come over? Hello, I'm ill. I'm dreaming about you all the time. Could you bring some stuff over for me? And, while you're at it, would you take me back?

I wouldn't believe me either, he thought. Actor, and all that. And if she doesn't want me when I'm healthy, why should she love me when I'm ill?

He gave a dry gulp. It was so hard to concentrate on anything. He had the feeling that he'd replayed the scene in the gazebo in his head a thousand times, and it was more different every time. Everything blurred. All his thoughts were so ... soft. Something wasn't right with him. This was no normal flu.

'Elias?'

Vera sounded surprised. But not very. He pulled himself together, tried to sound clear.

'Hey, Vera. I know this is silly, but I ... There's nobody who lives even remotely close by and I wanted to ask you if you...'

'Are you ill? You sound ill.'

'Yes,' he said. 'I think I've got a fever. Would you mind coming round for a bit? I need something to bring the temperature down. I feel...'

The word 'lost' was on the tip of his tongue, but that sounded so dramatic. But he couldn't find another, so he stopped talking.

'I'll come round,' said Vera. 'See you soon.'

No triumph in her voice, or at least not that he could hear. How few friends he had! He could have called Mareike, but he'd thought of that too late. Besides ... wouldn't she be in rehearsals now? He still didn't know what day it was, but before he could check on his phone, he'd fallen asleep again.

When he woke up, with even more of an effort than before, Vera was standing by his bed. She must have been there some time, because the cup of tea she handed him was lukewarm. She seemed a bit see-through, and he didn't understand right away what she wanted when she asked: 'Did you hit something?'

He shook his head and sipped the tea.

'Why? No. I just have some kind of bug. Don't know where I picked it up.'

Vera pointed to his hand. 'You've got some kind of bruise there.'

He looked at the back of his hand. It was true. There was a mark. And a couple of spots next to it. On his palm too.

'What's that?' he asked with an effort.

'I have no idea,' Vera answered nervously, 'But I don't like it. What did you do? Did you eat something funny?'

He shook his head again. It felt dangerous, as if it were too light and might fly off his neck and away.

'No idea,' he repeated. 'Maybe I'll go to the doctor tomorrow.'

She laid a cool hand on his forehead. 'You're burning up. When did you last have anything to drink?'

He didn't know. He also didn't know whether he'd even opened the door to Vera. How had she got in?

'Did you climb?' he asked.

'What?'

He saw that she was disconcerted. But he'd only asked if she'd climbed over the balcony.

'Elias, you've been talking really weirdly the whole time. You said a whole bunch of stuff about Clara and a tank. And about steps that you built. Not like in a dream. You're kind of rambling. It's scaring me, Elias. Seriously.'

Yeah, yeah, he thought. Steps. They were really dangerous. He remembered having fallen down them. An endlessly long staircase. Had that been at the theatre, or the gazebo?

Somehow, he must have fallen asleep again because, this time when he woke up, there was a doctor by his bed. And he was sitting upright. Had someone taken off his pyjama top?

'How long have you had these spots?' asked the doctor. If he was a doctor. Where was Vera? He didn't exactly know where he was himself. How had the doctor got in? Did everyone suddenly have a key to his flat? Or had he taken the door off its hinges because of the stairs?

'I don't have any,' he said, reluctantly fending them off.

'You do,' the doctor said, way too loud. 'All over. There are spots on your chest and your back. Mr Kornfeld, I'm going to admit you to the hospital. Do you understand me?'

'I can't do any more stairs,' said Elias.

'Don't worry,' he heard Vera say, 'they'll carry you.'

Carry is good, he thought, but I hope they don't forget my legs. He felt someone pull his top back down again, but then he drifted off.

36

New office. New city. New life.

It still didn't feel real, more like a holiday or work-experience placement. Not like anything long-term. The day had been filled with first meetings, a tour of the offices, a lunch with her future colleagues and a short chat with the managing editor she'd met at her interview. There hadn't been much time to think. The executive offices had a view of the elevated railway and the container port; from hers, you could at least see a semi-green inner courtyard. But it was all just as she'd imagined it. One of the secretaries had even put together a list of possible flats for her and pressed it into her hand.

'That's what we do here,' she'd said with Hanseatic brevity, but still friendly. 'You're not the first to come from down south and need somewhere to live.'

A breathless first day. That was good, it meant she hadn't had to think about Elias. At least until she finally stepped out of the building. Then there were suddenly time and space, and the kind of bright evening sky you only get in spring. It was almost seven, but still fully light, with that constant feeling of a surprise gift you could only be given when it wasn't that long since you'd put the winter behind you. The heavy, weighty blare of a ship's horn sounded from the river. As well as the gulls, there were a few swallows in playful flight over the housetops. From the nearby Michelwiese came the hoarse cries of lads playing football. Spring.

She unlocked the bike that Katrin had lent her and rode slowly along the Elbe towards Altona. She was in no hurry to get anywhere. As long as she was outside and in motion, she didn't have to think.

The city was in a rare state of peace. People were sitting outside fish restaurants and bars, having an after-work glass of wine, or a chic Aperol spritz, or simply a beer. At the corner by a café in what had once been a fish market, she carried her bike up some steps into a little park. She didn't get back on, just walked along the paths, pushing it beside her. The green space in any city called to her. She photographed the parks in any city. Because they were places where contradictions mingled: nature, wilderness and the untamed on one hand; and on the other, the city, the epitome of control. It had a strange attraction for her.

That's what I'm like. Sense and discipline. Passion and desire. Or something in-between. Except that the attraction I give off has its limits.

Don't think about that.

The path climbed. Scenes of the Elbe glowed in the evening light, framed in the gaps between the tree trunks as if in a film. A ferry in silhouette. A crane on the other bank, turning slowly in the wind. She wasn't so far above the Große Elbstraße, but from here she could mainly hear the rustle of the leaves. The wind in the trees sounded different in every season. In winter, it whistled tunelessly through the branches, and in autumn, it sometimes sounded mighty hoarse. But this soft, expansive rustle was the stuff of spring.

There was an open space with two benches up here. *Altonaer Balkon* said a noticeboard, covered in stickers. And it really was like a balcony. If you stood by the wall, you could see for miles over the tower by the old Elbtunnel and the Nordelbe, and beyond that, on the hazy evening horizon, the forest of cranes in the container port. Then she heard music. From an open window in the hotel on the edge of the park. The wind was blowing towards her, or she wouldn't have heard it ... *I can't believe you really gonna leave the town.* 'Rio de Janeiro Blue'. Not the Randy Crawford cover version. The original, sung by Richard Torrance. Hardly anyone knew it. It hit Clara unprepared and she stood very still as the tune drifted past her on the wind. She'd loved the song from the first. The grief in it. The longing for the lost lover.

Everyone knows that I'm nothing without you. She'd always had this image of it in her mind – alone on a mountain, above the sea … Rio, what it was like when you had no one to share it with anymore. At that moment, she was standing there in the wind over the water, and it was as though she'd walked into a different city, but that was exactly why it was as though Elias was singing in her, from her. Was it her own yearning or his that knocked her off balance like a sudden heavy gust?

But then … *parts of you with who knows who* … the thought of him with Vera was actually like an inner scream. Of rage or of whatever. And? Was it actually her fate to live her life alone?

She couldn't help it. She had to stand in this beautiful place, looking across the water into the distance, and listen to the song drifting from some anonymous hotel room behind her to the end.

Dusk was falling, but she was still coasting aimlessly, down broad, dreary streets where the cars were racing home, away from the city. Then down random avenues, which looked like money, where mansions stood in large gardens, behind elegantly discreet walls. Thousands of lives behind the lighted windows. Hers was only one of many. With no major significance. Elsewhere, there was war, or a ship was sinking, or a fire in a textile factory in the Far East was killing hundreds of women. Her own fate was nothing at all. She was well. She'd done almost everything right.

Almost.

When her phone buzzed, she thought it was Katrin. Or Jan. She hadn't been expecting Vera Steiner. She stared at the screen. What did she want from her? She was not in the mood for a conversation with her. Had Elias asked her to call? Didn't matter. She declined. It rang again almost instantly. She let it ring, it didn't stop.

'Ms Steiner,' she said with cutting politeness, 'what can I do for you?'

'I'm sorry that it's me, but I don't think Elias got hold of you. He's not at all well. He's pretty ill.'

Clara was surprised.

'Didn't he tell you? We split up.'

Vera Steiner said nothing for a moment. Had she really not known?

'Oh,' she said briefly, 'I'm sorry to hear that. But he's been talking about you the whole time. He's in hospital.'

Clara didn't understand.

'What do you mean, talking about me? So why doesn't he call me?'

She could hear Vera's breathing. Agitated.

'Maybe he wasn't ... He has such a high fever that he's babbling all kinds of stuff. He was hallucinating, and the doctor admitted him right away. They don't know what's wrong with him.'

Everything within Clara clenched together. They don't know what's wrong with him...

'I...' she began, but then didn't know what to say. 'Do you think ... how is he?'

'Not so good,' Vera answered right away. 'But where are you now? Can you come? I think it would be good for him. He talked so much about you.'

This feeling that she'd had back then too – like none of this was anything to do with her. As if one Clara was listening and another Clara was watching the whole thing from the outside.

'I'm in Hamburg. And I'll have to work some things out. Would you text me the ward he's on? And can I call you back later?'

'Of course,' Vera Steiner said simply. She paused a moment.

'Yes?' Clara asked impatiently.

'Maybe you could ... I don't have Jule's number. Do you? Someone should tell her.'

It sounded embarrassed. Like she was making a confession.

'I think I'll be able to tell her.'

'Thank you,' said Vera. 'I'll message you if anything changes.'

Once Clara had hung up, she tried to take a deep breath. To keep the panic down. She didn't know anything, after all. It was a fever. Fever wasn't that bad. You didn't get a fever when you had cancer. Pneumonia, maybe. Bad, but they could get on top of it. Jan. She had to call Jan.

It still wasn't quite dark, and only a little cooler, but she was suddenly shivering with nerves and fear. She didn't even know where she was. Some residential area. She leant the bike against a tree and tapped. Hopefully Jan would hear his phone.

'Sis!'

It was good to hear his voice. The warmth it always held. She crouched down beside the bike. Suddenly, her legs were very weary.

'Jan, Elias is in hospital. Can you find out what's wrong? His ex-girlfriend rang me. Apparently, he's got a high fever or something.'

'Haven't you spoken since then?' Jan sounded surprised. 'I'll have a look. I'm not at work at the moment, but I can go over there. Is it urgent?'

She hesitated, then took another deep breath. It didn't help much.

'I don't feel good about it, Jan. I'm scared.'

'Right,' said Jan. 'Do you know which ward he's on? Don't worry, I'll find out. I'll call you as soon as I know anything.'

'Can't you do that from home?'

Jan laughed.

'Clara, I'm not James Bond! I can log into my own computer from here, but the whole hospital? I'd need to be the big boss. I'll hurry, OK? And Clara, statistically speaking, most acute admissions leave us in full health.'

Speaking to Jan had helped, but there was a deep unease inside her, almost fear. She had to look on her phone to find out where she was before she got back on the bike. Suddenly, she was in a hurry, as though it mattered to her where she'd be when Jan called. She had to move, to at least take the edge off the unease – and the fear, which was rising again.

Katrin was already in bed when she walked into the dark flat. On the kitchen table, there was a plate with a note beside it: *There's some risotto left in the oven. And wine in the fridge.* Katrin was so welcoming, even though they'd only seen each other once every few years since their student days. All the same, she was glad to be alone. She didn't want to seem hysterical.

Her phone buzzed. An electric shock to her stomach. A message from Vera Steiner. *Infectious Diseases, ward II. Room 223. They're still investigating.*

She pulled the wine from the fridge and poured half a glass. She hadn't put the kitchen light on. There were a few glowing rectangles in the blocks of flats around the dark courtyard. It was very quiet. Only the fridge humming quietly.

Waiting.

She remembered Jule. She didn't have her number, but it would be easy to find her on Instagram via Elias. She messaged her. Cautiously, so as not to worry her too much. Asked her to get in touch. With a slight hesitation, she copied and pasted Vera's number into the message. Whatever. The main thing was for Jule to get hold of someone.

Waiting.

She was so edgy that she wished she could jump into the car and drive to him. But what would that achieve? And anyway, they'd split up. Maybe he wouldn't even want to see her. Vera was with him, after all. Even though they'd split up too. Hilarious.

Waiting.

She looked at the clock. It was over an hour and a half since she'd spoken to Jan. What was taking him so long? She stood up and walked quietly into the room Katrin had given her. From the window, you could see over the four-lane motorway to the old water tower in Schanzenpark.

Fever? What did that mean? Why did you get a fever? She withstood the temptation to look fever up on the internet. That would only make you crazier.

Waiting.

Why wasn't Jan phoning? She sent him a quick message: *Know anything yet?*

The answer came quickly. *Soon.*

That wasn't reassuring. Why soon? Why wasn't he phoning? The cars roared past down below. There was always traffic here, even at night. The people down there knew nothing about her. They weren't afraid. They were driving home from the cinema. Or to work a night shift. Or to see their boyfriend.

Monday! The earliest she could drive back would be Friday afternoon. The earliest. It was her first week and ... Her phone rang. She'd turned the ringer on, so as not to miss it.

'So?'

'Yes,' Jan began, and she could tell, just from that yes, that it was serious.

'Jan, what's wrong with him?'

'So, it took such a long time to find him, because they've transferred him already. He's in cardiology now.'

'What? Why?' Her voice sounded unnaturally loud. Shit, what was wrong?

'Clara, first of all, listen to me. He has endocarditis. I'll explain in a minute, but listen now. It's a serious staphylococcal infection, they're all over one of the valves in his heart, and so he needs urgent surgery. Sometime tomorrow morning. That's...' He paused as if to search for the right words.

'What do they have to do?' she cut in. 'What are they operating on?'

'He'll probably be given an artificial valve. Sometimes they can clean the valve when it's only been colonised, but that's dangerous. Mostly, they replace it.'

'Is that ... Is it common? Is it routine?'

She heard Jan take a breath.

'Uh-huh,' he said. 'The valve ... well, he'll be on blood thinners for the rest of his life. But the crucial thing...' He stopped again.

Clara felt herself spiralling with anxiety and fear. 'Jan! What?'

He was sounding calm again now.

'Heart surgery is always serious. But ... yes, it is routine. We do this very often here, and he's young. The critical thing is the infection. It's genuinely dangerous. All we can do is hope that the antibiotics will kick in. And he'll have to keep taking them for six to eight weeks. But staph is multi-resistant, and they don't know the strain yet, and that...'

Inside, she fell very silent, grew very cold. No way around it. No making excuses to herself.

'What's the mortality rate?' she asked.

She could hear from his voice that he didn't want to hurt her. That he was looking for a way out.

'Clara, that depends on thousands of factors. Age. Immune system. Mindset.'

'What is it?'

'Between twenty and twenty-five per cent.'

She put her phone down on the windowsill for a moment. Looked out. The cars were still driving past.

Two or three in ten. You always think it won't happen to you. The two phrases were playing catch in her head. Hilarious. Two or three in ten, you always think it won't happen to you. It won't happen to you. It does happen to you. It does happen to you. Sometimes twice.

She picked her phone up again.

'I'm coming. I want to see him.'

'Yes,' Jan replied. 'Call me. I'll come to intensive care with you.'

37

Driving through the night. There were no direct trains after nine. A nine- or ten-hour journey – she'd rather take the car. Anyway, she'd have found it unbearable to sit there on the train, not being able to do anything.

There wasn't much traffic on the motorway south now. She drove and drove. Sometimes there were advantages to having a doctor for a brother. Other people might have to find a dealer if they needed amphetamines. She always kept two tablets in her handbag in case of emergency. They were even legal. But she hadn't needed them yet. The wheel of images spun in her head. She and Elias in Tübingen. In the boat. In the garden at night. In bed in the morning. Elias, coming towards them on the café rooftop terrace and kissing her on the lips. 'Paul!' Mama had exclaimed. A wave of fear washed through her at the memory. As if it had been an omen. Elias was Paul. Elias was going to die like Paul.

No.

Nonononono. Mama was demented.

But the fear didn't leave just because she could say and think and shout 'No' as often as she liked. It was still possible. Twenty to twenty-five per cent.

She turned off somewhere near Hannover. It was just after two and the air was mild; even this layby smelled of robinia blossom. A May night, like something in an old folk song. Nature didn't care about anything. Paul had died on a glorious October day that had been so beautiful it hurt. Hurt the living, anyway. Those who were still able to experience it.

She typed an email to her boss. And to the team. Although it wasn't very likely that she'd still have her job at the end of the week. Then she checked whether Jule had replied. Nothing. She sent her another message. Instagram. Facebook. What else did girls use these days? TikTok? Could you DM people on there? She had no idea, and no time either. What was the situation with his parents anyway? They hadn't talked much about them. Not a very close relationship, she'd deduced that much. She remembered how patient and polite he'd been to Mama. Jesus Christ, what had she done?

She got in and slammed the door as hard as she could. I'm coming. Don't die. I'm coming.

By the time she was driving through the town to the hospital, it was just after six. At four, she'd needed to take a tablet after all. It was still quiet on the streets and she found a place to park right away. As she got out, she glanced quickly at her phone to see if Jule had answered yet, but it must still be too early.

Jan was waiting for her at the entrance.

'You look tired, sis,' he said with a tiny smile.

'You too. Thanks for being here.'

They walked down the hallway to the staff lift.

'How is he?'

The doors opened and Jan put his key in.

'He's been given a sedative and something for the fever. The op is scheduled for seven-thirty.'

'How can it go this fast? How does a thing like this happen?'

Jan shrugged. The lift doors glided open again. He pointed wordlessly to the sanitiser station and handed her a mask and a single-use gown.

'Nobody knows for certain. There's staph everywhere. On you. On me. Some open wound ... Doesn't make much difference, because there's not much you can do about it if your immune system doesn't get on top of it.'

The swing doors opened as Jan inserted his key again. He nodded to one of the nurses as they walked in. The ward was huge and looked very different from back then. The IV drip trolleys by every bed, which looked like bookcases on wheels. Folding screens between the beds. Everyone here was seriously ill. Her empty stomach contracted.

She spotted him at once. In a bed by the window.

Jan bent down to her.

'He might not remember you having been here afterwards. The anaesthetic generally wipes out the hours beforehand too.'

She nodded and walked to Elias. He looked so thin. Could you lose that much weight in a few days? She sat down next to him and took his hand without thinking.

'Elias,' she whispered, barely audible, more to herself.

Jan was standing at the foot of the bed.

'What's that?' she asked, pointing to Elias's hand.

'The spots?'

There were little black dots on the palms of his hands, and a bruise on his ring finger.

'It's from bleeding caused by the staph infection.'

Clara pointed impatiently to Elias's index finger. 'No, there!'

It was the infected nailbed she'd lanced that time. It still hadn't healed.

'I'll have to ask my colleagues if they've spotted it,' said Jan thoughtfully. 'That could be where the staph got into his system.'

Elias opened his eyes.

'Clara,' he whispered. 'Clara! How did you find me?'

She had to smile.

'Wasn't that hard. How are you? Are you in pain?'

Elias shook his head weakly. Looked around. Looked back at Clara.

'Is it true they're going to operate on me? I dreamt something like that. They ... I didn't believe them. Is it true?'

Jan stepped closer. 'The ward staff told you last night, and yesterday evening too. It's just that the meds keep making you forget. It's true. You need heart surgery. But they're very good at it. Really.'

Elias said nothing. He'd shut his eyes again. He seemed to have fallen asleep. But then, without opening his eyes, he asked 'Will you stay? Clara?'

It was hard to speak.

'Yes,' she said. 'I'll stay.'

He was asleep again.

They were standing on the cafeteria terrace. The elms tall and green in front of her. The sky wreathed in light veils of cloud that still made the morning light hazy. Jan had got her a coffee.

'I got them to show me the echocardiography images,' he said. 'It's like a string of staph hanging from the valve. The strand is a few millimetres long, which is quite a lot. Fragments loosen and come away all the time, and that's what causes the tissue haemorrhage – those dark spots you saw. And—'

He broke off. Turned to her and put his arm around her.

'Clara, they're very good at this. It's good that the doctor spotted the infection right away. Not every GP would have done. And it's a routine operation.'

Clara was holding on to her coffee mug far too tightly. She was staring between the trees. The last time she'd stood here, she'd been so in love. Everything had lain at her feet, open and new and wonderful. And it had all felt easy. There was none of that left, except a desperate love that might have come too late.

'Jan,' she began hesitantly. Speaking was an incredible strain on her. 'His nailbed was inflamed and oozing pus. So I ... lanced it. Is it possible that I ... Shit, is it my fault? Did I infect him?'

'Clara—' Jan began, but she stopped him right away.

'Tell me! Tell me the truth. I want to know if I...'

He gripped her by the shoulders. Almost angrily. 'I am! Let me speak. If you didn't use a knife that you'd previously dipped in staphylococci, then it's got nothing to do with it. There's staph everywhere. Was the blade sterile?'

She nodded. Of course.

'Did you disinfect the wound?'

'Yes,' she said with tears in her eyes.

'Then you did everything right. He should've gone to see a doctor about it, but the body can normally deal with that kind of thing. It's just fate. Just bad luck.'

'I didn't do everything right.'

She had to say it. Even if he hadn't been in hospital, even if he hadn't been seriously ill – the moment she'd seen him again, she'd known that he was the one.

'Jan,' she whispered chokingly, 'I can't bear it if he dies.'

38

Four hours. That's what they'd said. At least four hours. More like five.

She couldn't stand it in the cafeteria any longer. Jule had finally got in touch and they'd spoken. Somehow, Jule seemed a lot more composed than she was.

He'll make it, she'd said, Papa's strong. And that she could be there by midday at the latest, along with her mother. Clara had given them directions and told them where to park. She'd hoped it would take her mind off things for a while, but it hadn't worked. The fear thrummed within her like an over-tightened string on a violin. She walked, no she ran, around the grounds; constantly moving because everything else was too hard to deal with. She texted Vera Steiner that she was there, that Elias needed an operation. She had no idea whether or not Vera knew that, but she told her anyway. Not out of a sense of fairness, because Vera had texted her too. No, because none of it had any meaning anymore. As if they all had to stand together so that he wouldn't die. Jan hadn't said so, but the surgeon she'd met briefly had. If the strand came away from the valve and got into his bloodstream, there wouldn't be much left that they could do. And after the operation, it would be hard enough as it was to keep the infection under control. The fear was crowding out the hatred she ought to have felt at that moment. Then he'd put his hand on her arm for an instant and said: I'm a very good surgeon, Ms Wagenbach. He'll make it.

He'll make it.

He'll make it.

She knew that nobody could tell in advance. She knew it, but she kept repeating it to herself.

He'll make it.

She was outside the hospital grounds now. From up here, she could see far over the town. The tall church towers and expansive sea of red roofs that made up an ancient town were beautiful, but the beauty couldn't get through to her. None of it had anything to do with her.

She looked at the time. A little over two hours. And a message from Vera. *Please let me know if anything happens. Coming to the hospital at lunchtime.*

It reminded her that she needed to phone the office.

The conversation was far simpler than she'd been expecting: Good of you to call ... read your email. You started much earlier than expected anyway ... take the week ... get well soon to your partner.

My partner. It was no longer true. And right now, it didn't matter either way. She remembered standing with him at the rose garden wall in the driving snow, and suddenly there was this screaming panic inside her that that would never happen again. That he would cease to exist.

When her phone rang and she saw the hospital number, she knew that something wasn't right. Something had happened. Only two and a half hours – far, far, far too soon.

'Ms Wagenbach?'

A man's voice. Not the surgeon.

'Yes?'

Her voice shook. She couldn't breathe.

'I'm calling from intensive care. Your husband is here with us now and we're slowly bringing him off the ventilator. But so far so good. The operation went very well. As for everything else, we'll have to see.'

Clara had to sit down on the gravel path, and then she cried her eyes out in a way she hadn't done since childhood.

39

This evening at the earliest, they'd said. Anaesthetic. Painkillers. He wouldn't even know she was there.

She actually knew all that, or could have done if she'd been in a frame of mind to think clearly. Even so, she'd been drawn back to the hospital. At least they'd told her that Elias was off the ventilator and stable. Then she'd looked for Jan, but he'd been unavailable, had texted her that he could meet her at the end of his shift and then they could go to see him together. So, she was standing in the car park, waiting for Jule and her mother. She'd sent them the location and texted Jule that Elias had come through surgery well and was now in intensive care.

The sky was neither blue nor grey. A nondescript pale white with a few washed-out specks of blue here and there. Clara was still buzzing on the inside. The incredible relief from earlier had given way to a dull, deep-down unease. What had Jan said? It's a routine op. The infection is the danger. Or something like that. But at least he'd survived the first part.

She walked up and down at the car park entrance. Her phone buzzed. A message from Jule.

Nearly there.

When Jule's mother, Mona, got out, Clara was surprised by how young she looked. She knew from Elias what age she'd been when the two of them had been at stage school together, but she looked as though she was in her early thirties. Tops. And she was beautiful, truly beautiful. Even features that you might find in an early photo, from the late nineteenth century. His first great love ... Clara could see why.

Jule ran towards her, gave her a scared hug. You could tell that she'd been crying.

'How is he? We don't know a thing. What actually happened?'

Mona came over. Held out her hand. Her voice was as friendly as her face, with a slight accent that made her all the more charming.

'You're Clara, aren't you? He mentioned you in a message once. You don't mind me calling you Clara, do you? Can we see him?'

Clara didn't know what to say. Elias had told Mona about her?

She shook her head. 'Not till this evening, they said. Would you like ... we could get a coffee. I'll tell you everything. Is that OK with you?' she asked Mona. So strange to worry about etiquette and introductions at a time like this. But maybe that stopped you from just falling apart.

Mona nodded. 'Of course.'

They walked a little way up the Rothenberg, the way she'd been earlier as a distraction. There was an old villa that had been turned into a café. They found a spot on the terrace, from which you could see for miles, across the town and down into the valley.

'I think this is the first time I've been here,' Mona said, before they'd sat down. 'Pretty place.'

She has such an inner calm, Clara thought. Despite looking so young.

Jule was different. She seemed as uncertain as Clara herself. Just as overwhelmed by the pace of things. How quickly the fixed world around you could be blown apart. It had been like that with Paul too. She'd learnt that such things could happen, and yet this time it had hit her even harder. It must be similar for Jule.

She hastily told them both all she knew.

'Jan – my brother – is a doctor at the hospital. He's talking to his colleagues,' she concluded. 'I messaged him and he'll join us later, if that's all right with you. Vera Steiner too.'

Jule looked at her. 'Why? They split up.'

Yes. What should she say? That she and Elias ... Jule didn't know. It wasn't a good idea to tell her everything at once. And it didn't matter at the moment. But she still felt guilty.

'I was in Hamburg. So he must have phoned Vera. She went to

see him, and then called the doctor.' She hesitated a moment. 'She ... she's still very fond of him. She's just as worried as we are.'

'I don't know her,' Jule said in the end. 'But that's OK. I mean, it sounds like it was a good thing she was there.'

Vera and Jan arrived at much the same time, Vera first.

'I'm sorry I couldn't get away sooner,' she said, somewhat breathlessly. 'I've only just finished at the school.'

It was only then that Clara realised she hadn't even known Vera's job. She wouldn't have plumped for teacher. Maybe that was good. It said something in her favour.

Strange the way they were all meeting here. They barely knew each other. The only link between them all was Elias, and he wasn't here. It was slightly different with Jule, though. She felt a little closer to her after their day in Bayreuth together.

'This is Jule, Elias's daughter,' she introduced her. 'And this is Mona ... her mother.'

She'd hesitated a moment. Because she'd realised that all three of them were ex-girlfriends. Funny. Really funny to think of that just then.

Bitterness spread through her. She'd got it wrong. Again. First, she'd stayed with someone despite her feelings, and then she'd split up with someone despite her feelings. She was immediately ashamed of the thought. This wasn't about her. It was about Elias.

Vera Steiner looked at her, before sitting down.

'Can we be friends? I know I'm younger, but I'd like that.'

Clara studied her. No. She didn't mean anything by it. She was really like that. Almost naïve in her openness. There was no hidden barb, no you're older than me. I'm prettier than you.

Yes, I can understand him. That kind of thing can get on your nerves, but it can be very attractive too.

'Sure,' she said curtly. 'Clara.'

'I know,' Vera smiled.

Jule was looking awkward.

'So what happened? What's wrong with him?'

'May I?'

She hadn't seen Jan coming. Thank God he was here.

'I've just been with him and I had a chance for a brief chat with my colleagues. At the moment, he's still sedated and on a lot of painkillers, but everything seems to be OK. Mind if I join you?'

He pulled a chair up to the table, next to Clara. Squeezed her hand for a moment as he sat down. Almost whispered as he leant over to her. 'It's all OK for the moment.'

He looked around the table.

'You must be Jule. I'm Jan.'

He stood back up and shook hands with everyone. Clara smiled for the first time that day. Sometimes, Jan was like an overgrown boy. Jule seemed more friendly towards him than to Vera. Her face was an open book.

The waiter arrived. Everyone needed coffee. Nobody wanted anything to eat.

'It's a good thing you called the doctor so quickly, Ms Steiner,' Jan said appreciatively to Vera. 'Most people leave it too long.'

Clara couldn't stop herself in time.

'You can drop the formalities – we're all friends, apparently.'

Vera was too pleased by Jan's praise to respond to the slight needling.

'So here's the situation.' Jan leant in slightly. 'We now know what strain of staph bacteria we're dealing with. Some of them were extracted along with the heart valve, and we hope that not too many got into the bloodstream. But they're everywhere inside his body anyway, so he'll be on flucloxacillin for the next six to eight weeks.'

Jule looked questioningly at him.

'High-dose antibiotics,' Jan explained hastily.

He takes refuge in doing and explaining, like all men, thought Clara. But she got it. She wished there was something she could do too, rather than just waiting and hoping. And actually, so did Jan, he just wasn't admitting it. Or wasn't saying so with Jule at the table. Twenty to twenty-five per cent. A quarter of all patients die. The sudden fresh burst of fear made her gulp.

It was as though Jan had felt her fear. He paused a moment, then said pensively 'If he makes it to the weekend without running a fever, then it's all looking good. The first half is done. But the infection has to be flushed out of his body.'

'Isn't it bad to take antibiotics for that long?' Jule was worried.

Jan smiled wearily at her. 'Yes. But a staph infection is much worse. There's no alternative. Once the course is finished, they can start to build his gut flora back up again and all that.'

If he survives. Was that what you wanted to say, brother-dear? If he survives. She had to force herself to think of something else. Without much success.

'Do you think we'd be able to see him?'

Jan shrugged. 'Perhaps. But he'll have very little memory of it later. The first few days after such a major op are always a blur. Maybe not all at once.'

'And all that from such a little cut on his finger?' There was astonishment in Mona's voice as she asked.

Jan stared into the distance, across the town as he replied: 'We always forget that small, insignificant things can kill. A tick. A mosquito. A rusty nail.'

An unexpected separation. Or the tiny thorn from the dog rose in her hedge getting under his fingernail. Wasn't that where it had all started? She couldn't fight the dark thoughts.

Jan turned back to them. It was as though he was seeing them all properly for the first time.

'It's nice that you're all here. It'll be good for him. Some patients lie there alone for weeks. It really does help. There are studies—'

Vera interrupted. 'What about his heart?'

Yes. Clara was interested in that too. What was up with Elias's heart, in every respect?

For a tiny moment, Jan looked from Vera to Clara and back again, then said with a fine, barely perceptible smile: 'It will heal. That happens very quickly. The prosthetic valve is made of carbon and will last a hundred years. But he'll have to take blood thinners for the rest of his life. No contact sports. No skiing and nothing where you can bruise easily.'

Clara couldn't help thinking about sex. About their time in bed together. No contact sports? She'd ask Jan later, when they were alone. Sometime later. She was already wishing she could roll herself up into a tiny ball of shame and rage at her own stupidity, or else just give way to her tiredness, put her head down on the table and sleep. Just to get rid of the pictures in her head. All the pictures of her and Elias, in the knowledge that she would never be able to have that again.

'Come at around nine – they might let you see him. That's just after the change of shift, so it's quieter then. It might work. What will you do in the meantime?' He turned to Clara. 'Are you going to the flat?'

She didn't know. She'd made no plans beyond this morning.

'No idea. I could go to the flat. Or visit Mama. I can't get any proper sleep either way.'

Jan stood up. 'I have to get back. But I'll be around again this evening.'

They paid and walked back to the car park together. Clara could feel that she'd driven all night. Everything in this hyper-focused wakefulness was too bright and too loud.

'How are you?' Jule was walking beside her. She looked pale but with the assurance that probably only comes with youth. 'It'll be all right. He'll get better.'

Ahead of them, Jan was walking with Vera, who was asking all kinds of questions. Mona was listening in silence. Clara slowed down, let the rest of them get three, four paces ahead. She took a trembling breath. Jule had been honest with her. She ought to know. No clue if she'd understand, but she had to know.

'I did something very stupid,' she said. 'And right now, I'm scared that I won't be able to put it right.' Her voice grew hoarse. 'Or that it's too late.'

'What's that?' asked Jule.

'I split up with Elias,' said Clara.

Jule stopped. Total surprise.

'But you're … I don't think I'd ever seen Papa as happy. And you … you were too … It looked like you two were made for each other, so perfect. What happened?'

Clara shook her head. It was no good.

'I just wanted you to know. I can't talk about it now. Please.'

Jule gave her a long look, then a restrained nod.

'See you this evening,' she said, picking up speed to catch up with Mona.

She straightened her shoulders. What was this? It wasn't her lying in intensive care, fighting for her life. Her tiny sorrow was nothing at all. She had no right to have Jule or anyone else understand her.

They'd reached the car park.

'I'll go to see Mama,' Clara said curtly, walking to her car without saying goodbye.

40

The care home was in the leafy suburbs on the edge of town. Her parents had picked it out years ago, on their urging. So she'd been here twice before, but she still had to get her bearings as she walked through the large grounds. Back then, they hadn't been expecting Mama to end up in the secure dementia section. Nobody had been expecting that.

The carer who opened the door to her was very friendly, but when she gave her name and said who she was here to visit, he seemed kind of embarrassed.

'You're Mrs Wagenbach's daughter? Would you mind popping into the office for a moment before you go? The manager would like to speak to you about your mother.'

'Is she ill?'

Clara was almost too tired to be properly startled. Everything always happened at once.

'No, not ill.' The carer walked down the corridor towards the day room with her. No matter how expensive a place like this was, it still smelled of old folks' home. Bulk catering. Cleaning sprays. Disinfectant. And always a whiff of urine. Some of the people in the day room were sitting at the tables in wheelchairs, not moving. Others were walking up and down, and although some of them seemed younger than Mama, it all came as a shock because Mama had never looked that fragile.

'She's in the garden,' said the carer, pointing to a corner where there was a little wooden summerhouse. Clara could see her mother sitting there.

'Thanks,' she said. 'So, where exactly should I come along to afterwards?'

'The office is right by the entrance. I'll catch up with you then.'

The garden was large, almost a park. A shallow pond, gravel

paths, flower beds – they'd made an effort. Then she saw the bus stop. A bus stop in the middle of the grounds? A few elderly people were waiting there. It was only as she walked past them that she realised the bus stop wasn't real. The sign that would normally show the direction of travel merely read *Home*. That could mean one of two things – going home, or the home. Either way, it was clever. Clever and desperately sad. Her mother had always wanted to go home, wherever that was. That was why she'd run away. Except she'd never gone by bus. Not as long as she'd been able to take the car.

Her mother was sitting in the summerhouse, her cheeks flushed hectic and red, breathing fast.

'Hello, Mama.'

Her mother looked up at her. It was the first time that there hadn't been a spontaneous recognition, even when she'd said Toni or Paul or Hello.

'It's me, Mama, Clara.'

Mama said nothing. She was looking angry and tugging at the watchstrap around her wrist. Clara didn't recognise the watch. Her mother had always worn a slim, gold one. This was an ugly, bulky digital watch with a thick rubber strap. No wonder her mother hated it. Clara wanted to help her undo the clasp, but she couldn't. Apparently, it was locked and would take some kind of tool to open it.

'Mama, how are you?'

'Shit!' Mama said loudly.

Clara almost burst out laughing. The first logical answer in months. Her mother jumped up and almost ran to the fence. Threw herself against it. Then she knelt down and tried to pull the wire fence up from the ground, her tongue poking between her teeth with the effort. The way she'd looked thirty years ago, if she'd been trying to hang a garden gate on her own, or to heave the suitcases for their holidays into the car. Clara's father had never been any help. He'd always come along too late for Mama's impatience.

'Mama, stop. You can't go out that way. Would you like to show me your room?'

No chance. She didn't know if her mother had even heard her. She was running along the fence like a cat, looking for somewhere to slip through.

'Mama.' She tried to take her arm. 'Look, come with me.'

'Shit!' Mama shouted, furious again. Clara knew what she meant. If you looked at it from Mama's point of view, it *was* shit. She'd been locked up in a strange house, by strangers, surrounded by strangers, and had no idea how it had happened. No cat. No husband. No children. Just a prison that she'd wound up in, not knowing why. Clara would go mad too in a situation like that, she thought. It didn't matter how lovely the garden was. Clara let go of her.

'Mama, shall we go for a coffee?'

Maybe she could take her out for an hour, and get her calmed down. But it didn't work. She wasn't listening, just striding along the fence again, taking long, hectic steps. Clara let her. It had never done any good to try to talk to Mama when she was angry. You had to let her work it off.

Clara walked back through the day room, into the house, and found the manager's office. There was a Mrs Nowak sitting there at the desk. Small. Round. Resolute. She offered her a chair and came straight to the point.

'Ms Wagenbach, your mother is causing us concern. I've never seen anything like it, to be honest.'

Clara waited. The woman spoke rapidly and briskly.

'Lots of people are unsettled when they come to us. It's normal with dementia. But your mother ... she smashed the chair in her room. She won't let anyone touch her. She rampages. She even ... well, she didn't only wet herself, she went in the corridor, in a corner.'

She says went. Baby talk. They spend the whole day here dealing with all manner of excretions, so they really could call the thing by name.

'What are you saying?' Clara asked. 'That you can't have her here?'

The woman shook her head. 'No. But we can't manage like this. She needs medication and we can't prescribe that here. She needs mental-health care, in hospital.'

'I'm sorry?'

The sorry was disbelief, not incomprehension. Mama wasn't mentally ill.

Mrs Nowak tried to explain.

'This isn't uncommon. Dementia is linked to anxiety and depression. That needs to be treated. Who is her guardian? You? We need your agreement, and then we can transport her over today.'

Clara shook her head. Transport. The woman was talking about her mother like an object.

'My brother. And my father. I need to speak to them. I don't think we ... that they will agree without question. I mean, how long has my mother been like this?'

'Since the first minute!' Mrs Nowak was pretty agitated herself now. 'My staff can't deal with it. I've had a one-to-one carer with her for three days. There are no knives here and no scissors, and I don't know how she managed it, but your mother has cut the strap on her GPS watch twice. Or hacked it off. The straps are reinforced. I have no idea how she does it. I've never had that. I couldn't get hold of your father, or your brother either.'

No wonder. Jan never answered if he didn't recognise the number. Clara stood up. She really didn't need a semi-hysterical care-home manager today.

'Yes. My mother is a determined woman. Always has been. I'll speak to my brother and we'll call you later today. What is the alternative?'

Mrs Nowak threw her hands up exaggeratedly. 'We can't keep her here. We simply can't manage like this.'

Clara nodded and walked out of the room. Yet again, not

saying goodbye. Today wasn't a day for courtesies. On her way out, she looked around for her mother. She was still standing at the fence, full of wordless fury, and barely responded to her.

'Bye, Mama,' Clara said all the same, trying to hug her. Her mother fought her off. So she just stroked her back in a gesture of farewell. Which she accepted. Clara was incredibly tired.

41

It was the first morning when he felt he'd woken up properly. He'd certainly been aware of some things over the last few days, but it had been as if it had all happened on a stage. You were there, you were part of the cast, yet you knew that none of what you were doing was real. He'd felt like that when they'd moved him from the ICU to the high-dependency unit; when they'd told him that he now had a prosthetic heart valve; when, on the second or third day, they'd come to operate on his finger, local anaesthetic, ten minutes, done and dusted; and lastly, when they'd moved him to a ward. He'd woken up there.

Properly awake. For the first time in ... how long? He lay very still. His throat was still a little raw. That was from the ventilator, the nurse had said. One of the many nurses he'd seen in the last few days.

It must still be pretty early. It was light and the strip of sky he could see was a delicate blue. The brick wall a few metres from his window glowed a friendly red. He seemed to be on the ground floor.

He went back over it all in his mind. All he could properly remember of it. He had no memory at all of the day of the operation itself, but Jule had told him they'd all been there. Her. Clara's brother and ... Clara herself.

He cautiously felt for the tube in his neck. The antibiotics.

We have to put the cannula in your neck. It will be months. You don't have enough places on your wrist to set up such a long-term drip.

An infected nailbed. From a tiny thorn. And now he had an artificial heart valve.

He looked out. The top of the wall was gradually changing colour. The sun would soon be high enough to shine into the room.

He was alive. Jan – weirdly, Jan was his most frequent visitor, came at least twice a day – he had explained how seriously ill he'd been. He'd been in no pain. Only the fever. There was pain now though. With every breath.

We had to saw through your sternum. No swimming this year. No press-ups, no weight-training, no cycling, don't lift anything one-handed. Not even shopping bags. Or something might shift out of place and make it heal wonky.

Cycling ... as if he could. He was weaker than he'd ever been in his life. Yesterday, they'd let him stand up for the first time. Just standing. After three minutes, he'd been so out of breath that he'd been glad to lie back down again.

Press-ups. Clara on her parquet floor in her flat. In leggings and a sports bra. She hated it, thought she looked silly. He liked it.

He used to like it.

Yesterday, Jule had come to see him again before she had to go back to school. Mona had been there too, but he couldn't remember it.

What day was it today? He sat up a little. That hurt too. Really hurt. They'd shown him yesterday how to raise himself up on the bars, so as not to strain his chest, but it was still awful.

He pulled open the drawer in the bedside trolley. No phone. He couldn't even remember how he'd got to the hospital. The last image in his mind's eye was of Vera in his flat. Oh yes, and the doctor. He'd have to ask someone to bring him some stuff. Mareike maybe. He could call her at the theatre.

The theatre. Mareike. Clara. Vera. Jule. Something had grabbed him and whacked him around the head and plucked him out of his life. Completely. That was how it felt. Like a pawn that's been taken off the chess board.

Four to six weeks here. And then six weeks' rehab. We'll have to see where we can put you. We'll have to see how well the antibiotics kick in. We'll have to see how well you recover. We'll have to see when we can get you on the blood thinners.

We'll have to see.

The window was slightly open. He could hear a cuckoo calling. He'd read somewhere that cuckoos still kept arriving at the same time in spring, even though other birds had already started coming sooner, because of climate change, and so the cuckoos couldn't lay their eggs in their nests in time.

Cuckoo, cuckoo, tell me true, how many more years will I live through?

A children's rhyme.

But he'd always had a superstitious fear of reciting it. Because the cuckoo had always been calling for a while already by the time you asked him. So he could quite easily stop really quickly and then you'd know you only had three or four or five years.

Cuckoo, cuckoo, tell me true, how many more years will I live through with my new heart, half flesh, half carbon?

He pulled a face. Not a real smile. He'd never have bought it on stage: what's the problem? You wanted a new life. Here you are – here it is.

What now?

He didn't know how he felt. He should be happy. Everyone – everyone here had told him how lucky he'd been. What a close shave it had been. But he hadn't known the danger he'd been in. He'd only been dreaming. Maybe that was why he was short on the happiness that everyone else seemed to feel.

And perhaps he was short on happiness because Clara had taken it from him not long before. He lifted his hand and looked at the bandage on his finger. The dog rose in the fence he'd climbed. He'd been carrying that little pain around with him for some time, yet he hadn't even managed to get through the hedge of thorns to her.

'Good morning!' Jan walked in. 'How's my personal private patient this morning?'

'You're here more often than my ward round,' said Elias. His voice was still a lot hoarser than he expected. Hopefully that would get better soon. He couldn't talk like this.

Jan stood beside his bed and checked the drip. Presumably as a doctor you just did that, even though it wasn't your ward.

'I don't know how I am. Everything hurts.'

'That's good,' said Jan, opening the window wide. 'That's how you know you're still alive. But seriously, you're making good progress.'

'I can't stand up for even five minutes. That's not progress.'

It helped to talk to him.

'For someone who could've spent the rest of his life dead or in a coma, five minutes are excellent.'

Jan was unfazed, and Elias had to laugh. It hurt. Jan sat down beside his bed.

'My sister wants to know if she can visit you.'

'What day is it today?' asked Elias.

Jan took his hand and pretended to take his pulse.

'Maybe the infection got into the brain,' he said gravely, as if to himself. 'The man is talking nonsense. I ask him if he wants a visitor and he asks for the day of the week. Saturday.'

Elias tried to explain his thought processes. 'She's still in Hamburg, though, right?'

Jan sobered up. 'She's been here all week. Since the morning of your op. She drove through the night to be here, and she's been here ever since.'

'We split up. You know that, don't you?'

The memory of the gazebo was the last to be sharp and cold and clear. After that, things had started to get fuzzy and feverish and nasty.

Jan nodded. 'Yes. I do know. Do you want to see her anyway? I mean, your other exes pop in now and then. Once you're back to full health, would you mind letting me in on how you do that?'

Clara. Of course he wanted to see her, more than anyone. He missed her so much. But at the same time, it was as though the fever, the illness had started with her. Or rather, at the moment she'd distanced herself from him. Their first serious row, about

Hamburg, the day after the storm. He tried to shake his head, to clear his mind. But a sharp pain immediately stabbed his chest and he groaned involuntarily.

'Is that a yes or a no?' Jan enquired.

'Sure,' Elias said, 'tell her she's welcome to come.'

Jan smiled. 'Great. I'll tell her. She's waiting outside.'

'Now?' Elias was alarmed. He didn't know why.

'Did you have plans?' Jan retorted teasingly.

Elias tried to sit up straighter.

'OK,' he said, 'OK.'

Jan went to the door, opened it, then closed it behind him as Clara stepped into the room.

It was the first time she'd seen him since right after the operation. He'd looked so awful – the infusion lines, the catheter, the orange of the disinfectant up to his neck and down his legs, the deep exhaustion in his face. Today, he seemed more like himself, although he still looked thin.

'Hello,' she said, very uncertainly.

The sun was over the top of the wall. The morning light was making the place about as bright and friendly as a hospital room could be. Elias studied Clara, unable to answer right away. She looked very elegant in her pale-grey suit, and very serious.

'Hello,' he croaked.

'May I sit down?' She gestured to the chair beside his bed.

He nodded. Between them was ... well, what was it?

'How are you?'

That was the one good thing about this situation. She could open with that question without it sounding funny.

'Your brother says I'm doing well. I think—' He broke off. He wasn't in the mood to tell her that he'd never felt this weak and vulnerable in his whole life. His body was the tool of his trade, his capital. Movement. Voice. Strength. None of that was left. He didn't even know, hadn't dared ask himself, if he'd ever be able to act again.

What's up with him? I'm getting it all wrong again. I want to get it right this time and I can't find the way.

'My mother is here too. In the hospital. On the geriatric mental health ward.'

Why am I telling him that? I'm looking for a beginning. I'm looking for a place to start.

'Why?'

It didn't sound inviting, he knew that. But why was she talking about her mother? What kind of visit was this?

She filled him in briefly on her visit to the care home and explained that they had, eventually, decided on anti-depressants. Because there'd been no other way. He smiled briefly as she told him that her mother had smashed up a chair in her rage.

'You're not dissimilar,' he said. Elias looked at her, sitting straight-backed in her chair, her knees barely twenty centimetres from the edge of the bed. Her beautiful knees. 'Clara, why are you here?'

Because I love you.

Because I love you and I hadn't even realised how much.

Because I love you and I wish I could take it all back and put us back in that gazebo and kiss you and just say: Yes, let's try it.

She sought his eyes. They met hers for a moment, then he looked out of the window into the sunshine.

'I think I made a mistake,' she began hesitantly. 'No, I don't think so, I know I did. It was all wrong, Elias.'

'Because I got ill?' he interrupted hoarsely. 'When I was fifteen or sixteen, I was in love. Or so I thought. Very unrequited. Anyway, she didn't want anything to do with me. And I kept imagining what it would be like if I had an accident or was dead or something, and how sorry she'd be, and then she'd notice how much she loved me. But love doesn't work like that.'

Did that matter? She'd so love to take his hand. As if that would get her thoughts through to him more directly. Not via the uncertain means of words, which always sounded different to the way you meant them.

'I know,' she started again. 'But on the Monday evening, when I realised my mistake, I didn't even know you were ill; I was standing in a park. Where you can see over the water, and across the port, and I missed you so badly. I wanted to share it with you. It didn't mean a thing, all alone, but with you...'

She paused. He waited. Because it wasn't that simple. Because the last few days had changed everything. As if he first had to rediscover his emotions. As if his heart was still numb. A great spotted woodpecker was hopping around on the wall. It looked like an amazing spring day and a furious longing for the outside world engulfed him.

'What changed, then?' he asked. Speaking was still something of an effort. 'They say I'll have to be in here for the next four to six weeks. And then at least six weeks' rehab. Maybe three months. You're in Hamburg. And then ... I don't even know if I'll ever act again. I don't know a thing.'

Now that he'd said it aloud, it really hit him: he had no future now. He'd been sidelined. The world was moving on without him.

'Jan says you'll be totally ... that you'll be able to live a pretty much normal life. But it'll take a while.'

She wanted to be encouraging, but his thinned-down face closed off even further. She heard his tone change.

'You know,' he said slowly, 'I can understand much better now what you were saying in that gazebo. That I should be realistic, and how often we'd really get to see each other, and how we'd get through it and that you don't want a relationship like that. You want everything.'

He paused and looked out of the window again. The

woodpecker had gone. The sun was high enough to paint a cheerful rectangle of light on the lino floor.

'Yes,' said Clara, 'I said all that. But it was wrong.'

'No,' Elias said wearily. He had hefty chest pains with every breath, but that fitted. 'It was true.'

A quick knock, a nurse came into the room. Without saying much, she changed the bag on the drip and vanished again. The silence that had come with her was impenetrable. Why couldn't she touch him? It wasn't that long since every touch they'd shared had been perfectly natural. In a way she'd never known with anyone else. And now they were like two magnets with the same polarity. They could no longer come close without resistance, and they could no longer touch.

'Like you said – how's a relationship like that meant to work? Even if I wanted to – I can't just move to Hamburg any more. I—'

He interrupted himself and looked at her. This beautiful, upright woman he could no longer reach, without being able to explain why not. It was a bitter feeling.

'What do you even want with me? You know, you told me what it was like for you back then. With Paul. Do you think ... do you really believe either of us could bear that? Do you want to nurse me and check in on me every two weeks? Or give your job up again and push me around in a wheelchair until I can walk? And give everything up, yet again, for a sick man? Clara, it'll destroy everything we...'

He couldn't finish the sentence. Caught in my own words. I'm caught in my own words. I said all that and externally it was true and internally it was false.

'You're not Paul,' said Clara helplessly. The words were intended to convey everything he was to her and the whole enormous and wonderful feeling she'd found for him in herself, but it just sounded flat.

I'm exhausted. She looks so lovely in this light and I can't feel a thing and I don't know a thing either.

'Clara,' he said. 'It's not so good for me when you're here. We've lost something, haven't we? First you couldn't trust my love. You split up with me because you didn't believe that I could love you when we were far apart, or because you're older than me, or maybe just because you didn't trust yourself. And you know the funny thing? Today, I think you were right. Maybe you can't ask everything of love, after all. Maybe it can't sustain too many bad days, after all. Mine or yours. But I don't want to live through it growing tired. That's what you said. I think...' He hesitated, but then spoke quickly: 'I think it would be better if you didn't come again.'

She stood up slowly. Looked down at the box of sunshine and then out into the blue.

'That's it?' Her voice was raw too. 'That's it for us?'

Elias just glanced up at her. Nodded. He couldn't trust his voice.

'Goodbye, Elias,' said Clara, but it sounded like a question.

When no answer came, because he still couldn't speak, she went, shutting the door quietly behind her.

42

The days blurred. The hospital routines were so set and structured that even the smallest variety was a welcome change. He could stand for longer now, but how far he could wander was limited by needing to wheel the drip stand with him. He felt like a slapstick character in an old black-and-white comedy, and he was starting to hate the thing. Quite apart from the ever-present needle in his neck.

'You're going to have a series of extremely interesting scars,' Jan had said on one of his recent visits.

How strange that was. He hadn't seen Clara for almost two weeks now, but Jan came almost every day and his flying visits were their highlights. It was like a delicate, budding friendship between them, even though Jan's visits constantly reminded him of Clara. Jan never asked what had happened between him and her. Conversations with him had a weight of their own because Elias could sense behind Jan's flippancy the person who'd become a doctor because, in his restrained way, he liked the people he treated. You really couldn't say that of every doctor in this hospital.

'Why aren't I allowed to cycle when they make me go on this thing every day?'

He was sitting on an exercise bike outside the ward door, trying to pedal evenly. It was tiring.

'Because we need the energy you're generating to power this place,' said Jan, who was slumped in a visitor's armchair, watching him. 'If you stop, we won't be able to resuscitate anyone else. So, keep going. And keep your pulse under a hundred and twenty.'

Every time he went on the bike, they attached a heart-rate monitor to him. No going to the max. Never again, in fact. The max! He'd worked up a sweat, but according to the display, he'd done less than seven hundred metres. If Jan hadn't been there, he'd have given up in frustration by now. Seven hundred metres. There'd been days when he'd ridden a hundred kilometres. Thinking about it at night sometimes brought him to tears. He couldn't help it. He'd never been this weak in his life before.

Jan sensed his mood and leant forwards. 'Because in real-world cycling, you occasionally have to turn around or look over your shoulder. That could make your sternum twist out of alignment and stop the bones healing as solidly as they should. Give it a year and you'll be fine. You'll be able to get back to all that, I promise.' He stood up and looked at the speedo. 'Today you'll do two kilometres.'

'Two kilometres to where?'

Elias almost turned around in the saddle as he heard Vera's cheerful voice, but remembered in time what Jan had just said.

'I see you're making progress. He is, isn't he?'

She rested her hand very gently on his back as she walked past, an almost tender gesture of familiarity, before saying hello to Jan, to whom Elias pointed breathlessly.

'Progress! He's just informed me that in a year or two, I'll be able to participate in society again. In the best case.'

'There's not much going on out there,' said Vera.

It was as though they'd reached a silent agreement that she could visit as if there'd never been anything between them. Vera acted as light and optimistic and cheerful as ever. The good part was that he no longer had to look behind the scenes to find out if that was all a façade, if she was hiding certain thoughts and wishes behind her open smile, and expecting him to guess. That was over, and in a strange way, it hurt.

'I brought you something to read.'

She put a bag of books on the glass table between the armchairs.

It seemed like she'd stopped wanting him at all costs.

My market value has dropped considerably now that I can only cycle two Ks. Cool phrase. You could use it in a play. If I can ever get back on stage. And even if I can, they might not want me anymore. Like Vera.

How bizarre his trains of thought could be. He didn't love Vera and had never loved her. But to feel that she suddenly no longer loved him – that had shaken him.

He kept pedalling in silence and watched Jan and Vera chatting, not listening to them.

So that was what he'd been like. Someone who could easily get what he wanted. Not always, obviously, but more often than other people. He'd taken it for granted, made use of the effect on others. On stage, you were always seen in a good light, and that didn't wear off right away. It was easy to be modest when you were the focal point. Now that he'd been taken out of the game and was watching on from the sidelines, it no longer felt so good. Modesty had been like a flattering suit; he'd known he looked slim and handsome in it. It didn't come from the inside. He'd only dressed himself in it. And now? Now he had real grounds for modesty – he looked pitiful.

'I'm stopping now,' he said breathlessly, getting cautiously down from the bike.

'And I've got work to do. I'll pop in again after my shift. And if you like,' Jan added to Vera in passing, 'come along to orthopaedics later and I'll show you what you need to do.'

Apparently, they'd been discussing her recurrent back problems. Her coccyx. That was so typical of Vera. Totally unself-conscious. If she met an orthopaedist, she told him about her orthopaedic problems. Perhaps that was how everyone should be.

Vera picked up the bag of books and walked him back to his room.

'Seriously, you look so, so much better.'

Elias had to smile. She always did that.

'Vera, I might have believed one "so". Because I want it to be true. But two ... well, that tells me how things really are.'

'No,' she contradicted vehemently, holding the door for him. 'Seriously! You do look better.'

He pushed the drip stand over to the bed, sat down and raised his legs. The nurse had shown him how to get onto it without putting too much strain on his chest. He felt like ... no, he *was* an invalid.

'Thanks for coming that day. And for calling the doctor. Good job you did. I don't think I've ever said thank you.'

Vera opened the window. It was a rainy day and the cool air streaming in smelled good.

'You'd have done the same,' she said with a shrug. 'When do you start the physio?'

'As soon as they've found a place for me. It might be here. Don't mind either way. Doesn't make a difference where you're not allowed out from.'

Vera sat down and crossed her legs. It wasn't that warm a day, but she was wearing a thin dress. She liked buying clothes. Not usually the best quality. She always cared more about how a dress looked than how it felt.

'Why did you split up?' she asked in a tone that was aiming for nonchalant. 'Want to talk about it?'

Elias lay back slightly. He still tired easily.

'Wrong way round, Vera,' he said, not sure if he should be annoyed. It wasn't worth it. 'You have to ask me if I want to talk about it first, and then ask the question. God! Why do people split up? She got a job in Hamburg and long-distance relationships never really work. Certainly wouldn't now.'

It was only half the truth. He wanted to correct himself and tell her that it had been Clara who'd broken up with him, but Vera seemed to draw her own conclusions and get in first.

'You didn't get involved with her either. Good that she realised sooner than I did. You're incapable of getting involved with anyone, Elias.'

No, he thought, that's not true. I wanted to commit to her. Completely and truly.

'But at least she got to meet your daughter.'

He almost laughed. 'Vera! Seriously? You ask me if I want to talk about it but really, it's you doing the talking. About you and me. Yes, you're right. I didn't get involved with you because we weren't actually well suited to each other. You wanted a man you could buy a house with. A man you could have kids with, and settle down in that house with. That was never me. I didn't want a house and I already have a child. You thought I'd change if you just loved me enough. And I ended up dishonest because I let you believe that. Look, I'm glad you were there. You did everything right. You saved my life and I'll be eternally grateful for that. Truly, with my whole heart. Isn't that enough for you?'

She was quiet a moment.

'And now everything's changed anyway,' he added. 'First, I have to get my head around what I can still do. I don't know what's going to happen.'

Vera nodded. Smiled.

'You have to start by getting well again. I've read a lot about it. Most people get back to a normal life. There are just some things where you have to be a bit more careful.'

Yes. Thanks for not spelling it out. They'd given him brochures. You can travel abroad if ... There's no problem with the occasional glass of wine if you take care not to ... Moderate levels of sport and exercise are fine if ... These foods are best avoided if you don't ... If. If. If.

He smiled. The way he'd used to smile when neither of them knew what to say because their views were too far apart. But at least it was an honest smile.

'Go and see Jan and let him treat your coccyx. I'll just hang around here and get a bit of R&R, OK?'

She approached the bed for a hug. He did his best, with a needle in his neck.

'Thanks, Vera,' he said again. It was more than just thanks for having called the doctor. It was a heartfelt thanks for her patience and for the good times too, perhaps; and maybe it was also something like an apology that they hadn't been right for each other. She might have understood that, because when she pulled away, her eyes were glittering.

'See you, Elias,' she said as she left.

'See you,' said Elias.

A fine drizzle was sparkling on the elm leaves by the redbrick wall. Wafting through the open window was the fine, sharp smell of wet, mown grass, and he couldn't help thinking about Clara all the time, and he was desperate and alone.

43

She was cycling around the edge of the park. She'd been avoiding the park itself since coming back to Hamburg. Even though she'd never been here with Elias. But the day she'd sat alone here in the café after her interview and phoned him she'd still felt as though all the promises made by that early spring would be fulfilled. Now it was the beginning of June and the summer to come had broken all its promises. It was still chilly enough to ride fast. It rarely got as warm here, up north, as it did at home. She cycled beneath the trees leaning over into the park and occasionally looked up at them. This strange interval when all the explosive force of the first blossoms, the overflowing of colour and scent on every bush, every tree, on every meadow, when that wave of colourful desire had ebbed away and the trees were just plain green. That was how she felt. Yes. Alive. But not blooming.

Four weeks since she'd last seen Elias. Five since his operation. There were times when she didn't even ask Jan how Elias was doing. Not because she was afraid of seeming weak. That wouldn't bother her so long as she knew herself to be strong. She and Jan had always told each other everything. But when it came to Elias, she really was weak. She wanted to know how he was, but was afraid of thinking about him. Because it wouldn't stop hurting. Jan sensed that and only spontaneously mentioned him now and again.

Guess what, he'd said, last time they'd spoken: Elias went to visit Mama in mental health. It's right next to the rehab clinic, and he asked after her. Because she doesn't get so many visitors. And then he actually went.

She'd had to end the conversation hastily, because she'd abruptly lost control of her voice. She'd been so surprised by what Jan had told her, that she couldn't utter a word for yearning and supressed tears and God knows what else. Elias had gone to visit Mama.

She looked up again before putting the park behind her. You couldn't see whether or not the unobtrusive plane-tree flowers had started forming into little balls.

Not everything that blooms in the spring bears fruit.

Four weeks. As if the pain would go away if she counted the weeks in between. It wasn't wrong, what people said about time healing wounds. The strange emptiness that had remained after Paul's death had imperceptibly filled with the years. But then she'd wanted the pain to go. Paul was dead. Elias was not.

She was coasting downhill now. It was good to be out this early, and Clara preferred getting to the office first thing to working late. When she reached the English Church, she braked. Then, she didn't know why, she leant her bike against the wall and gave the door a doubtful try. It was really very early, but to her surprise, the church was open. She'd often ridden past, but never gone in. Inside, the church was predominantly white. The ceiling was flat, not vaulted, but still high, and the lamps hanging down from it were also white. There was red carpet in the aisles and the pews were in simple wood, yet despite it all, the nave seemed bright. If there was such a thing as a calm, courteous church, this was it. As if the entire interior was trying to say have a seat, if you like. But don't let me keep you if you have other things to do. We'll still be here later.

She sat in one of the pews and looked at the altar. The painting of the Virgin Mary was the only really colourful thing in this church. Even the pipes above the white organ in its white loft between the white pillars were such a pale silver that they didn't stick out.

The only times Clara had been in any church in years, she'd been sight-seeing, or there for work, to photograph it. 'Just because' hadn't happened for a long time. She sat very straight, absorbing all the images.

I am where I want to be.

The job was a lot of work, and she had far less opportunity for photography than she'd expected. Most of it was looking at photos, negotiating with agencies, coordinating freelancers, but she didn't mind. It was good to organise things, to give them a structure. And then – the company did still have a studio. It wasn't often used these days, but it was there. And she had plans for it. She was building something entirely new, and she was good at it. No job was perfect, but this was exciting. A thousand times better than the overly sloppy routines back at the newspaper.

The silence in the church was deep and beautiful. But it was as though she could only see that from the outside. As though it could be beautiful for someone, so long as that someone wasn't her.

I'm where I want to be. Just without the man I want to be with. Maybe that simply doesn't exist for me.

How many thoughts could race through your mind at once when you were this still! He's not dead. Maybe someday ... time heals ... there comes a time when it's a scar and no longer hurts ... if you were here, you'd take my hand ... maybe you'd sing. For me. Like you sang in the car once, do you remember ... on that Saturday, you were standing there between the trees and I don't need a single one of my photos of you to know what you looked like. Your smile, Elias. That smile without the politeness that you can have with almost everyone else, but not when you look at me ... looked at me. Your hands crossed on my belly when you hug me from behind...

She bit her bottom lip until the iron taste of blood came.

Stop!

Almost six weeks since that day in the gazebo. And only the few short words since then, when she'd been able to visit him. Her visit to him that had cleared nothing up between them. It had been like an inversion of their conversation in the gazebo. Then, she hadn't believed that Elias could love her. An older woman. And a distance of six hundred kilometres. And then, once she'd finally found the courage and the faith in the memory of his laugh, his face, his hands, and come to him with that trust, he had lost it.

Ha, missed the moment. Not for the first time in her life.

After talking to Jan, she'd drunk too much wine and then written another letter. Which, the next morning, furious at herself, she'd thrown away.

She stood up. Time to get to the office, if she wanted to be in before the others. She was almost at the door when she turned back. By the quire, there was a slender sand tray on long metal legs. There were a few burnt-out stumps stuck in it. She dropped a coin into the offertory box, picked up a fresh candle and lit it.

For you, Elias.

It was the only candle burning in the church when she left.

44

'When d'you think you'll be up to acting again?'

Mareike had come to see him, and they were sitting on a bench in the clinic garden. The cuckoo was calling from the copse on the hill. It was a very warm day; the grass was starting to show yellow at the tips because it was so long since it had rained. Elias shrugged. Of course, he felt better in general, but he still had the drip at his side and the canula in his neck. On the other side now – it was in its fifth site by this point – but it was still there. Even if he'd wanted to, he couldn't have exercised properly. He was still so thin that he got cold much sooner in the evenings and mornings than ever before.

'Let Tom take the part, and I'll do the voiceover from here.'

Mareike laughed. Tom couldn't deliver a line, but he'd been at the theatre for approximately a century, and therefore had to be cast again and again.

'I have no idea, to be honest. I hope they might discharge me in three or four weeks. And then it might be another fortnight or so before I'm fit for anything. It'll all be different. I'm not allowed to cycle for a year. Or swim. And I'm bored to death here. I can't sleep at night because I'm not tired enough, and the thoughts start circling, and my emotions suck me into a whirlpool, and then I write letters that I never send or texts that I always delete. Whatever. Nobody said it would be easy. I'm alive. Lucky sod, huh?'

'Oh,' said Mareike, pointing to the entrance, 'look, here's your daughter. I'd better be going.'

Elias had to smile. 'Hospitals aren't really your thing, are they? You've been here precisely twelve minutes.'

Mareike turned to him, smiling as if in apology. 'No, they're not. They scare me. You just get on with getting out of here, and then we'll go for a drink.'

'Sure, I'll get wasted. On an apple spritzer or something. A real piss up,' he said sarcastically.

Mareike looked questioningly at him.

'I'll barely be allowed alcohol,' he explained. 'They say it's a problem with the blood thinners.'

'OK,' said Mareike, half in astonishment and half in pity.

'Yeah,' said Jule cheerfully, having approached and overheard the last part, 'life's not worth living without beer, is it, Papa?'

She hugged him. It was good to see her. She was wearing frayed denim shorts and a plain T-shirt, but she looked so fresh and pretty that he felt a little twinge. So carefree – it would be so lovely to feel that light again. But those days were long gone.

Mareike left. Jule sat beside him.

'Has Vera been visiting too?' she asked with unabashed curiosity. 'I just saw her.'

Elias shook his head in surprise. 'No. She does come now and then, but ... Oh, hang on.' He laughed as he put two and two together. 'I bet she's here to see Jan. I've had the impression that they ... well, it looks like she's got over me,' he said.

'How are you, Papa? And Mama says hi.'

'Thanks,' said Elias. 'But that's enough hospital talk, OK? How are things with Anna? Are you an item?'

'Papa!' Jule exclaimed, half laughing. 'That's none of your business. But yes. Yes, sort of. It's not that simple.'

'Really?' Elias feigned astonishment. 'Welcome to my world, daughter of mine. Nice that you're here too.'

Then he stood up.

'Fancy a visit to psychiatrics with me? I go there sometimes when there's nothing on TV.'

'You're so weird, Papa,' Jule said in surprise. 'Seriously?'

He pushed the drip stand along beside them. If he was ever allowed to act again – *The Hypochondriac*, perhaps – he'd insist on taking this thing on stage with him. There was nothing more awful, and no better proof that you were among the sick.

'Seriously. I sometimes go to visit Clara's mother.'

Long corridors linked the various clinics and you could easily walk from rehab to old people's mental health.

'Are we allowed to just turn up?' Jule asked as Elias rang the bell by the glass door.

He was leaning against it. He was longing to get back to a bit of sport. He was out of breath, just from walking a few metres.

'They're glad if the old folks have visitors. Means they can go off for a smoke.'

A carer opened the door. She nodded to him, as they'd met a few times now. 'Brought your daughter today?'

'Oh yes.' Elias gave an exaggerated sigh. 'The child hasn't seen her grandmother for years. You know what these youngsters are like.'

Jule nudged his back. 'Papa!'

The nurse laughed. 'Mrs Wagenbach is in the garden.'

'Why do you visit her?' Jule asked as they walked out through the dining area. There was the quiet of midday.

Elias shrugged his shoulders. He didn't really know. 'Because Jan told me she was here. And that she doesn't get much company. I can sympathise a bit,' he added. Nobody knew how uneventful hospital life was.

'Sorry I can only come at the weekends, but school's pretty stressful at the moment.' Jule felt got at.

Elias reached for her arm. 'I don't mean you, kiddo. It's good that you come at all, and it won't be for much longer. Hello, Mrs Wagenbach,' he added. Clara's mother was standing by the most pointless table-tennis table in the world. Nobody in here played table tennis.

'Paul!' Her face relaxed. She was pleased to see him.

'This is Jule, Mrs Wagenbach,' Elias said softly. 'You haven't met her before.'

'The guinea pig ... I know her. Yes. Yes.'

Jule had to laugh. Mrs Wagenbach laughed too, although she clearly had no idea why.

'Shall we go for a walk, Mrs Wagenbach? Bust ourselves out of jail for half an hour?'

'Cat?' she asked, but she seemed to have understood all the same, because she linked arms merrily with Jule.

'Doesn't she need shoes?' Jule asked on their way to the door. Mrs Wagenbach was in her tights.

Elias waved dismissively. 'Don't worry about it. She keeps hiding her shoes. They once found them in the big tea urn in the dining room. It's warm enough for her to go barefoot.'

They weren't allowed to leave the hospital grounds, of course, but a bit of a walk was good for him, even though it was more a case of dragging than wheeling the trolley down the gravel path. Jule was chatting to Clara's mother. Or rather, they were chatting past each other. Jan had said that she felt a lot better on the ward here than in the home. It wasn't just the medication. It was just less oppressively old here.

They were attracting quite a bit of attention as they reached the café terrace. Mrs Wagenbach in tights that were now ripped to shreds. Him with his drip and the zombie tube in his carotid artery. And Jule in between.

'Pretend we're your lunatic parents,' he whispered, when he saw how uncomfortable she felt being stared at.

Jule laughed. It was a strange dialogue. Like something by Ionesco.

'Would you like a coffee, Mrs Wagenbach?'

Clara's mother looked down and tugged at her ragged stockings. 'My winter tyres!'

Her coffee arrived, along with orange juice for Jule and espresso for Elias.

He nudged Jule, whispering: 'Keep your eye on the spoon. This is my favourite scene, and it happens time and again.'

Elias didn't know why, but Clara's mother always stole the spoons. And she was so matter-of-fact about it, that nobody ever noticed. This time, they just disappeared up her sleeve. It was great.

'But you give them back afterwards, right?'

Elias laughed. 'No way. Mrs Wagenbach and I have a very lucrative spoon dealership running on eBay. How else d'you think I can pay for our drinks?'

Clara's mother was chatting away, making no sense at all. Jule listened and Elias looked out over the town and yearned ... for everything. For his life before the gazebo. For Clara. For the stage.

'Little cat,' Mrs Wagenbach suddenly said to Jule, putting her arm tenderly around her shoulders. There was so much of Clara in the gesture, in the unexpected affection, that Elias had to look away.

Once they'd delivered Mrs Wagenbach along with the spoons, and a fork that neither of them had known about, back where they'd come from, and were walking back down the corridor to rehab, Jule asked, out of the blue: 'Why *did* you split up, you and Clara? I know...' she hesitated, 'it's not really any of my business. But the two of you ... you know, when you came to see me, you looked like you were exactly...' She didn't have the words.

Elias waited. Jule took her time.

'You looked,' she said in the end, 'like two broken halves that somebody sticks back together and then you can hardly see the crack because they fit so perfectly. That's what you looked like. And I don't get it,' she concluded, almost helplessly. 'Is that what relationships are like?'

They'd reached the lift. Elias was tired.

'I don't know, Jule,' he said. 'What you said about the halves, I felt like that too. I had the feeling that, for the first time in ages ... no, actually the first time ever, it was right. That she...'

He didn't finish the sentence. But Jule understood anyway.

'That she was the one?'

He nodded. Jan opened the door to his room.

'Oh,' she said. 'Hello!'

Jan was there, and he'd apparently been waiting for Elias.

'Hey, Jule,' he said amicably. 'Listen, could you wait outside a moment? I need to speak to your dad, OK?'

He was giving off a strange tension. Elias suddenly felt jittery.

He nodded to Jule. 'See you in a mo.'

She walked away and Elias sat down on his bed. Did Jan want to tell him something about Clara?

'Elias,' Jan began cautiously, and suddenly Elias was scared that something really had happened to Clara. He was almost rough as he said:

'What is it? Spit it out!'

Jan was looking at the paper in his hand. Then he straightened up. 'I shouldn't really be telling you this, but I accidentally ... well no, not accidentally, I'm always asking questions. Anyway, the thing is, your bloods weren't where they should be. And that's not so good.'

Elias didn't know what to say. He understood the words, and yet he didn't get the meaning.

'What's not good? What does that mean exactly?'

Jan sat beside him on the bed and pointed to the infusion bag above him.

'To cut a long story short, the antibiotics aren't working as well as they should do. The staph ... the concentration isn't decreasing. It's actually started to climb a bit. And that's just not good.'

'Does that mean I'm getting a different antibiotic?'

Jan raised both hands. Elias recognised that gesture.

'That's what they'll try, yes. But the thing is ... actually, the one you're on already is the best option. Staphylococci are multi-resistant. You need the big guns, and that's what you're getting.'

He fell silent. Elias was trembling. That was why he was so tired. So out of breath. He thought back to the gazebo. Not again. Shit. Shitshitshitshit.

'Does that mean they could ... they could get back into my heart valve?' he asked, weak with fear.

He heard Jan take a deep, trembling breath.

'Elias, to be perfectly honest, yes, that's possible. But it's also possible that you just ... that there's nothing more they can do. Not necessarily. Truly not,' he said hastily, loudly. 'We'll have to wait and see. It's only a slight increase at the moment. But it shouldn't happen. It's telling us that the drugs are no longer having the desired effect. And that's dangerous.'

I'm going to die. He's telling me that I'm going to die. I'm going to die.

Suddenly, the fear was omnipresent and overwhelming, and he didn't know how to deal with it.

Jan put his hand on his back. 'Elias, it doesn't mean a thing. We'll take more bloods tomorrow and the day after. But I didn't want anyone else to ... I wanted to tell you myself.'

Elias gulped and gulped. Only then could he speak.

'I don't want you to tell anyone. Promise.'

'Sure,' said Jan. 'I have to get back to the ward, but I'll come at the end of my shift, OK? Please, Elias, you just have to rest. Tomorrow, they'll probably change the drug, and then we'll see.'

Elias understood that Jan was lying. Jan didn't believe it himself, but didn't know what else to say. How do you tell someone that he's going to die?

'You go. Yes, we'll speak later.'

In the doorway, Jan turned back.

'I'm sorry, Elias. Really. I'm sorry.'

Elias nodded. What are you sorry for, Jan? For telling me? That I'm going to die? That you have to go? That ... God knows. Is this what it feels like? This dying business?

Jule came back in. He pulled himself together, but she could see that something had happened.

'Papa? What's wrong? What did Jan say?'

He gathered his thoughts.

'Jule, I'm pretty knackered. Do you mind coming back this evening? I need sleep.'

'Papa,' Jule insisted, 'what did he say?'

'My blood test wasn't quite right. I need to rest. So you come back later, OK?'

She left very hesitantly, and only after he'd promised to call her later.

Then he was alone.

45

Jule picked up at once. He'd left her hanging a long time and she'd already messaged twice. But he'd needed the whole afternoon. Screaming fear interspersed with calmer moments when he listened to his body and didn't feel all that ill, just a bit light and dizzy, and couldn't believe that he really ... that he might die. Would die.

You always think it won't happen to you. The night in the garden in Tübingen. She'd been speaking about Paul. You always think it won't happen to you. That night was possibly the closest they'd ever been.

'Papa?'

'Jule, I need to ask a big thing of you, and you can say no.'

'Papa, what's wrong?' She sounded scared and furious at the same time because she didn't know what had happened.

'I'll tell you everything on the way. Can you drive here in my car? And then...' He paused a moment because it was crazy, but on the other hand, what exactly was normal right now?

'Papa,' Jule interrupted, 'I'm not allowed to drive on my own. I'm only nearly eighteen.'

'Listen,' Elias tried to sound as calm as possible, 'I know that, but it doesn't matter now. You can drive. Nobody will stop you. Just fetch my car. The key is by the door. Come and pick me up. And then we have to go to Hamburg. I can't do it alone. Can you? Will you?'

She was silent for a moment. When she replied, she sounded much firmer.

'OK. I'll be there in half an hour. If your car starts.'

She hung up. He'd have liked to laugh.

He got properly dressed. Phone and wallet in his pockets. Went to the bathroom and washed. Doing these everyday things helped.

Then he looked at the drip. A quarter left. He thought for a moment, then unplugged the bag, emptied the rest of the solution down the sink, hung it back up again and rang for the nurse.

'The drip,' he said, as normally as possible, pointing to the stand. She nodded, smiled and came back five minutes later with a full bag. Routine. She'd done it umpteen times before.

Funny that you could never give up hoping. That you acted like it might maybe, maybe, maybe actually help. You're going to die anyway. But maybe only because you gave up too soon and took yourself off the drip.

That was why he didn't dare travel without the thing. That would be admitting that he really did have no chance now.

But come on. Be honest. Why else would you go? This is no different. Last rites. Doing whatever there is left to do. You could just leave it behind.

His phoned buzzed. Jule. I'm here.

'Let's go,' he said defiantly to the drip stand, 'you and me, we're going on a road trip.'

They drove through the rain and the night. There'd been a thunderstorm as they set off. Here on the motorway, it was only raining, heavily and steadily. The drip stand hadn't been easy to manage. It wasn't collapsible. Now the infusion bag was hanging from the grab handle above the door, tied on as best they'd managed with a piece of string, and the frame was behind them, lying right across the back seat. Jule was driving. Much more cautiously and considerably slower than he'd have gone, but he said nothing. They hadn't said much in general since setting off. There was a funny atmosphere. The motorway was almost empty. They were racing through the pouring rain, and at night and in weather like this, it was always like you'd been set apart from the world, you were alone. He'd always liked this kind of journey.

'Do you remember when we drove to Croatia? You were twelve, I think.'

Jule nodded. He looked out of the window because the memory had suddenly unleashed the terrible feeling that he'd never be able to experience anything like that again.

'We're going to Clara, right?'

How long had it been since he'd been this close to his daughter? Nobody else, just the two of them. Jule and Papa. This incredible feeling of unconditional belonging. Of being family. He could only think of Croatia, when they'd camped in this tiny, grotty campsite. Every day they'd swum across the bay to the big inflatable water park, which you were supposed to pay to go on, but they'd always snuck in from the other side. He would have loved to go camping with Clara someday. He didn't even know if she liked it. But given the way her garden looked, she must do, surely?

'Yes. And you were right. We looked happy because we were happy. And neither of us properly realised, I don't think. She didn't at first, and then I didn't.'

Now and again, red rear lights glowed faintly in the far distance. Now and then, they hissed past a heavier, slower vehicle. Now and then, the few lights of a village at night whizzed by.

'What does that mean?' Jule asked. Then hesitated, before asking, feeling her way cautiously, falteringly, 'Is that ... Are we ... Papa, what are we doing here? What's going on with your blood? Is that why we're going to see her?'

What do I say now? Jule, I'm probably dying? Jule, listen, it's possible that I ... Jule, I'm dying. It all sounded wrong. Way too dramatic, and simultaneously too banal. Like dying was some everyday thing. Which it was – except only for other people and not for yourself.

'My blood test results weren't very good. These bacteria are getting resistant to the antibiotics and that...'

Jule was concentrating so hard on her driving. He'd have to take over at some point; she'd never keep it up the whole way.

'And that? What does that mean?'

He took a deep breath. As if to calm himself. It didn't work.

'That means that...' He couldn't say it. Not to Jule. 'You can die of it.'

He'd read up on it. In patients with a replacement heart valve ... prognosis is not that good ... three quarters ... eighty-five per cent ... in the end, he'd had to run to the bathroom, where he'd puked from fear.

'But you look so well! You're getting better. I mean, we were in the garden only this afternoon, and you're getting fitter all the time.'

He leant back wearily. 'I wasn't expecting it either. Oh, Jule, I don't know. I have no idea. But it doesn't matter anyway, because we can't change anything right now. I didn't even notice how ill I was. The heart valve thing – most of the time, I've just been annoyed, but I didn't really understand. Because somehow, things kept moving forward. But now...'

He looked out at the rain. Outside, everything was perfect, and why, for fuck's sake, did you have to be dying to finally properly understand how fucking beautiful life was?

'You want to put things right between Clara and you?'

Jule had taken his hand. It was such a fearful, tender gesture that it made him cry.

His shoulders twitched. 'Yes. What else can I do? She came and told me that she loves me and that she'd just made a big mistake. And now I want her to ... I don't want it to be my fault, Jule. I just want her to know that what we had was real.'

Jule said nothing. Her hand stayed on his. At some point, the lights of an oncoming lorry lit up her face and he saw the tears rolling down her cheeks, and then he found himself thinking that there'd be a time when, for him, it was over, but that Jule and the rest would be left behind with the pain. No comfort.

46

It had rained all night and left the morning very chilly, but it was clearing up. The shorter the nights, the earlier she left the flat. The swifts were swirling and swooping through the air above her: summer was on its way. Their shrilling, soaring screams had always filled her with yearning. Now, they sounded like the bells in the ruins of the Nikolaikirche, from a different, unrepeatably beautiful era, lost and unspeakably sad if you listened to them for too long. She pedalled as fast as she could. Running, cycling or swimming to the point of exhaustion were the only things that helped. The wind was cold in her face and her ears were burning as she rode between the redbrick façades, down the last side street to work. Saw the car out of the corner of her eye, felt a burning stab in her belly, and rode on. Everything reminded her of him. All the time. Even if it was just a car that looked like his.

'Clara!'

She looked over her shoulder as she rode, braked because she couldn't immediately tell where the shout had sounded from. Turned, and then she saw him. Elias. Standing by his car, leaning against the roof, the passenger door open. The deep shock as she recognised him flicked a switch and, at a stroke, all the tension in her body turned to internal trembling. She dismounted. Leant the bike against the wall and walked over to him. He no longer looked quite as thin as he'd done four weeks ago, but still just as fragile.

Such an unusual beauty. He hadn't forgotten but she was still, always and afresh, surprisingly beautiful. No, not beautiful. It was far more about that stern clarity that he'd fallen for, once and for all. In a suit, far too elegant for the mountain bike she was riding.

What a contrast, and how much he'd missed her! She was coming towards him and he could see no surprise in her. What could he say?

'I thought maybe it was my turn to drive through the night to see you.'

Why couldn't you just put your arms around her? Even now? Even now, when it was almost at the end? Why wasn't that possible?

Jule got out too. Clara could see that she'd been crying.

'Hello, Clara,' she said. 'It's lovely to see you.'

'Hello, Jule,' she replied. She didn't understand a thing. What was wrong?

'I'm going for coffee,' said Jule.

It was only now that she spotted that Elias still had the canula in his neck. The tube disappearing inside the car.

'Can we talk? I texted you, but you had your phone off.'

Yes. She switched it off when she went to bed these days. Because she'd been unable to bear waking up at night and reaching for it and then not reading a message from him, and then lying awake for hours, watching her thoughts running in circles.

'And I didn't know where you live, so we waited here.'

'Seriously? Why? Why now, all of a sudden, Elias? To ... to do what to me? I can't do it. I can't have another conversation like in the gazebo, or your hospital room. What's changed?'

She hadn't wanted to say all that. The wrong words were coming out of her mouth.

'Will you help me with this thing?'

Elias had opened the rear door and was pulling the drip stand out. Then he untied the half-empty bag from the handrail. Clara reached for it almost automatically and hung it up. She was on the edge of laughter.

'You two drove here with that? Do you still have to have it?'

Elias shut the car doors. Then he turned back to her.

'How about a little walk?'

It was still pretty quiet. The rustle of the gentle wind in the lindens around the Michelwiese mingled with the sparse morning traffic. No din yet. A city waking up, speaking softly and sleepily. They walked towards the church tower. The first huge awkwardness between them was lessening because walking side by side, the symmetry of their strides, was like a memory of their intimacy.

'I'm probably far too late,' Elias began cautiously. 'I've probably missed the right moment again. You were so brave when you came to me. It … I'd dreamt of it and wished for it, and then you saw me like that. So broken and I had no idea…'

He was hunting for the right words.

'Why has Jule been crying? Did you argue?'

'What?'

Her question came so unexpectedly that it took him a second. He hadn't wanted to tell her about it. That wasn't what this was about. He'd needed a long time yesterday afternoon to understand himself and to know why he needed to see Clara.

'She might tell you later. Or I will, but that's not all that's important right now.'

She waited. The pale, summer-morning sky above the spire was unusually clear. A transparent, cool, beaming blue. When she was younger, mornings like this had always held a huge promise that had only rarely been fulfilled and never in full. She turned to Elias. Still in silence.

It was as though Elias was seeing her through different eyes. How well her name suited her. Suited her severe features, as clear as water, which had stilled every thirst inside him from the very beginning, as only water could, water that tasted of nothing more than clarity.

To be clear.

He leant against the church wall.

'Clara, I love you. I think I've loved you right from the start, without really knowing it. That's the only reason I came. Like you came to me in the hospital. Because I wanted to say that – without the need to talk about anything else. Not about you being here in Hamburg. And not about my illness. And not about what happened before.'

Above them, the bright whistle of a kestrel as it threw itself into the wind from a louvre. The dew was still sparkling on the meadow. The church roof was starting to shine in the rising sun – it was an early summer morning as if there'd been no such thing until now.

'Clara. I love you, and I want you to know that.'

For this one moment, here with her in this June morning, that really was all that he wanted.

He looked so tired. But he was radiant. Maybe it was just the light, and because he'd grown so thin, but it was as though he was glowing from the inside. Everything inside her was topsy-turvy. As if her heart was suddenly beating from her belly.

'That's why you came?'

He was quiet. Looked up at the drip bag and briefly felt the canula in his neck. She would have wished for him to be rid of that thing and free again. Free to just run off with her and pick her up, and drop to his knees in front of her, in some grand gesture.

'You know,' he said then, and the way he looked at her was as though he was caressing her with his gaze, and she would happily have reached her hand out for his, 'I kept thinking about it in the last few weeks. We're so modern and ironic. We know that it's all just hormones and pheromones and that being in love ends after two or three years, and that a third of relationships break down after six, seven years, and you lose the lust for each other and ... and I've experienced all of that, and I thought that's just how it goes.'

He paused for a moment. As if he was out of breath. She was just as churned up and was breathing far too fast herself.

'But – then you came.'

She understood what he meant. She would just have found it hard to put into words.

'Neither of us really believed in it. First I didn't, and then you didn't,' she said slowly.

He nodded.

'Clara, there's no other way I can say this: you're the one. Before I got to know you, I thought I needed to change my life. And then you came. Then I thought you had changed it. And then this fever came along and my life...' He faltered.

She moved suddenly to stand beside him with her back to the church wall. At this moment, she wanted to see what he was seeing.

'Yes?' she asked quietly.

'The hospital changed my life again. Yes, I know it's a cliché. But that doesn't mean it isn't true. Probably nobody knows that better than you, Clara.' He turned towards her. Their faces were very close now. 'You know, there was a day when everything was empty and I just missed you,' he blurted suddenly. 'Every single day, every hour, every night. Always. And there's nobody else who could fill that emptiness. It doesn't work without you. Because, you know, it has your physique,' he concluded with a sudden smile.

Then kiss me, or hug me, she thought, I don't want to think any longer, kiss me or...

She put her hands on his shoulders and turned him away from her, and for a heart-stopping moment he thought that she was going to push him away because she wouldn't or couldn't speak to him anymore, but then he felt her hands push their way under his arms and cross over his stomach. Her face soft against his neck, where it was scarred from the canula, and he'd forgotten how warm she could be.

'Thank you,' she whispered in his ear.

A ship's horn. Powerful and deep. The whistle of the young kestrel. The soft rustle of the lindens in the offshore breeze, and the two of them with the church at their backs and the first light of the morning on their eyelids.

Now, he thought, if it's coming to an end, let it be now, and if not, then treasure, hold, never let go, never again, treasure this moment until the end.

When Clara opened her eyes, Jule was standing a few metres away on the meadow. The tears were running down her cheeks, but she was smiling. Her voice shook as she said, 'I brought you guys coffee too.'

The three of them were sitting in the sun and drinking coffee. A good way to let the colours and sounds of reality slowly trickle back in. He and Clara were sitting side by side, shoulder to shoulder.

'That's why I like the theatre so much,' he said.

'Because you can bring down the curtain after a big scene, but it never happens like that in real life?'

Clara had the same feeling. Because after a moment like that, everything felt profane, cheap and unimportant.

Elias nodded. The church clock struck eight.

'Are you two staying here?'

Jule shook her head before Elias could answer. He hadn't thought beyond Clara and this morning. He hadn't wanted to.

'Papa has to go back. He needs his drip refilled.'

Clara looked at Jule. 'Why are you so sad? Or is that too personal?' she added hastily.

Jule shook her head again. Her eyes glittered anew and Clara felt – as sometimes happens – that her own were welling up too, for pure sympathy.

'We have to hit the road,' said Elias, standing up. 'Will you walk us to the car?'

'In a minute,' said Clara, shuffling over to Jule and taking her hand. It was so obvious that she was fighting for self-control.

'Leave her,' said Elias. 'It's not that important.'

'Yes, it is.' It burst from Jule like a shout, and suddenly she was so shaken by sobs that it was hard to understand her.

Clara knelt in front of her. 'What?' she asked softly. 'What is it?'

'Because Papa's dying,' Jule screamed desperately in her battle against the tears. 'Because he might be dying.'

'Nonsense,' Clara said automatically. 'He only...'

She looked at Elias. Jule's hands clenched around hers. Her crying was quieter now, but that was all the worse because she sounded so hopeless. She froze on the inside with sudden fear.

'Why?' she asked Elias. 'Why?'

'I didn't want you to know. I didn't want that, but I had to see you. I wanted to do the right thing for once, and now I'll have to hurt you again, and I didn't want that, but I couldn't go on without you.'

He saw her kneeling in front of Jule, holding her and looking up at him; almost as if she wanted to ask him to lie to her. But she didn't do that. Never had. She was much stronger than him.

'Jan told me. The antibiotics have stopped working. But they're trying a different drug. That's why we have to go back.'

As if he could downplay it to her. Her of all people.

Clara stood up slowly.

You always think it won't happen to you. But it does. And then you think that you've paid your debt to fate and that it won't happen again. Because even the first time was so unfair. But then it happens to you. A second time, and maybe a third, and it never stops because fate or God or life doesn't actually give a shit how often it happens to you. Her mouth was bone dry.

'Why didn't you tell me?'

Elias looked so tired that she was asking herself how she could have been so blind.

'Because it isn't about that,' he answered. He was exhausted and done in, but it was still important. 'Because it isn't about that, it's about you and me. And nothing else.'

Clara was trying to breathe more calmly. And to think. There is one advantage to it keeping on happening to you. You know what you have to do.

'Elias and Jule,' she said, as calmly as she could, 'go back now. On the train. We'll book in a minute, and I'll give you a lift to the station. I have to go into the office, but I think I can get away at lunchtime, and I'll bring your car, OK? I'll speak to Jan, and then I'll come. I'll be there this evening.'

He could see Jule relax slightly. Clara was anchoring her. And he was so tired that he was just glad of Clara's idea.

'Clara…' he began, but she raised her hand as if to fend him off.

'We'll speak this evening,' she said curtly.

She turned back to him, looked at him. He was smiling like someone who had nothing left to lose.

She took his face between her hands and pressed her brow against his. 'Even if you hadn't driven through the night to see me, Elias – I love you.'

47

They were standing on the cafeteria terrace. It was getting on for half past ten, but not yet quite dark. A warm June night. Jan had one foot resting on the wall, his elbows on his thighs and his chin propped in his hands. In this uncertain light, beneath a strangely bright night sky, he looked picturesque – and tired. Suddenly, everything was reminding her of the time when they'd been around fifteen or sixteen and spent summer nights like these roaming the town, driven by an unutterable yearning, on a quest for adventure in the well-behaved streets; on a quest for true love on the banks of a river that flowed far too tamely.

The cafeteria windows were dark; it was long since closed. The grounds were as quiet as a hospital at night could ever be. The nurses on night shifts were speaking quietly. Even the ambulances were quiet at this time, before the first bleeding drunks or broken noses and jaws from clubland punch-ups were dropped off around midnight. And you wouldn't hear the silent despair from certain wards anyway.

'I'm sorry that it's like this for you again,' said Jan quietly. 'That it's happening again.'

The tip of his cigarette glowed red. Jan hardly ever smoked. They both had as teenagers. Roll-ups. He handed it to Clara and she dragged on it. The taste was yet another reminder of the summer promises of the past. None of which had come true.

No. That wasn't right. The one big one had come true. This morning when he'd come to Hamburg. And then it had been immediately snatched away from her.

'Jan...' she began, hearing the scratchiness in her throat from all the screaming she'd done in the car this afternoon. The wordless, frenetically furious screaming at the motorway traffic, at the fear and, above all, at everything that was stronger than her and out to prove it: God or fate or life, or just the lottery of bad luck in which she had, yet again, got six correct numbers.

'Jan, I can't ... I can't give that man up.'

Jan made a tiny, defensive hand gesture, but Clara wouldn't let him speak.

'I know. I know that fate doesn't give a shit what I want or don't want. If I'll give him up or not. If I love him or not.'

Jan took his foot from the wall and stood up straight. A slim figure in a white coat that shimmered against the soft, dark outlines of the elms. He didn't look at her.

'I didn't love Paul by the time he died,' she continued, 'but his death still blew my world apart. If Elias dies,' she said and looked up at the sky for a moment, where the Plough was appearing to their left, above the tops of the old trees, 'I might survive it. But I'll never be whole again. It'll be half a life, and that's less than I had before. I'm not giving Elias up. The pain will be the same if he does die. But there's no way I'm giving him up. I want them to do everything possible. Everything.'

'There isn't a lot more than they're already doing,' Jan said, very quietly, after a brief pause. He was still not looking at her. Only the lighter clicked brightly a second time.

Clara felt the rage rising up inside herself again, but she held it back.

'There's always more, and you know it. I ... Jan, I know you're doing a lot already. Elias told me how often you've been there. But I want us both to do everything, everything, everything even remotely possible. Can't they do that thing they did for Paul? Stem cell transplant or whatever?'

Jan shook his head. 'Paul had cancer. So that made sense. This is ... Clara, I don't know what else can be done.'

She took a deep breath. Then she stepped up to him, took his face in her hands as she'd done when they were little. Forced him to look her in the eyes.

'This time, I'm only giving up once he's dead.'

She held him briefly, then let her hands sink down.

Jan smoked, looked out into the night and was silent a long time. The light, aromatic ribbons of tobacco smoke blurred into the delicate, unmistakable and yearningly sweet aroma of robinia in flower. Then he nodded slowly, as if to himself.

'See you tomorrow, Clara.'

She quietly opened his door. A strip of light fell from the corridor into the dark room; she shut it quickly so as not to wake Elias. The window was open. She slipped off her shoes and walked over to his bed. It was never fully dark in a hospital, and she could at least make out the lines of his face. In a strange way, he looked beautiful.

'Hello, Clara.'

He hadn't opened his eyes, but his voice sounded awake.

'I didn't want to disturb you,' she said softly, sitting on the edge of the bed.

'You didn't,' he replied, equally quietly. 'I can't sleep. I'm scared.'

'Me too,' she whispered.

He threw off the covers. 'Come in next to me.'

Her head on his shoulder, her incredible warmth beside him – how long had it been?

'I can hear your heart ticking. Like a clock!' she whispered in amazement.

He smiled in the darkness. 'It took me a while to get used to it. I always hear it at night.'

They lay side by side. Nothing but them and the ticking of his heart.

'In the past...' he whispered '...in the past, when I imagined what I'd do if I was dying, I always thought I'd definitely want to have sex. One last time. And now...' A whispering laugh.

She was lying right there, where she wanted to be. By his side.

'And now?' she asked.

'Now? Now you're beside me. The only woman I'm desperate to have sex with, and the only one I could ever tell that I'm far too scared to even think about sex. The only woman who ... You know, Clara,' he turned to her, 'there are a few more places I'd like to have shared with you. Now I'm sharing my fear with you, and it's shrinking because I can do that and because you're lying next to me.'

She couldn't say a word. She could only snuggle up to him, as hard as she could, and hold his hand and listen to his heart as it ticked through the night. And so they stayed until morning.

48

He must have fallen asleep. When he opened his eyes, Elias saw Jan sitting at the table in his hospital room, his hands in his coat pockets.

'How sweet,' he said. 'I've already posted a photo of you two.'

Clara woke up. The bedding, her blouse, Elias's pyjama top – everything was damp. They'd sweated horribly. When she touched him, she jumped. He had a temperature.

'I have to talk to you both.'

Elias sat up. 'Good morning to you too.'

It was good to play at normality for a moment, with irony and all that, as if nothing was wrong.

'Elias is burning up,' said Clara.

Jan stood up quickly, walked over and touched his forehead. He nodded absentmindedly then sat back down at the table.

'I'm not a specialist in either internal medicine or infectious diseases. I have no idea of the literature or the current state of the research. Clara suggested something yesterday that I initially thought was nonsense.' He nodded towards Clara. 'But then I did some reading. It's like this.'

He stepped to the foot of the bed. Elias and Clara were sitting close together. Jan shrugged in a gesture of hopelessness as he turned to Elias.

'Listen here, Elias, this is a really desperate idea. Just because I want to try everything. But…' He faltered.

Clara understood him. She squeezed Elias's hand.

'He's trying to tell you that you shouldn't get your hopes up,' she said, her mouth dry.

Elias shook his head, pulled a face and opened the metal drawer in his bedside table.

'No,' he said. 'That's not quite it, is it? If I shouldn't hope any longer, I might as well just down all the sleeping pills I've been hoarding, right? Jan, I'll take everything. I'd be really miffed if I ended up dying just because I didn't try out all the options.'

It wasn't that hard to make a joke.

Jan smiled. 'It's not just up to you. I have to suggest it to my colleagues first. These aren't approved treatments. They have to go along with it first and then ... then we'll see. And another thing – is Jule eighteen? If everything works, we might need her as a donor.'

'What kind of treatment is this then?' asked Clara.

Jan hunched his shoulders again, as if embarrassed by his own idea. 'There's a particular type of stem cell. MSCs. That won't mean anything to you. Mesenchymal stem cells are different from the rest. They're normally responsible for repairing bones, but there have been experiments in using them to fight severe infections.'

'That sounds good!' said Elias. 'Did it work?'

Jan nodded. 'In rabbits,' he explained wryly. 'But the other thing, which it might be possible to use in conjunction, would be apheresis. Blood filtering,' he continued hastily, as if he was scared they'd interrupt. 'Let me say again – this is a wild idea, and my colleagues will probably think I'm out of my mind. But I'm going to speak to them now. If they agree to it – *if* – then it needs to be done fast. Can you call Jule and get her to come? We'd need a donor, and she might be a match. Besides...'

'What?' Clara hastily asked her brother. She knew that hesitation.

'Nothing. We won't be able to find anyone else so quickly. And even if she is a match, it'll take four days to get enough stem cells.'

Elias nodded. It was a strange feeling, mingling with this light, feverish non-presence that he could do nothing about.

Clara stood up. 'Thank you, Jan,' she said.

Once Jan had gone, Elias lay back and looked out of the window. How familiar the view was now. He'd lived in so many places. He'd moved from theatre to theatre, and he'd always had the knack of settling in quickly. But here, that was like a curse. The room was saying: you belong to me. You're at home. You're not leaving this place.

Clara was in the bathroom. He could hear the birds through the window; it was still early. He could make out yellowthroats; the merry, monotonous up-down of a chiffchaff; and the cheerful chirp of a willow warbler. And the bluetits. It was all song this morning. Breeding season. Most birds only sang to find a mate and when they were brooding eggs or chicks. Maybe even for fun, and just because they were alive and there was life all around them and they were bringing forth life.

He knew what Jan had done. It wasn't for him. It was for Clara and maybe for Jule. So that later, they wouldn't have the feeling of not having done enough. So as to leave nothing untried and, above all, so that they wouldn't just have to sit there and watch him die.

Thanks, Jan. I never knew how clever you were. Or how much you loved your sister. As much as I do.

He felt the slight temperature warming his whole body. It wasn't a bad feeling. Coming from the bathroom were the small, wonderful sounds of Clara after a shower. The showerhead dripping. The door banging. The hairdryer. Peaceful sounds, and it was hard not to wish to hear them forever and ever, in the coming weeks and months and years and for a whole lifetime.

He looked back out of the window. A piece of blue-and-white sky, as there should be in southern Germany in June. Thank you so much, dear God, for dressing the heavens up so prettily and meanwhile forgetting that there are people dying down here. Doesn't matter. Maybe that's why you don't exist.

His thoughts were a bit all over the place. Still. If dying was going to be like the fever right at the start, then he needn't be afraid of it. No pain. It was only the horrible stairway dreams that scared him. But after a while, they'd be over.

Clara came out of the bathroom. Naked. She moved so naturally. There were droplets of water on the skin of her forearms.

Such fucking shit. He'd love to keep living. Just for that. Just to be able to keep on seeing that.

'Have you phoned Jule yet?' she asked.

Elias exhaled. 'No. I'm just about to.'

He wished he could pull the needle from his throat and go down to breakfast with her, in some café down there, on this summer morning, with this beautiful, clever woman. But he could only stand up, pull the drip stand along behind him and press her naked body to him, as hard as he could.

49

Jan's office was tiny and its only window looked out over the courtyard.

'We've come a long way,' said Clara ironically. 'My office in Hamburg looks much like this. So, what's up? What do they say?'

Jan sat behind his desk and fiddled with a pen.

'They were interested. More than that,' he corrected himself, 'they thought it was a good idea.'

Something wasn't right. Jan sounded far too resigned.

'That's a good thing, right?'

Jan looked out of the window. Clara saw to her surprise that his hand was shaking.

'What?' she asked loudly. 'What is it, Jan?'

'They won't do it. They can't do it. It's...'

'Why not?' Clara shouted furiously. 'What's wrong? Why?'

'Let me speak,' Jan snapped. 'It's too expensive. It's not a recognised treatment. Of course not. No health insurance will cover it. Harvesting stem cells, filtering out the bacteria, cell expansion – it would come to somewhere between twenty-five and thirty thousand euros. If it works. His insurance won't cover it. So we're not allowed to do it. End of.'

'What?'

It was as if he'd slapped her on the forehead. Like he used to do when they were kids. The dry pain deep in the bridge of her nose and being unable to breathe for a moment.

'But you can ... he can take out a loan. Or I can—'

Jan interrupted. He was angry too. 'Will you get a loan through today? Or by tomorrow morning at the latest? It's Friday. It's not a recognised treatment. It's simply a wild experiment. It's not like an injection that you just dish out on the side without anyone noticing. It's not just some packet of headache pills. The money has to be there before they'll start up any machines. It's complicated.'

She was silent. Thinking.

'Have you spoken to Elias?'

Jan hurled the pen at the wall. 'Sure!' He was shouting now. 'Hey, Elias, sorry, that's that for you. We can't afford your life. What d'you think? How can I tell him that? I shouldn't have mentioned it to you in the first place. I'm so stupid.'

Clara calmed down, perhaps because the whole thing was affecting Jan so much.

'Jan,' she began. 'OK. I don't have the money yet. But listen. I'll give you the house. Whether you then want to keep it or not is up to you. We can always sell it, and then you'll get the money. But you've ... would you have that much? Could you lend it to me? Look, I don't need the house. And I know you'd give it to me, if it were me.'

She paused. Jan said nothing. Then he turned to her.

'I never wanted a house,' he grinned suddenly. 'Yes, I might have somewhere in the region of twenty-two thousand. I can turn it into cash by Monday. And you'll have to max out your overdraft. You have one, don't you? Shit, what am I supposed to do with your house?'

Clara shrugged and smiled, despite or precisely because of the tension. 'Not my problem anymore.'

They looked at each other. Jan leant against the window.

'Someone like you,' he said quietly, 'the way you are for him. I've never ... That would be nice.'

She walked over to him and they stood shoulder to shoulder. Childhood. Teens. Today.

'I only got through it all with Paul because you were always there,' she said. 'And it's the same now. I couldn't do it without you. The two of us, hm?'

'I'll speak to the team.' Jan rested his hand on her arm for a moment. 'And you talk to Elias, OK? Let's hope he gets through the four days until we're ready.'

'You must never say that to him, Jan. Never.'

Jan knew what she meant.

'I'll just tell him that I've always wanted a place in the country, if he ever asks.'

'Yes. Perfect. You're the world's worst liar.'

Jan dug her affectionately in the ribs.

'I don't have time for you now. I have to go to the bank.'

50

They both looked awful. Jule lying pale on one bed, cannulas in both arms. Elias on another, cannulas in his arms, in his neck, cables hanging from his chest to keep an eye on his heart. Now and then, a nurse looked in, but otherwise, it was quiet in the treatment room.

'Hey,' said Clara as she came in. She'd gone into town for ice cream. Just to bring part of the outside world into the hospital.

'Hey,' said Jule weakly. 'Sorry, I can't eat at the moment. I feel sick. But it's OK,' she hastily added, as Elias looked at her.

'I was about to be proud of you, kiddo,' he said, 'and now you're moaning just because you feel a bit ropey.'

Elias was trying to sound light, and it was kind of working.

'Shut up, old man,' Jule retorted. 'I'm sacrificing myself for you.'

'That's just what we produced you for, Mona and me. For replacement parts. That's the only reason. Did you think we just wanted a child?'

Clara leant in the open doorway and had to laugh. This was why she loved this man.

'Don't you want ice cream either?'

'I do,' Elias said hastily, 'I'll take anything I can get.'

Jule laughed too, but that was a bad idea and she had to grab for the kidney dish.

'Still want ice cream?' she asked Elias, smiling with an effort as she straightened up again.

He looked at Clara, who was bringing Jule water and cleaning up the sick bowl. Not repulsed, just matter of fact and competent.

I don't dare hope, he thought. They're doing all this for me, and they're all acting like it's going to work. Jan and Jule and Clara. They're doing it all and they're acting the part. Or else they really believe it. But that's how it should be.

Clara sat beside him.

'I have to go back to Hamburg. They say the apheresis will help until you can get the stem cells. Elias, I wish I could stay, but I have to at least stick my head in at the office door, so that they remember who I am. I'll come at once if anything happens, and I'll be back next weekend either way.'

'Let's hope I still recognise you.'

He couldn't help it. He knew she couldn't be there the whole time, but he remembered the fever. How quickly he'd lost the ability to distinguish between dreams and reality. He didn't want to be without her.

'You're still scared, aren't you?' She spoke very quietly so that Jule wouldn't hear her.

He looked away. It took a while before he could look back at her.

'Yes,' he whispered. 'And you are too. Clara, you know as well as I do. It's all pointless, all this.'

Her face hardened and she bent down to him. 'No,' she hissed, and he was startled by the sharp anger in her voice. 'No. You do not give up. You can give up once you're dead. Your daughter is lying over there, giving her blood for you. Jan's done more for you than you can imagine. You do not give up!'

Her grip on his wrist was iron. He saw her knuckles whiten.

She whispered as quietly as ever, but with hot intensity: 'We belong together. That means I'm yours. And you're mine. You don't go without my permission. You fight. For me. For your daughter. For Jan. And for Vera, for all I care. But you don't give up!'

Jule looked over to them, pale and curious. But the machine was buzzing so loudly that she couldn't have heard anything. Clara's face was still very close to his, and he felt her rapid breathing.

'Yes,' he whispered in the end, exhausted. 'All right. I'll fight.'

51

The bag was by the bed. The cupboard doors were open, and he'd opened the window wide too, to let the grey-damp air in. Wonderful rain. Rain, just as it should be on a summer's day like this. On autopilot, he lifted his hand to his neck, as he'd done thousands of times before. It had been almost two months in total. Now he had three scars on one side and four on the other from the various insertion sites. It felt good: the little raised patches were all that there was left, nothing extraneous to feel.

He folded his trousers and shirts, and stashed them in the bag next to the books, the notebook and all the other little odds and ends. He'd accumulated a few things, but it only took ten minutes until he was done. He walked over to the window that he'd looked out of so often. Full of anxieties, full of despair and at least a few nights with the certainty that he was going to die. If you stood up, you could see over the wall to the trees in the hospital grounds and the forest on the horizon. The rain was steady. The earth was drinking. Life.

He left the window open as he picked up the bag and walked out. Simply walked out.

I don't want to forget this feeling. I want to keep hold of it. What it feels like just to be able to walk away without that thing tagging along behind and a tube in my neck. Without the leaden weariness in my legs that comes from the fever.

Saturday morning. It was very quiet in the corridors. So quiet that beneath his own footsteps, he could hear the quiet tick of his heart valve. He smiled. That was it, right? If he ever forgot this wonderful feeling, it would be the ticking of his heart that would always remind him. Remind him that his life wasn't just a matter of course, it was a gift. From Jan and the doctors who'd treated him. From his daughter. But most of all, from Clara.

Clara had put her umbrella up and was leaning against the wing of her car. She'd driven up to the main entrance; it wasn't that busy today. She looked up at the front of the hospital. She'd been here so often. But today, she got to pick Elias up. Not just for a few hours, always in the all-pervading fear of what might happen tomorrow or next week. She was standing here and she finally got to take him home for good.

She was very quiet inside. The steady rain tickled the fabric of her umbrella. A friendly sound. The weather meant that nobody wanted to be out here, even though it wasn't at all cold. This moment belonged to her alone.

The automatic door slid open. Elias came out, stopped a moment and looked around for her. He was moving like his old self. The slight spring was back in his step, and his movements were rounded again. His strength was returning. She glanced at the asphalt in front of her for a moment. Her grey umbrella reflected uncertainly in the puddles. Now he saw her and smiled. She straightened up fully and walked towards him.

'What would you like to do?' she asked him.

'As a matter of fact, I was planning to spend the next half hour looking at you,' he said, 'but as you might have noticed, it's raining.'

'You've gone soft, stuck in that clinic,' she retorted. Their faces were very close. 'If you like, you can look at me in a café. Come on.'

They left the car down by the river and took the little rope ferry to the other side. There were generally a few confused tourists here too, but it was as though the rain hadn't just slowed everything, but had emptied it out. They had everything to themselves. The steep steps up into the town. The lanes between the little houses and their tiny, terraced gardens. They walked past weathered fences and high walls, and once, Elias lunged up to grab a handful of cherries, so dark they looked almost black. They'd burst open from the rain, the flesh shimmering red. He gave Clara one.

'I know this will eventually become everyday again,' he said softly. 'The cherries. Walking up a few stairs without getting out of breath. Walking through the rain with you. But I never want to lose the underlying feeling, the gratitude.'

They were holding hands lightly. She'd never liked that with anyone else. With him – it was like he'd said – it was a gift to be able to hold hands, for ten steps, and then to let go again. It was a gift and he was a gift. Nothing you deserved. That was the essence of it – a gift was something you were just given.

They found a new café that neither of them had ever been in before. To Clara, it felt as though she'd left the town such a long time ago. It wasn't much different for Elias. It was as though they were visiting.

'You only ever notice how much something's changed when you haven't been around for a while.'

He held the door for her. Half in jest, half in old-fashioned courtesy. They walked in. It was a large space, almost a hall. If it hadn't been for the music, they'd have left again, because there was nobody else here.

'That's what you like though, isn't it?' She was remembering their conversation on the way to Bayreuth.

He smiled. 'You remembered.'

They sat by one of the large windows. The hum of the coffee machine. The quiet clink of porcelain being tidied. And the music. Timeless, relaxed. Nothing he knew. Just background music, composed by someone who hadn't made a name for themselves, and wouldn't deserve one for this. And yet – the notes pearled like raindrops on a tulip petal, leaving no trace, but had a wonderful, transient beauty, disappearing instantly – the notes sounded like a quiet happiness. Clara had crossed her legs and was looking very ladylike in her grey, fitted, high-necked woollen dress.

'I feel underdressed. We should have stopped off at my place first.'

Clara smiled teasingly. 'My dear, I've spent two months seeing you in gowns that were open at the back. Or hospital pyjamas. For me, you look absolutely perfectly dressed – you have no idea.'

The waiter, a young man with a hipster bun and pleasant manner, came and took their order. Once the drinks arrived, Elias took a sip and stared out of the window into the rain.

'I never expected to get to sit in a café with you again.'

She looked seriously at him. Me neither, Elias. Will this small, quiet fear ever go? This fear for you?

He pulled a black notebook from his pocket and handed it to her. It had been folded in half, was well worn, the corners long since rubbed off.

'Funny you remembering our car journey together. Do you remember that I said I'd like to write you a song?'

She nodded. Of course.

The music lay in the air like a scent. Like the pale, sweet scent of robinia blossom with a hint of bergamot.

She took the notebook. Elias looked at her hands.

'I can't write music, but these are all the poems I wrote for you. All of them, right from the start, through the fever and the dark nights, to yesterday evening.'

She opened it and flicked through. His writing was unusual. There weren't many people who still had nice handwriting. Some were written in pencil, others in ink, others in biro. But there was one that caught her eye. 'To Travel with You'.

A day-bright night. Afar, I hear the screeching trains.
Their rattle stutters softly on the tracks.
A whisper through the window, what time with you remains.
To her. To her! The breeze breathes pictures in my mind.
I travel...

'Nobody's ever written me a poem before.'

Her hands were shaking slightly as she clapped the booklet shut.

'Now they have,' answered Elias.

Clara laughed softly, as something occurred to her.

'What?' asked Elias.

'Ha,' she said. 'Now you have to come to Hamburg with me.'

Elias was playing with the sugar shaker. He set the rippled glass purring against the table.

'I was planning on it anyway. If you still want me to. What's keeping me here ... well,' he said, light-hearted all of a sudden, 'if in the last three months, I hadn't noticed what really matters, when would I ever?'

He paused a while. She wanted to say something but he was faster. His smile was a little askew.

'I want to be with you, Clara. Will you still have me?'

She laughed. 'All I meant was, you need to come and visit me in Hamburg. See my new flat. But ... yes.' And hastily, she added: 'Otherwise, it wouldn't have been worth all the fuss!'

Elias stood up and walked around the table.

'What?' she asked.

'I just want to see if I can still kiss you.'

52

It was a funny feeling, returning to the flat. He hadn't been there in almost three months. The stairwell smelled dusty and of linoleum and the old wood of the worn treads.

'I can only hope the fridge hasn't exploded,' Elias said darkly, as he unlocked the door.

'Surely Jule's been in a couple of times,' said Clara.

Elias grinned. 'Jule is only eighteen. If she bears even the remotest resemblance to what I was like at that age, she certainly won't have paid any attention to the fridge in the last three months. Unless it was to see if there was any bubbly or beer lurking inside it.'

He walked into the kitchen and opened the window.

'Would you like tea? I'll put the kettle on. And then I need to change. I'm throwing away everything I ever wore in hospital. Everything.'

Clara stood at the window, felt the rainy air, looked over the rooftops to the belltower and thought that, despite everything, it was a beautiful town. Smiling, she called into the bedroom: 'That's pretty theatrical, you know. I'll be glad when you can get back to acting.'

The water was boiling. She was hunting in the cupboard for the teapot. Elias walked in. She could see that he was still thinner than he had been. His shirt hung loose. But he was looking good. Really good. He took two cups from the cupboard; she poured the tea. Her phone rang as she set the pot down on the table.

'Ms Wagenbach?'

She didn't recognise the number, or the voice.

'Yes?' she asked.

'My name is Tobler, I'm calling from the Luisenheim care home. Ms Wagenbach, I am very sorry to have to tell you that your mother has passed away.'

Clara understood the words, but didn't immediately take in the meaning.

'What?' she asked in reply. 'What?'

Elias looked enquiringly at her.

'But she was ... she was only just discharged back there!' She still didn't quite understand. 'She was perfectly healthy—'

The man broke in gently. 'It was very sudden. Just after dinner. We tried to resuscitate her. We have laid her out in her room. You are welcome to come at any time to see her.'

Clara hung up.

'My mother is dead.'

And then it was the same as when she'd heard that Elias had survived the operation. She couldn't do a thing about the tears. Even though she knew it was good. That her mother had hated the dementia, and that she'd never, never, never wanted to be in the home.

Elias took her in his arms. He said nothing. He just held her.

How close everything was to everything else. On this rainy, grey yet bright day, when he'd been allowed back into life, and when Clara's mother had died. He didn't know how to feel.

Clara was crying soundlessly. She hadn't cried at all for so many years. And now, in these last few months, she'd cried more than in the previous decade.

'Shall we go over there?'

She nodded.

'I have to call Jan. And Papa,' she said. 'Oh, Elias.' The tears wouldn't stop. 'She was such a strong, crazy woman.'

'She certainly was,' he said. 'An amazing woman. And I'm glad I got to know her.'

Having met Clara's mother, he knew where Clara came from and what had made her the woman that she was. It was as though it had brought him closer to her.

The home wasn't far from the hospital, and just that made it feel funny to drive over there. But on the other hand – he'd got better there. It wasn't the hospital that had made him ill. You forgot that sometimes, because so much had happened there that had scared him.

They walked from the car park to the front door. Clara close beside him.

'I never expected it to throw me this much. She hadn't actually felt like Mama for such a long time. Or at any rate, not the way she always wanted to be.'

'In the last three months, I wasn't the person I wanted to be either,' Elias replied. 'But your mother ... the way I got to know her, I believe I could still recognise the special woman behind it all. Despite the dementia. But perhaps you're right.' He thought of certain nights when the despair had been so great. 'Maybe you're right, and what counts is still being able to live with yourself.'

They climbed the stairs to the secure dementia section on the first floor. One of the nurses opened the door almost the moment they rang the bell.

'She's in her room,' she said. 'My condolences.'

How many times a month must they say that here?

The blinds were down in the bedroom; it was a peaceful semi-darkness.

Clara walked up to the bed. Her mother was just lying there. No trace of any death throes. Her mouth was slightly open and her eyelids weren't fully closed.

'They always say "it's like she's sleeping". But that's not true,' Clara said softly. 'You can see at once that she's dead.'

Elias nodded. Suddenly he had the oppressive feeling that it could have been him lying there. He could have been lying there and Clara would have been standing there and he'd never have been able to see her again. That was the thing, wasn't it? Not death. That was over and done with. No more pain and no fear. But that he'd never have been able to see her again, or anyone else, that was the thing. The sudden gratitude hit him so abruptly and so unexpectedly that he was afraid of losing his balance. It hit him much harder than two weeks ago, when they'd told him he was over the worst of it. He reached for Clara's hand.

They stood there in silence with the dead woman. Then Clara's mother sighed and they both jumped.

She's not dead at all! They made a mistake!

For a second there was a wild hope as the thought darted through Clara's head, but then she realised that it had only been a last remnant of air that had gradually worked its way out of her system. Mama was dead. Then the tears came again.

'Oh, Mama!'

Clara would have wished to be stronger, but Elias was there, and he couldn't hold the tears back either. Perhaps from the deep relief that he was alive and could be with Clara; perhaps, because he'd liked Clara's mother and the fact of having to die was still something terrible.

The sun shone through the blinds, painting clear, bright stripes on the lino floor in the half-dark. A death room. A summery image. They were sitting by the bed. Everything was peaceful.

'She liked you.' Clara smiled at the memory.

'I liked her too.'

'She was a negligent mother,' Clara said.

The emotions were gradually finding their places inside her. Strange. It was as though she had no longer felt right in the years before Elias. As if love and grief and despair and courage had only been pictures; like photos of emotions that you could look at but not touch. Now she was feeling them again.

'She was a negligent, crazy mother, who preferred reading to parenting. But when you needed her, she was there. Always.'

'Like you,' said Elias, and he meant exactly what he said.

Later, Jan arrived, and her father and relatives that Elias didn't know. The room filled up and candles were lit. An aunt had brought angel figurines and laid them on her mother's chest. Then she scattered flowers around the room, weeping fiercely. Elias looked over at Jan, who, almost imperceptibly, rolled his eyes and lifted his hands somewhat helplessly, as he exchanged another quick glance with Clara. Clara only raised an eyebrow and whispered to Elias that everyone got to grieve however they liked.

'I'd better go,' he said quietly.

Clara nodded with a slight smile. 'I'll come over to yours later, OK?'

'You don't have to,' he answered hastily, glancing at the many people in the room, 'but I'd be very glad if you did.'

'I'll definitely come,' she said.

Then he left.

53

The cemetery chapel bell chimed thin and regular. Clara remembered how often she'd heard that bell when she'd been at school, on warm days when the classroom windows were open.

'That sound always meant summer to me.'

Clara and Elias were the last, following the others out of the chapel after the funeral service.

'That bell was the sound of my yearning for adventure. Whenever I dreamt my way out of boring lessons, away into the distance, out of this small town, that bell was the lure.'

Elias said nothing. He'd slipped his arm under hers. Like that, he needed no words to show her that he understood. That it had been just the same for him in a village with different sounds, a different image. That huge, sometimes rending yearning for real life.

The coffin had been carried out and lifted onto a trolley. He was surprised by the number of people. There had been many fewer earlier, when Clara's mother had been laid out again in the chapel of rest.

The trolley moved off soundlessly, and everyone started walking. It was a special picture. The many spanned umbrellas were colourful splashes of paint in a small sea of black. It was drizzling. No wind. The birch leaves, still young, hung motionless from their branches. They shone pale and green in the grey air. It was a pretty cemetery.

'She did quite a good job,' said Clara unexpectedly. 'Didn't act like she knew Mama.'

The birds are still singing everywhere, he thought. Summer still isn't quite here yet.

'Do you miss her?' he asked Clara.

She thought for a moment, then shook her head. 'No. I think she just wasn't in the mood any more. In the mental-health unit there was one time ... she actually spoke again. Laughed. As if she'd perked up again for a bit. But the home – she hated it.'

She laughed.

'It's typical Mama. She determined when she was going to die. Like she forced her heart to stop. I'm sure she had her tongue between her teeth, like she always did when she was putting her weight behind a stuck door, or all her strength into opening a jam jar.'

'You do that too, sometimes,' Elias smiled.

'Me?'

He nodded. Clara didn't reply. But they were walking closer than ever now, and that had nothing to do with the rain.

It's nice that you know a thing like that about me. That you're here, she thought.

The grave lay at the edge of the sculpture garden, under an old linden. Her father was right at the front, swaying slightly, but he was holding up well. Perhaps he felt like she did. Perhaps he'd also had the feeling that her mother had decided she'd had enough. That she didn't want to live like that any longer, because it was no longer her life, it was a stranger's, and she didn't want to be forced to live it.

Elias hung back slightly behind Clara as she joined her father, her sister and Jan. These minutes belonged only to them. The pastor was standing at the head of the open grave, between two hills of fresh soil. The coffin was resting on the two beams laid over the grave. Pale birch. Only a single wreath on top of it. Elias folded his hands, not to pray but because he wanted to pay his respects to the woman in the coffin there once more.

The pastor spoke the old words about earth and dust, and they didn't sound quite genuine from the lips of this young woman. How old must she be? Mid-thirties, perhaps. But that wasn't the reason. None of what the living said about the dead could ever sound genuine, however old you were. Clara looked up. There was Elias, standing among the friends and relations. His gaze was fixed on the coffin, and he looked very serious and introspective. A warm feeling filled her. It was quite right. As if Mama had put everything right again. As if she'd heard her voice once more, firm but with a hint of amusement: What nonsense. People don't die when they're barely forty! Let me do it. I'm old, I'll die now for the man.

She had to smile. Toni saw it and smiled back, with a rapid glance at the coffin.

Once the pastor had finished, Jan took her place. He beckoned to her and Toni to stand at his side.

'Our mother,' he said, his voice shaking slightly, 'grew up without her mother or her father.'

To her surprise, Clara heard Jan fighting back tears. She touched his hand.

'A wartime child. Her father had left the family during the war, her mother was living with another man in another town, so she had to be brought up by her grandmother. Her mother didn't come to fetch her until she was fourteen.'

Jan raised his voice slightly.

'And despite this childhood without much by way of love, despite that, our Mama was a woman who could truly love. We might not always have realised that as children. She much preferred reading to cooking, and we learnt young to take care of ourselves.'

Toni met Clara's eyes and they smiled in shared remembrance.

Jan continued: 'She loved her dogs and her cats so much that, occasionally, on her old twenty-minute Super-8 films of the animals, you might see one of us stumble fuzzily through the picture for a few seconds. But on the other hand, she preferred taking us to the theatre to doing homework with us. On the other hand, she got us out of police stations and drove two thousand kilometres in her beloved red VW van to bring us home from Greek hospitals. On the other hand, she spent the nights at our bedside if we were ill, even once we were well into our twenties. I reckon she loved us as much as we did her.'

Clara's father threw a scoop of earth onto the coffin and once she'd followed suit – a funny feeling, despite everything – she made a little sideways tilt of her head that Elias knew well by now. He looked in that direction and saw Vera standing next to Jan.

'Surprise?' she asked, a touch of mockery in her voice.

Elias shook his head. 'No, actually. I saw them together at the hospital a few times.'

'She didn't even know Mama.'

Clara didn't know exactly what bothered her about that, or whether anything did at all. It was thanks in no small part to Vera that Elias was able to stand here beside her now.

Elias shrugged. Vera – that all seemed so far away.

'*Nil pluriformius amore*,' he quoted. 'Nothing is more various in its forms than love, right? And she would so much like to be part of something. Of all this.' He waved his hand, taking in all the mourners.

A thought occurred to Clara and she laughed.

'What?' Elias asked.

'I can't help thinking about the cottage. Look, we first met because Vera wanted my house. That's how we found each other. She brought us together, didn't she?'

Elias raised his eyebrows melodramatically. 'A stroke of luck!' he declaimed.

'Be quiet,' Clara said sternly. 'This is still a funeral. What I'm saying is: now she'll get the house after all. Cosmic justice, or what?'

Elias didn't understand.

'What? Why?'

Clara felt simply light-hearted for the first time in ages.

'Because I made the house over to Jan,' she smiled. 'I don't need it anymore.'

'She'll be pleased. But how come? Why did you...?'

'Long story,' said Clara.

The rain was growing heavier. It was falling through the leaves of the lindens, the chestnuts and the exotic tulip trees. It was falling on the colourful umbrellas and into the open grave. A comforting sound. The congregation started to scatter.

'Long story,' she repeated, putting her arm around him. 'I'll tell you another time. Come on, let's go.'

54

The flat didn't seem that empty; he wasn't taking much. Jule was sitting on the kitchen windowsill, her feet on the stool, and was drinking coffee.

'I say this only reluctantly, kiddo, but you're going to have to clean the fridge out now and then. It wasn't all that pleasant, opening it after three months. I don't know if I should actually let you have the flat.'

Jule smiled. No trace of guilt. 'It's my fridge now and I'll do what I like with it. Besides, I gave my blood for you. So it's only fair that I get your flat.'

Elias took the mug from her and drank from it.

'It would be fair if you were paying me the full rent. I'm currently unemployed,' he said darkly. 'But that's young people for you. Perverse, work-shy and inconsiderate. I don't know what's happening to Germany nowadays.'

Jule laughed. 'I'm not moving in until uni starts. In a few months. But then I will.'

Elias smiled at her. 'No. Don't worry. I have a well-paid girlfriend now, and she'll have to keep me. Maybe I'll never work again!'

Jule jumped up from the windowsill and hugged him.

'Old man,' she said softly, 'I'm so glad you're well again.'

Daughter, he thought tenderly. My daughter. How much their relationship had changed in the last few months.

'Mostly well,' he said as she let go of him. 'I'm a walking clock.'

'That's true,' said Jule. 'I can hear your heart ticking from here. Perhaps you should just sing all the time, then you won't hear it as much. Imagine you're lying in bed with Clara at night, warbling away.'

Elias pushed the second suitcase down the hallway to the door.

'I'm already looking forward to being introduced to your girlfriend. Then it'll be payback time. In full, OK?'

Jule came after him and took one of the cases.

'I'll help. But just to make sure you actually leave.'

Once they'd shoved the case in among the boxes in the boot, Elias looked up at the façade.

'I'm glad you're moving into the flat. I liked it a lot. Come and see me soon, Jule. I seem to have got used to you in the last little while. Such a bothersome emotional bond between father and daughter,' he sighed theatrically.

'Tell me about it,' Jule sighed back. Then she gave him a peck on the cheek. 'Drive safely, old man.'

She went back inside, and he saw her jumping up the stairs. World's best daughter.

It was late afternoon when he reached the building where Clara had found a flat. Rush hour on the Elbe bridges. He looked at it from the outside. The arches over the window and the white cladding meant that the late nineteenth century could pass itself off as Art Nouveau. The balconies had playful wrought-iron railings and there were green glazed tiles climbing in broad arches at their sides. Showing its age a little, but not shabby. He was surprised to find himself suddenly anxious. It wasn't like it was their first date. But all the same – as he pushed open the street door, his heart was ticking a little faster than normal.

The stairs were wide. He'd left the suitcase in the car. Fourth floor. He was a bit out of breath once he got to the top, but that was finally perfectly normal again – he'd always taken two steps at once.

She'd just got home from work, and had been really hurrying to get there on time. But as she reached the stairs, she could hear him above her. Unmistakably his step. Once she reached the last flight, she could see him standing at her door.

'Elias!'

He turned around and saw her standing, leaning on the banister, one foot a step higher, wearing the same suit she'd had on that day in the garden. The palest grey. The fitted jacket with a flared skirt, like something from the fifties.

'Clara!'

He came towards her and she bent her knee slightly. Laughing.

'You see, now I could drop to my knee before you. By way of greeting. Like you, that time.'

'By no means!' he exclaimed, was already down on one knee before she could react, hamming it up: '"With love's light wings, did I to Hamburg fly, for stony limits cannot hold love out."'

'What's that?' she asked with a laugh. 'Shakespeare?'

He nodded and stood up. 'Romeo and Juliet. The balcony scene. But you haven't got one so I'll make do with the stairwell.'

'I've got a balcony,' she said. 'What are you? A poor man's Romeo or something?'

She unlocked the door. 'I'm not Juliet. I hereby invite you in.'

She walked ahead and he followed her into the flat. And stopped in the hallway. It was like a gallery. Framed black-and-white photos on the walls on either side. She was bold with colour – the walls of the little corridor were painted dark green, and the light was skilfully arranged to make all the pictures stand out. And they were all of him. On stage as Willy Loman. Wonderful shots of him in mid-performance, just the way he'd imagined Loman to be: pretentious and yet petty, and secretly always begging for recognition. Others were of him in the park. In an avenue of trees. He often hadn't noticed her photographing him. There were portraits of him while driving. Pictures of him and Jule running a race in Bayreuth, carefree and full of movement. Him in profile, quiet, vibrant, taken while they'd been in a church. And all the photos looked as though the camera had been in love with him. He suddenly felt very small; this gallery spoke with such urgent force of Clara's feelings.

She turned in the kitchen doorway. Made an uncertain hand movement.

'I had all the pictures framed when I came to Hamburg. I wanted to have you around me. Always. And when you gave me the poems, I thought ... you should see them. They tell everything. Or try to, at any rate.'

He said nothing at all as he walked over to her and she turned her back to him so that he could cross his hands over her stomach and he felt his face against her cheek.

'Welcome, Elias,' she whispered.

Much later, they stepped out onto the balcony. It must have been after eleven by then, but it was still not quite dark. The silhouettes of the neighbouring buildings stood out black and sharp against a pale evening sky in which the stars were only faintly to be seen. Music was playing from one of the many open windows below and beside them. It rose up to them with a strange clarity. Light and summery. A melody that wanted nothing, that only gave. Bats darted through the mild air. In the distance, the tip of a church spire peeked over the rooftops across the Alster. Nothing special. Just an early summer night on the balcony of a flat in a big city.

They were standing side by side, their hands on the slender iron railings. Their fingers were touching as they'd done back then.

'You always think it won't happen to you,' Elias said quietly, 'but then it does.'

'Yes. You always think it won't happen to you.'

She turned to look at him. He turned to her and saw her soft, almost invisible smile.

'And then,' she said, 'it does happen to you after all, true love.'

The song below them came to an end. They stood in silence. And then it started again from the beginning.

Acknowledgements

This book is not only my own. There were – and still are – so many helping hands.

First of all, I would like to thank Annette Weber, who so patiently talked the manuscript over with me again and again, happily sometimes while sharing a bottle of wine.

Secondly, Karen Sullivan, for believing that my books stand a chance in the English-speaking market and for being so wonderfully enthusiastic in everything she does with literature.

Of course, there is Rachel, who must be thanked from the bottom of a writer's heart, because she is so scrupulously exact about translating this book not only into English but into *literature* (which I have to admit I sometimes find more beautifully written than my own text in German). She is one of the rare diamonds in this business, a person who would rather write a dozen emails to make absolutely sure that her translation finds the exact tone of the original.

Again, and as usual: all of you booksellers up and down the country. You, out there, who are willing to be persuaded by a translated work, who are willing to give it a try, and who are willing to persuade your customers into becoming fellow readers. Thank you so much! I appreciate your work and your passion!

Lastly, all the lovely members of Team Orenda, who are always as passionate and enthusiastic as their publisher Karen. Thank you, too!

Translator's Acknowledgements

I'd have been stuck on matters medical and theatrical in this book without the help of

friends and colleagues. Thank you to my GP friend, to Ulrike Peters Nichols for putting me in touch with the ITI Medical Network, and to Jean Walters; and thank you to Charlotte Collins, Roland Glasser and Peter Walton. Any misunderstandings remain mine. And as always, thanks to West Camel for his sensitive edits, making this translation the best it can be.